A LICE TÉLOT,
ALIAS
JACQUES FRÉHEL

THE INN OF TEARS

STORIES AND PROSE POEMS

TRANSLATED AND WITH AN INTRODUCTION BY
BRIAN STABLEFORD

I0591183

THIS IS A SNUGGLY BOOK

Translation and Introduction Copyright © 2022
by Brian Stableford.
All rights reserved.

ISBN: 978-1-64525-090-6

CONTENTS

INTRODUCTION

THE stories in this collection were published in various periodicals under the pseudonym "Jacques Fréhel," a signature that the author also used on eight books, five of which were novels and three collections of stories. The narrative voice of the early stories sometimes pretends to be male, but that pretence was eventually abandoned and the first-person narrators of many of the later stories are explicitly female. The actual sex of the author became manifest when she became a regular contributor in 1898 to *La Fronde*, a feminist newspaper entirely written by women; the editor, Marguerite Durand, occasionally rendered her by-line as "Madame Jacques Fréhel," presumably in order to reassure her readers that the rule was not being broken. The reviewers of her later volumes were, therefore, well aware that the owner of the pseudonym was female. The three collections were *Dorine* (1890), *Tablettes d'argile* (1894) and *Le Cabaret des larmes* (1902). The five novels were *Bretonne* (1891), *Déçue* (1893), *Vaine pâture* (1897), *Les Ailes brisées* (1903) and *Le Précurseur* (1905).

Information regarding the author is exceedingly scarce, and the sparse data reproduced in numerous reference books and documents available on-line are almost all copied from a single source, notorious for its unreliability: Abbé Louis Bethleem's eccentric bibliography of *Romans à lire et romans à proscribe* [roughly, Books to be Read and Books that Ought to be Banned], first published in 1904 and expanded several times as it went through numerous editions in the following thirty years. Bethleem stated—for the first time in print, as far as I can ascertain[1]—that "Jacques Fréhel" had been baptized Alice Télot, that her real name was "Madame Jules Martin," that she had been born in Saint-Malo in Brittany, and that she was from a family of mariners. The first of those data was subsequently confirmed by the anarchist novelist and philosopher Han Ryner (previously Henri Ner) who revealed after her death that he and Alice Télot (1861-1918) had been secret lovers for more than ten years, before the Great War. He did not, however, confirm or deny any of the other details published by Bethleem, either because he was respecting the wish of Alice Télot to keep the details of her life secret, or because she even kept them secret from him.

We have no way of knowing where Bethleem acquired the information that he published regarding Alice Télot—surely not from her—but it is probably not a coincidence that he spent most of his life in Brittany and had extensive connections in the region. His reportage is almost certainly hearsay. Modern internet genealogy sites can find no trace of any marriage in Brittany between an Alice Télot and a "Jules Martin," but one of them does record banns published there for a marriage between an Alice Télot and one Léon-Jules Mathis. It would not be the first time that multiple reference books had blithely copied an item of accidental misinformation, but as there does not appear to be further trace of Léon-Jules Mathis, any more than there is of Jules Martin, it is impossible to be sure of the truth of the matter.

---

1 No copy of the first edition of Bethleem's book is currently available online, but the third edition of 1906 is, and the article as it appeared therein was reproduced verbatim in all subsequent editions. The reference to *Le Précurseur* must have been added in 1906, but it is probable that the rest of the entry had appeared in 1904. When later editions of Bethleem's book were taken over by a different publisher, he added a preface admitting frankly that previous versions had contained many errors, of which he had only been able to correct the most glaring.

Bethleem comments that it would be obvious from reading Jacques Fréhel's books that she was a Bretonne, but in fact, it is not so very obvious, and the strong suggestion of some of her early publications, including several reproduced herein, is that she probably grew up in the coastal town of Granville in Normandy. However, the stories she set there, especially "Un Duel de marsouins" (tr. as "A Duel of Marsouins") suggest that she might have been a result of intermarriage between a Norman and a Bretonne—something that would have been regarded as a trivial matter by all other Frenchmen, but would have been a circumstance of great consequence in Granville itself, where Bretons were particularly loathed, partly for reasons indicated in "Un Coup de pistolet" (tr. as "A Pistol Shot"). Whether she was Breton or Norman, however, or a little of both—and her spiritual Breton allegiance was certainly to an ancient, mythical Bretagne that included what subsequently became Normandy, rather than to the modern département—her work strongly implies that she felt like an outsider in her own land long before she became an exile in Paris.

The present collection of translations is not a complete collection of Alice Télot's short fiction. Although the title story of *Dorine* is included here, the other stories in that collections were not available to me for consultation, and although at least one story reportedly reprinted in *Tablettes d'argile* is included, at least three are not. Although I have employed the same title-story as the third Jacques Fréhel collection, I do not know what else the original collection contained. None of the collections is available on-line, and I have not been able to obtain full contents lists of any of them in order to ascertain the exact extent of their overlap with the present volume. It is, however, worth noting as an additional remark that although *Dorine* was the author's first book to be published in France, it had been preceded by a novella entitled *W Sudanie*, published in volume form in Warsaw, in Polish, in 1888. That publication is interesting, not only because the title provides further support for the implication of several other stories that Alice Télot had spent time in North Africa during the 1880s but because it implies that she must have had connections in Poland.

Nothing is documented regarding Alice Télot's literary acquaintances in Paris, but when she was one of a small stable of female writers who contributed fiction to the pages of *La Fronde* while Marguerite Durand was imitating the policy of *Le Journal* of frequently using a short story as a lead item on page one, one of the other leading members of that stable was the Polish-born Marie Krysinska. The two writers certainly had an influence on one another while they were writing for *La Fronde*, as is clearly evident by comparing the translations herein with those of Krysinska's parallel stories,[1] but the existence of Fréhel's Polish publication might suggest that she and Krysinka had already been acquainted for some time before then, and that one of them might have introduced the other to Marguerite Durand as a useful recruit. Together with "Myriam Harry" (Maria Shapira) and "May Armand Blanc" (whose real name remains unknown) the two writers made a very significant contribution to the development of French feminist short fiction in the *fin-de-siècle*, and influenced later writers in that vein, including "Renée Vivien" (Pauline Tarn) and Lucie Delarue-Mardrus.

Alice Télot's association with *La Fronde* also has a strange connection to her liaison with Han Ryner. If the information on the website located at *hanryner.over-blog.fr* can be trusted—and it is presumably based on documentary evidence—Ryner and Télot began their affair in April 1899, which must have been either immediately before or immediately after Ryner published *Le Massacre des amazones*, a demolition of "bas-bleus" [blue-

---

1 Marie Krysinska's contributions of fiction and prose poetry to *La Fronde* are translated in the Snuggly Books volume *The Path of Amour* (2020); May Armand Blanc's stories, also written in parallel, are translated in the Snuggly Books volume *The Last Rendezvous* (2021).

stockings], one chapter of which mounts a scathing attack on "les Frondeuses," in which "Jacques Fréhel" is the only contributor of fiction to the newspaper to be given partial relief from the hail of abuse. Even apart from her general tendency to secrecy, therefore, Télot would have had every incentive in 1900 for not letting her colleagues on the paper know that she was sleeping with the arch-enemy.[1]

Not a natural writer of vignettes in the 1200-1700 word range favored by newspapers for short stories, "Jacques Fréhel" had slight difficulty adapting to the slot made available to her in *La Fronde* for a period of just over eighteen months. Her difficulties are evident not only in the eccentric range of her work, but also in her categorizations. Many of her items appeared under series headings, some of them devoid of any further title, but only one of the seemingly-projected series had more than three detectable inclusions (the stories from *La Fronde* reproduced here might not be the full set as several issues of the paper are missing from the archive reproduced on *gallica*, and my search of the pages might not have been as exhaustive as I wished). She adapted swiftly, however, and soon cultivated a measure of expertise. The material contributed to *La Fronde*'s fiction slot by the other regulars was also interestingly varied, but none of the others showed such sharp contrasts as the discrepancy between Fréhel's sternly Naturalistic "Rustic Images" and her hallucinatory tales based in the ancient mythology and pseudohistory of the "Bretagne" of Druids, bards and early Christian Saints.

In stripping down narratives to fit the slots made copiously available to them in newspapers of the 1890s, writers like

---

1 The hanryner.over-blog website alleges that Ryner and Télot collaborated on a number of projects, including ghost-writing for a feuilletoniste, but gives no details at the time of writing; as the website is a work in progress, however, more information might be forthcoming in the future. It states that Alice Télot worked at the time of the affair for a Society for the Protection of Children, and there is supportive evidence for that allegation elsewhere.

Catulle Mendès, Octave Mirbeau, Jules Richepin and Edmond Haraucourt had already developed a battery of useful narrative strategies, and those developed by Blanc, Krysinska and Télot are an obvious evolution of that armory. Their tactics of feminization are, however, of some technical interest in terms of their further avoidance of narrative twists intended to surprise the reader and their almost-absolute refusal to employ the kinds of ending that had become stereotyped in longer kinds of fiction: romantic, competitive or commercial success. In general, feminist fiction of the relevant brevity is unremittingly bleak in its attitude to redemptive amour and its intense sympathy for the victims of fickle male lust mounted a stark challenge to the masculine mythology of amour as well as enhancing the evolving genre of the *conte cruel*. Even in the early novelette, "Dorine" Jacques Fréhel could only bring "himself" to pay skeptical lip service to the conventional literary mythology of amour; in her terse work for *La Fronde* her demolition of it is relentless, albeit often witty rather than lachrymose. Her work is ingenious, original and often of high quality.

Of the three most prolific contributors to *La Fronde*'s fiction slot, "Jacques Fréhel" was the most intense and the most inclined to unashamed melodrama. She was not the only one to mingle lyrical and fantastic material with laconic Naturalistic accounts of female tribulations, but she was the most venturesome in so doing, not only in her raw materials but also in her manner of presentation. Although Blanc and Krysinska also edged into the fringes of surrealism occasionally, neither of them ever conceived a story like "Kemp Owyne," and nor did any of the other Symbolist writers who dabbled in revisionist recycling of the materials of Medieval romance.

When Han Ryner gave "Jacques Fréhel" a grudging compliment in *Le Massacre des amazons* he only did so on condition that she refrained from "further excursions to ancient Egypt," but fortunately, she took no notice of the prohibition, and not only wrote "Servantes de Hathor" (tr. as "Servants of Hathor") but placed it in *La Nouvelle Revue* rather than *La Fronde*, where its feminist revision of Herodotus would have seemed unusual and a trifle daring, even in the era when Pierre Louÿs' *Aphrodite* had made "antique moeurs" exceedingly fashionable. Alice Télot was no more afraid of the hallucinatory, or even the frankly insane, than she was of the stark tragedy of her most brutal Naturalistic tales. Her two "Lettres égarées" (tr. as "Crazy Letters") and "Dernière lumière" (tr. as "Last Light") are some of the most remarkable contributions to the subgenre of literary accounts of mental disturbance, which thrived in the *fin-de-siècle* under the influence of rapid developments in psychiatric theory.

"Jacques Fréhel" received a certain amount of critical praise in her time; *Les Ailes brisées* was awarded the Prix Jules Favre by the Academie Française, although the fact that two of the three brief items of information appended to that notice on the Académie's website are probably false reflects the fact that her work suffered such great neglect thereafter that she is almost forgotten today. Her quest for secrecy was, in the end, too successful for her own posthumous good. There is, however, every reason why she should be included in the quest undertaken by modern feminists to uncover more of the buried heritage of early feminist fiction and she ought to be given the credit she deserves for the verve, style and inventiveness of her work as well as its fugitive ideology.

All of the following translations were made from the relevant copies of the periodicals contained on the Bibliothèque Nationale's *gallica* website.

—Brian Stableford

THE INN OF TEARS

DORINE

(*La Nouvelle Revue*, 1 June, 1888)

I SIGNY is in the depths of the wide open gulf at the confluence of the Aure and the Vire. Served by magnificent meadows shaded by centenarian linden trees, with its château two centuries old, its little port sheltering twenty coasters in all seasons, its butter known throughout the world, and its mussels of which Aurigny is jealous, the little town is as neat and orderly as an honest bourgeoisie, rich by virtue of being economical, sometimes with a hint of luxury by virtue of one of the trading coups incited by unsentimental cunning an ever-alert rapacity. Usury and sorcery march hand-in-hand there; chicanery holds the high ground, and—a characteristic detail—in a population of three thousand inhabitants, six bailiffs live well on the exploitation of obtuse, stubborn, debauched and thieving Norman peasants.

William the Conqueror, on his deathbed, depicted in incisive and mocking strokes the Normans of those days. We are no better able today to portray them with the pen: "Vain and fond of good cheer, it is necessary at all times to master them, for they are very difficult to govern."

Everyone goes to his justice of the peace on the most futile pretext, and those who do not do so on their own account on Wednesday, market day, accompany their friends; they go there as spectators to amuse themselves before dinner. The audience is

17

held in the large drawing rooms of the château, on the first floor. They only emerge at the last moment, when the bailiff rattles his big keys, ready to lock up. As soon as the judgment is rendered the insults rain down, and often blows as well. The intervention of two splendid gendarmes—the gendarmes are very handsome in Isigny—only aliments the quarrels.

The peasants' clogs clatter on the staircases of the old building; women in short skirts utter shrill cries, and more than one cotton bonnet whose victorious hank of hair dominates the struggle for a long time ends up remaining on the tiles. The children, whose mother and father never fail to bring them, their hair shiny with pomade, red-faced and dressed like little old men, are dragged around, their hands in their pockets full of hazel-nuts. Once outside, the sabbat continues; invectives seem to rebound from mouth to mouth in a deafening jargon. The calves that have been brought to be sold, attached in the square to wooden pickets, raise their white muzzles patched with black and brown, bellowing; in order to chase away flies they beat their flanks with their long tails soiled with mud; the sheep bleat, hobbled in pairs by their feet, with large red crosses traced on their backs.

Under the shady lindens, butter is sold. On trays placed on the ground, emerging from damp cloths, enormous blocks of butter loom up, like golden milestones. Is it not the wealth of those country folk, and the brightest part of their income? That malleable gold will be changed there, before their eyes, into solid, hard, shiny metal, also yellow, which their callused fingers will slide into their leather purses, and in the evening, once back at the farm, the week's profit will go to join the treasure buried between the piles of sheets in the old oak cupboard scented with washing soda, lavender and iris.

Master Jean Belhache, the rich farmer of Gebosses, found himself summoned to the tribunal that day with regard to a boundary hedge that the cows of his neighbor Gardinier sacked during the night. That old swine Gardinier used his cows expressly to do harm, like the ugly wretch that he was.

The justice of the peace, very pacific, had started by asking for the complaint, and, in spite of the introduction of a request to reconvene, he sent the two Norman plaintiffs away.

Master Belhache, furious, his face congested, strode across the square gesticulating.

A tall, slightly stooped fellow accompanied him.

His son, of course: Pierre Belhache, at your service, twenty-five years old, the pride of the family; long black hair slightly wavy, falling over the collar of his jacket, an oval face, splendid dark eyes in which the pupils stood out vigorously against the blue enamel, a curly beard barely furnished, of simple elegance, resembling no one, least of all his father.

Disembarked from Paris that same morning, the young man, after an absence of several years, let himself go to the charm of rediscovering his homeland in the midst of the hubbub of the market, and he was enjoying that spectacle, familiar in his childhood.

The peasants saluted him, raising their black caps.

"Bonjour, Master Pierre—back again! Good! You'll get plenty of pure juice—that'll put the color back in your cheeks!"

He responded to them all, smiling mildly.

At the extremity of the square, a tooth-puller, mounted on a gilded carriage, dressed in a magician's robe, with broad sleeves, was exercising his cruel profession. On top of his cart, two negroes were beating a big drum during the operation, in order to drown out the patient's screams. The unfortunate fellow was gesticulating like a man possessed, waving his arms desperately. He went away without saying a word, very pale, his head empty, clutching his jaw.

The charlatan possessed a marvelous facility of elocution, and he talked incessantly, capturing the Norman by means of all his cunning, all his fears and even by means of his avarice. In front of him, two immense baskets full of hundred-sou coins were sparkling; his large red sleeves thrown backwards, he took a basket full of silver and poured it into another, empty one, making the metal stream and glitter above the crowd.

"You see," he said, "I don't want your money, I'm richer than you."

And the peasants came forward, their hands hooked as if to grab it, dazzled by the sight of that money exposed in the sunlight, forgetting that they had brought their pistoles.

Very amused, Pierre stopped his father in front of the conjurer. Flattered to see a gentleman in his audience, the man with the hundred-sou coins emptied his bag, delivering himself to coarse jokes, mocking the country folk without them perceiving it, scattering his salesman's wit, his old stager's philosophy and his inexhaustible Gascon verve.

Master Jean Belhache, spotting a group of girls, took his son in that direction. He tapped one of them on the shoulder.

"Hey, Dorine, it's necessary to tell Père Duchêne to bring a sack of mussels to Gefosses on Friday; in the morning, you hear?"

The child had turned round, surprised in the middle of a loud laugh; it was still vibrating, her neck half-stretched, her lips fleshy, wide open in an expansion of gaiety.

On perceiving Master Belhache accompanied by his son, however, the little fisherwoman went very red, troubled by Pierre's admiring gaze.

Hands in his pockets, the young man fixed serious eyes upon her.

Dorine responded that she would bring the shellfish in person, her father not being able to walk for the moment because of his cramps.

Her voice was soft, charming in its timbre, very personable; she expressed herself well for her condition, having stayed in school until the age of fourteen, exceptionally. In spite of her rude métier as a fisher, she was still slim and delicate, her ankles thin and her hands dainty in spite of the calluses put there by the oars.

The sunlight caused her dark curly hair to blaze on her head with ardent coppery reflections.

The dazzled Pierre murmured, with a smile: "It's not Dorine that it's necessary to call you but Dorée, all gilded!"

"It's midday," the farmer interrupted, consulting his large silver watch, retained by a leather thong. Let's go have lunch, my lad—and you, little one, don't forget the order."

"Who is that pretty girl?" Pierre asked, while his father headed with him to the Couronne-d'Or, the best hostelry in the region.

"Cha!" said Master Belhache scornfully. "She's a Les Hogues girl!"

In addition to the society of farmers and bourgeois, there exists in Isigny a population with a very special cachet, which inhabits a quarter knows as Les Hogues; it is there that the mussel-fishers live. Separated from the town by a bridge, almost entirely surrounded by the Aure, that swarming suburb, whose houses are built on piles, resembles on sunny days a wretched scrap of Venice.

Superb chubby children covered in rags play in the fishing boats moored next to one another with thick rusty chains; a dozen of them fall into the water every year, but they are always fished out in time.

At every tide the heavy boats—*picoteux*, to use the local jargon—emerge from Les Hogues, manned by their crews, man and women. Long iron rakes are fitted to the stern of each skiff. A tripod, a cooking-pot, bread, cider and a little broken wood are arranged in one corner; for the rest, the sea will provide.

Having gained the open sea, going from one channel to another, the picoteux penetrate the vast estuary that forms the mouth of the Vire during the ebb-tide. When the waves have withdrawn, exposing the mussel-beds, the fishers of both sexes start manipulating the rake. The long iron claws sink profoundly into the sea-bed, bringing back at every stroke stones, sand, and glaucous green or bright pink seaweed, mingled with mussels, which it is necessary to extract and wash summarily before throwing them in the bottom of the boat.

The semi-naked children, with little baskets on their backs, also take part in the pillage of the sea; they splash about in puddles of water, in which their troubled image dances or floats like tresses, like golden threads.

Winkles, sand-eels, cockles and shrimp are piled up in the deep baskets. Edged in narrow fissures in the intervals of little rocks, where carnivorous cephalopods grasp errant crustaceans in their arms, on the sandy bed laminated with resplendent mica with a dark gleam like polished bronze, crabs and little blue eels are adroitly seized by the young fishmongers and thrown into the baskets. They swarm pell-mell in the wicker over the meager spines of the children, close to their skin, with a continuous noise of colliding shells and sticky flesh, quitting and grasping one another again in viscous combats.

When the fishing is concluded, each family comes together to take a little nourishment. On the driest sand the burning faggots heaped under the tripod crackle around the cooking pot full of mussels. The succulent mollusks open, offering white and flavorsome flesh.

Everyone sits in a circle around the flame.

They are streaming, the worthy seamen, their rags soaked with sweat and spindrift, sticking to their backs, a warm mist emerging from them. The labor is rude and makes them pant like wheezy horses. The old ones whine.

What is the point of complaining, seaman? Summer brings back winter and winter prepares spring. The snow is on your head, man! Your profile of a centenarian bird, your tanned face, and your sinewy neck are ripe for the tomb. Everything wears away, you see, but everything is also reborn, and whether your old carcass reposes in the depths of the sea, enveloped by seaweed and somber wrack—a true seaman's shroud—or you are taken to the blessed earth of the parish cemetery, where the great ecstatic Christ opens his arms to humanity, it doesn't matter. Life is in you, old man; for if the greatest preoccupation of human beings is the fear of annihilation, the constant will of nature is to rejuvenate images and forms incessantly. In your dissolved being, creation will well up, and you, a frosty ruin, will prepare the renewal; dead, you will still give life to youth.

Of all that marine court of miracles, the oldest, the most tremulous, the most lamentable, the most withered and the most tearful was Père Duchêne. Shrunken, stunted, with a long nose, further prolonged by the collapse of toothless gums like empty scuppers; a small head, rounded like an old wrinkled apple; his sunken eyes, where a thousand radiating wrinkles came to furrow the temple; the fleshless ears, crenellated and ragged, from which dry cartilage emerged, missing pieces all around, as if some voracious seabird had pecked them during the night while he was rowing; his limbs were frail and his shaky head leaned over the ground with the mechanical gesture of a man carrying a heavy burden. His attitude did not vary, just as weary whether he was burdened or whether he was moving freely, his arms away from his body and his arms folded behind his arched back. His hair was sparse and short, very white; a single fleecy wisp stood up over his forehead like a feather. A little bonnet covered his unsteady head: a strange little bonnet of gray wool made of three pieces sewn together, in the form of those that are put on little children. With that bizarre coiffure, one might have thought him Dante travestied as a sailor. Escaped from an inexhaustible spring, a drop of yellow liquid swayed at the tip of his nose; he sometimes wiped it away with the back of his hand, but it formed again immediately. The urchins of Les Hogues called him "Père la Roupie."[1]

Père Duchêne often talked to himself while walking; no one understood what he said. His faint speech was decomposed, and evaporated, mingled with the great voices of nature. They clamored: "Shut up, then, old dotard, can't you hear our howls? We're the storm, the wind, the rain, the tempest, the typhoon and the waves! Cease your murmurs, poor human rag animated by a vacillating breath. It's our prerogative to moan! When you see our forces, our terrible din, united on those apocalyptic nights full of black horror that sea dogs like you know well, that's matter in revolt, caught by an impetuous need to lament. Then we thunder desperately in the shadow, and our imposing breath upsets the world. Understand us, sailor, and say to yourself: 'That's the tormented soul of the of earth, making efforts to break its moorings in order to drag its anchor into infinity.'"

And he did, indeed, shut up.

The furies of the sea took hold of him; and when the fishing left him some leisure, an occasional spectator, he went to watch the coasters come in from the end of the dike, on which the white-painted lighthouse stood. Tottering on his soft legs, awkward on land, habituated to being carried by the soft springs of the sea, pushed to the right and the left at the whim of capricious gusts of wind, he breathed more heavily, bent double.

Sometimes a three-master came to engage in the channel, all sails aloft, advancing straight toward him as if launched with a heroic and sure impulsion by a giant. The waves were fleecy, the ship seemed, from a distance, to be gliding over the water in the midst of the foam, without oscillations, seemingly insensible to the furious impact of the waves. The pilots chatted at that place. One of them would have to wait for the ship at the entrance to

---

1 Roughly: "Old Snotty."

24

the pass, in order to guide it and bring it into port; access to it is difficult, especially when it is a matter of turning abruptly before engaging with the channel. On days of bad weather, when big waves hollow out profound furrows in the sea, like those traced across a field by a gigantic plow maneuvered by a titan, ships have been seen opening their hulls on the môle.

All the old mariners are there, attentive to the peril of others. Père Duchêne, fascinated, advances as far as he can to the edge of the platform, his eyes riveted to the three-master getting closer and closer, the disorderly movements of which can now be discerned.

"Watch your feet, Père la Roupie, you'll fall in the sea!"

He responds with a grunt to those charitable warnings. The wind rises and causes the unique wisp of hair emerging from his bonnet to turn over on his head, white with yellow reflections. He is not afraid of the sea; he knows her well, the slut. She does not like the old! Good for a handsome fellow like his Barthélemy, an honest and brave sailor, married, useful to his family, very bold with his broad red face dotted with freckles, his heavy stride rhythmic with a perpetual roll. What a fine child, poverty of God, always ready to laugh, and so adorably awkward when he played with his little one in the evening!

That was the good time; the robust son earned the living for all his family. One bad day, without any warning, the sea took him in the full flush of youth—an ambush of the traitress—and he had never been seen again.

With despair, poverty had entered the little house.

By excess of affliction, Barthélemy's young widow died two years later, leaving little Dorine, a five-year-old girl, to the charge of Père Duchêne.

Ten years had passed since the catastrophe. The poor old man had toiled in order that the child would not lack anything, serving as both father and mother, with touching tenderness and the puerile dreads of an old man alarmed by the slightest danger that might have threatened his beloved little Dorine.

She was about to turn fifteen now, and the woman was blossoming abruptly in the child; she adored her grandfather and did her best to support him. Sitting on one of the benches of the picoteux, handling the oars as boldly as a man, she rowed firmly, stiffening her thin adolescent arms. Her nascent breasts were designed, exquisitely round, under her fustian bodice; the sea wind raised crazy curls around her forehead and nape; the sun, vivifying and penetrating her freely, had gilded her like an antique marble exposed for several centuries to the light of the blue countries; her hair, gathered artlessly on top of her head, would have made a Parisienne despair, as much because of its opulence as its undiscoverable Rembrandt hue, which the brunettes of today try to borrow by means of the secrets of the art.

And how well it suited her, that pretentious name Dorine, spotted by Barthélemy on the prow of a ship on the day of his daughter's birth. "You," the young father had cried, proud of his find, "will be called La Dorine."

Master Jean Belhache wanted to keep his son on the farm henceforth, without permitting him to exercise any profession, uniquely to see, hear and admire him. When one has enabled a rare plant to grow in one's garden, one likes to contemplate it and to respire the perfume of its flowers. Miserly for himself and for others, prodigal for his son, the vain countryman prepared to satisfy all Pierre's desires and to spare no effort to keep the young man at Gefosses. The latter, in any case, devoid of ambition, an enemy of struggles, delicate by nature, and something of a poet, did not seem to put up any opposition to the ardent wishes of his father.

When they both returned to La Miseraigne on a glorious autumn evening the sun set ablaze the little jaundiced panes of the arched windows of the old farmhouse. An immense portal draped with ivy gave access to the courtyard abandoned to poultry; it is a large square surrounded by outbuildings, in which the tables are found, surmounted by forage stores, the cowshed where the young calves are reared, and the milking shed.

The milking shed, the object of every care, is paved with stone, drained by little cemented streams full of rapid and refreshing water. A double row of granite supports receives the earthenware vases that the farm girls, called milkmaids, scour every day with freshly-cut nettles and iris roots; the foamy milk is poured into them, drawn before dawn in distant pastures, brought in bright bronze pails covered with frost for having been placed in long damp grass where chilly buttercups close their yellow eyes and daisies stiffened in their slenderness tighten their tiny petals modestly while awaiting the kiss of the sunlight.

Distant noises were perceptible: a cock standing on the compost heap, raised up on his spurs, his wings extended in a hieratic pose, launched his victorious cockadoodledoos with a full throat; the pigeons kept quiet, arranged on the walkway of their wooden loft; some were as black as swallows, some wore blue mantles over white waistcoats, others, a scintillating gray, were cooing very gravely.

A stout girl with red hair, occupied in some task, crouched in a corner of the courtyard, was singing in a shrill voice:

In low Normandy
The land where I was born
There were three gentlemen
All in love with me
Oh, vertigo!
Oh no, in faith!
Oh, quioup, quioup, qioup! Oh, quioup, in faith!
Oh, oh, how they were in love with me!
Who couldn't sleep, who couldn't sleep, oh, quioup,
    quioup, quioup

Who couldn't sleep, who couldn't sleep, oh, quioup,
   in faith!

Pierre, intoxicated by youth, in a complete expansion of happiness, had turned round, having arrived in the middle of the courtyard. Before him, the countryside, restricted by the portico of his dwelling, was reduced to the proportions of a graceful landscape. The steeple of his village, around which a flock of crows was circling, surmounting the charming thirteenth-century church whose slender ogival windows are impeccable in their finesse, delighted his artistic eyes.

In the meadows, the motionless cows were inhaling the sea breeze with avid nostrils, and their large half-closed and tranquil eyes were gazing into the depths of the horizon. Sometimes, as if responding to impenetrable meditations, one of them raised her broad white forehead toward the sky and lowed languidly.

At the foot of every apple tree the fruits harvested therefrom had been piled up; the apples thus accumulated formed little cones in the green grass, some the color of pale gold, others bright red, according to the species; the morning dew put some russet therein. The abandoned nests of goldfinches could be seen, allowing cottony threads to hang down from twisted branches, tangled with slender roots and damp feathers.

In the hedges, the virgin vines, already turning crimson, spread over the black pearls of the elders and there were violet brambles laden with mulberries—the leaves of which, turned over by the wind, were tinted underneath with a cobalt green mingled with brown—oak leaves with cadmium hues, and privet leaves with long ridges of emerald. The tallest birch, clad in a robe of silvery white satin with black fissures, dominated those bushes and shook its quivering branches, from which gold coins hung down, full of frissons, at the decline of the year. Then, at the foot of the hedge, amid the grass and the violets devoid of flowers, there were wild strawberries patched like the wings of butterflies with hues of carmine, lacquer and orange.

A cart passed by heavily, making the shiny red porphyry pebbles creak, piled up on the damp edges of the path.

In the background of that scene, as impalpable and light as threads of spidersilk fleeing rapidly toward an unknown goal, a gracious image was blurred, vague and indecisive, in the distance of the landscape. Pierre, without paying any heed to it, without knowing why, evoked the fisher girl glimpsed that morning at the market of Isigny, with the pretty laugh on her lips of a young bacchante, which Carpeaux enabled to blossom on the mouths of his statues. He confounded her with nature herself; she personified for him the sea and the fields, and his memory left in the utmost depths of his soul, like an uncertain hope, a rocking full of charm for his heart in the reconquered peace of the paternal house.

Before a great fire crackling in the kitchen fireplace, a chicken was roasting, turning slowly; a dripping-pan placed underneath it was receiving the juice; suspended from a hook. An immense cooking pot containing cabbage soup was simmering, while a maidservant, standing by a window, was carving thin slices of bread into a basket. When the basket was full, she set about dividing the contents into the bottom of eight or ten soup tureens, which she arranged around the hearth as she went along.

An ancient poet of Villedieu-les-Poëles has sung that national dish, the soup of fat and green cabbages that is eaten in all Norman farmhouses:

To my taste, green cabbage is a food of kings
And my Colette loves it as much as me.

The man whose appetite labor augments,
And a green cabbage soup every day contents,
Cannot be seduced by the allure of your gold
And his frugality takes the place of treasure.

Medals obtained in regional competitions put dark patches on the ocher-coated walls; copper letters stood out thereon, relating the farmer's agricultural successes. They could be seen everywhere, in the intervals between the saucepans and around the crockery.

The father and the son dined copiously, served at a small table near the fireplace.

The domestics took their meal at the back of the room in semi-obscurity; they did not speak, maintaining the extraordinary silence of ruminants. A few got up, soup bowl in hand, and went out to wander in the courtyard while eating.

The farmhouse had a drawing room. When Madame Belhache was alive it had been clean and tidy; now it was rarely opened, fruit and preserves were kept in there.

Pierre spent the day after his arrival settling in and taking care of correspondence, but on Friday morning he set forth, whistling, toward the sea. A velvet jacket floated around him and a brown felt hat covered his head.

He reached the dikes raised to defend the muddy meadows reclaimed from the sea; the waves came to expire at their base with a light splash, on a carpet of pink sand where herbaceous saltwort and rock samphire grew.

The young man was apparently idling; he was walking slowly, skirting the channel. The breeze agitated his black hair.

Suddenly, a little dot appeared on the horizon and then grew: a picoteux manned by a woman and a child.

Pierre sat down in the grass at the edge of the dike, his legs dangling. Dorine's back was turned to him as she rowed. He could make out her exquisite nape, on which the sun, cooled by autumn, darted pale oblique rays.

Gulls with velvet robes flew around her gracefully, inclining their inexpressibly tender faces over her.

A strong muted heartbeat raised the breast of Master Belhache's son, as if wings within him had begun to impel his heart, suddenly struggling like an imprisoned bird. He closed his eyes, surprised by so much emotion, and in order to reassure himself he began to smile incredulously. Was his head about to be turned upside down by a little fisherwoman? Get away! He had wanted to see her again, yielding to a purely artistic curiosity, drawn by the plastic amour of the beautiful, and nothing more.

Without seeing him, Dorine leapt out of the boat, helped the child unload the mussels, and then, winding the end of a cable around one of the buoys in the channel, holding her shoes in her hand, placed her bare feet, red with cold, on the sand. She tucked up her short skirt slightly, showing a firm leg in which the high-set calf rounded out, veined with blue.

"Oh, what a pretty leg! Oh, what a pretty girl!" the young man murmured.

And then Dorine's eyes were raised, summoned by Pierre's eyes.

The daughter of Les Hogues bowed her gilded head, her forehead crowned by a virginal blush. Like the triumphant dawn invading the sky at daybreak, the blood of youth rises to the brows of children.

The young boy accompanying Père Duchêne's daughter suspended the basket full of mussels from his shoulders and clambered up the bank, shouting: "Wait for me, Dorine." And without further delay he launched forth across the fields, heading straight for the village, from which could be heard, beyond a curtain of mist-shrouded poplars, the distant barking of dogs spreading through the farmyards.

The tête-à-tête embarrassed Pierre; he invited the young woman to sit down beside him, but she remained indecisive, frightened, her eyes fixed on the child who was drawing away, walking rapidly, curbing the rushes in his path.

The farmer's son began to speak in a low and soft voice, musical and measured, with a metallic vibration so profound that his words appeared to come from further away than him. The fisherwoman, accustomed to the rude accents of sea folk, marveled as she listened.

She remained silent, very emotional. It had never been given to her to co-ordinate the vague ideas floating in her ignorant brain. Her intelligence, enclosed within her like a hidden treasure, did not bring back any fruit; however, that simple girl had the entire poem of the sea in her eyes. She did not know the savant combination of words, but she knew how to keep quiet, and her face, mobile and expressive, showed by turns and without constraint the sentiments by which her soul was agitated. She glimpsed in Pierre's conversation a world of unknown and attractive things; it was like an ideal kingdom with gates closed to the daughter of the poor; and he drew her in his wake into that blessed realm of chimerical dreams and blessed amours.

A rare diamond emerged from a vulgar matrix; for the first time in her life, Dorine cast an eye over her worn garments, the poverty of which caused the triumphant charm of her young body to stand out with an ironic splendor.

Divining her shame, Pierre reassured her hastily, saying to her: "What does it matter, my golden one? You're the more beautiful for it, and I'd like to contemplate you always as you are today."

Seeing tears of joy and pride rising to Dorine's eyes then, the sage Pierre lost his head slightly; drawing the tremulous girl forcefully into his arms, he kissed her moist eyelids.

The boy appeared, marching briskly through the green meadows; he rejoined them, whistling.

"Tomorrow," young Belhache said to her, "you'll bring as many again."

✳

Pierre went back to La Miseraigne in a state of indescribable delight.

Adorable grace, intelligence, beauty and candor, all that was Dorine; and he had found Dorine.

A fisherwoman, her? A daughter of Les Hogues, her? No, neither a fisher nor a daughter of Les Hogues, nor a bourgeoise with tight-fitting clothes, nor a country girl stiff in her lace, but rather a unique individual, fortunately created for him alone; a charming soul attached to a perfect body, not belonging to any social status, nor related to any vulgar hierarchy: a woman . . . *the* woman!

Behind the farm he went through a little clump of trees adjacent to it. In the middle of a pond, two swans were plunging their black-crowned red beaks into the water, or sweeping them voluptuously over the surface in order to catch a few insects. A creeper had climbed into a pyramidal fir tree and fell back majestically like a curtain.

Chestnut trees with black trunks retained their luminous and gilded leaves, as if the last autumnal light were languishing there, forgotten; a few remained green, at the tips of branches, sensing the sap withdrawing but wanting to continue living.

On the following days, things happened in the same way. The boy came to La Miseraigne, bringing mussels, and Pierre went to meet the fisherwoman on the water's edge.

The farmhands sought to explain the change in their nourishment, to which their stomachs adapted poorly; they could not succeed. Lads returning from labor saw Pierre and Dorine talking on the dikes; they looked at them without surprise, and joked about it between them.

Finally, the season for hunting waterfowl arrived. The farmer's son hired Père Duchêne's boat in order to shoot the aquatic game found in great abundance in the marshy bay of Veys, bathed at the equinoxes by great floods of sea water, where the Vire, becoming sinuous, expands, designing several Vs in the crude handwriting of an ignorant child. That expanse of terrain, cut by the arms of the river, stitched with little lagoons, covered by verdant islets carpeted with fine grass, species of meadow-grass, goosefoot and sandwort, serve as shelter in winter for the great family of sea- and river-dwelling birds. There are curlews with long plaintive cries; lapwings with tapering crests, whose wings imitate the noise of a winnowing-basket agitated in order to purge the wheat; golden plovers with white undersides and black beaks; rails that are seen running, light and agile, over dormant water on the leaves of water-lilies; nightjars, great hunters of moths and butterflies; grebes, which make use of their wings as oars, so marvelously that they seem to be flying in the sea, and whose floating nests carry pale green eggs flecked with brown amid the reeds; and solitary snipe swooping in the dusk and bleating through the muddy pastures like a goat-kid forgotten in the darkness.

In the boat, the hours went by too quickly for the liking of Pierre and Dorine. Amour floated around them, as subtle as a perfume spread in the air and as soft as a kiss; that redoubtable name had not yet been pronounced, however. They had never asked anything of themselves; they had not even sought to know of what their attraction was born; they merely submitted to its mute charm.

Sitting facing one another on the bench of the boat, their eyes exchanged poems as, writing in the heavens on great golden books, the angels meditated with folded wings and those beautiful white voyagers came to sing, to the music of divine harps, into the ears of poor mortals, doubtless to give them the illusion of celestial felicities.

Sometimes, in the clear limpidity of the waves, they admired jellyfish with pure rainbow hues affecting the form of long ribbons snaking through the water like the cestus of Venus, or they gazed at the stars of the carmined sea. Pierre told Dorine that the lights of the sky, in being reflected in the water, had imprinted their form on the living substances of the sea, and that the figure of all the stars rotated thus, shrunken, in the depths of the waves. Often, too, there was a diving bird, falling heavily nearby like a stone thrown from the height of a cloud, and everything was a subject of joy for them.

During these long excursions Père Duchêne said very little. He lowered his wrinkled head over his breast, or raised it to gaze at Dorine. Every day a new charm embellished her; her eyes had acquired an exquisite veiled languor; she no longer laughed with the loud explosive laughter of a bacchante, but a tender smile parted her lips in the plenitude of her happiness.

In the evening, the young man was disembarked on the dikes near an abandoned building where he kept his hunting equipment and where he lay in ambush during the night waiting for game.

Père Duchêne remained in the picoteux, holding the oars, while his granddaughter helped Pierre and illuminated him by means of a little lantern.

That moment of solitude and shadow threw them, maddened, into one another's arms. The farmer's son clasped Dorine against him passionately, kissed her on the lips, and ran away, distraught.

Of marriage there was no question. Dorine dared not think of it, and Pierre, in spite of his amour, frowned in thinking about the future. With a tacit accord, they expelled all preoccupation from their minds, knowing full well that those amiable hours of the present would never return in their blessed candor.

Sometimes tumultuous desires whirled in the young man's head; fever took hold of him, bringing hot blood to his arteries, beating the charge of youth; then a great lassitude invaded him. On those days, the hunting was poor; he scarcely thought of shooting a few ducks with webbed feet. Often, he remained thoughtful, his gaze lost, and Père Duchêne shook his clownish head, considering that strange hunter.

Their passion followed its ascendant march; everything depended at present on the hazard of the occasion. Like the majority of lovers, they did not hasten the denouement, sensing with the generic instinct of beings, that nature, the great purveyor of amour, would take charge of everything.

※

One day, when Père Duchêne was occupied in some lucrative labor in a neighbor's house, Dorine arrived alone in the picoteux under a tranquil sky. Joyfully, Pierre embarked with his griffon.

Toward evening, the sea suddenly became choppy; at sea, the noisy waves rose, subject to the attraction of the full moon. The pale light of the star traced a broad, mobile and livid route over the surface. The wind began to blow tempestuously.

The fisherwoman perceived the danger rapidly and cried, fearfully: "Take the oars, Pierre, and let's make haste to reach the channel, if there's still time—and may Saint Marcouf aid us!"

They bent over the oars in silence, uniting their desperate efforts. Splashes of sea water slapped them in the face with a dull sound, filling their ears with a confused buzz, and bitter droplets entered their open mouths; convulsive shudders shook their shoulders. The young man stiffened, as pale as a moribund, and the exhausted Dorine felt that she was dying.

Every wave bore the heavy boat to another; that one seized it furiously in its turn, balanced it momentarily at the top of its crest of foam, and then sent it into a profound fall into a disdainful crease of its green robe with innumerable ripples.

Fortunately, the tumultuous squall was pushing them in the direction of the channel; they found a refuge there without knowing how the tempest had thrown them into it.

The imprudent lover succeeded in anchoring the picoteux. It was just in time; Dorine, at the limit of her strength, fell backwards and fainted.

What should I do? thought the farmer's son. *Where can I find help? She's doubtless going to die.*

The sky opened with a flash of lightning and Pierre perceived, not far away, the old abandoned building, a former shelter of a solitary shepherd, where he spent part of his nights in ambush. He seized the fisherwoman in his arms and leapt out of the boat, the heavy keel of which sank limply.

The storm was raging; the wind surrounded the young man on all sides, like a diabolical round of fays and dwarves singing in discordant voices; it was engulfed in Dorine's wet skirt, and hurled it abruptly, flapping, over the head of the blinded hunter. The griffon, his fur bristling, fuming, trotted on his master's heels, his tail lowered.

With his knee, Pierre shoved the door of the hut, and, groping in the obscurity, he deposited the young woman on a camp bed set up for him; then he lit the hooded lantern hanging from a rusty nail driven into a crumbling wall. Into the hearth containing cold ashes he piled a few dry apple-tree branches forgotten in a corner, and a fire began crackling joyfully while the smoke, driven back by the storm, rose toward the blackened ceiling in a vertical column and was crushed there, reaching the corners.

Pierre approached the bed and set about warming Dorine up; he removed her soaked garments one by one and accumulated blankets over her. In spite of his cares and appeals, the young woman retained her rigid immobility. Then a frightful anguish, further magnified by the solitude and the darkness, slid into the lover's heart. Wrapping his arms around the child's naked torso, he drew her pretty head nearer, inundating it with tears and kisses. She opened her eyes very wide, eyes the color of the sea, speckled with gold. How beautiful she was thus, the daughter of Barthélemy the fisherman!

Outside, the elements were unchained in a racket similar to the muted skirmishes of squadrons, with prolonged metallic impacts, and the lamentable cries of curlews pierced the night between the panting gusts of the squall.

Her hands wrapped around the young man's neck, Dorine tightened their enlacement. An unspeakable need for tenderness gripped the breasts of the lovers, and an infinite, intoxicating sweetness circulated in their veins. Their moist faces were almost touching; they gazed at one another with searching, profound eyes, as if they had never seen one another as clearly as at that moment. Something august passed through them, with a frisson, and annihilated them, as if at the approach of a sacrifice: the child offering herself in her confident ignorance, the man grave and mad, seized with terror at the supreme moment and stopping, like impious individuals profaning a tabernacle, on the threshold of the virginity.

I feel sorry for you, bruised voyager, having reached the extremity of the road of life, if you have not known that instant of amour in which two young souls try to fuse and burn together in the fires of a grand passion; my pity will accompany you to the term of your sterile existence, disenchanted man!

"Dorine," said Pierre, "how I have desired to contemplate you without dread, hidden from all gazes, as at present. I cannot live an instant apart from you without languishing; your memory haunts me during the night and your beloved image troubles my mind incessantly. As ivy around the rim is mirrored incessantly in the black water of a well, the subterranean spring causes the water to rise, the ivy grows and descends toward the surface, and they unite in a kiss; thus our lips have come together, obedient to the interior attraction of the amour that attracts them."

The fisherwoman, mute, listened to those sweet words, and taking her lover's hands in hers, she put them over her breasts with a possessive and ardent gesture.

※

The next day, the weary sea was moaning faintly. Pierre and Dorine found themselves back in the boat, as calm and modest as young spouses, and also without remorse, because true passion does not know any.

Often, after that day, the young woman quit her grandfather's little house on dark nights without making a sound, traversed Les Hogues with her heart beating rapidly, and flew to join her beloved, who was waiting for her on the dikes. The young man enveloped her in the folds of his large cloak, and they went, pressed together tightly, to parade their amour in the darkness while the waves sang nearby.

A fisherman who was in love with Dorine perceived that maneuver. Driven by a jealous fury, he lay in wait for the young woman one evening, and after having seen her go out he ran to Père Duchêne's cottage. He opened the wooden shutters attached by a piece of rope, and, seeing that one of the broken panes had been replaced by paper, the rogue passed his fist through it; then, sticking his mouth to the gap, he cried: "Hola, Père la Roupie! You're sleeping too deeply; necessary to move a little. Hola, Père la Roupie!"

"Who's calling?" asked the old man.

"It's me, Napoléon, Lelandais' son. I've come to tell you that Dorine's bed is empty. If you want to find her, run after Pierre Belhache along the dikes, unless they've put to sea. That's a fine haunting!" The fellow added, sniggering: "When's the wedding?"

The old man moaned dully; he opened a door and closed it again abruptly. Then, after dressing in haste, with jerky movements, he launched himself outside. His gaze made a tour of the house; Napoléon had disappeared.

Light dawned in the poor old man's brain. He knew very well where to find Dorine. Putting his hands to his trembling head, he started marching with all his might, shaking his wrinkled head, curbed by the weight of age and destiny.

A man had stolen Dorine from him: a strangely pale man whose vibrant voice seemed so distant . . . and every day, receiving that demon in his poor boat, the old man had not perceived the sorceries that surrounded his child!

Ah, the remainder of his forces crumbled in that last blow; life abandoned him, like an old tree devoid of sap; his will became weary, and his limbs, devoid of flexibility, used up the final effort of his exhausted being.

A mariner says little; he is a thinker and a fatalist. He listens to what the waves say to him; perhaps he responds to them; we are not initiates to their mysterious language. Those speeches are doubtless worth as much as many others, since those old rollers of the swell believe in God, respect honor and practice charity in aiding one another and loving one another like brothers. But it is in the hour of danger, in the tragic moments of existence, when his intimate sentiments are in play, that the humble matelot becomes heroic, superb, eloquent, generous and grand, like the sea.

There does not exist in humankind a sentiment more touching than the love of a grandfather for his grandchild. It is a paternity more tender and more indulgent than the first, and also more exclusive: the last enchantment after all disenchantments, the sunbeam of old age, the anxious and supreme pity with which those departing surround those who remain.

Snow was falling in thick flakes, padding the dikes. Père Duchêne skidded as he ran. At his feet the Vire seemed a black highway. As he passed by, teal rose up in pairs; coots and rails, breaking the dry, frost-covered reeds in their flight, ran over the frozen streams.

Now he has arrived at the building. No light filters through the narrow loopholes pierced in the wall. Napoléon has said it; they are in the boat at sea. The grandfather lends an ear, and his infallible matelot's hearing perceives a distant sound of oars, lazily pulled. In vain the old mariner hails the boat; the contrary wind draws his voice away, with the snow, in another direction; and the waves, breaking on the rocks, repeat in a voice infinitely varied in its intonations the same fateful cry: "Ahoy . . . ahoy . . . ahoy . . . !"

The matelot shows his fist to the great oscillating liquid mass; the night swallows his appeals; only the sea responds to him.

Then, solemnly, his figure straightened, the long hank of his hair frozen where the snow has suspended flakes, his Dantesque, bristling forehead raised, Père Duchêne throws himself into the sea in pursuit of the boat.

For that supreme moment the old man recovers the strength of his prime. He swims vigorously. The feline waves bear him and lick him like a dog recognizing its master; perhaps they will soon serve as his coffin.

The white swirls have suspended their flight; a few golden stars appear between the silver clouds, and a faint gleam, frightening the darkness, expands over paralyzed nature.

In the boat, the oars are suspended in the hands of the rowers; the young couple are about to be joined by Dorine's grandfather; the vessel sways a few brasses away.

Pierre has heard the splashing water displaced by the old mussel-fisher as he swims. Is it a sea-monster? A seal gone astray in the waters of the Manche? A human being, the living victim of a shipwreck? What miserable creature is struggling thus with the Ocean on that polar night?

Dorine's lover, leaning over the waves, interrogates the shadow: "Who goes there?" he cries, at the same time as a vigorous thrust of the oars propels the boat forward.

The old man, exhausted, breathless and frozen, cannot respond.

To illuminate the scene, the moon suddenly uncovers its broad, sardonically placid face of a floury miller; and Pierre and Dorine, terrified, see Père Duchêne before them. His small round head emerges from the waves; his sepia brown face seems carved in rock; his blue eyes are fixed; the yellow sou'wester in which he is clad is inflated stiffly around his body. He clutches at the side and hoists himself painfully into the picoteux.

Standing at the prow, which drops and rises like a chest swollen by a powerful breath, the old man, streaming, looks at them silently, his arms folded.

The swell rocks the small boat at the whim of its caprice.

The silence of the old fisherman is frightful. Imagine a damned soul who is not lamenting.

An eternity of anguish in a few seconds weighs upon the guilty parties, dismayed.

Master Belhache's son has made his decision. "Père Duchêne," he said, "we can't explain here; every instant's delay puts your life in danger. I can only tell you one thing at this moment: I swear on my honor and before God that I will marry Dorine. And you, my beloved," he added, addressing the tearful young woman, "hoist the sail; the breeze is strong and freshening; we'll be in Les Hogues in ten minutes. Hurry."

"No, no," replied the old man, very softly, shaking his head with hallucinated movements. "We're here, you see, Monsieur Belhache, over the tomb of my son. It will doubtless be mine too, for the sea is the common gave of all mariners. Adieu, then! One lets go of everything, sinks to the bottom, and that's it! So, you understand, it's only just that we discuss that brave fellow's daughter here, in view of my being her grandfather."

The fisherman changed his tone, and emphasized his use of the familiar form of address, which inflated his language with irony and scorn. "You said, I believe, that you would marry Dorine. May Saint Marcouf confound you! Your father possesses five hundred acres of land, two hundred cows and who knows what else! I'd give you in exchange my rotten picoteux and my daughter, devoid of dowry and honor. I don't believe you," Père Duchêne continued, forcefully, extending his arm toward the young man. "You're deceiving me as you've deceived her. Liar and thief!"

Carried away by a tail wind, the boat sped like an arrow, its sail deployed; and the old matelot, rigid in his frozen sou'wester, remained standing.

"Father, father," Dorine intervened, "he isn't lying..."

His back to the mast, Pierre, profoundly moved, responded in a tone warmed by pity and amour: "No, I haven't lied, poor man. I implore you, wait to judge me; don't destroy my dream, and above all, don't penetrate my soul with the hideous thought that I've deceived your child; for, you see, I'd deny my own existence, I'd believe that my body had become the plaything of a demon!"

"Well," continued the matelot, "I want to understand you, to excuse you if you can be excused; perhaps you have reasons I don't know. By what right have you taken her from me? Have you taken care of her? Have you cradled her? Don't you know that I held my breath in the long silent nights in order to hear her light respiration; that I got up, as mute as a mother, to lean over her cradle and watch over her sleep? A thousand times I defied death at the peril of the sea in order to earn her bread! And then, you don't know, young man, awkward as a seaman, that a grandfather is twice a father and that the old heart of an old man allows itself to be caught in the last trap that a little child sets for it..."

"Don't condemn me, she loves me..."

"She loves you? Impossible! Why would she love you more than me? You do her nothing but harm! And I, you know, my good God. I have done her nothing but good!"

And the poor old man lost his thoughts in an obscure labyrinth, in meditating that supreme injustice.

But the young man went on: "It's the fault of passion, you see, which has driven us toward one another; but I shall make Dorine happier than a queen, for I love her..."

Père Duchêne burst into a laughter full of madness, more heart-rending than tears.

"You love her! A fine reason! How could you not love her? Everyone loves her! She's admired like a flower blooming in a garden, or a fruit suspended from a tree in the middle of a walled orchard; but if you cut that rose, if you pluck that fruit, what are you called? Thief! Well, she is my flower, my fruit, my unique treasure, my only joy, my wealth and my everything!"

Tragic and hallucinated, the old fisherman went on, in a sort of evocation: "My Barthélemy, brave and worthy boy, I have not been able to protect your child! Forgive me, and may your soul not draw away from mine like a fire follet wandering through the darkness when I go to seek yours in the land of shadows."

Then, addressing Dorine mercifully: "Why are you weeping, my child? You never wept when you loved me. You seem as feeble as a new-born; it requires courage, however, to quit the house of one's aged father in the middle of the night, and confront the sea, when even the marine birds are forced to land."

"I have done that, Grandfather," replied the child, naïvely. "I would have braved all deaths to see him; I have not been afraid of the spells that the wicked cast by night, nor of phantoms, for something pushed me toward him. Cold does not chill those who love," she continued, excitedly, "and the sea respects whoever scorns her. I have not thought of what might happen; I did not believe that I would cause you so much chagrin. Father, I knew nothing . . ." Her face radiant, superb in her egotism, indicating Pierre, she went on: "He is so handsome; look at him, look at him . . . and he has said that I shall be his wife," Dorine added, placing her hands over her heart.

"He has said that!" repeated the pensive man, like an echo.

They fell silent suddenly. The picoteux reached the harbor, traversed the hedge of coasters aligned along the quay. To either side, newly-disembarked coal formed large heaps; wood from the north, arrived from Norway, edified bizarre constructions there, and from one end to the other of the beams, unequally superimposed, the snow had left narrow white strips. The customs officer's hut was silent; a slumped form could be divined within it. The bridge of Isigny designed its arches ahead of them; the boat was engulfed beneath a narrow vault, and, obedient to the action of the rudder, like a horse to the bit, it came to rest in front of Père Duchêne's house.

A peace replete with torpor enveloped Les Hogues; the strong odor of the sea, exhaling iodine, arrived from all directions. Every hut was covered with broad brown nets from which a little obstinate wrack hung down; in their shadow small flower-beds surrounded by shingle could be glimpsed, and the skeleton of a climbing rose, the thin and abruptly angular branches of which supported with difficulty, until Christmas, rare pink buds that would never blossom, as well as round clumps of thyme, and a border of dried and blackened carnations, or pyramids of wall-flowers powdered with white frost. Poorly-closed doors defied malefactors, and mussels destined for the market in Caen had been carelessly left outside, contained in large damp bulging sacks. Confidence is the sister of poverty.

The old mariner began to feel the repercussion of his pro-digious effort; the temporary vigor that he had imposed, by a miracle of will power, on his overworked body, fell away with the overexcitement; a release was triggered within him; he tried to speak again; Pierre and Dorine put him to bed like a child and imposed silence on him.

"Be tranquil, Grandfather," the young fisherwoman repeat-ed. "Rest. You know that he has promised."

The lovers leaned their tenderly anxious faces over him, and, seeing them so beautiful and so amorous, their actions seemed less odious to the old man. Memories came to him of his youth and his distant voyages, when, as a matelot, in the Oceanian is-lands, under skies clement to amour, he had encountered savage couples, enlaced and wandering in the shade of flowery forests.

Fever gripped him, with delirium. He agitated, rolling his head over his pillows

With a slow movement; then, addressing an invisible inter-locutor, Père Duchêne, turned to the wall, repeated: "He has said that! He has said that!"

Slumber invaded him gradually. When day was about to break, Pierre Belhache quit the cottage and returned to La Miseraigne.

It was not good to approach Master Belhache that morning, so Pierre decided to postpone until the evening the conversation he wanted to have with his father on the subject of his marriage.

The farmer had just been subjected to a frightful scene. An eighteen-year-old farm girl, sacked for misconduct, was the au-thor of it. The wretched girl had given birth during the night. A mother for the first time, she claimed that she had been seduced by the farmer of La Miseraigne. She was also being dismissed because, in the circumstance, she had not acted in accordance with custom. The case is, in fact, anticipated; in every Norman village there is a midwife who draws an income for all the farm girls, mothers every year, and provides a nursery in which all the poor babies born of those creatures are deposited, destined to perish before long for want of care. Some of the poor disinher-ited individuals suffer the torture of childbirth in the meadows. Nothing is less rare than infanticide, and the farmers, the cause of all the evil, placidly see the pregnant companions of their vulgar pleasures taken to prison.

Master Belhache, pacing back and forth in the yard, vocif-erated: "I have ten girls, ten milkmaids, and one of them has the effrontery to give birth here, instead of going to Mère Gallu in Isigny? Look at Mélie, who's on her eighth, and isn't incon-venienced. Go find the midwife, I tell you. You claim that it's mine, but you don't know that, and nor do I. Hey, Picot," he cried, interrogating a valet who was standing open-mouthed at the door of the stable, "You're married—do you have children?"

"Excuse me, Master Belhache," the fellow replied, touching his cap modestly, "my wife has three of them."

That amiable repartee sparked general gaiety, and vulgar laughter erupted from all corners of the building.

Then the servant girl, an energetic brunette with big bones and intersecting eyebrows sheltering eyes like coals, approached the farmer with menace in her eyes, darting a sharp and hateful glare at him.

"No, Master Belhache," she said to him, "I won't do as the others do; I won't go to La Gallu, the child is yours, for sure; you're sending us away haughtily, well, you'll remember me. See you again!"

She disappeared, trudging.

Every Norman cultivator, every petty merchant or journeyman stuffed with excessively rich nourishment has the obstinate egotism of a hundred bourgeois and encloses himself arrogantly in his material wellbeing, insolent and pitiless with the unfortunate. For those vulgar natures, down-to-earth and devoid of ideals, to be poor is a crime recognized by the Low Norman code. To have heart and delicate sentiments is a phenomenon much more curious than a heifer with two heads.

Needless to say, no one felt sorry for the poor milkmaid.

The farmer of La Miseraigne did not show himself, in this case, any worse than the others; he was following the tradition; and within Cotentinais memory, I don't know that things have ever happened otherwise.

Unfortunately for him, Master Belhache had fallen, in this instance, on a grim, masculine and intrepid nature. Instead of groaning, submitting and accepting all the shame for herself, the dismissed maidservant departed from the customary rut. All day long she remained in the vicinity of the farm, lying in wait.

The farmer did not imagine that he had anything else to fear than sorcery. He would have been very astonished had anyone told him that the tall brunette with a sturdy and lithe figure wanted to make an attempt on his life, but he believed her quite capable, for example, given her irascible nature, of going to find a celebrated bone-setter in Caenchy. That individual, known throughout the region for the singular facility he possessed of changing into a dog, would come into his pastures in the morning, having adopted the form of the quadruped; with his paws he would overturn pitchers full of milk without the frightened maidservants being able to prevent him. Furthermore, it was a fact averred by everyone that a peasant fatigued by the evil spells of the animal who lay in ambush in a hedge had wounded the mysterious black dog in the shoulder, and that, having gone to the dwelling of the sorcerer, the country-dweller found the latter in bed and ill following a gunshot wound he had received—which proved peremptorily that there was no mistake in attributing to him, as a new Proteus, that surprising faculty of changing form.

Perhaps the milkmaid would even give him a hundred-sou coin in order for him to put that pistole, with some groundsel, in a box placed in a corner of the bone-setter's cupboard. If, after a fortnight, on opening the box, a live toad was found instead of the vanished coin, it would be an infallible sign that the spell elaborated by the sorcerer had succeeded fully.

Then, at Le Miseraigne, terrible things would be seen; the yellow cream fixed in the large pots would begin to turn; the cows would perish while calving; the chickens would catch pip; everything would go wrong until Master Belhache paid the bone-setter richly, begging him to lift the spell.

That prospect was bound to make the farmer seriously anxious, but he did not have the leisure to examine all those misfortunes in depth.

That same evening, Master Jean Belhache was sitting, as he was accustomed to do at the end of the day, on one of the large mossy stones rolled in front of the gates of the farm. Replete in the brutal slaking of his passions, his stomach confident and his vanity satisfied, he was inhaling voluptuously the heavy odors coming from the meadows, where the soil is excessively fecund.

The darkness, accomplice of vengeance, was blinding; at night, only hearing counsels and guides. The farmer of La Misteraigne had lazy ears. He did not hear the rude and angular peasant girl approaching him, gliding as silently as a snake. When she was very close to the cultivator, who was dreaming, calculating his wealth, his head in his hands, she raised her two muscular arms into the air, stretching them, armed with one of those enormous spades rounded in the form of an oar, employed in the cultivation of gardens, and then she brought it down with an effort of her entire being, delivering a formidable blow to the nape of Master Jean Belhache. The cutting edge of the instrument plunged in all the way to the ears; gray matter spurted out; the farmer collapsed without uttering a cry.

Pierre and Dorine were married in the church with svelte ogives, before the altar where the Virgin in a black robe held a beribboned infant in her arms, the same one at which Richard, Duc de Normandie, mad with love, married the beautiful Gonnor.

Their union caused great rumor in the region; people regretted that Master Belhache had died before being able to prevent such a scandal. Marriageable daughters were indignant, and put away, with chagrin, the precious bonnets destined for their wedding celebrations. That coiffure, of folded lace, hides the hair and poses on a black velvet headband enclosing the temples; above the forehead a golden brooch holds the orange blossom. Which of them, in fact, refined by three years in the convent, had not coveted for a husband that handsome pale youth with the long black hair?

The occasion passed very simply.

Dorine, apt for all transformations, had slipped her delightful body into a long white dress without any ornament; her adorable hair, put up, made a nimbus for her, and amour an aureole; nacreous pearls with a discreet gleam, sown in its silky torsades, sparkled with a soft radiance; one might have thought them drops of milk in which a flame was floating.

Pierre straightened his indolent stature; the blood ran rosier under the epidermis, rendering his amber pallor warmer.

A few old mariners, accompanying Père Duchêne, stood behind the spouses, bare-headed, bonnets in hand.

Kneeling beside one another, Pierre and Dorine looked at one another with eyes full of gratitude, surprised to be giving one another reciprocally such a great joy. In them, amazement prevailed over ecstasy; there was no longer an abyss between all and nothing, time was indifferent to them; perhaps the sea no longer existed; perhaps the flowers were blooming again, for gusts of spring were stifling them. Who, then was Napoléon Lelandais? Had anyone cried to Père la Roupie: "When's the wedding?" Had there ever been a rotten picoteux in Les Hogues? Had anyone weathered the tempest in it? Had the grandfather been seen, by night, struggling against the icy waves? Had an abandoned building sheltered their amours? Had Père Belhache died with his skull split?

The present happiness absorbed the past. An untranslatable and unconscious need to laugh and to weep found an equilibrium in their hearts, preventing them from yielding to one or other of those two natural expressions of the movements of their souls. The infinity of their joy was decomposed into a thousand unanalyzable sentiments; kaleidoscopes passed before them in which their entire lives filled past in rapid points of view, and in which the scenes were shrunk in the perspective of the years. In spite of the sanctity of the place and the gravity of the circumstance, distant and puerile memories obsessed them, to the exclusion of more serious events.

It was thus that, in the worm-eaten confessional, with the excessively short green curtains, the young groom recalled having recounted improbable sins in a low voice; having slyly suspended himself, in the deserted church, on the thick, shiny, blackened rope, for the sacrilegious pleasure of feeling himself lifted from the ground in an ascension full of charm and fear, to the great alarm of laborers and crows, skillful measurers of time. Pierre also thought, with remorse, that he had killed couples of grebes and broken their fragile eggs.

For her part, Dorine recalled that one day, when she was six years old, she had been brought to the church on the day of the festival of Saint Marcouf; the large gilded vases on the altar had been ornamented with flowering whitethorn, and for two sous, a gospel had been read for her in honor of the patron of the village; distracted by a fly she had raised her head and seen floating overhead a pretty schooner in precious wood, with its sails and rigging, and the delicate little ship was still there, except that it seemed smaller and not as high.

In the confusion of their reflections, the idea of death brushed both of them for an instant, but they rejected it, convinced that death would never attain them.

O youth, apotheosis of life, season in which amour makes the soul lurch, in which faces are devoid of melancholy, in which eyes full of mirages see the future strewn with flowers and the indefinite multiplication of joys! O youth, you are the supreme wealth, the treasure of which time, alas, robs us too rapidly.

Père Duchêne, more curbed than ever, withered like a dry herb, considered his granddaughter with resigned eyes; his round head was slightly elongated by suffering. In the end, the sacrifice was consummated. Dorine seemed happy; so much the better, doubtless. She had changed proprietor and amour. The new beloved had put pearls in the hair of his Dorine, frozen drops of the sea; he, the poor old man, had often shaken his oar over the child's head, and liquid pearls, iridescent in the sunlight, had rendered her as beautiful, but had only shone for a moment in the burnished gold of her tresses. Everything was finished now, and of her tenderness, Dorine would only give him alms in passing; for the child was running to an unknown life and the grandfather was remaining alone, nailed in the past. It was necessary for him to renounce unshared kisses and charming caresses, the prelude to amour in which the grace of young women is exercised, catching old fathers in deceptive nets, through which they cannot see the tomb.

The priest had finished. The bride descended the narrow nave, entered the old oak benches, carrying in her dress the blue flakes of the odorous smoke of the incense. Dorine's footsteps were as lively and light as those of a bird ready to take flight; Pierre's, proud and assured, caused his varnished boots to click slightly on the large flagstones with Gothic inscriptions. The old mariners, marching on land with an uncertain gait, waddled in cadence, obedient to the unforgettable rhythm of the great cradle-song intoned by the waves. In the wake of the joyful and naïve guests, a grave heavy tread was perceived, that of an old man who would not march for much longer, a bleak tread that hope no longer hastened, the tread of a father who would no longer follow his child; it was that of the old fisherman.

In the large granite font in the form of a bowl, where the lustral water evaporates gradually in the shadow of great pillars, everyone dipped their fingers and bore them to their foreheads; abruptly, outside, the wind wiped away the trace of the moist touch, producing a sharp sensation of cold.

At the farm, a lavish dinner had been prepared. The old sea dogs did honor to it soberly, and when dusk came, they departed again for Les Hogues, along the Vire. Père Duchêne went with them, in spite of the protestations of his children, who made every effort to keep him with them.

"Later," he responded to them, with an enigmatic and dolorous smile.

52

Dorine hung around his neck, as coaxing as in the best days. "Soon, isn't it? Say soon, dear good papa."

"Soon," conceded the old man, kissing the young woman's hair passionately.

For as long as they could, the spouses accompanied him with their eyes, but at the end in the sloping path. The pale head of Père Duchêne, coiffed in his strange little three-piece bonnet, from which his long wisp of gray hair emerged, did not take long to disappear.

The disabled picoteux has been retired. The wounds that the sea had opened in its flank, the singing caulker could no longer fill with his lint of oakum and pitch; very solely, it is rotting before the house of its former master, without the hope of any last graving, devoid of paint and tar; in their play, children make its split and caved-in carcass creak; people stick out their tongues at its timbers. Never again, in the interval between the tides, will the fisher go to seek the mussels with dark violet shells, nor the blondes, nor the transplanted tulips wedged in the holes in stones and madrepores; for since the terrible night on which Père Duchêne had hurled himself into the water to go in search of Dorine, he remains weak; on fine days he can be seen warming himself in the sun, atonal and mute. But when a three-master comes in the channel with all sails aloft, the matelot emerges from his torpor and rediscovers a residue of life; he drags himself painfully to the white-painted lighthouse where the pilots are conversing gravely.

March has returned; violets are budding, hidden under the new leaves; daises are blooming on the banks of the dikes, covered in thick grass where mint mingles with wild thyme, sea oats with darnel, meadow foxtail with marine club-rushes, water plantain with bog-stars, and phalaris with groundsel; sheep graze there without hindrance; often, some of them descend as far as the bank of the Vire, and are seen stretching their heads out curiously over the water.

On certain days, the sea, like a silky and silvery sheet, remains pure and unwrinkled; little light clouds suspended in the pale sky remain motionless in the depths of the limpid mirror; the picoteux with white sails and yellow sails, the fishermen and fisherwomen with tanned skin, and the gulls with golden beaks, are reflected faithfully therein.

On other days, the deceptive calm disappears and the tempest suddenly bursts, furiously. It is the season of unexpected shipwrecks, cyclones and typhoons; the sky and the sea seem to plot the doom of the mariner and collaborate in order to deceive his vigilance.

On an equinoctial high tide, the *Charles-Jean*, a Norwegian navigating between Christiania and Isigny, was signaled. A north-easterly wind was blowing violently; the muddy yellow sea was carrying algae and wreckage; waves with glaucous reflections launched forth madly against the stone ramparts, spring impetuously over the obstacle that the dikes opposed to them and falling back in fine white dust; the buoys of the channel disappeared under the foam; and as far as the eye could see, there was nothing but waves without number, overtaking one another, uniting, dispersing, hollowing out, rising up like walls and mingling their snowy fleeces.

A dull rumor full of tumult reached the ears of the matelots grouped anxiously at the end of the môle.

Solitary, Père Duchêne was also listening to the great furious voice of the storm.

The *Charles-Jean* was in sight. Everyone said his word:

"A brave hull, lads!"

"Look at that; she's diving like a gull!"

"Be bold, lads!"

"Oh, hoist! She's taking in a reef!"

"Cargue all! The canvas is adrift!"

"Another wave washing the deck!"

"A rude porpoise!"

"Solid in clearing the deck, lads!"

"Bravo the topmen!"

The ship draws nearer; the guttural voices of the northern sailor, the blond Norwegians, known and loved, are audible.

"Prepare to come about!" commands the pilot.

The attention of the spectators redoubles.

Still alone, Père Duchêne advances to the edge of the jetty, unsteadily. A little more and he will be precipitated into the swirling current.

"Watch your feet, Père la Roupie! You're going to fall into the sea!"

Too late . . . the old man has disappeared.

Mooring-ropes are thrown; a boat is launched; men dive—wasted effort. The waves keep their prey, for the sea, you see, is the common grave of mariners.

ROSE
(*La Revue Bleue*, May 1889)

HALF-BURIED under the twisted apple trees, very humble and very low, the Breton cottage, with its thatch rod drawn back over two dusty windows like a felt hat over an old man's eyes, seems more rickety and decrepit in this spring full of sap, in the midst of nascent crops.

Winter, which fecundates the glebe and rejuvenates nature eternally, hollows out the wrinkles of unrepaired old buildings cruelly, aggravating the cracks, protecting the sly collapses in which a few ancient stones fall soundlessly, a distressing material defection.

The cottage threatens ruin; however, a numerous family finds shelter there by night and bread by day: eight children, six boys and two girls, an exhausted father and an infirm mother, paralyzed in the legs since the birth of Rose.

Oh, that child has caused a great deal of affliction; they have all suffered because of her, deprived of the woman's activity and heavy share of the labor that makes a laborer's rustic house rich.

She knows that very well, the girl. Her humble, very soft gaze resembles a perpetual apology. She multiplies herself, employing herself in the hardest tasks, looking after the pigs, taking up the compost heap, cleaning the stables, and it is not her who dresses up to go to the town to sell the butter, the eggs and the flour of the black wheat. The father does not like the sight of her; although he is a Christian he has a fashion of shaking his sad head silently when he reposes in the evening by the fireplace, sitting on the leather-clad bench, when she pokes the fire with the tips of the shiny tongs, inclining the wings of her head-dress toward the flames.

But the invalid agitates in her bed or makes the shaky boards of her old armchair with straw cushions creak, and Rose turns to the paralytic, smiling. The continual caress of that smile diminishes the affliction of the peasant woman. Rose is the child of her heart, the enchantment of her eyes; the ingenious care with which she surrounds the invalid lightens the latter's woes; the girl willingly deprives herself of all pleasure in order that the mother can sometimes have, secretly, a cup of hot coffee, abundantly sugared, which the old woman awaits with a kind of touching quasi-animal sensuality. It is the best part of the day, the moment when, behind closed doors, she delivers herself to that clandestine feast.

One evening, while they were supping on boiled chestnuts crushed in milk, the father, careworn and a little tremulous, spoke.

It could not last; the soil was becoming miserly, doubtless weary of having measured its gifts. It was necessary to make a decision. They never had money in reserve, the garments were worn out, the house itself was falling apart. It was necessary that the boys stay, because of the fields. Furthermore, Jean was about to do military service, and that would be one mouth less. But the girls! They did not need two housekeepers, since misfortune had determined that the mother was incapacitated. So one of them must decide on a change in condition. The daughter of Guillaume, their neighbor, earned a good wage in Paris and did not complain about the work. With good conduct, one thrives anywhere.

The old woman, very pale, sitting up, wrung her wrinkled hands. The boys, in a naïve gaucherie of attitude, looked at their sisters with a certain malaise. The coquette Annik turned a deaf ear; she had a gallant and did not care for such a distant exile. Then Rose, her lips trembling, after having looked at the paralytic for a long time, with an infinite love, said simply:

"I'll go, Father, whenever you wish."

⁂

She departed one morning when it had rained lightly over the region. It was the time of the grass-cutting, when the scythes were mowing the moist meadows with broad gestures. Vapors blanched the distances slightly between the poplars and the willows, and, as she passed the presbytery, the warm odor of the flowering lindens suddenly descended upon her in intoxicating gusts.

Rose climbed into a third class carriage, among mariners who were singing and agitating in the smoke. At the moment of departure her father embraced her more tenderly than he had ever done. The train drew away in silence after one last strident screech, and in the evening she met a fellow countrywoman, a good soul, who took her, utterly bewildered, to one of the hotels frequented by Breton domestics, in the depths of a cul-de-sac in Batignolles.

"It's a good quarter to go into service," her companion told her. "Tranquil people, many from the homeland."

They had, in fact, encountered a few coiffed in bonnets with tapering wings, mounted over smooth blonde tresses.

The next day, Rose went to the nearest placement bureau, two rooms on an obscure entresol overlooking a gray courtyard. The agent, an old woman surrounded by numerous little dogs, got up from an old yellow sofa encumbered by fripperies and drew the young woman toward the light.

She had a client who was very difficult to satisfy, who had the custom of only engaging as domestics maids arriving directly from the country, in the flower of their ignorant credulity.

"Have you served before?"

"Never, Madame."

"How are your parents, my girl?"

"They're very well, thank you, except for my mother . . ."

"That's not what I mean. How are they in their affairs? Good or bad, comfortable or poor?"

"Poor, Madame, unfortunately."

"Good," said the old woman, with satisfaction. "And you, my girl . . . Rose, I believe . . . are you docile? Have you a good character? Are you not too susceptible?"

"I don't believe so, Madame. I haven't come to Paris of my own will, but that of my masters. As for what I think myself, I'm free, and I keep it to myself."

"That's good; you'll do. Go right away to this address, on the fourth floor, door to the left. Above all don't speak to the concierge."

"Don't worry; I don't know him."

Rose hastened through a maze of little streets with black and viscous paving-stones, above which the dazzling azure sparkled of a sky that appeared to the Bretonne more profound, more elevated and more accessible than the ceiling of the fields, which inclines so softly toward the horizons behind curtains of tall trees.

She was seen to traverse the square, giving signs of a profound admiration. Unfortunately, the wheezing of locomotives, arriving breathlessly in the nearby railway station, or the harrowing whistle of a train in flight caused her to stop dead.

Not without vertigo, with her eyes shut and her hand on the rail, she climbed the four staircases indicated, without counting them, imagining that she was in a tower with no exit.

It was on the top floor, an apartment with a balcony. After an instant's reflection, Rose tugged on a hind's foot which hung down the wall. She saw without surprise the little black hoof of the gentle animal remain in her hand, and she kept it there until someone came to open the door.

The door opened by a crack; then Rose, rapidly and silently, held out the foot of the stag's companion, curved like the butt of a weapon, in the obscurity of the vestibule. A hand came down upon it, and just as the young woman opened her mouth to say: "I'm Rose, the maid sent by . . ." a wild scream resounded, and a large form collapsed, crying: "Murder! It's a revolver!"

That was Rose's first interview with her mistress.

The lodgings were vast and comfortable: no children; Monsieur always absent, Madame always present, followed by a she-cat with large perfidious green eyes and long silky hair.

Madame Chamaillot was one of those housewives simultaneously sentimental and harsh, unhinged by modern and fantastic reading, of which she had only grasped the unhealthy and false aspect. Not good, with that, kneaded by the strangest pretentions in spite of the forty years vigorously emphasized on the features of the bony brunette.

A provincial, never emerging from her quarter, which she mistook for the center of the high life, except to descend from an omnibus into one of those great bazaars of novelties that collect every day the dangerous idleness of so many women.

Ludicrous ideas and a hint of aggressive madness had created a void around her. Friends of both sexes had been dispersed; even her husband only appeared at meal times, during which he gazed straight ahead with an innocent expression and a puerile smile. Then, exasperated, abandoned alone with her maid and her cat, Madame Chamaillot had made an equitable division of her unemployed tenderness and her unslaked rancor; the former descended upon Minoute in a rain of treats and affectionate words; the latter fell, thick and wounding, upon the shoulders of the maidservant, often dismissed or resigning of her own accord, who was seen, her eyes as large as Easter eggs, tumbling down the staircases behind her trunk, flying on the shoulders of a porter, shedding torrents of tears, while the irascible bourgeois hurled her final maledictions from the top of the stairs.

Rose set out to please with all the obstinacy of her race; she ran to the appeal of her mistress, served her in bed in the morning, made the gift to Minoute of a beautiful collar on which was engraved the word fidelity; she chose for the angora's meals the most delicate morsels, and, knowing that Madame liked the parquets well waxed, launched herself through the rooms with her two brushes every morning like an audacious skater.

But the strange Madame Chamaillot, like a capricious beast, jibbed at everything and never disarmed. She harassed the young woman, spied on her, eavesdropped on her and humiliated her by pointing out, to the benefit of her own charms, the physical flaws that she discovered in the poor Bretonne.

Sometimes, Madame Chamaillot stopped Rose in front of the long looking-glass and, dominating her by a head, said to her in an imperative tone: "Look at yourself!"

Rose, with her short stature, wrapped in a fustian bodice tailored like a nun's coat, her red hands sticking out of sleeves with black wrists, raised a timid gaze toward her image.

"Now look at me. There! Well, what do you think? Is there the slightest relationship between you and me? Are we even of the same race? What have you come to do in Paris, poor girl? You're ugly, short, knotty as a bundle of sticks, with no intelligence. In your place, I'd throw myself out of the window!"

Rose, whose robust common sense was not curbed by that wind of folly, then looked without vertigo, with a secret irony, at the palms and green plants agitating their foliage near the perforated railing of the balcony.

At other times, the cat with the green eyes served as a pretext for obsessions of another sort.

"Rose, Minoute has spots on her head, you can't have cooked her liver well enough."

"Madame is surely mistaken; she's out of sorts, the animal; it's necessary to make her take medicine."

Or: "Rose, Minoute has abscesses in her mouth, inside her cheeks. Where has that come from? She doesn't want to go into the kitchen any more; there's a bad smell there that she doesn't like—she's so sensitive!" Or even: "You must have beaten her."

One night, Madame Chamaillot had the maidservant get up, and, huddled under her bedclothes, fixing her with haggard eyes, she enjoined her to look under her bed.

"Madame," said the girl, flat on her stomach in the carpet, without departing from her usual calmness, "there's nothing at all, except for a little dust."

"Dust, Rose? That's how you do my room? Go to bed."

And Madame Chamaillot, relieved, her nerves soothed, stretched herself out and went to sleep.

✳

In September, Rose received a letter from the paralytic conceived thus:

> *Dear daughter,*
>
> *It is with maternal love that I am conversing with my cherished Rose, in response to your letter, which has reassured us in our anxieties. The affairs of the house are much the same; we have two cows and a beautiful heifer. The work is abundant. The season isn't good, because of the prolongation of the rain; the wheat isn't producing much grain and the potatoes are rotting; the best thing is the fruit. In a word, the season is thin, but it's necessary to ask God*

for health and his mercy, one will always be content by means of good conduct. Your brother Martin is still the same ignorant; little Yvon is only too awake, by night in his studies . . . a singer to infinity . . . at present, it's the vacation, he goes to the field, and the king isn't his cousin, for he has taken out the savings that he's put away over two years in order to buy a little lamb. Oh, how content he is.

Everything in the region is passing coldly, as usual; the inhabitants are bleak. Nothing new that merits your attention. Louisa has married old Méry, who is twenty years older than her; he's rich, she's content.

My child, your old mother is languishing since she no longer has her Rose. Save up your little sous in order not to lose the fruits of your labors, and don't forget the poor infirm woman in the midst of your pleasures.

If my family is doing well, I shall say to God, when I leave this world, that I am dying content.

Adieu, dear girl.

A short time later, Madame Chamaillot, in the wake of an argument with her dressmaker more impetuous than usual, fell into a crisis so violent that she had to be put away in a sanitarium.

Monsieur took her there in a carriage, and when he came back, in a disengaged fashion, with his placid smile, he dismissed Rose, who wept like a gutter.

She went into the home of good bourgeois, simple folk, in a house that had no cat or looking-glass, and as Christmas approached, the young woman stopped every day before the window displays, somewhat perplexed, wondering how she could get some money to her dear invalid to buy a small provision of coffee and sugar, that treat of old people, which warms up their worn-out bodies momentarily. She saw her in thought dragging herself to the hearth, curbed over the fireplace, while the men slowly maneuvered the plow in the field or threshed the grain in the barn, while moaning.

One evening, while bringing the children back from school, she perceived in a grocer's brightly-illuminated window, between a Christmas tree and a personification of Winter, an object appropriate to symbolize her offering and to conceal it. It was a little coffee-mill in mat sugar, like masonry, with ink and yellow reliefs: one of those touching and vulgar surprise bonbons that it does not seem possible to break into.

She bought it and, before sending it, slipped two louis into the ingenious hiding-place that it contained; she wrote to the village the same evening, by the light of her smoky lamp, in her attic, while blowing on her fingers, on a beautiful sheet of paper decorated with designs and flowers.

Everyone had a gift: a jersey for the father, shoes for little Yvon and socks for all his brothers.

For you, dear mother, she said in conclusion, *I've only found this little mill, which is good to tell you that I'm miserable. Eat it very slowly, when you're alone, and take care, above all—for it's hard in places—not to break your teeth.*

A PISTOL SHOT

(*La Nouvelle revue internationale européenne*, September 1891)

IT HAPPENED in Granville last Sunday, before the departure for the Banks.

After reading the offices in her large prayer book, my grandmother replaced her spectacles in their tinplate case, adjusted her immense bonnet of fine cotton with a coquettish gesture, as if it were able to give her the proudest youth, flicked away a few grains of snuff that had fallen on her pigeon-throat fish-tail blanket and smoothed her green silk apron over her knees.

We sensed a story coming. The cat purred on the foot-warmer between the good woman's slippers; two burly matelots, as strong as Turks, were smoking their long Jersey pipes silently; a young woman who had no need of anything, I assure you, to occupy her mind, standing by the window, was gazing without seeing it, at the snow falling behind the little green panes; the old uncle was asleep, holding an almanac upside-down; and I, a bad cabin boy, the latest arrival in the house, perched on a chair, was painting a fine ship.

The lads, at the start, murmured against the wasted evening. "Brigand of time! Come on, Mother leave your paternosters, and you, uncle, leave your book in peace. Damnable man, nose always buried in politics."

"What politics? I was sleeping blissfully."

"Well," said my grandmother, with the prompt gesture of a valiant old woman, "aren't a good fire in the heath, a well insulated room, and warm *flip* in an earthenware pot made with sweet cider, brandy and sugar, enough for a snowy evening? In my day, youth was less morose."

When she evoked that lost youth, her gaze seemed to take on all the fire of its first bloom; she was no longer the old woman that one saw every day sitting in the doorway or in the tortuous street, enveloped in her black *capot* and curbed over her stick, worthy of a rare engraving or etching to revive an eccentric figure full of vigor; one might have thought one were contemplating what is known as a beautiful "*conée*," one of the pure Graveillaises of La Roque, who still speak half the language in which Wace[1] wrote, mingled with a host of mariner terms and colorful expressions in a style more Moorish than Spanish, with the figure of Venus, jealous black eyebrows and an imperious gaze, before which men wilted, without a well-defined character and seemingly part of a colony of silent slaves tolerated on that shore by a seething people of amazons.

"Tell them, then Grandma," I cried in an important manner, "the story you've told me a hundred times. You know! That will cheer them up a little."

Everyone supported me with voices and gestures, and silence was re-established more profoundly in the old granite house suspended from the rampart. Nothing could any longer be heard inside but the clock agitating in its fir-wood box, and nothing outside but a grand rumor like the tumultuous sound of wind racing through an oak wood—but more extreme and more menacing: always the same anthem, of course, our

---

1 Wace was a tenth-century Norman poet, credited with two important romances. One of them, Roman de Brut, is a vernacular rendering of the legendary history of Britain invented by the Anglo-Norman Geoffrey of Monmouth, which made a considerable contribution to the popularization of Arthurian legend in France; the other, *Roman de Rou*, includes a long account of the Norman conquest of England.

neighbor the sea growling as she beat against the robust flanks of La Roque!

In order to get herself in the mood my grandmother offered a pinch of tobacco to the uncle, her old friend, and smiled agreeably. He responded to her politeness with a fine bow and a few compliments on her appearance—for it was once the custom of old people, although poor, to exchange civilities between them, often with as much wit as any other kind of person. Then she scratched a little blue mark at the tip of her nose, of which she had always been proud, and commenced.

It was the twenty-first of Brumaire in Year Two of Liberty—as your grandfather, a man of the old school, who had known hard times, would have said—and the Vendean army was headed for Granville in order to open the door to the English. In fact, Lord Moira was waiting at Guernsey with his flotilla of forces composed of Germans and émigrés. Well, those dirty dogs had the courage to send Frenchmen to break heads in their stead. For they were Frenchmen, those Vendeans, those Whites, and that was why the Rue des Juifs wasn't up in arms for the landing and they weren't smoked like herrings, whereas, for the redcoats, you know, children, it was: "Up! Up! All hands on deck! Axes between the teeth! Fire at will!"

My father came in that evening in great excitement. He said that the Chouans had gone around Avranches and would be with us in no time. He scarcely had time to swallow a bowl of soup before he started to empty the dresser, the cupboard and the chest of drawers and to make parcels of everything that we possessed, which a neighbor was to come and collect in order to hide it in the country with his own effects. I was fifteen years old and I helped as best I could, without sharing his apprehensions, so easy was I with the stir that had been made in the town since morning, the animation of the streets where carts full of flour and vegetables succeed one another without interruption. The continual passage of soldiers relieving the posts and taking orders to the square where the scouts were being dispatched, as well as the fantastic supposition of old wives, to which those comings and goings gave rise, whipped up my curiosity and filled me with a certain joy.

So I was to witness terrible events! I experienced all the emotions, mingled with dread, of a young soldier on the eve of his first battle. Many women of Granville felt the same; many showed a courage equal to their brothers in serving the batteries and transporting munitions; one widow is cited, nicknamed La Vigoureuse, who was killed on her artillery piece defending liberty. I stayed by the fire knitting for a long time, sitting on the stool on which my late mother had once sat, while my father spent his time inspecting his rifle, sharpening his hatchet and casting bullets from all the spoons in the house.

The rude man made his preparations silently, with a terrible expression. Suddenly, he turned to me and said, softly: "What, not yet in bed, funny little girl? Put a log on the fire and go to sleep. It's not a time for staying up late."

"Tell me, then, Papa, I asked, with a serious expression, plying my needles, "is it not until tomorrow that we're fighting?"

"Yes my little citizeness," he replied, taking me in his arms, "And *Vive la République!*"

I heard my father go to bed; he blew out the candle and started snoring, as usual, neither more nor less. *Good*, I thought, on hearing him, *the fire isn't yet in the well; let's imitate him.* And I went to sleep like a log.

The next day at eleven o'clock, the cooking-pot was on the fire and we were putting the cabbages in when my comrade Mathieu, father's godson, three years older than me, came in. He was a pulley-man in the docks, as tall as the doorway, square-shouldered, slim and supple in the back.

Oh, my good Saint Anne, it was no longer the time when, as simple kids, we played *galinettte*.[1] We'd been seen in the Nères-Vaches, at the rendezvous of loyal lovers; we'd danced, me in plum-wood clogs, him in leather brodequins, on the heath at Donville while the violin scraped all day long—the two step, the *Carillon de Dunkerque* and the *Gigne*—while father played cards under the arbor.

He had seen a hussar at the gallop, heading for the commandant in the square, where he arrived out of breath from following him. It was about to warm up. All the mariners in the port were like freshly-sharpened hatchets. Palisades were defending the outlying districts; Chouanerie was about to have news of him, Mathieu, without delay.

"Yes!" I said, blushing proudly, "there's going to be fire and sack here!"

A few moments later, however, the general summons was sounded; the drums beat furiously and the clarions. Then Mathieu ran to the attic to change clothes before fighting—not wanting, he said, if he were captured by the Chouans, with his work clothes in rags, to be mistaken for an onion-seller, nor to resemble the hordes of beggars whom the Vendeans dragged in their wake. My father put up much less opposition because he was dressed carefully himself: a broad-brimmed waxed hat, a cornflower blue jacket with tails and brass buttons bearing an anchor in relief and wide britches; a piece of carrot inflated his cheek, with which he was livening up his plug of tobacco—such was his costume of war.

We ran to the door. An order of the municipality forbade women and children to leave the houses. No one appeared

---

1 Literally, a galinette is a kind of fish, a species of gurnard, but it also referred to a kind of dance, and it is the latter meaning that provides the basis for the metaphorical usage here.

disposed to obey it, for there had never been more young pale brunettes in the streets, coiffed with "cones" or "dauphines," chattering like magpies, not so many old "*capotées*" wagging their chins and raising their arms to the heavens.

"Alas, good people," said one of them, "what's wrong?"

"Oh, Mother," replied another, "don't you know what's happening?"

"Nothing at all. I haven't put my nose outside and haven't seen a living soul all blessed day."

"Well, Granville's in a state of siege. The citizen representative declared it this morning."

"That's nonsense, my poor woman—does anyone even know what it means?"

The feminine gathering was driven back, mouths closed, in an instant by the march past of troops that were going out to reconnoiter the enemy forces, which were thought to be considerable. Cavalrymen, infantrymen and artillery caissons, were descending from La Roque with an admirable briskness; the faces were placid and almost joyful, the brass sparkling, the weapons shiny; one might have thought that the men were going to be passed in review as a prelude to a civic fête.

Mathieu emerged from the loft as handsome as a star, holding his old clothes under his arm, which he threw into a corner. I ran to kiss him, hanging round his neck like a medal. Father grumbled: "That's how it is! Come on lad, enough silliness. Go fetch a bowl of cider."

They drank with a grave expression, swearing: "Death to the Chouans! Live free or die!"

I thought them very fine, at that moment, as bold as people in stories; in any case, the idea of death awoke nothing, nothing at all, in my heart. Foolish and blind youth! They seized their weapons and their ammunition, and departed without looking back.

I wasn't to go out under any pretext; I had promised—well, yes—but I couldn't remain in place; my knitting was burning

70

my fingers; one instant saw me at the hearth, another in front of my cracked mirror, in which a worried face looked at me, hair in disorder. Then I smiled to cheer up my company, but it was a forced smile. I adopted a detached attitude, like a man who finds his creditor in a place where he didn't expect him. My eyes had never seemed so dark or so wide.

Suddenly, *boom!* That's when we heard the cannon: *boom!* And again, *boom!* What a fine echo in the sea, what an imposing sound!

No longer able to stand it, I ran outside.

I had scarcely taken ten steps when an old whaler with a wooden leg stopped me in passing.

"Hey, young citizen, where are you dragging your trawl? Back to your berth, my girl, and quicker than that!"

"Let me pass, Maser," I said, sketching a brief curtsy. "I can carry stones to the wall like anyone else or serve the soldiers; I'm afraid at home."

He lifted his stick, swearing like a pagan against me and my wheedling sex, and I went home, very sullen.

Then the idea came to me to put on Mathieu's clothes. A demon had got hold of me, I wanted to see the battle.

In the blink of an eye the woolen bonnet took the place of my dauphine and hid my hair; Mathieu's trousers, which, fortunately, only went down to the knees, fit like a glove—at least, I thought so—and the jacket, whose holed sleeves let the whiteness of my elbow show through, seemed to me as desired.

I returned to the mirror and, lifting my arms, shaking my fist and grinding my teeth I shouted, like Mathieu: "Death to the Chouans! Live free or die!"

A loaded pistol, forgotten on the table, which I stuck in my belt, completed my equipment.

Abandoning the upper town I ran to the Plat-Gousset—a little square in front of the great gate with the portcullis—in the direction of the cannon- and rifle-fire; the smoke could be seen upriver of Saint-Pair.

A few cannoneers of the Social Contract, sitting on a bench in front of the post, joked about my outfit. Then the crippled old whaler, who was there, retorted: "Leave him alone, damn it! Plenty of cabin boys like that have already seen fire aboard, and fought like father and mother."

I started to laugh, running toward the old quarters.

I soon saw several cavalrymen arriving at top speed, going past the shipyards of Port Foulon; many others were following. From another direction, the soldiers of our garrison were returning at the double toward the square, pursued by the enemy, who were beginning to press them closely. No one looked at me. Retracing my steps, I started running with the soldiers, half-carried by the great movement of men.

General Peyre, the commander of the Blues, who had initially arranged his little army in battle order in the plain of Saint-Pair, in the presence of the Vendean army, was beating a retreat toward the Calvary. There, he was proposing to engage the action when someone came to warn him that the enemy cavalry, slipping along the shore, was threatening to cut him off—those were the horsemen I had seen galloping over the sand a few minutes before. Fearing to compromise the security of the square, he immediately gave the order to fall back.

He was just in time. We had difficulty getting over the bridge, which the Whites had reached. The enemy, hoping to be able to slip into the square at the same time as the Republican army, threw itself after us, and a few Chouans were even confounded in our ranks.

We had almost reached the great gate, through which everyone was entering in haste, when the fusillade burst forth more furiously. A battery above the barricade fired at the mass of cavalry that we had on our heels.

Unfortunately, I was with the rearguard. Suddenly, seeing the enemy so close and so numerous, the gates and barriers were closed, and I remained among those who had been unable to get through.

Then our soldiers, sacrificing themselves for their brothers, turned to face the enemy. I imitated them. "Courage!" they cried. "Live free or die! Down with the bandits! Let's get them, lads!"

They launched forward.

But the fire of the cavaliers decimated us. They abused us while reloading their weapons. "Catch this, bell-founder! Paper-muncher!"

We responded with other insults.

No fear attained me—oh, no, my blood was boiling, I was blaspheming with the others. My smock was torn over the chest and my breast was bare, but I paid no heed to it.

At the head of the Vendeans, an officer distinguished by his temerity and the irresistible impetus that he imparted to his men dragged them after him under the murderous fire from the square. He was a fine soldier with big blue eyes and blond curls falling over the embroidered collar of his coat, mounted on a superb horse.

At the moment when he charged us, saber held high, in order to slash at us, a gust of hatred seized me, on seeing that the majority of my unfortunate comrades were lying on the ground. I took my pistol from my belt and took careful aim at the young leader.

"Madman! Catch this in your turn!" I said.

He tottered momentarily, as if suddenly stunned, then leaned over in the saddle, very pale.

"Damn!" he murmured. "A woman! It was predicted to me."

A sort of contracted smile passed over his arrogant face and he fell from his horse.

At the same moment I received a discharge full in the face and collapsed among the dead.

After a time that is impossible for me to specify, I came to and realized that I had no wound. I saw with horror the Plat-Gousset inundated with blood and encumbered with poor dead soldiers.

The wounded had doubtless been picked up after the battle, for no one was sighing in that terrible place.

I sat down in the midst of the cadavers and my hand, which I placed on the ground, collided with another, icy hand, ornamented with rich rings: that of my victim. We had slept side by side in that sinister bed of the battle, but the officer would never get up again; his blond moustache tapered over his pale cheek, his wide blue eyes were staring at the sky with an unusual gaze, and diamonds were scintillating on his long, fine, aristocratic fingers, as if to give more luster to death.

Rifle fire was still continuing. The Vendeans, masters of the outlying districts, had established batteries on the surrounding heights, particularly in the direction of Les Houles and Roche-Gautier, and were bombarding the square obliquely. Stofflet was waiting, before commencing the assault, for the arrival of La Rochejaquelein.[1]

I could not think of getting back into the town through the main gate; the idea occurred to me of trying to do so from the side of the Windmill, the old sheer slope. So there I was, climbing along the cliff, instinctively ducking my head on hearing bullets whistling through the air. My face was burning from the gunshot I had received; Mathieu's clothes were hanging about me in rags, and when I arrived near the Isthmus gate, I was leaning sadly on the bridge above the Douve when I distinctly heard my fiancé's voice saying: "Godfather, there's the citizeness!"

Dressed as a pulley-man, black with smoke, he could have added.

---

1 Jean-Nicolas Stofflet and Henri de La Rochejacquélin were two of the major military leaders of the Vendean revolt against the first French Republic launched in 1793; their failure to take Granville was a major turning-point in the conflict and the beginning of the end for the revolt. As the story suggests, La Rochejacquélin had expected, when his forces reached the town, to be supported by British ships, which failed to arrive, and they met unexpectedly strong resistance from Republican troops and irregulars. Their retreat, harassed by the Republicans, was disastrous.

In that state I was not a least a very pleasant sight, but I threw myself into my father's arms.

I was given a little brandy laced with gunpowder to reanimate me, and the old whaler, who was there, said with emotion, without recognizing me: "It's that scamp, though, who stood up to the cavalry and killed their leader with a pistol shot."

Mathieu kissed my hands; I scarcely looked at him; it was as if all the chill of the dead had passed into my heart.

A good woman whose house was nearby washed my face and lent me a girl's clothes, and I continued to watch the combat—or rather the assault.

The enemy cavalry was directly under the rampart again; the infantry, hidden in the houses outside the wall, caused a hail of bullets to rain down on the cannoneers serving the Cavalier battery; that of the cemetery received cannonballs from the artillery established on Les Houles and Roche-Gautier by the Chouans.

Finally, a cannonball fells the tree of liberty, which is immediately reattached like a mast broken by a tempest. It is crowned with a flag and the bonnet of the patriots.

A little more and all is lost; the Whites reach the Douve, they set up ladders; the heroic Clément Desmaisons has been hit, the artillery pieces smashed, the cannoneers exterminated; a few Vendeans reach the rampart, but they are tipped back; they retreat; the fire of the besieged redoubles, two companies of grenadiers arrive; night falls, the fusillade continues by moonlight.

Frightened by the resistance of that population of corsairs, seconded so bravely by a little garrison of only four thousand men, the enemy falls back to the outlying districts, taking shelter.

The representative then decides to set fire to those quarters in order to flush out the Chouans. Cannonballs are heated red, sulfurated chemises are prepared, and Adjutant General Vachot launches forth outside the walls at the head of a few heroes with torches in hand. In a moment, flames rise from all parts, and the Vendeans, surrounded by fires, finally decide to beat the retreat.

The victory is ours. Granville has served the fatherland and the Republic well!

What a strange and magnificent night! The moonlight floated serenely on the open sea like an undulating silvery gauze, while its edges, crimsoned by the reflection of the conflagration, rolled waves as red as blood.

It was by that light and in that red flamboyance, while everyone yielded to the intoxication of the triumph, that I saw for the last time, and with what inadmissible remorse, my victim, the handsome Vendean chief, whose fate was to perish at the hands of a woman.

After all, I thought, *he died for his idea—that idea visible in its entirety, as if palpable, in his last and immutable attitude, in his impenetrable and obstinate gaze—and then, these Whites are also Frenchmen!*

Bong . . . Bong . . .

The large bell of Notre Dame had just started swinging, and sounded a dozen strokes. My grandmother stopped.

"Where does he repose, the poor Chouan?" the young woman asked.

"Under the old flagstones of the cemetery with letters corroded by moss, which your footsteps efface slightly every day. I alone know the place."

"But," I reflected, "my grandfather wasn't called Mathieu."

"I only married much later," she replied, pensively, with slight embarrassment, "and . . . not Mathieu."

Everyone went to sleep. I put my boat on the window sill to dry, and I thought, as I went to bed in my turn, that in grandfather's place I would have been very jealous of the Vendean.

NILOS AND PAÏMA

(*La Nouvelle Revue*, 1 February 1892)

THE old man and the young woman lived in a house situated in the Ammonium, adjacent to the Naret quarter, to the north of Thebes, near the temple forge.

His name was Artée, hers was Maâï.

Artée's garments were borrowed from what plants have offered humans of the purest and the whitest. A narrow tunic of fine linen enveloped his body, and his feet were shod in sandals made from papyrus bark. His head and face were completely shaved, and he surpassed all other men in height, although stooped by his great age. In his immutable face, with ruddy tones, only his large black eyes remained alive, youthful and sparkling. Someone seeing him sitting motionless in his large armchair at the back of his dwelling, might have thought that he was contemplating a freshly-embalmed mummy, when the embalmer, before wrapping the bandages, had just placed between the eyelids artificial eyes resident with enamel. Devoted to the cult of Ammon, he guarded the god's golden chambers; in addition, as a master of the secret language of horoscopes, he occupied the first rank in the hierarchy of pontiffs.

All his children had died. All that remained to him, to conserve his memory, was his great-granddaughter Mâäi, and two fifteen-year-old twins, whom a Phoenician trireme with a golden tent, doubtless similar to the rapid vessel that had abducted

Io from the shores of Argos, had brought him very young, after having received them from the hands of nomads, which brought them back from a distant country, in the direction of the Zephyr, where their father, Artée's youngest son, had died.

However, all the old man's tenderness was directed toward Mâäi. The fifth of the month of Paophi had seen her born, and the seven Hathors, as they were seen gliding lightly over the wall bright with syringas, inclining their grace of nymphs over the gilded cradle, to the great alarm of nurses and head-shakers, had determined her destiny without their calm smile of arrogant detachment ceasing to shine for an instant on their enchanted lips.

This is what they said:

"From this day on, our heart will be more fragile than the most delicate urn emerged from a potter's hands; so, do not quit your house; repose while the hours go by. Offer gifts to the gods. Whoever is born when Paophi has seen the boat of the sun triumphant over the darkness five times while traveling the celestial ocean will perish in her flower, in the hands of amour."

Such was the oracle.

And the seven sisters disappeared, as light as a leaf chased by the zephyr.

The child was covered with talismans, for it is permissible for mortals to struggle against fate; a wax figure was suspended around her neck to ward off evil influences, and as soon as she could talk, a little girl dressed solely in jewels, Artée taught her a psalm, which she recited piously to the gods with woven beards, in order not to allow her heart to be stolen.

Fifteen times Mâäi had seen the Nile crowned with gladioli and irises spread through the fields like a sea over a shore, and fifteen times, too, the harvests, ready to fall under the sickle, had brought back the fatal date.

The young Egyptian woman had the refined beauty, the ideal flesh, the contained life, the excessively heavy head, the discreet and disenchanted mouth, the saintly smile, the eyes full of dreams that are not uninvolved in the crease of the lips, and the round and gilded cheeks that are all distinctive features of the ancient race, from which sculptors have drawn such a neat and precious estheticism. The long line of her thin eyebrows faded away beneath the embroidered headband that surrounded her coiffure and thinned out her temples; her neck supported a triple row of alternating lapis and red quartz beads mounted on golden threads. Suspended from enlaced rings of the same metal beneath her large collaret, a bird with a woman's head descended between her breasts, which, lifted up by enameled straps, were brought closer together, like two electrum cups that are about to be clinked at a feast. Her robe, or calasiris, tailored in a fabric as light as a veil, woven in raw silk embroidered with flowers and fruits, was terminated by a broad blue border, from the bottom of which hung fringes sown with little scarlet pomegranates. That garment hugged her hips and her knees, giving her gait a slightly gauche grace, and the steps of her richly-shod little feet fell upon the marble paving stones as hurriedly as raindrops.

The gardens of the temple of Ammon were only separated from Artée's by a low wall. The smoke of the incense burned in the amschirs, carried by the wind, sometimes passed in blue shreds over the brick wall and hung momentarily in the crowns of the palm trees. Mââi watched it disperse from the height of her stucco balcony while she distracted herself listening to the chanting of the priests, which sometimes rose up in a powerful and broad rhythm and sometimes lowered and almost died away, vaguer and more tremulous than the last pant of a goat-kid with its throat cut. Sometimes, a warm gust of mystical perfume fell upon her abruptly, like the breath of a god upon her ember cheek; and from granite dovecots in the form of crenellated towers a flock of domesticated birds flew away, casting a thousand patches of shadow over the clear and shiny water of large fishponds.

The young woman followed with her large dark eyes the games of Artée's grandsons, whom she cherished like brothers. They chased one another, running through pathways strewn with a pink dust of crushed granite; they hit balls to one another with wooden spatulas covered with pieces of colored hide, or dragged garden implements noisily, and when they were tired, a slave brought them an Achaemenid cup carved in the form of a seashell and filed with knucklebones.

Since they had become as tall as man those relaxations of their childhood occasionally became repugnant to them for a while, although they brought to them an impetuosity of young barbarians unknown in peaceful Egypt. Then they preferred hunting birds with Hyrcanian dogs and fishing with a line or a trident. Mâäi could scarcely retain them with her in the evening around the table at which an old scribe sat, with a face of profound malice, recounting a fashionable ghost story of the era, or the adventures of the Predestined Prince, until the time came for them to recite some passage of astrology learned with great difficulty from books, which they declaimed with a sullen docility. Then, in the great hall illuminated by golden lamps suspended from the heads of goats, they were heard repeating, in their slightly harsh voices, what happened in the heavens at the commencement of things, when the moon was in the sign of Cancer, the sun in Leo, Mercury in Virgo and Venus in Libra. But they stopped quickly, not understanding anything of those mysterious lessons, although they were struck by the most superstitious fear.

It was thought that they belonged, via their mother, to the savage Tamhou race,[1] tattooed and clad in ox-skins, which is

---

1 Tamhou, rendered elsewhere as Tamahu or Temehu, meaning "white people," was the version of the ancient Egyptian term for Europeans

seen depicted in bas-reliefs in which the god Horus is guiding the nations to the four corners of the earth. Very different from the Egyptian, the Nahasi and the Asiatic was the menacing Tamhou, the European, our ancestors, with bright complexions, blond hair, with a slender waist and eyes that gave a passionate and grim gaze to the soft color of beryl.

Nothing in those orphans recalled the features of the son of Artée, the man *par excellence* of the banks of the Nile, of the Rot-eh-ne-rôme,[1] in a word, the most civilized of mortals. However, Mââi found in them a beauty superior to all the officers of chariots or the scribes, and Artée could not help recognizing that they possessed the bravery of lions and a heart as resolute as that of the gods.

At first those twins only had one name between them, for no one could tell them apart. Only the old Libyan maidservant, Taba, sometimes claimed, when she put them to bed in the evening to recognize some particularity in their bodies. In their barbaric and sonorous idiom, however, the two brothers gave one another a sonorous appellation. Finally, a necklace formed by little jasper cats with emerald eyes was hung around the neck of one, and he was called Nilos, while a tress of the fine blonde hair of the Tamhou woman, their mother, passed through several hundred gold ringlets, was passed around the neck of the other, and he was named Païma. But they sometimes exchanged their adornments with a mischievous intention.

Mââi loved them as much as one another at first; then, unintentionally, a preference was established in her heart. She lavished marks of the most vivid tenderness on the fortunate

employed by François Champollion in his translations of hieroglyphic inscriptions, deciphered in the early nineteenth century with the aid of the Rosetta stone. In the same context, Nahasi, rendered elsewhere as Nehesu, was assumed to mean Negroes.

1 Another term identified by Champollion, which he determined as meaning: "the race of men, the men par excellence—which is to say, the Egyptians."

Païma, and one evening, in the depths of the gardens, at the extremity of the main pathway, under the vine arbor, near the lake, they exchanged oaths of betrothal under a green and mobile moonlight.

But Païma, becoming suddenly sad in the midst of the sweetest felicity, said to the young woman: "My brother Nilos also burns with the most violent amour for you; let us hide our projects of marriage from him, if we don't want him to go away soon to recommence among the mânes."

"O my friend," Mââi replied, smiling with a resigned expression, "do you not know that it is me who is to die of amour in my flower? For it is just that oracles are accomplished. Let us therefore allow the good Nilos to live in peace, and enjoy ourselves the days that the gods reserve for us."

Then the young man got carried away, shed tears, and removed from his breast the Tamhou talisman, which he wanted to attach with his own hands to the breast of his beloved.

"If you believe that you're going to quit me," he sighed, sobbing, "what is the point of wearing that wax figure and reciting psalms? Why pray to inexorable gods? Is it not better to break their images and shout insults at them, since they're impostors and are unable to defend us? But I shall avenge myself on them."

Gradually, the dolor of Nilos' brother eased. The young Egyptienne, lying on a slender day-bed, maintained silence, and they remained thus, contemplating the crystal heavens until the crescent of crowned Isis was extended above their heads like a silver sickle.

"Rejoice your heart, O my prince, for we have finally reached Thebes, the sacred city of Ammon, after having held firm at the poop of the ship and beaten the water for a long time with oars."

At those words, addressed to him respectfully by the chief of the sailors, a foreigner emerged from the gilded naos of the cage; an air of supreme grandeur was spread over his entire person; his thick hair fell in regular waves over his neck, and the adaptation of his long beard with staged curls seemed as immutable as the beard of a god patiently sculpted in stone. For coiffure he had a high tiara; a long cloak thrown over his shoulder and knotted over his breast by cords, allowed the perception, as it opened, of the Median robe descending over the thighs in equal pleats.

A Nahasi guide offered to escort him.

"Take me to the dwelling of Artée, priest of Ammon, master of horoscopes," commanded the voyager.

And as soon as he was in the presence of the old man, the foreigner said to him: "Do you know who I am?"

Artée raised his arms to the heavens and cried: "Who does not know the Persian conqueror?" Then, in a lower tone: "King Cyrus! One cannot easily forget your face; I can still see you barefoot, at ten years of age, holding the hand of the oxherd you believed to be your father, entering the palace of Astyages . . . But tell me, Prince, what motive made you quit Persepolis so modestly and your cherished residence of Tschil Minar, in the depths of which you are enthroned under an awning bordered with roses?"[1]

"So you have recognized me, savant and mild old man, to whom I owe my life and all my crowns, since it was you who convinces the magi to send me to my mother Mandane. I have come to you because I encountered you on the threshold of my life as a good omen. I have great plans, but the heart of the greatest conqueror is not exempt from weakness; no one bears the burden of destiny more rudely.

---

1 The account of Cyrus the Great given in this story is derived from Herodotus—the author's primary source for all her tales of ancient Egypt—and differs in several respects from the one assembled by twentieth-century historians.

"I have subjugated Ionia with the lapis sky, Caria, Xanthe and all of high Asia. Now a god is pushing me toward Assyria; the mere name of Babylon has burned my soul. I want to intone the hymn of combat under the walls if Imgur-Bel; I want to overturn Nabonide! Tell me, then, O Artée, faithful guardian of the old science of Ascelpius and Necepto, whether fortune is not weary of serving my broad sword, for having delivered so many blows?"

"Come up with me to the summit of the temples," replied Artée, "and I will respond to you. Excuse the sadness of my face; the fifth of the month of Paophi is a deadly day for my family."

They both crossed two ebony steps and found themselves at the entrance to Artée's gardens, which a secret door connected to those of Ammon.

At the corner of a grove of cypress, Cyrus perceived a young woman of great beauty, who was singing and feeding bullfinches and blackbirds contained in palm-wood cages suspended from the branches of a mimosa.

"Is that your daughter?" cried the Persian, admiringly.

"No, it's my slave," replied the priest, with a sort of harshness, for he feared attracting the king's attention to Mââi, knowing that he had been the husband of Cassandane for a long time.

At the same time, he moved a long curtain of flowering convolvulus away from the wall and opened a low door, the location of which was not revealed by any exterior sign. Then he traversed a hall sustained by columns, the capitals of which formed lotuses and tufts of papyrus, surmounted by a stone cube presenting on its four faces the pensive head of Hathor. The vault of a staircase led to the highest of the sanctuaries hollowed out before them; they climbed it all the way to the last platform, only surrounded by a porphyry rail. Below them, all around, Oph was displayed in the middle of the plain.

It was the season when the Nile, in full flow between its banks, parades the splendor of its divine waters throughout Egypt.

Cyrus admired the giant city in a mute ecstasy. His sharp eyes scanned the prodigious panorama with a strange covetousness. How many vanquished capitals had he not already contemplated like this, from the height of towers, through a smoke of glory and blood? How many new gods had he not adored in order to dream incessantly of others?

On the eastern bank of the river there was the temple of Karnak with its propylene preceded by a long procession of sphinxes, its forests of columns and its accumulation of palaces and porticos, and Luxor, with its variegated obelisks, resplendently gilded, at the end of an avenue of sycamores, dominating the confused domes of a thousand other monuments decorated with caryatids, pillars with human faces, and goddesses with the heads of lionesses sitting on the edge of sacred pools; then, at the feet of granite colossi, a fresh pleasure habitation buried in palm trees, provided the eye with recreation by means of the dazzling tiling of its courtyards, its verandas shaded by floating curtains, its kiosks with balustrade, its lakes, its arbors and its orchards scintillating with fruits. Innumerable boats overflowing with foodstuffs were hastening toward the city like a herd taken by its drover at a run toward its byre.

On the left bank, toward the west, everything seemed more severe and more formidable: the palace of Memnon, with the colossal statue of Sesostris, which seemed to be protecting the rein of the last of the Pharaohs, stood out on the hills, not far from the royal hypogea—for the sovereigns whose life is inscribed in stone in fine hieroglyphs, sculpted in relief on columns as high as towers with a cameo delicacy, were already participating in the immortal life of the gods.

Artée followed, on the features of the conqueror, all the movements of his soul.

"Patience, Cyrus," he pronounced, slowly, with a bitter sadness. "A few more years and the sacred city of Ammon will be in your hands. The future is open to my eyes; already I can see Persia in Pelusa! But go toward Babylon; it awaits you, on the bank of the Euphrates, like a rich courtesan. It is there that you will see men adore you as a god."

Then, as if responding to his thoughts, the old priest added extending his arm toward Thebes: "And yet all this is not worth a soul: a divine and impalpable particle, a jewel fallen from the heavens, a radiant atom of the great mystery. A treasure contained in a putrefaction. A marvel! A marvel!"

Nilos and Païma have chartered for Memphis a large and rapid vessel manned by five hundred sailors, the best in the land of Egypt. From there they will go to Phoenicia, where a well-known road leads to the plains of Chaldea, toward Babylon.

Their eyes are inundated with tears; they are not speaking in the excess of their affliction, each spending entire days without any other companion than his own heart.

The seven Hathors have prevailed upon the gods with the woven beards, the figure of wax and the Tamhou talisman.

On the fatal date of her birth, Mââi, abducted by Cyrus—who mistook her for a slave—had plunged the house of Artée into mourning.

While the Persian's boat extended its crimson sails, the temple blacksmith affirmed that, while beating metal on his anvil, he saw the Egyptian maiden, thin and paler that day than a new moon, descend from her palace by the basalt steps where the ruddy waves of the river come to expire with the profound plaint of a breaking heart, doubtless with the design of awaiting the return of the two brothers, departed the day before with their greyhounds to hunt ostrich and gazelle.

Cyrus' camp extends infinitely under the walls of Imgur-Bel, in the plains of Shinaaar, where Nimrod, the violent hunter, had reigned over the children of men.

Cyrus' tent was erected in the center of his army. The hero is asleep, covered by his weapons. His tunic is crimson, his breastplate bronze. A javelin of cormier wood reposes under his hand, next to his short sword and his helmet with a white plume.

The Euphrates, deflected into the basin hollowed out by Nitocris, will be fordable at daybreak. At that moment, the Persians will penetrate into Babylon. The password for the night is *Artée*.

While struggling in the midst of the soldiers, a young man, almost a child, has been able to introduce himself into the camp by pronouncing that name and has reached the king's tent.

It is Nilos.

As in the fine days of their mischievous childhood, when he and Païma slept in palm beds and traded by way of malice the adornments that served to identify them, Nilos is wearing around his neck, whiter than a Greek marble, his brother's necklace, which he cleverly exchanged for his own under cover of darkness: hundreds of gold ringlets retained by a thin cord of woven hair.

But today, with what grave and supreme design does the old priest's grandson want to establish a confusion between himself and Païma? His features are contorted by fury, his beautiful hair, which he has allowed to grow as a sign of mourning, has the undulation and clarity of flames.

"Wake up, Cyrus! Defend your days, wretch!" he cries in a loud voice. "The hour of appreciating words has come for one of us, for you have dishonored the house of the virtuous Artée!

What have you done with his daughter? What have you done with my sister, the sweet Mââi?"

Scarcely has the young man pronounced those words than armored men, raising the alarm, came running crying: "Treason!" and surround him on all sides; one of them pierces him with his sword and he falls without Cyrus, who has launched himself toward him, being able to cover him.

Then the generous Persian knelt down beside Nilos, shedding abundant tears.

"Your sister is safe and sound, O unfortunate and noble son of Artée, for I soon perceived my mistake, and already, if the war had permitted it, heaped with my gifts, she would have resumed the road to Egypt. On a rich chariot, beside my wife Cassandane, the maiden of Thebes is guarded in my camp, safe from enemy blows."

"If it is thus, powerful king, have my brother Païma fetched. No, Cyrus, you hear," the young man went on, wildly, "no, Nilos, that's his name, I am Païma. He resembles me in every point. Return his beloved to him . . . and may the gods give you victory!"

Resuming then his barbaric idiom, a soft and maternal tongue, the grandson of Artée murmured, with a strange and feeble smile:

"I shall not see the beautiful land of the sycamore again, and, joyfully, I shall recommence among the mânes, for Mââi will now share her amour with Nilos, since Nilos is Païma! The two twins are henceforth more linked in her heart than they were in the womb of their Tamhou mother. Mââi will cherish the one who gave his life for her in sacrifice to the seven Hathors, and the tears destined for Païma will fall upon the mummy of Nilos; then, finding in the eyes of that brother, whom she will call Nilos, the soft and innocent charm that emerges from the eyes of Païma, it is me whom she will love in him!

"Adieu, Cyrus," he added, in the Persian language, "already my heart is no longer in my breast and I know the life of death! Let the old Libyan servant Taba keep the secret of the immobility of the heart!"

THE FESTIVAL OF THE VULTURES
(*La Nouvelle Revue*, 1 December 1893)

I WAS warned by my domestic, Bechir, the evening before. The news was circulating in Constantine with a sort of mystery, especially in essentially Arab and Negro quarters: tomorrow would be the festival of the Vultures.

The ceremony was to take place in a location habitually left to solitude, beyond the gates of El Kantara, on the culminating point of the highest rock overlooking ancient Cirta.

I immediately sent word to my new friend, a young Hungarian doctor, very curious about Arab matters and capable of comprehending them all. Indefatigable, not very talkative, a nomad like me but more knowledgeable and less of a dreamer, Monsieur Drobeczki seemed to me to be the best of companions for an excursion of that sort.

At eleven o'clock in the morning, Bechir gave the signal to depart. It was mid-August, the sun was burning the city; the streets were almost deserted and very silent. We went through the gates and the grandiose bridge of El Kantara, thrown toward the Orient over theatrical depths to give access to a golden land; then we reached a plateau on which pines grew with difficulty amid sand and rocks. The pines ceased and only a few needlegrass bushes still showed; they disappeared in their turn; the rock infringing on the sand devoured to the entrails; soon, nothing more could be seen but an expanse of burning stone, as tawny as the hide of a dromedary, covering the hill where the festival was to be held.

We finally found ourselves on an esplanade flamboyant with light overlooking an immense horizon. There, normally a rendezvous for lizards, kestrels and crows, on that bleak summit, a worthy halt for eagles and vultures, a bizarre population was grouped, in which black was dominant, travestied with a barbaric pomp, delivered to strange preparations.

I remarked right away that the Arabs present appeared to have come more as curiosity-seekers than devotees, and that there were no women of quality, but only a few old women, delegated by families to represent them. I learned eventually, to my great amazement, that the negresses charged with the ceremony, performing the function of priestesses, were none other than bread-porters, renowned for their strength and height, whom I saw every day in the streets doing their job; there was, therefore, reason to expect some vulgar masquerade.

Very large tents made of dark fabric with crimson stripes had been erected; they were open and full of unveiled women, very beautiful for the most part. Seeing those charming faces united in groups, Bechir leaned toward us and, speaking in a low voice for the sake of modesty, designated them by the old Hebrew word *nakria*, the literal meaning of which is "foreigners," but which had a different and more scornful one for him.

We immediately recognized the prostitutes of the desert, the Ouled-Nayl, the A'Zarlia, wearing around their necks as a sign of their industry necklaces made of European louis sewn on black velvet. A man of rude aspect, with a snub nose and a bronzed face, was standing before them with the air of a master. I learned later that he was known by the name of a conqueror: Alexandre. It was doubtless that mercenary who had brought them from Tougourt, where they arrive in winter.

They were born in the shade of date-palms in the gilded villages of the Sahara, cradled by the sound of the wind in the palms. In the evening they practiced dancing to the sound of flutes and tambourines; then, one day, with the assent of the family, they departed to seek their fortune, joining the other "foreigners." I suddenly saw mentally the caravan emerging into the cleft of gorges: the camels laden with gourds and the bizarre fruits of the desert, also bearing women with supple and light bodies, whose veils undulated in the slightest wind; from the height of their mounts, the voyagers overlooked funnel-shaped ravines were oleanders grew, under which invisible waters rippled, impassibly leaning over the abysms of the mountain.

"But what have these women to do with the vultures? What is this parable?" said Drobeczki, very interested by the spectacle unfolding before our eyes. "Do you remember the etymology of the word vulture?"

"Of course," I replied, shaking off my dream. "*Vultur.*"

"From the Sanskrit *Gardhra*, which means 'enemy,'" Drobeczki added, with his mysterious smile.

At that moment we envisaged another part of the tableau, the principal and more interesting part, for the presence of the Ouled-Nayl, toward whom our esthetic eyes were initially directed, appeared to me to be purely fortuitous and foreign to the astonishing ceremony that was in preparation: eight or ten negresses were completing the final apparatus of a sacrifice with an unknown meaning. Before us rose pyramids of cucumbers and watermelons with pink pulp, cut into slices, alongside a putrid heap of animal entrails and meat, covered by buzzing flies.

Those women were of colossal stature, further heightened by the head-dresses they wore, which completed their costume of priestesses and added a sort of barbaric grandeur to the scene, all the perfume of an ancient rite faithfully retained. All of them were standing upright on the rock, draped in sumptuous fabrics in bright colors; they were inspecting the sky as if searching it for a signal and appeared to be waiting for the sun to reach a determined point in space; with its perpendicular rays, the star struck their polished skin, which seemed to reflect the flames like a mirror. Their faces, hideous and funereal masks, were surmounted by gilded tiaras, and they extended their long bloody hands toward the city, as if for a conjuration.

Of vultures there was not a shadow, as far as the eye could see, but at the feet of the black fanatics, a cascade of rocks similar to corals at the bottom of the sea, overhung the spring of Sedim-Sid; then raising the eyes, there was Numidian Cirta, in a motionless and fiery atmosphere, designed in neat lines, without indentations, reigning over the immense plain drowned in ardent mists; toward Setif, other masses of rock extending, ever larger, and the road to Batna, the desert road, undulating in endless meanders.

The high esplanade that carried us was covered with an ornamented population and tents; deafening music produced by metallic castanets, reed flutes and onager-hide tambourines, filled our ears with strident notes, like the song of cicadas, sometimes as languorous as the sighs of the wind in osier-beds.

Everything was ready; the fodder of the vultures was fuming in the sunlight, like a holocaust.

Everyone was still waiting.

"You see," Drobesczki said to me, "it's necessary that the bird of Juno has the necessary pasture. We're going to witness the feasting of an eternally powerful race."

"Do you really believe that we're going to see vultures arrive here, close to us, to devour this flesh before our eyes?"

"I feel adequately assured," replied my friend, who, like the veritable scientist he was, had none of the slight doubts and negations that characterize boastful ignorance. "Do you remember that, the day after the battle of Pharsalia, vultures came from a hundred leagues around to devour the cadavers? They fly so high that they cannot be seen; their senses are so powerful, their instincts so ardent, and their maleficent life so voracious of innocent lives, that no prey escapes them; they are always assured of the triumph. For all those reasons," Drobeczski added, with a melancholy smile, "they resemble our enemies."

I understood that the mild and inoffensive young man had already been torn apart by vultures with human faces.

While waiting we wandered through the fête, like an immense peaceful camp. Part of the scene was fully illuminated, in a splash of radiance, the rest in the soft shade of open tents. We soon came back to the house of fabric that sheltered the Ouled-Nayl, and we studied them in a more leisurely fashion. The sunlight came to die at their feet; it dissolved there into golden dust, like an impalpable sand. It was as if they were bathed by an atmosphere of blue liquid, traversed by a rain of red jets, which colored them with warm reflections. They had tawny complexions, ardent eyes, a gaze of tranquil impudence, cold arms, perfect hands tinted with henna and laden with rings, and flesh saturated with perfume, which they exhaled like flowers; they were ornamented like idols. Everything—beauties, costumes, colors, jewels, barbaric caprices of adornment, movements and attitudes—was various and harmonious, in spite of the garish crudity of certain hues.

I distinguished one of them in particular. She formed the center of the group, as the principal subject of a ballet is offered to the eyes when the curtain rises. She did not seek to please; she did not look at the brilliant circle of young Arabs of quality who were crowding around. Her grace had nothing languid; her chin was energetic; her admirable eyes, fixed on the grave horizon, had a strong and enigmatic expression; she was pale, and smiling in the inexpressible, slightly bitter, fashion of a woman remembering the past. In terms of expression, the exquisite purity of the features and perfect forms, she was the most beautiful, and her attire, thanks to I know not what elevated research of simplicity, by an assembly of rare and discreet jewelry and silks with melted tones, also made her stand out among her companions; she was clad in green and gold, a green so fresh that she seemed to personify an oasis; she made one dream of shade, palm trees or long reeds plunging their roots into the water of springs. She attracted admiration like a rare precious stone in the middle of a rich desert necklace; young men of distinction, with nonchalant manners, enveloped in fine white burnooses, turned their languorous gazes toward her.

Drobeczki and I only had eyes for her, but she was doubtless subject to the irritating magnetism of pupils infinitely wilder. A somber cavalier in a brown burnoose emerged from the midst of the fête, which he dominated from the height of his mount. He was the only mounted man among the spectators, but no one wondered how his animal had been able to bear him to the summit of the rock; the horse was thin, sturdy and ardent, with fiery eyes, and the cavalier was similar, with a poor and proud air—but the harness of his mount, his damascened stirrups and an expensive weapon glinting under his ragged haïk marked the distinction of his origin.

He arrived from the south on his violet-black mare, which seemed, like him, to be nourished on sand and fire. A vast hat ornamented with ostrich plumes hung over his back, between his shoulders, and his bronzed arms, naked to the neck, emerged from the folds of his garment. He paraded his sharp eyes over the flamboyant landscape and the African ceremony, but was evident that he had not come in search of a fortunate presage for his distant tribe or a subject of edification; no vain curiosity attracted him, any more than participating in the feasts promised by the open-air cuisine.

"He's a horseman from the tribe of the Ouled-Moktar," Bechir told us.

I knew the renown of those indefatigable centaurs and considered the newcomer with a keener interest. He had the nose of a hunter, ears extended to the wind and an emphatic jaw.

Leaning over his saddle, his gaze devoured with a savage passion the beautiful, impassive young woman placed in the center of the tent, while carefully avoiding being remarked by her.

A movement in the crowd alerted us to move closer to the black officiants as quickly as possible if we wanted to witness all the details of the ceremony. They no longer had any sex, and benevolence was effaced from their features. Illuminated by fanaticism, penetrated by their sacerdocy, they now appeared to be enormously tall, with their Assyrian miters and the coils of fabric that dressed them, forming ample pleats.

The fateful moment had arrived. They advanced nobly, with the faith that makes miracles, toward the city to which they wanted to attract unknown benefits, and stopped on the edge of the abyss. They supported then, in their inverted palms, copper trays, polished and sculpted, of antique workmanship, covered with a part of the meat, in the midst of which incense was burning, the smoke of which rose up in vertical columns. Without weakness, they held them in the air at shoulder height, their hands folded, their backs braced, as motionless as Ethiopian statues.

Those humble and taciturn negresses, whose path we were accustomed to cross in the shady margin of the streets, covered in coarse blue veils, near the fountain, laden with a koulla of water or carrying bread from one shop to another, appeared to us magnificently transformed in their barbaric role of priestesses accomplishing an extraordinary and primitive sacrifice. On the polished and elevated rock, where they took on colossal dimensions, enveloped by the sterile splendor of the region, from which one could only discover bleak mountains with bare and fiery flanks, roads winding in long ribbons of fire, and, in the valley, like a serpent deploying its coils infinitely, the blue-gray Rhummel approaching the ancient Numidian city as if to recall the myth of the reptile crushed under the woman's foot.

At that moment the shrill fanfares redoubled, covering the voices of the impassive black caryatids, who were pronouncing sibilant syllables; the tambourines resonated more loudly, the castanets tore the ears of the spectators pitilessly, while the gentle flutes exhaled swooning sounds, like the last vocalizations stifled by emotion in the throat of a nightingale.

Then, instantaneously, the vultures appeared. They surged forth at our feet in hundreds; they covered all the ridges of the rock; they came from all directions; they soared over our heads as if above a charnel-house; they mingled with us; they stood beside us boldly, their tails touching the ground.

The orchestra ceased making its discordant sounds heard. A mystical joy spread over the faces of the negresses; they began to sing gutturally, while throwing pieces of meat to the vultures, which devoured them voraciously, with assurance. What mysterious advertisement had they received in the crevices of the mountains where they made their nests? What sense of prodigious acuity had guided them to this place at this precise moment in such great number? Was it smell or the piercing sight of their orange eyes? Or did they take count, in concert with the black priestesses, of the days and the moons that had gone by since their last feast? They doubtless came from the violet summits of the Djebel Aures, and perhaps also from the thick dunes of El A'reng, beyond the Zibans.

Some had pale brown and ash gray robes with russet wings, half-extended, confounded with the color of the rock, others a blue back, an almost white belly, and black wings and tail; there were also some that were uniformly brown, with a crest on top of the head, reminiscent of monks.

Their robust beaks soon caused the dust-soiled flesh to disappear, to the last scrap, and their crops distended by nourishment proved that they were sated and that their frightful broods would participate in the copious meal. By means of a few awkward leaps, the most important members of the troop began to give the signal to depart, and they were seen to rise up slowly, beating the air with a rhythmic movement of their long russet wings. Their flight obscured the inexorable azure of the sky momentarily; then they rose to a great height, until our fatigued eyes ceased to follow them.

Immediately, the negresses seized one another by the hand and formed a radiant and hilarious chain; their fleshy mouths opened in the broad laughter of sphinxes, and they began a frenetic round-dance, whirling before us and singing, exalting in an increasingly hoarse and passionate tone, sustained by the instrumentalists. That went on for a long time. The dance and the songs attained a paroxysm of delirium; then, gradually, the cries caught in throats from which nothing any longer emerged but intermittent roars of a sort; the somber breasts began to heave beneath the necklaces of glass beads and seashells; the basalt masks of the priestesses of a day twisted, expressing all the nuances of madness, passion and the transports of a superhuman joy; they tore off their miters, and their white hair fluttered in bizarre wisps around their foreheads; finally, by degrees, their physiognomy was petrified, their eyes became bewildered, their pace relented; they tottered and, succumbing to the weight of a mystical intoxication, fell down, backwards or faces to the ground, and remained there, stiff, in catalepsy, like antique statues struck by lightning and tipped from their pedestals.

The music burst forth again, and a savage and triumphant hymn rose up, while the fanatics were carried away, as rigid as chilled cadavers. They were transported under the tents, and women employed themselves in bringing them round by means of frictions and making them inhale perfumes; then no one paid any further heed to them, except for us, who watched the scene, worthy of being inscribed by a graver on a basalt slab twenty centuries before, in mysterious Egypt. With sharpened investigative regrets, we scanned the vividly colored scene again, so harshly bitten by the sun.

The Ouled-Nayl had not budged, but a denser circle of ad-
mirers surrounded them; they were nibbling sweetmeats and
desert fruits, bananas that retained a chilly perfume in their
slightly fibrous flesh. Laughing, they showed off the tattoos
imprinted on their delicate arms between the bracelets, on the
forehead or in the velvet shadow of their ears; sometimes it was
a heart, a bird, a sword or a star, following the dream of the temporary lover who had marked them with his sign.

Only the serious beauty of the troop, the woman in green
and gold, as supple as a willow branch, did not take any part in
the feast, nor the gaiety of her companions: she stared obstinately, with anxious eyes, in the direction of the endless roads
fleeing southwards. As for the horseman of the Ouled-Moktar
and his thin horse, they were still standing, motionless and unified, like a sinewy statue of a centaur. The man's eyes, sculpted
like those of an eagle, were plunging ardently into the tent of
the Ouled-Nayl. He presented his bronzed profile to us, with
the excessively aquiline features, the nose forming a curved line,
with palpitating almond-shaped nostrils, a thin mouth, more
cruel than voluptuous, and the neat design of the black beard.
With his brown burnoose, which draped him amply, I could not
help comparing him to the birds of prey that we had just seen, to
a belated vulture that had not yet found its fodder, waiting for
its share of the carrion.

The afternoon was already well advanced. The azure of the
sky was paling, without the heat diminishing; it was covered
with white sweepings, like snow disseminated by the wind,
which the mariners of the shores of the turbulent Manche call
"marionettes," and do not see them form without anxiety for
the security of their boat. All the colors paled; the prestigious
brightness of the scene was tarnished; a wind rose, agitating the
fabric of the tents, which seemed to bear anguish on its leaden
wings; a bleak and ashy light also spread over us, and it seemed
to me that the flames were extinguished in the covetous eyes of

the nonchalant young men and in the eyes of the "foreigners." The entire brilliant assembly suddenly appeared to me as an uncertain population of phantoms.

A new individual of great importance appeared, with an air of authority, in the middle of the incessantly-swelling crowd that surrounded the Ouled-Nayl. He exhaled a violent odor of musk and his entire person respired the most inexpressible indolence; his eyes were large and tranquil, his hands were beautiful, charged with diamonds and precious stones. He scanned the troop of women with a gaze full of disdainful mildness, which stopped with fixity on the one whom the horseman of the Oued-Noktar held under his eagle eyes and who fascinated a thousand others with eyes of fire. He advanced in her direction, a madrigal on his lips, and, removing from his little finger a ring ornamented with emeralds, he held it out to her, as if to complete her ideal adornment, the color of green reeds and vermilion oases. He compared her to the banana tree with long leaves, which yields clusters of golden fruits. She had a pale smile, and extended her narrow amber hand toward the rich Arab.

Scarcely had he slipped the ring on to the desert-woman's ring-finger, however, than there was a violent stir in the crowd, accompanied by cries of dolor and fright, and we suddenly saw the horseman bound on his mount toward the woman. His meager arm was upraised, armed with a sword; he leaned sideways from the saddle, very low, without losing his equilibrium, like a master horseman, and struck twice. A great agonized scream was heard and the woman in green stood up very straight, applying her hands to her wounded breast. She pronounced a few words in a loud voice, which were heard by everyone, and as she clasped her breast, the assassin seized her violently in his arms; we thought that he wanted to carry her away on his infernal horse, down toward the south. But he suddenly put the small amber hand, where the emerald still glittered, to his lips; a further cry was heard, very faint, and the inanimate body slid to the ground.

The women had risen to their feet in disorder, gathering with fearful moans in the corners of the tent; the men, with their delicate effeminate hands, were trying in vain to stop the rude cavalier in his flight. He escaped them with a bound, like a bird, and stimulated his horse, which seemed to have wings, with a hoarse exclamation; it seemed to strike large sparks from the rock. He passed like lightning through the multicolored crowd, which opened abruptly before him with a long frisson of silk. Then we saw the admirable horseman, enveloped by a hurricane of sand and fire, disappear as if he had plunged head first into the precipice.

A violent stupor had taken possession of everyone.

"What did she say to the murderer?" I asked, loudly. "What did she say?"

Then the handsome Arab, the possessor of the deadly emerald ring, turning in my direction, replied to me in pure French, fixing his large Hindu eyes on mine, very placidly, in a voice that did not tremble: "She said. 'My life did not belong to you.'"

A great silence fell on those words, as if they had opened up a source of unknown reflections to that mass of people. The young victim was picked up; help was given to her, but everything was futile; she was dead. It was perceived that the ring-finger of the left hand was missing, and that it had been severed by teeth. The ring was on the ground, glittering on the sand like a satanic eye; no one dared pick it up.

At a gesture from the barnum, men of good will picked up the unfortunate woman and transported her to the tent where the negresses who had officiated before the vultures were completing the recovery of their senses.

Night fell then, the dusk unfolding its violet mantle; the hills turned brown and the enormous plain filled with shadows; the noble lines of the mountains were no longer perceptible. The storm accumulated during the day burst out in all parts, but it did not succeed in dissipating the assembly; fires were lit, scintillating like stars. The fête was prolonged through a long evening, in which everyone seemed plunged in a sort of hypnosis.

Before departing, a desire came to us to see the young dead woman again. Bechir lit a torch and, lifting one of the tent-flaps, illuminated the funereal spectacle.

In the midst of the demonic black women, like a peaceful soul suddenly abandoned to the furies, the foreigner appeared. Her adornment, of the varnished green of a young plant, tarnished by the dust into which her body had fallen, was now similar to the pale gray branch of an olive tree; her eyes, which no one had closed, seemed to be directing their mysterious pupils southwards, toward the burning country where camels bray, and where amorous palm trees lean toward one another, quivering, where young women dance barefoot to the suave orchestral sounds that the wind produces in the palms; her gilded nostrils seemed still to be dilated to respire the aroma of the odorous desert, the bitter perfume of almonds; and her delicate and mutilated hand displayed on her breast, as if to indicate her wound, a red patch in the place of the heart.

The negresses, like ancient weepers, formed a circle around her; someone had charged them with guarding the favorite of a satrap. They were sitting on the ground, clutching their knees between their fleshless arms; the savage fanaticism had fled their eyes, along with all expression of life; their souls were enveloped by a profound and unfathomable nostalgia. They no longer resembled the priestesses intoxicated by enthusiasm that we had just seen officiating, interrogating the protective divinities, collecting fortunate auguries delightedly, bearing guarantees of prosperity to the homeland. Those were the same ones who had once meditated, crouching at the feet of pilasters surmounted by fabulous animals, gliding between the fluted columns sustaining the antique peristyles of the palaces of the master, decorated with pious inscriptions, the same ones that camped in the wake of the armies of conquerors in the immense

Asiatic plains, celebrating the gods and the invincible glory of their kings with panegyrics. But with their hair scattered, their tiaras fallen, watching over the barbaric young woman whose face was ambered by the ardent sun, with bleak gestures and bewildered gazes, those aged negresses, glimpsed by torchlight and the intermittent clarity of lightning, now gave the impression of mourning the lying presages, the faith that had fled and the dethroned monarchies.

For us they were truly the sisters of others who, in remote times, after a defeat, rhapsodized faithfully the names of the vanquished gods over the ruins of their collapsed temples, while in the distance, the immense battlefield was covered with avid vultures.

THE SIGN[1]
(*La Nouvelle Revue*, 1 January 1895)

THERE was great rejoicing when the child was born—the first, a boy, after a year of marriage—for the farm was rich. The next morning—he had disembarked in this world in the middle of the night—he was sumptuously dressed in accordance with the Breton custom. His thin body was covered with a long-sleeved chemise, a swaddling-band, and a collaret of old lace, rigorously folded and weighed; finally, on his feeble head, three bonnets were fitted, the last of which was a masterpiece. Around a backcloth of pale mauve silk a silver embroidery snaked, sewn with violet cabochons; beautiful coral ribbon bordered it, forming a knot behind with two falling ends. His face, beneath it, made a hideous grimace of bitter displeasure, and if he opened his eyes, he closed them again rapidly in great terror, while his crumpled hands opened and closed, as if he were falling into an abyss and trying to catch hold of someone. It was visible that he did not like it at all on our earth, and he seemed firmly decided to shed as many tears and to utter as many screams as the most recalcitrant of brats before being habituated to dwelling there. The despair of which those wailing beings give evidence in their cradle is a suggestive mystery.

---

1 *Intersigne*, the word I have translated here as "sign," has no exact translation in English; it refers to a significant mark or event implying a mysterious ominous connection.

The beautiful young woman, the sister of the mother, who carried him while playing with him, was scarcely occupied with these grave problems; she did not ask where that stranger came from who had been sent among us, or for what task; nor did she notice how much he resembled a strange scarab, with his brilliant adornment and his ugly little black and hairy face. She only paid attention to what was happening around her, and the spectacle was very moving, very joyful.

The house was crowded with people, the doors remained wide open even though it was the depths of winter; Tables had been set up downstairs, upstairs, and in the room of the woman who had given birth, who remained motionless, as if inert, very pale, in her closed bed, the sculpted woodwork of which represented vultures. It was necessary, however, that she respond to each new arrival who appeared on the oak bench and who slipped a head into the bed, headgear removed, to congratulate her. Three housewives, with white aprons over their best dresses, were working hard around saucepans and cooking pots, in which heaps of raw victuals were engulfed. The men drank while waiting for the stews to cook. Midday arrived and they had not yet succeeded in putting anything on to cook but piles of carrots, onions and cabbages.

The church bell ringing in the nearby village advertised the baptism. People set forth under the snow, but the rector made it known that he had started breakfast and could not be interrupted. There was great desolation, everyone knowing that it took a long time to fulfill that important duty. The cortege met up on the church square with the funeral procession of a choleric, who could not be buried for the same reason, and also because the Maire, jealous of his slightest prerogatives and living some distance away, had not yet sent the permit.

The people of the burial and those of the baptism took refuge in the inn, where they sat down at table. The women who were nursing offered their breasts to the child out of politeness to the father; he was also given adulterated wine to drink, which he spat out all over his white collaret. Finally, the beadle summoned them, the lustral water flowed over the child's forehead, and they returned to the farm.

The celebrations lasted three days, day and night, so long as the cooking-pots received further supplies and there was still a glass of cider left in the barrel pierced for the occasion. On the fourth morning, the house emptied. The high and light charabancs were harnessed in the courtyard and everyone went home.

The next day, the bedridden mother was very ill and announced to her relatives that she was going to die. They believed it, all the more so because they knew that she had seen her own sign, so no one thought of dissuading her. Someone ran to fetch the priest, and a messenger on horseback launched forth flat out to inform the guests of the day before, who were sleeping off the drunkenness of excessively copious meals. She made a new and more precise description of the warnings she had received of her death. By night, when everyone was asleep, she had heard the charabanc, the cart of death, stop outside the door, and the sound of the nails that were being hammered into the smoky ceiling beams in order to hang the curtains that were disposed around the deceased, exposed rigid on trestles. One evening, at a crossroads, she had seen lights going past that no one was carrying, and heard bells ringing before them, like those rung before coffins.

Sitting in the bed, she spoke with an astonishingly sonorous timbre, with grand gestures. The phenomenon of jactitation was produced, and the peasant woman, habitually taciturn, spoke and spoke to her entourage, which became numerous. Sometimes she asked her mother for holy water and sometimes her rosary, which she recited nervously.

Finally, the rector arrived, and behind him a flood of undulating head-dresses that formed white eddies. As on the day of the baptism, the house filled up; there was not a place to be taken in the dying woman's room; the purist could scarcely succeed in fraying a passage to her in order to administer the sacrament. A great noise of sobs invaded the habitation, the doors remained open, the dogs wandered between legs and the children kicked while weeping. The new-born exhaled a bitter and anxious plaint.

"If the hour has come," said the moribund, "I'm content to go. Don't weep, you'll all be coming to join me."

She appealed for aid to all the saints that were venerated in the vicinity as being the most familiar and the most helpful, and also the beneficent Saint Anne, whom her imagination represented to her descending toward her from a throne of light, from cloud to cloud, clad in a golden robe, with her arms outstretched. She promised to go to find her in her sanctuary—more venerated than a holy Mecca—if she recovered her health; she dispatched a relative toward an ancient chapel lost in the woods, where an old worm-eaten idol reigned, a rustic divinity whose mystery was attractive. A young woman, in tears, held a blessed candle inclined, which was consumed slowly, the thick droplets of which fell upon her fingers.

When the rector had gone, one of the men in the audience, who had done military service, remarked in a low voice that it might be as well to go in search of a doctor. That idea had not occurred to anyone. It was agreed by the family, however, with a sort of pride, as a formality less important than the first, but which it seemed good to fulfill, no matter how futile and costly it might be.

After an hour or so, the rolling of a cabriolet was heard. Then the women hastened to make all traces of the priest's passage disappear, as if they were of a nature to indispose the newcomer. The sobs also stopped; the handkerchiefs resumed their customary places, and something hostile and anxious slid over those physiognomies, illuminated by fanaticism, which the approach of cold science, perfectly represented by the old practitioner, rendered stupidly grim.

At that very moment, a noisy delirium seized the invalid. An immense fear appeared on her face, her voice attained the strangest diapason, while retaining the most striking sonority. The Devil introduced himself to her and tried to drag her away. She uttered heart-rending cries then, as if she were being subjected to physical violence and as if a hand-to-hand struggle were taking place between her and the invisible enemy. Then a great calm followed for a few moments, and a very particular expression of pleasure—but a licentious pleasure, ordinarily forbidden—appeared in her striking gaze, and slid over her lips, which split in a smile. Songs burst forth, French songs, with daring implications, which she emphasized with an immodest gesture.

Eyebrows frowning, the doctor watched her while taking off his overcoat and gloves; then, perceiving on the table a wad of cotton wool forgotten there and still steeped in oil, he threw it in the fire, shrugging his shoulders, paying no heed to the disapproving murmurs that accompanied his gesture. He climbed up on the oak bench, as the priest had done, and, after a thorough examination, declared that the invalid's days were not in danger. He left behind remedies and prescriptions, and departed.

A few days went by and the farmer's wife did not die; people were forced to yield to the evidence, and the house emptied again. Meanwhile, the delirium was reproduced from time to time, but feebly. The approach of the brief energy was recognized at the outset, by the shrill timbre of the taut vocal cords. The haggard eyes bulged, and she trembled like an infant, asking in a halting voice who could remove her "frightenment."

With that end in mind, it was proposed to her to fetch a renowned sorcerer who, by suspending round her neck a small bag full of magical herbs and reciting a few words, could remove the terror to which she was prey. But someone made the observation that the specialist in question only operated on Tuesdays and Fridays, fateful days, with the consequence that, because it was Saturday, they decided on the reading of a gospel in order to expel the demon sooner.

Again the priest appeared in the cottage, carrying his book, his surplice and his stole on his shoulder in a small sack of black wool. He put on the white vestment, passed over it the violent ornament fringed with gold, and started reading the good news of the day. The invalid fixed her eyes on the minister of God with ecstatic joy. He was the one who had the power to dissipate the perverse shadow that had held her terrorized for so long. She drank his words—the sonorous Latin syllables, incomprehensible and sacred—which the stout man mumbled, mangling half the phrases, until the final words of the benediction, which he emphasized, detaching them one by one.

The next day, the evil of terror took hold of her again. The diviner was summoned

And alternately, the presence of the priest and that of the sorcerer chased away the phantom of the sign that agitated before her in the cloud of her tottering mind. A violent conflict was engaged in her afflicted soul: which would prevail in the substance or the vertiginous mystery, life or death? Her strength was sapped and she became very pale, bloodless, with thin fingers and eyes full of stupor.

Finally, one night, a drunken domestic attached a horse by mistake in the abandoned stable adjacent to the cottage. The noise that it made kicking the wall appeared to the hysteric more terrible and more supernatural than all those she had heard thus far. A violent frisson seized her, her blood began to flee in disorder in her veins; she abandoned herself, vanquished, to the magnetic power of the suggestion of death.

She expired. And as she had lived them in advance, the events happened: the charabanc rolling over golden straw stopped outside the door, under the mossy roof, to wait for her; with great hammer blows, nails were driven into the ceiling beams to retain the drapes above the trestles where she reposed; and, at the verdant crossroads, a procession passed, preceded by an old man ringing a little bell, in cadence.

THE INN OF TEARS
(*La Fronde*, 18 March 1898)

THE Breton inn was near the church and the cemetery. The beadle often clinked glasses there with the gravedigger. People arrived who had made a long journey carrying the dead, in order to rest there, sponging their damp foreheads and emptying glasses in a taciturn fashion. No Bacchic songs ever emerged from them. The mistress of the place, a widow with flat hair, had large tearful eyes; she often groaned, hearing all sorts of sad stories. So many tears shed for others had made her face pale, already hollow and monastic, and cast a melancholy shadow full of softness over her forehead. Her establishment was known as the Inn of Tears.

The sea beat the cliffs of the shore nearly and its broad lamentation penetrated the inn when the door was opened; the cemetery also sent its sepulchral sadness there in a whirlwind of dead leaves; it penetrated all the way to the drinkers of morose intoxication who found the bitter taste of past chagrins at the bottom of the glass. Because of its proximity to the strand, that famous inn had sailors for clients who told stories of shipwrecks. The sous they poured on to the counter had an odor of the sea, impregnated with the powerful emanations of toil. Those of the beadle and the gravedigger were scented by incense and the soil.

All of them recounted how the evil of drink had seized them and how none of them could escape that magic of lamentation, that thirst for tears.

They narrated their dolorous losses, their ruinations, the treasons that had broken their hearts, their amorous chagrins and their passions, the contained ardor of which was reinforced by the age-old stubbornness of the most obstinate of races—the trap in which misfortune had caught them.

Twenty times the gravedigger had made the audience of regulars shudder by telling them about the day when he had disinterred his own daughter in order to make room for another body, pausing in his task to weep and resuming it grinding his teeth. Twenty times the beadle had related how the dead curé left him neither cease not respite, and tormented him every night, pulling away his blankets and pinching his feet, reproaching him for his misdeeds to the point of driving him mad. Then there was the mariner who was haunted by another nightmare. One day of shipwreck he had let go of his cabin boy, a boy of twelve, and abandoned him to the gulf in order to save his own life. Now, he heard the child's last plea incessantly, and believed he recognized him in all the boats with red sails that turned around the rocks or lay dormant, rocked by the swell, under the wind from the green isles.

Many of those sad drinkers had wives and children at home, plunged by their disorder into funereal and chilly poverty, and came there to eke out their money, their sap and their reason. In their folly they were quite conscious of leading a wicked life; some, as if illuminated, slapped their foreheads at times and shouted insults; above those the immediate consequences of their vice floated, vague and terrifying, the menace of losing their soul.

But one day, the widow's clients saw a tall fellow come into the place of Kergaladu named Lanloup the Hermit. He ordered a large glass of eau-de-vie, plunged his lips into it, emptied it almost in a single draught, and said: "Life is stupid, stupid, stupid . . ."

As they knew him to be sober and steady, his arrival caused a great astonishment in the Inn of Tears. He was an old shrimp fisherman; he knew better than anyone else the holes in which they lodged in the rocks in the vicinity of Cabello Point. The rare good fortune of his fishing had procured him an ease; his cottage, the only one at the extremity of a little cape, overlooked a superb bay that he had considered for forty years to be his domain.

As soon as the tide went out his meager silhouette was seen outlined against the sand. The rocks presented their immobile backs to him, covered in wrack dried by the wind, like a bearskin, and in the minuscule bays that opened between them, a young blue water entered, the scarcely foamy flow of which kissed the shore on its lips of shellfish. Doubtless he sensed the beauty of those things powerfully and obscurely. Over those Breton shores, the only adornment of which is a kind of metallic blue thistle that grows in abundance, and the rich colors of little pebbles rolled by the tide, which sparkle at the water's edge, he marched like a king invested with an undisputed possession, for even the people of the region rarely ventured into those parts, and the poor widows whose métier is also to search for shellfish turned back when they approached the area conceded implicitly by everyone to Lanloup the Hermit.

He was tall, strongly muscled, almost majestic, like a divinity of the sea; his white hair came to join his long muddy beard over his chest, where the time of his youth remained fixed like a golden reflection; his eyes, still full of fire, were those of a Breton of the old race, as glaucous as the waves and profound, for having always reflected vast solitudes.

He returned the next day to the Inn of Tears, filled his glass, emptied it, uttered the same exclamation as the day before, listened attentively to the stories of the gravedigger, the beadle and the mariner, shook his head and remained silent, giving the impression of saying: *My affliction doesn't resemble yours, and I want to keep quiet.*

But they soon learned that strangers had built a house on Cabello Point near the hermit's cottage. It was a frail construction with turrets and a pretentious belvedere on which a telescope was perched—what is known as a villa. Bourgeois retired from business came to install themselves in the dwelling; they boasted, after some apprenticeship, of becoming redoubtable fishermen. Everyone understood Lanloup's chagrin.

Never had a lover constrained to abandon his beloved to an abhorred rival felt a heartbreak more tragic than Lanloup's on seeing his cherished beach profaned by the footprints of accursed gallics. To see the owner of the chalet pulling up his gilded wrack with fat, pink idler's fingers, and troubling the sapphire water of his little inlets with his heavy feet rendered Lanloup insensate; then he fled, seized by a savage jealousy, seeing red. Only one thing avenged him; the newcomers could not find shrimp; they came back exhausted in the evening to their beautiful rich house with their ridiculously red-painted fishing-baskets as light as in the morning. They persisted, however. At first they had attempted to seduce Lanloup with promises and capture him with flatteries; the old man had avoided them with an undissimulated hatred. Then they had started spying on him; but they had spied on him in vain with their Apache ruses; they could not discover his secret.

What did the shrimp matter to the unfortunate hermit, though? His torment came from elsewhere. He no longer experienced pleasure in seeing, once his basket was full, the sea rising over the eternally rejuvenated shore. Once it had been a pure delight for him to contemplate the invasion of the strand, step by step, whispering in the hollows of the rock with ineffable murmurs. Now that it did not belong uniquely to him, that spectacle, which had filled his heart for such a long time, no longer offered him anything but the atrocities of sharing. He fled the strand and the appeal of the elegiac voice of the waves to take refuge with his dolor in the Inn of Tears and numb himself with the drunkenness that draws obscure tears from unknown sources.

The alcohol burned his albatross lungs and the mortal fever of chagrin weakened his strength, corroded his muscles and rendered him debilitated and tremulous.

He was soon confined to bed; he was no longer seen at the inn, and the widow, more anxious for her client than a nurse for her nursling, went one autumn evening toward the place of Kerlagadu in order to visit Lanloup the hermit. The cold fatigue of recent labor hollowed out his features, the sweat of agony inundated his face, and in the penumbra, a form was leaning over him and speaking to him almost in a whisper.

The devout innkeeper thought that it was the priest and was already kneeling in the shadow; but the meaning of the words that reached her could not leave her in doubt for long. The last moments of the old man were troubled by the owner of the chalet; he was begging the moribund to reveal to him the secrets of his fishing, the retreats of the ungraspable crustaceans. Was he not the old fisherman's heir, and since he was about to die, could he not yield his treasure to him?

Then a residue of life galvanized the body of the ancient king of the strand; he suddenly got up, extended his long arms, which formed an immense wingspan, and, shoving his enemy away with an abrupt gesture, he said, in a voice that made the cottage resound, in a tone of infinite majesty: "Go away; the sea is mine!"

The fat man ran away, utterly bewildered. The widow remained, who received the Hermit's last sigh. Oxen drew him, in a cart in the form of a boat, over roads hollowed out by ruts, to the field of rest not far from the Inn of Tears, where it stopped. He was laid in a bed of sand with a large pebble of blue granite for a monument; his soul in torment doubtless mingled its lament with the sepulchral one borne toward the morose drinkers of oblivion by the dead leaves, those blonde and moaning turtle-doves of winter.

LAST LIGHT
(*La Fronde*, 28 April 1898)

THE carriage had rolled along the quays and passed the bridges; very pale, with a crease on her forehead, the young woman sitting in the depths of the fiacre had said to the fat stranger placed heavily beside her: "Let's see, I no longer remember very clearly, my friend: where are we going?"

She passed her hand over her forehead with a strange gesture, as if to move veils aside, and a great tension was painted on her face, in her mobile and anxious eyes.

"You know very well, my little lady," the man replied, in a persuasive tone. "We're going to the Prefecture of Police to make a complaint against your neighbors, who are preventing you from sleeping."

He tried to soften his rough voice as he spoke, and crossing over his red hands, emerging from sleeves that were too short, he whistled as he looked through the window.

"Yes, yes, that's it," the lady had replied, in a very simple tone. "If necessary, I'll write to the Czar about it."

"Of course."

Another stranger was sitting on the seat. He was the one who had given the address to the coachman: three words whispered in the ear: "The depot infirmary."

A more sonorous rumble, the shadow of a vault, the ringing of a bell, bolts drawn, and then she had been pushed very gently into a profound and dimly-lit room, in the depths of which disquieting shadows were agitating. It resounded with shrill cries of torment, bursts of laughter, stifled ululations, and fearful and childish appeals: "Maman, help, I'm frightened!" Mute hand-to-hand struggles were perceptible, and in the muted light, the blue and black flutter of nuns' head-dresses.

Stupefied, shivering to the marrow, the young woman advanced meekly, brushing extraordinary beings with flamboyant eyes. Suddenly, a cell opened underfoot: walls, shadow, a bed. Then she jibbed, throwing herself backwards, clutching at the garments of the people holding her. But after a struggle devoid of violence she felt herself lifted up like a child by powerful hands and deposited in the bleak room, the door of which fell back with a cavernous sound, brutally evoking the idea of a definitive retrenchment.

In those surroundings everything became silence and immobility again.

Until those horrible minutes a sort of consciousness persisted in her: a frail tissue that would rip at the slightest shock. She felt mortally exhausted. However, her perceptions were sharpened morbidly; she counted the rustle of the habits and the gliding footfalls of the nuns, the buzz of distant voices and the infantile sobs of other wretches similar to her.

The following day, a cellular vehicle took her to a suburban asylum.

Again she found mental death floating there, crushing and invisible, and in the long days, the silence and the immobility of beings and things, broken by the abrupt audition of sonorous cries, projecting the horror of the inferno, and brief supplications.

"Help!"

"Quickly, quickly!"

"For the love of God!"

It was in those first days that the young woman felt her true name and her sane being decidedly detached from her, to make way for the vampire-madness that sucked her thought for such a long time.

The vampire howled with her voice, yapped for hours like a dog at the moon, scratched with her fingernails, bit with her teeth and pronounced base insults with her tongue. A padded cell had become her habitation, and the years passed without her perceiving their duration. No help descended upon her from the paternal bosom of Providence.

A kind of tragic beauty still floated over her dolorous pallor, around her bruised eyes and through her long, scattered hair.

Often, a word escaped her arid lips, and when she pronounced it, her voice became once again the melodious and passionate voice that had once enchanted those who loved her: *Before.*

Then she put her hands to her creased forehead in the effort of a profound and vain research; an expression of expectation was fixed on her features, and she remained standing, motionless, like a visitor behind a closed door. "Before" was lost for her, departed in the evening mist, via the dusty roads of the past, toward who knew what distant counties, from which it would never return.

It happened that she followed for long moments the fantastic play of the light on the wall; sometimes she thought she recognized cherished features there.

It was a grave profile of a thinker that interested her most of all, but she no longer had any idea who that profile resembled, nor what name to give that shadow.

It was in spring above all that she experienced the greatest troubles, when her soul of long ago lifted its broken wings of a dying dove. The buds of the trees glimpsed n the crowns through the bars appeared to her to enclose in their satiny sheaths familiar treasured mingled with impressions that had fled. As for flowers, by dint of considering them, she shed blinding, inexhaustible tears over their fate, so easy did it seem for them to be wounded and bruised, exactly like the virgin hearts of women.

One day, when the serene earth was delighting in the first enchantments of spring, when Ariel had wept in the morning and laughed at midday, when the vaporous air carried light perfumes of fecund humus, nascent lilies of the valley and partly-open wallflowers, the madwoman was sitting on the ground, gazing at the sky.

In the corridor, the ill-assured footsteps of a child were skipping, and a pleasant rising voice full of delight sang, stammering: "Quasimodo! Who broke the pots! Quasimodo, Quasimodo."[1]

The child, a little hospital attendant, never ceased repeating his refrain as he ran. When he drew away, the sonorous notes were mysteriously stifled, and then they returned, sounding richly in the young throat.

At first, for the insensate, they had only been syllables similar to others; then they struck her more forcibly, and in being assembled, acquired a complete meaning:

"Quasimodo! Quasimodo!"

Then she extended her infirm will and her suppliant hands toward the past, and, stammering with hope, she lay down in the dust, impotent to climb the giant steps that rose from her darkness toward the light and toward God.

However, her confused plaint found an echo somewhere in that vast universe, where, from tears and suffering, the prosperous seeds of pity emerge.

From all the obscure forms that populated her delirium, one was detached, and that phantom said, softly: "Oh, how was the memory of our amour lost?"

---

1 *La Fronde*'s readers would have been familiar with the name of Victor Hugo's legendary hunchback, but they would also have known what his name actually meant, being derived from the first words of the Introit of the mass sung on the Sunday after Easter: *Quasi modo geniti infantes* ... [In the manner of new-born children ...], taken from *Peter* 2:2, for which reason that Sunday was known as Quasimodo Sunday.

Overwhelmed by joy, she was only able to respond: "Beloved, oh, beloved!"

"Quasimodo!" sang the child. "Quasimodo!"

Yes, it was on such days, between flowery Easter and Trinity that she had lived the springtime of her amour.

O spring without rival, unparalleled flowers, violets on the edges of roads bathed by tears of pleasure, roses with burning calices, velvety palms, odorous mosses, diamond stars on the forehead, intoxicating vapors of the lost Eden: she sees you again and respires you again!

Her thought had become an enchantment again, and the past, emerging from the limbo of time and the abyss of her madness, enlaced her in a suave and strong contact.

She remembered, she revived their first embrace, when he had dared to take her hand, clasp her in his arms and kiss her face.

They had been very pure kisses, falling like rain upon her cheeks and hair, only brushing the lips by chance; they exchanged few words of amour, but they hugged for a long time, like two flowers of life sighing for another life . . .

Why had that sweet happiness not endured? Why, from the conquered Heaven had she fallen into this solitary Gehenna? That, that was what she could not comprehend.

But what did the ambiguity of reminiscences matter? The unknown had approached her and, as in the blessed days of happiness, he had clasped her to his bosom, brushed her face and hair with his lips, infusing her again with youth and beauty.

Thus he had rediscovered her; through the forest of sepulchral darkness, their wandering spirits finally found one another again . . . !

Before the past had reattached its impenetrable mask, she lived an hour of Paradise.

However, the vision glided toward the barred window, murmuring scarcely intelligible words, promising eternal reunions, an invisible bond stronger than terrestrial attachments . . .

As soon as the pensive phantom had disappeared, the chain of the madwoman's ideas was broken again; they fled in disorder like a crowd escaping through faintly lit doors.

All that survived in her was a formless aspiration toward the delectable repose of the tomb.

"Quasimodo! Quasimodo!" sang the child with the joyful voice.

Soon, everything fell silent, the sun sank, night descended, the bats flew through the ashen air, and the April rain, softer than the tears of human amour, streamed over the silent foliage . . .

PAMENES' HARPER
(*La Fronde*, 12 May 1898)

IT WAS the season when the Nile, flowing at full breadth, paraded the splendor of its divine waters through Thebes. Innumerable boats serving to transport foodstuffs hastened toward the city, all drawn in the same furrow, like cattle led by a herdsman toward the cowshed.

On the bank, the shops of artisans and metalworkers, whose patron was the bellicose god Horus, fishers of catfish, captives devoted to cyclopean works and criminals who had paid their debt under the whips of soldiers in the diorite mines of Wadi-Hammamat or the gold and emerald mines on the shore of the Red Sea, prolonged in miserable suburbs the city of the hundred gates: Thebes, Oph, Diospolis Magna.

In one of those huts with walls of between earth and roofs of interlaced rushes and asphodel leaves the old potter Amentou had just died.

An improvised coffin and an abandoned tomb had been his lot. No one had been there to offer him sandals of painted cardboard and a traveling staff. No gilded envelope of laudatory papyrus, protective effigies or inscriptions. No delectable provisions, legs of gazelle, fruits of doum palms, grapes or dates; no enameled glass libation vases, curly wigs or perfumes.

Injected violently with horse-radish and plunged into a bath of natron without any precaution, nothing remained of him but skin and bone. From the tower of Persée to the drier of Peluse, no poorer dead man had ever departed for the fields of Yalou, in which, an innocent soul, he would reap the corn of the celestial harvest.

In the meantime, the taricheutes from the Memmonia quarter, after having granted him that mediocre sepulcher, had taken for their salary his beautiful urns painted with rigid flowers and his canopic jars with lids like human heads.

His daughter E'A Lil yielded them all, weeping.

The chief of the embalmers made a grimace. "Is that all?" he said. "That's not enough to pay for our trouble."

E'A Lil went pale and trembled under the insult. She had nothing else except for her harp, the gift of a fugitive stranger once received in the hut of Amentou.

It was a superb instrument, yellow with blue and green chevrons, ornamented at the top with the head of a young man with a bronzed face and at the bottom with a garland of lotus flowers.

"That comes from a palace," murmured the master to his acolytes, "and is worth a good number of gold rings; let's take it."

But E'A Lil threw herself at his feet and begged them to let her keep her harp. She clasped it to her heart, sobbing, and kissed the insensible bronzed head that ornamented it, sculpted with a scrupulous artistry, the enamel eyes of which simulated the gleam of a veritable gaze.

They yielded to her tears and a scribe intervened to draft the document establishing the debt of E'A Lil, daughter of the potter Amentou. Curbed under the opprobrium that attained Egyptian children who could not pay for their parents' funerals, she swore to acquit it by Khouit, the protective goddess of the dead.

When dusk descended on the Delta, refreshing the grasses and the mint of the shore, she put a veil over her face, picked up her harp and headed for Diospolis Magna. Behind her, the paternal hut was enveloped with mist; the battered door was half-detached from its hinges, and the old Typhonian figure, the hideous face of the demon of the wind, inflating his cheeks to blow ruination over the rich fields, placed in the window to ward off the deadly action of gusts, no longer guarded anyone. A boatman, her neighbor, passed her on the right bank. Nothing was exhaled by the bleak city of the dead except the evening hymn sung by young Levites on the threshold of some temple . . .

She followed the vast streets of the city, full of movement and life. She stopped at a crossroads. Donkey-trains were halted there, guarded by children and shaking their harness; a fountain added its freshness to the shade of sycamores. Ethiopian slaves were reposing, eating fruits; women were drinking from clay pitchers; a troupe of young women wearing make-up were dancing to a drum and a flute while others rattled castanets and agitated silver bells. An odor of musk and rose-oil floated.

That bold troupe was succeeded by jugglers, exhibitors of monkeys and bears, and then a void formed again.

Before the circle of spectators broke up, E'A Lil appeared.

Round her neck hung a Chimera, at her waist a statue of Anubis, who shows the way. She let her fingers wander over the strings and played a brief prelude, listening in her dolorous memory to what the demon of the wind suspended from her father's door confided to the reeds of the Nile

He had taught her all his voices, from the intoxicating breeze of spring that returns the leaves and the flowers and resembled a kiss on the face and a word of amour in the ear, through whistling laments, growling and mysterious murmurs, to redoubtable moans seemingly coming from the "land from which no one returns."

She communicated them to the crowd; it was no longer a lively prelude, cheerful modulations celebrating voluptuous pleasures, the intoxication of desire or dancing, but an evocative song, strong and tender, an unknown language with expressive

124

tones. The young woman, who wept as she sang, a radiant image of youth and poetry, captured the heart of the crowd. Those who were passing by paused; the litters of nobles stopped; a harvest of flowers covered her bare feet.

"Isis!" people cried, "Isis!" comparing her to the goddess whose tears enable closed calices to open.

Encouraged, E'A Lil improvised further.

At present, the wind was weeping, weeping over the harp. They sensed it seated there, somewhere in the midst of the reeds; then it suddenly rose, taking its crazy course and skimming the plain with its rapid footsteps. Sometimes it scattered, scarcely growling, shaking the trees, mocking the pale moon, and sometimes it gathered itself like a wild beast, in order to pounce in a devastating whirlwind, striking the faces of the sphinxes, already mutilated by time. It filled the solitude, belling like a stag, raging. Then there was something tragic and heroic in the powerful harmony of its confused voices, far beyond the reach of human dreams . . .

The harper fell silent. Large jewels, pieces of silver, and gold rings flew toward her. Someone threw her an emerald plaque from a terrace.

She collected those riches in a fold in her tunic, thinking about her father's funeral. The door of a palace opened; a servant took her toward an elevated throne where an exceedingly handsome, grave and delicate young man was seated.

"Sing," he said.

E'A Lil seized her harp; she symbolized the wind in a flock of spirits. Into their wordless language passed the soul of the world and scattered atoms of amour; they seemed to hold the torturing mystery of the beyond.

Penetrated by impotence and shivering with anxiety, people despaired of being able to comprehend it.

Prince Pamenes kept her with him; he assigned her a place in a chamber of columns with multicolored walls and every day

125

he came to hear her, sitting facing her, without taking his eyes off her face.

E'A Lil loved him, without being aware of it.

He was the vague and divine dream, the flood of delights in which she wanted to dissolve, and to please him, she drew from her soul exhausting songs in which the sap of life flowed. Every day she opened an unknown vein, and everyone except the master remarked that as her inspirations were elevated, and as her genius grew, her smile became paler and her hands more transparent.

Pamenes was a strange man, haunted by an incurable melancholy.

He said to her one day: "Your name is Music; you are not named woman. Who could desire your body, having sensed your soul swooning over those strings, and having possessed it, while you delivered yourself to the sublime fever of your art?

"Do you know," she said, "that those reckless sounds are only a vain echo of what they contain? O Pamenes, I shall never find the necessary tones to depict my amour."

The prince was silent, traversed by the terror of seeing a soul of genius adapted to a superior form.

One day, E'A Lil sensed a chill spreading through her veins, and in her weakness she went to see her father Amentou, who now reposed at the bottom of a rich syringe in a basalt sarcophagus.

Oh, the abandoned hovel on the edge of the river where she had grown up between the potter's urns, the creviced walls from which she watched the boat with sails furled like wings! How she loved those very poor things, a thousand times more than the superb palace! To see them once more, lying on the bank, to die on the Nile . . .

She ordered a litter.

The Nile, bordered with flowers, flowed through the fields, as majestic as an embalmed poem, paled by the gold of the setting sun; birds were flying toward Libya with the red soil; jackals were prowling around animals reserved for sacrifice, confined near temples. The circling swallows were crying, as if to distract the city of the dead from its dream of eternity.

Amentou's hut had almost fallen apart, but the old Typhonian figure, the hideous face of the demon of the wind, was still swaying in the abandoned doorway. An ineffable breeze was exhaled that evening from his thick lips. When E'A Lil penetrated beneath the paternal roof, the shadow of Shu could no longer be seen between Sibut, the Earth, and Nuit, the Sky . . .

At daybreak, the prince went into the chamber of columns. He did not find E'A Lil. Her harp was lying on the floor, and her palace robe heavy with diamonds.

The young woman's spirit was palpitating over things, suspended in an atmosphere of death.

The master suddenly went pale, shivering; a flash illuminated him, and as he launched himself forward to join her, a servant replied in a low voice: "She's dead."

RUSTIC IMAGES 1
(*La Fronde*, 26 May 1898)

THE QUEST

IN warm downpours, traversed by summer lighting, strip-ing the heavy sky with vivid fiery serpents, the harvest is completed. With great blows of the flail, shirts stuck to the spine, making great efforts, men and women have threshed the wheat in the barn, and also the barley and the rye with pale blue ears.

One sapphire morning, in the dusty sunlight, on the floor, the oats have been winnowed, its flying blonde robe surrounding the laborers like a swarm of golden insects, the grain-loft is overflowing. Nothing any longer remains in the fields but vain and deflowered grasses that no one cuts, the white down of which snows on the bushes.

After the morning mass, murmured before the choir of sculpted and gilded wood in the Breton church, where a Christ marching on clouds reigns, the village curé returns to the presbytery and eats breakfast in the cool kitchen scented by thyme and laurel, with the sour reek of dairy produce.

The beadle, with the head of a ferret, shows himself in the doorway.

"Monsieur le Recteur," he says, without approaching, "the chestnuts are ripe. Han the redbreast has not been singing any longer for some time, the oven is idle, there is no more wheat to carry to the mill; my opinion is that this is a good time to go in quest."

"Well then, saddle the mare," responds the master, laconically.

That is a little red horse, a little legendary horse with delicate feet, caprine hooves, with a white shiny mane that falls back over the eyes, large savage eyes. For the first time, she is separated from her frolicsome foal, and the rector bestrides her.

The beadle appears in his turn with an old emaciated horse that he is dragging by the mane with difficulty. Throwing large canvas bags on to the animal's meager back, ragged and cheerful, he hoists himself on to the starveling mount, paying no heed to its disapproving nods of the head. A choirboy leaps on to the rump.

The old horse, taught by experience, knows very well that it is a matter of departing like the devil downwind, to return in the evening exhausted, succumbing under the triple burden of the full beggar's wallets, the drunken beadle and the sleepy child. No matter; it is its ineluctable destiny of a domestic animal, a servile beast fallen under the domination of man, and, resigned, he limps away in pursuit of the red mare.

Here they are, at the top of the hill. What a beautiful morning! A last veil of mist is tearing apart in the distance; A mild autumnal serenity reigns over the glebe. All of the summer sunlight has remained in the foliage. The moss of the woods is verdant, the mushrooms are appearing, the heather reddening the slopes, the osiers rustling. As the silent riders pass by, jays with blue wings take flight.

Finally, a farmhouse shows its mossy roof. At the noise that the choirboy makes, the farmer advances, simultaneously humble and proud, anticipating the request of "the one who does not sow." The horses are tethered near the door to an iron ring sealed in the wall.

It is one of the richest farms in the village; there are eight horses in the courtyard, a dozen cows and more than twenty ewes. Servants are agitating, hooves ringing on the ground, geese screeching, the cock clarioning the last triumphs of the sun. In a room sparkling with copper, the standing priest responds to the toast of the laborer who, in accordance with the ancient rite, fills his glass first, empties it gravely, and then spills the last drops on the ground.

The staircase resounds with heavy feet, the bolts are drawn, the grain-loft opens, revealing the fertility of the furrows. For the priest, those conical heaps of opaque, russet, precious grain—new grain harvested with such tender care and ardent preoccupation—are eroded. Joylessly, but with a decent urgency, the daughters of the house remove the tithe and fill one of the bags borne by the old horse to the brim.

The rector shakes the hands that are held out to him, kisses the little children, praises the livestock and mounts his beast again, while the beadle, rendered loquacious by libations, heaps the masters of the place with the customary benedictions.

He says: "A cry of joy in honor of the mother, the father and the children of the family!"

"Iou, iou!" cries the choirboy.

"May your sons respire health, and your daughters lavender!"

"Iou, iou!" vociferates the servant,

The mounts set forth; from the sunken road the voice of the beadle can still be heard, continuing his litanies: "Year of beetles, year of dew, year of oats and wheat for you," while the *iou ious* of the child add a joyful cadence to the distich.

THE PURIFICATION OF THE MANOR

KATOUT the lame has headed toward the curé, hastening on her holly staff.

"Monsieur le Recteur," she says, "there are new masters at Kerthomaz, gallics who don't know our faith; although I'm only a poor beggar-woman I'd rather spend every night defending the moon from the wolf[1] than lie under that old roof before it's been blessed."

The priest is newly ordained and very ingenuous. "I'll go to purify the manor tomorrow. Perhaps these foreign owners will be more respectful than you think of our holy customs, and I'll be as cordially welcomed in their home as in a clog-maker's hut."

The little manor with the blue bell-turrets is situated on a narrow hillock that it occupies entirely above a salmon-stream. It is surrounded by oaks, maples and wild cherry-trees. After long years of abandonment its gardens have run wild; giant brambles and foxgloves prosper there; the hawthorn continues to flower, and clumps of centenarian box-trees speak of extinct splendors.

Through the sunken roads the curé goes forth with his choir-boy. In his pale, thin hands there is a large book bound in black sheepskin; the child is carrying holy water, incense, the surplice and the stole. They go up toward the manor through odorous

---

1 Author's note: "Sleeping under the stars."

ferns, under arborescent rushes, the golden heads of which shine like blazing torches.

The hosts—the husband at the dawn of happiness, mildly skeptical—consent to the purification of the manor. The priest, young, like them, with an unsmiling face, contemplates them bitterly, arm in arm.

He puts on the surplice and the stole; he opens the book, and his speech, in which blind faith vibrates, goes to render the atmosphere pure, in which the heaviness of the past is stagnating.

The rooms are swept and the ancient dust thrown to the wind, the inviolate parasols of cobwebs snatched away and cast down.

Here there were banquets, feasts and frank mouthfuls. The Day of Necessity often dawned there, as elsewhere, curtaining the doorways and bringing the funeral cart in the form of a boat, drawn by white oxen.

There were life and death here, tears and smiles, long suffering that devours, joy as fleeting as lightning, renunciations of solitary hearts, secret lacerations that silence lips ripened by modesty. The truth was sealed here, as it is everywhere, and so many secular sentiments lived under these sculpted beams, dormant in impalpable molecules, impregnating things with germs of grief, amour and death . . .

The voice of the priest rises; he holds the book in one hand and flowers in the other, which he dips in the lustral water with which he sprinkles everything. He goes at a rapid pace, without fixing the objects, from which a sort of troubled charm emanates, proffering the formulae of an entirely pagan exorcism in the language of the consecrated liturgies. He abjures all the obscure forms of sin to flee, all the tribulations that overwhelm humans to go away, and he blesses the beds in which people sleep and make love, the mirrors that reflected so many vanished scenes, the cradles in which disappeared individuals wailed, the closed harpsichords whose keys might retain the mortal passion with which beautiful hands fallen into dust made them vibrate, the armchairs where people dreamed of pleasure, and the hard stools where they knelt in order to do penance, weeping, in mourning and abandonment.

The choirboy mutters the responses and swings the censer, and the priest is even more livid for having believed that he has raised those enviable phantoms who lived, by means the power of his speech . . .

But the light enters the manor in liquid floods; a new peace settles; the soul of things appears to have forgotten the stories of the past, the importunate shadows vanish; the echoes give the impression of no longer remembering that names that the wind taught them and the secrets they had retained.

It is as if the old domain is swearing fidelity to the newcomers by all its mute hearths.

Tightening their embrace, huddled fearfully together, the spouses have gone pale. That is because, whispered by the ancient dead, the mysterious and profound warning that everything must end, remains in the manor, present and ungraspable.

AETERNUM VALE
(*La Fronde*, 10 June 1898)

I KNEW less about her than a woman who was a stranger to me because I had heard talk about her, and the inept and murderous judgments that are borne against people of the elite had fallen upon her noble soul, which did not want to yield, heavy, gluttonous, hypocritical and deformative. One day, someone said to me: "She's dead," and an interest that I had never had before for her destiny was born in me. Then, when one of her relatives, talking about her loss indifferently, asking me to substitute for her, pronounced these words: "Go and regulate everything," I accepted and left immediately.

The house was very small, of an Oriental discretion, between the sea and the woods. On one side, limpid, flat and somnolent waters filled the bay like a precious wine in a golden cup; on the other was a living countryside over which a bucolic charm floated, where green springs sang untranslatable eclogues from morning until evening. But I knew that for a long time, for the one who was asleep there, nature had lost its brilliant colors and the esthetic contemplations of its charms.

I crossed the threshold; a vast silence floated, the placid waves of which my passage seemed to break. I knew the illusory value of that funereal peace. Between those walls, which had enclosed her entire soul, the passionate tumult of her thoughts was still quivering, for she had never descended into the inferior regions of apathy and had sought her center of gravity in vain. I only remembered her ardent pale face and her inexpressible grace. I rediscovered those two distinctive features in the cold and motionless image that was no longer able to respond to me.

The bedroom had a severe simplicity, bathed by a bright white light, and the silhouette of an old woman in tears ran over the wall like a Chinese shadow.

Crammed bookshelves, a *Melancholy* by Albrecht Dürer, a *Placement in the Tomb* by Andrea Mantegna, and two further prints of the Florentine school, ornamented the vast room, with a portrait of the dead woman made at the moment when she had withdrawn from the vague ostentations of society.

I contemplated that beautiful face at length, which seemed to be animated by a blood purer than the sap of spring.

The dream of youth was there, exhaling the perfume of the white flowers of May, only one aspect of which blindness had destroyed, but which death had dissipated forever.

By virtue of a double confrontation, my eyes lowered upon the cold image that lay there, a symbol near to disappearing of the fragile phenomenon of personality. Over the forehead floated the serenity of deliverance; on the mouth an equivocal smile was fixed, the mute irony of dead lips whose weary enigma, a problem beyond time, which we cannot resolve.

The old woman who had served her for a long time hastened toward me. A reflection of the soul of the dead woman passed into her humble speech. In urgent words, punctuated by long sobs, she praised her mildness, her tenderness, her abnegation, her courage, her virtue, her reserved and melancholy manner.

In simple terms, she sketched a depiction of that sacrificed life. Before me, the mute drama of the shadowy days she had lived unfolded, of intimate meditation and proud stoicism.

"No one consoled her," she said. "She only had me to love her, and her bird . . . but I loved her like a dog, like an ignorant person, Jesus, without understanding her. Oh, poverty, what poverty! What misfortune! Where is the bird?" the old woman cried in a strident voice, suddenly, seeming no longer to have her reason, looking in all directions. "Lord, he's departed with her! Chimera! Chimera!" she called, leaning out of the window.

There was no response.

"I was sure that it was a spirit hidden in the body of a bird, that it would leave me all alone," she murmured, even more dejected. "How fortunate it is: it has wings!"

"She succumbed to pneumonia, did she not?" I interrogated, to put an end to her divagations.

"Yes, that was at the end," said the old woman, shrugging her shoulders, "but, you see, she had something that was eating her away inside. Look," she added, opening a drawer, "You, who know writing, read all that and tell me of what she died."

I followed her advice and I read avidly for long hours. I discovered the enigmatic misunderstanding that had separated two beings uniquely worthy of belonging to one another.

Transported by pity, I approached the bedside of the dead woman, and I said to her: "Pale bride of Nature, here you are again in the hands of her inspiring genius! Indestructible being! From the dust will emerge the brilliant gem from which will spring the azure spark similar to your eyes; your flesh will fashion flowers, in which the ermine of your skin and the incarnadine of your breast will be rediscovered. Have no fear! The dew that will cover them in the morning will not have retained the bitterness of the tears that you shed in solitude, for God alone!

"Tell me, did you not have in the lassitude of grief, in the eternal aspiration of your being toward life, in the intoxicating springtime, the mad desire to be the grass scorched by the sun, the butterfly intoxicated by the April wind, the calyx that dies in the evening in the arms of the night?

"Did you not, woman with the cold breasts, the burning heart and the illuminated mind, envy those brief and perfumed lives, those lives without regrets, without revolts and without memories? Death has realized your prophetic wish!"

136

Then, with a mortal fright, I heard a voice rise up to respond to me, breaking the sepulchral mutism of the place.

"Yes, adieu forever."

The words spilled out one by one, pronounced in a dying tone, which seemed to transpire the tragic laceration of the solitary soul on the edge of eternity.

I moved closer to the body with a respect mingled with fear. The head of the dead woman, sunk into a red velvet cushion, had not budged; the mouth, which displayed the bitter silence of Job, had not stirred. The maidservant had gone; I was alone. What was the meaning of that prodigy? Whence came that distinctive voice with such a strange notation?

Terror number my senses for a time whose duration escapes me, but a sudden courage rendered me thought. A kind of delirium took possession of me, and, questioning once again the woman lying there, I said to her:

"Misunderstood heart, partial heart, heart submerged by bitterness, exile of happiness, never weary of loving, tell me, did you endure the torture patiently? Even when you were thinking of nothing, did you not feel something icy and dolorous within you? Tell me about those unknown struggles in which you measured yourself against the Angel of Pain. What did you think about fidelity devoid of hope? Did you give unlimited credit to the man who owed you an equitable judgment? Confide in my weakness. What became of you when it was necessary for you to tear yourself away from another heart and you remained alone with your roots broken, spreading a bloody rain? I implore you to reply in a low voice, even if it is as vainly as you appealed for aid, while cursing it, to the oblivion that liberates.

"Yes, adieu forever!"

Even more stifled and more pathetic, bearing within them the infinite exhaustion and the vanity of mute combats against the invincible adversary, those words, the same ones, reached my horrified ears. And I did not know, in my alarm, whether they had entered through the open window with the breeze, or risen from the abyss, whether the curtains had whispered them, or whether they really had sprung from that cold breast and still heart!

I lost the notion of what followed for some time. When I came round, the candles had gone out and an Oriental night-light was swinging a violent radiance from the ceiling; night had fallen.

The maidservant, crouching in a corner, was asleep, without ceasing to weep in an anguished dream. Outside, water was splashing, beating a moored boat, and a nightingale was singing in a hedge of syringas.

We waited for daylight, praying. When the sun rose, every-thing was disposed for putting her on a bier. I laid that dolorous sister in the coffin; I braided her beautiful hair, I ornamented her with flowers and lavished her with the tears that another owed her.

Sure of being heard, I wanted to talk to her again, promising her to undertake the defense of her outraged soul, since it was going completely disarmed into death, as it had been in life, retaining a child-like heart in spite of its abstract meditations and its profound culture.

"Listen," I said to her, holding out my hand, "you will not always be disavowed. That which your lips cannot say, closed by the dolorous scorn of the degrading plea, I shall say. I shall expel the false image from his heart and I shall substitute your veridical and resplendent portrait.

"His soul has been the labyrinth in which you have wan-dered, weeping, I divine that; it is because the fire of yours burned more brightly in his brain than his sensibility. That is why he did not understand you. Absolve him, for his error has made him suffer. Disappointments have plunged him into a profound dejection; he has cast himself into weary sophisms, deceptive skepticism and bitterness. At this moment he is torn apart by the antagonism of his ideas, his senses and his heart.

"Rest in peace; I shall invite him to love you in triumphant detachment from carnal bonds, in the eternal recommencement of beings, when your terrestrial lives are no longer anything but a forgotten dream . . .

"I shall say to him: 'The ideal is not dead; you shall not lose your Eurydice twice.' I shall tell him . . ."

"Adieu forever!"

Those two words, imprinted with a superhuman expression, passed over our heads with a great sound of wings, and a superb white macaw—the dead woman's cherished bird—launched itself through the open window and flew away toward the sky.

"Chimera, O Chimera!" cried the old woman, in a desperate tone.

The coffin was closed.

In the green countryside, the springs, little futile souls, laughed breathlessly.

The grave sea declaimed to the attentive shore an interminable and religious poem, in which it celebrated in undulating strophes, through innumerable forms, the indestructibility of all the divine particles confided to life and the mysterious revenges of unique amour.

RUSTIC IMAGES 2
(*La Fronde*, 18 July 1898)

I WOULD certainly not have woken up so early in the miller's close bed, the curtains of which resembled too closely—*aiee, aiee*, how they scratched!—his flour sacks, if a voice, and what a voice, like a nearby bellow, had not shaken my dreams, and if the blows of fists, and what giant fists, had not shaken the door, which yielded without any commentary. The daylight suddenly entered, no less indiscreet, splashing everything with white patches. The trenchant radiance of the sun pierced the obscurity like the sword of an archangel, and the rural postman, a tall, handsome fellow with a low Roman brow, blue eyes and a savage air threw a letter on to my blankets.

A letter! I raised my arms to the heavens. A letter, here, in the miller's bed! Discovered! Adieu peace and forgetfulness!

It said:

Jacques, you know what there is to know about ribbons: grave, antique ribbons with large passé flowers, large and religious ribbons, only woven to make girdles for virgins and angels, light and noble ribbons, detached from the height of crimson banners in order to be held by dainty little girls crowned with roses and eglantines, ribbons embalmed with incense and lilies, moist with the holy water of the baptistery and lemon-water, in ribbons . . .

I passed on.

Well, whether you know it or not, depart! Have the outlook of
a nomadic sculptor who wanders like a vagabond with his chisel
over his shoulder and a large holly staff in his hand like a prim-
itive shepherd's crook. Buy me those ribbons, Jacques, buy me lots
of them. They won't be profaned, I swear to you. I shall put them
in my oratory—a fin-de-siècle oratory, it's true, which resembles
a studio and will resemble a room full of bric-à-brac. I have an
awning there overhanging a divan reserved for my crepuscular
meditations. I'll suspend them from the baldaquin and they'll
float over my dreams.

And, post-scriptum, an address followed, flushed out by
some touring painter and confided in secret to my young friend.[1]

It was three leagues by road to the village of Pont-Avon,
beloved by artists, whose women, with their bare and snowy
necks, their huge collarets, resemble delicate meadow daisies:
Pont-Avon, where Bretagne laughs via all its chatty windmills,
all its dancing streams, its waterfalls and its woods, all its fêtes
and songs, which respire the most delightful paganism; Pont-
Avon, where the unknown hermits of old, in the depths of their
icy sanctuaries, had more joyous expressions than anywhere
else in Armorica; where the old saints, the honor and the joy
of the Breton pantheon—in stone, fortunately—are heaped
with presents, caresses, praises and spangled robes of flowers,
intoxicated by incense and kisses from fresh lips, stirred by
passionate and quivering canticles; Pont-Avon, an oasis where
the eternal Viviane, in the depths of woods filled with golden
immortelles, still enchants enraptured old Merlin; a little corner
of Cornouaille that still seems to be ruled by the poetic laws of
Moemud and Hoëldu.[2]

---

1 Amie [friend] is rendered in the feminine; the fact that the letter-writer has
addressed the narrator as "Jacques" might be capable of causing readers some
confusion, perhaps not entirely dispelled by the fact that an interlocutor
subsequently addresses its recipient as "Madame" and that the editor of *La
Fronde* routinely took the precaution of rendering the author's by-line as
"Madame Jacques Fréhel."
2 Moemud or Moelmud was allegedly an epithet of the legendary chief

I departed across fields and heaths. The country was still covered with dew, but the sun was beginning to drink its joyful tears. All the fine flowers of the heath, open in the cool morning, stood up proudly, guarded like the princesses of chivalry by the halberd of rushes. The pines sighed softly, agitated by the sea breeze, and the voice of a pastor sang octosyllabic lines to the nearby hills, rhyming them two by two, the rhythm of which awoke the memory of the best pieces of the bard Lywarch-Hen.[1]

When I went into the village eleven o'clock was chiming. That was the signal for a flock of pigeons gathered on the roof of the laundry, which flew away with a noise of rustling silk. I awoke the malevolent attention of enormous sows that were trailing their pink-snouted piglets through dried-up streams, and I kept company with a flock of angry turkeys that were walking along the street making a great racket. The houses were asleep in the sunlight, full of mysterious shadows. Under the bridge the river passed, lifting a silvery dust over the large opaline pebbles.

Clack, Clack, Clack! That is a noise I hear to my right; one might have thought it the impact of metallic elytra. It is simply a woman's clogs ringing on the stony ground. Above the clogs there are naked legs, then a flamboyant skirt, hands holding a loaf of rye-bread, a black corselet, a youthful face and flying hair.

"The house of Marie-Rose le Mao?" the young peasant replies to my question. "It's at the turning of the bridge, Madame; I'm going there myself."

What a dream of a dwelling! Imagine a leaning and mossy gable, above which three giants raise their sheaves of swords, a

---

and lawgiver Dyfnwal, the first of the sea-kings of Britain and founder of Druidism, it supposedly means "supreme wisdom." Hoëldu or Hoel Dhu was a lawgiver mentioned in twelfth-century Welsh documents. The fashionable French Celtology of the 1890s unified all relics of proto-Breton culture into a single mythology.

1 Lywarch Hen was an invention of antiquaries, the alleged works of his not appropriated from twelfth-century Welsh literature being nineteenth-century forgeries; some writers of the day attempted to promote him as a rival to James Macpherson's similarly-spurious Ossian.

large black rotten wheel garlanded with pink flowers hanging in clusters all the way to the water. Three rickety steps to climb.

"Marie-Rose de Mao?"

"That's here, come in," says a *basso profundo* voice, "come in."

The interior is not at all similar to what I dreamed; it was much more beautiful.

As among primitive peoples with rare and slow actions, one found the tableau ready to be fixed forever, a perfect composition. The scene, faithfully transcribed by a painter of merit, would have stopped you by virtue of its serious grace. Completed by the infinite nuances of life, it was worthy of emotion. The light, only entering from one side, left the back of the room in a tawny shadow. The walls were bordered, as in all well-to-do Breton dwellings, with furniture sculpted in shiny oak, giving things a church-like air. Ribbons unfurled here and there gave a lively note to the superb dressers. Above the fireplace, on the hearth, stood an armchair, an oak stall used for generations, in which an old man was sitting enthroned, holding a book. He had just interrupted the reading he was giving to two women, one of whom was the young woman in a red skirt to whom I had just spoken in the village, the other an aged woman who was doing the housework, noiselessly, in her socks.

When I was able to approach I saw that the volume was the *Lives of the Holy Fathers of the Western Deserts*, and it was open at the page on which Saint Paul de Léon is represented dragging out to sea, rolled up in his stole, a dragon that was ravaging the isle of Ouessant.

My desire having been expressed, I was shown the ribbons. The beautiful young woman opened the sculpted dressers and plunged her young arms into the mass of silks. There was an immense choice. On velvet backgrounds there were large flowers, as if passed through incense and the mystery of the tabernacle; ragged poppies with hearts of lace; anemones, open peonies like the bleeding hearts of the mystical passion; celestial vines with heavy clusters of grapes; chaste rigid flowers, all purity, like the confused hopes of virgins; lilies and tulips; sunflowers, golden dreams to make the sun jealous; and there were also nameless flowers, the distant flowers of lost Atlantis, isles of dream the flowers of mysterious lakes, paradisal waters scaling triumphantly the margins of nacreous silk.

I made my choice slowly, for a curiosity had come to me. The young woman fled again, flown like a bird outdoors; we chatted. That child, Marguerite, whom they called Gaud, was not related to them, they had had her to nurse when they were already old. The mother—a Paris slut, they said—had paid for her for a few years, and then nothing more. They had believed her to be dead, and it was a great joy for them to think that little Gaud would remain to them as a daughter, brought up in the Breton fashion, in a colleret and a headscarf. One day, when they were no longer thinking about it, the bad mother had remembered Gaud, had been seized by a sudden maternal fever, and had written that her daughter should be sent back to her right away.

It had been necessary to return her. Oh, how they had wept in the old mill! They would have preferred, for sure, to see the pretty little girl sleeping with the dear dead in the cemetery.

Years had passed and it was then that the old man had "fallen into devotion," and read pious histories aloud from morning till evening, filling the mill with his voice.

After three years, while the mourning had borne away that living joy, a letter had come. The sad mother had left, abandoning Marguerite to the concierge of the house in which she lived, and the latter no longer wanted her, for she was a fine rascal, spoiled by bad example for all time. Now she was wandering the streets and went to sleep at the Public Assistance. On learning that, the poor old folk had run to the Maire's house: "Write quickly, and let them give us back our Gaud."

144

Their child had been returned to them, in silk stockings with holes and the pink rags of a ballerina. She had a bold face, and an eccentric way of talking; they no longer recognized her. For a week she had wept on putting on her headscarf, although it was so pretty and such fine lace. She no longer liked the Breton country. She had never given them her heart as she had before—they felt that keenly—and they saw something in the depths of her green eyes that made them fearful. They dreamed of going away to the depths of an inaccessible village of lost Cornouaille, where no one ever pronounced the name of Paris, a village unknown to young men who, under the pretext of painting the rivers and the woods, sought to please coquettish girls. Poor folk!

In the evening, after having wandered in the village, I came back to the old mill to fetch my ribbons. The door was open. I stopped on the threshold. The old man, illuminated by a resin torch fixed in the hearth, was reading in a loud, slow voice the story of Saint Paul de Léon:

"His master Saint Hiltut, having sowed wheat in a field, for fear that the birds might come to steal it, ordered young Paul to stand guard there. By night, while he was asleep, the birds came to ravage that plot of land. When he woke up, he perceived the damage done to his crop, he said his prayers while circling the field; the birds remained impotent to fly away, and he chased them before him into an enclosure, where he shut them in like sheep."

He was reading again, the old man, in order to numb himself and expel the threat planted like a diamond nail in the cherished eyes of Gaud. Sitting on a bench, her hands abandoned, she was dreaming, without listening. A bird of passage, an exotic bird, it would have required a new miracle to retain her in that hospitable land, to cure her of her nostalgia for the perverse . . .

I went out with my heart constricted, and like the drone of a gigantic insect, the deep voice of the old man, emerging from the hearth, continued the legend.

145

All the joy of the morning had vanished. Storm clouds remained out to sea, kept back by a contrary wind. Fog blue-tinted the extremities of the streets. Over the silent countryside, where the sunlight had poured the sparkling illusion of the prism all day long, the dew was falling in tears of chagrin with the gray crepes of dusk.

RUSTIC IMAGES 3
(*La Fronde*, 27 August 1898)

GRISON

O UR house was called Abundance because of a spring that
never dried up, which ran through the garden, and the
farm that depended on it had been known since time imme-
morial throughout Cotentin as the farm of the High Pear Tree,
because of the giant tree that sheltered it, charging its hoary
head every year with an infinity of little stout fruits full of fibers.

In front of it a vast open space shaded by centenarian linden
trees separated us from the little Norman town gathered upon
itself as tightly as a citadel, strong in its arrogant wellbeing.

It was in that place that the animal fair was held every
Wednesday. The oxen, the cows and the heifers flooded in,
with the sheep and the horses. There was a sea of curved horns,
shiny coats, a swell of spotted backs, an animal swarm exhaling
a violent odor of the cowshed, bellowing, whining and bleating, formidable or plaintive, expressing in a fashion singularly
intelligible for my ten years nostalgia for familiar pasture and
anxiety for the obscure tomorrow.

That year, the farmer had a colt to sell, which I had seen born,
and which I loved with all my heart. Every Wednesday he decided to take it to market the following week, and on the eve of
the designated day, he yielded to my pleas and tears, and put off

our separation until later. Master Pigault was not proud of his ward. Imagine an awkward animal, with excessively thick feet, a sad expression, a slightly tilted neck, which, in gray weather, displayed a dirty gray coat, and on bright days, a strangely pink coat. The worst thing of all was that, by virtue of a deformation of the skull, he had a hole above his eyes, deep enough to put a walnut in it.

The sight of him made people laugh, like that of certain humans heaped with disgrace. The farmers of the area said to Master Pigault, tapping his belly; "Damn it, Pigault, it's funny, your little horse!"

He was treated unfavorably. He never received any caresses other than mine, and in order to disqualify him more, he had been given the name of a donkey. He was called Grison.

I loved him as one loves a pariah, with a sentiment mingled with a little dolor; I thought that he would always be unhappy and that I alone could understand him. In order to go to see him I ran down the long garden pathway, bordered by yellow lilies, a summer palace of ladybirds burning their maddening perfumes in the sun. I let myself fall over the sunken wall. Grison was waiting for me.

"Grison, my Grison!"

He whinnied with joy, placed his nostrils on my cheek, and sniffed my pocket, where I hid bread for him, and the game commenced.

We launched ourselves through the hemlock, the fine grass, the sow-thistles and the horsetails. A large green pond covered with a thick curtain of lentils stopped us, and we remained motionless, our souls full of obscure thought, watching the "green ladies" jump.[1]

The countryside was striped with indecisive green, brown and gray lilac. The river kissed the flat banks, meadows over which deflowered apple-trees curbed. Sometimes it had slate-

---

1 Author's note: "Frogs."

gray water and sometimes glaucous waves in which the silvery gray of the willows and the dark green of other verdure seemed to have dissolved.

In the distance the crops formed a variegated mosaic in which silver, blue and green mingled in the wheat, the barley and the rye. An impression of opulence and security for the human race emanated from the landscape as far as the eye could see.

The Magdalen fair was approaching; the sale of Grison could not be put off any longer.

He was taken there. I went with him. I hoped that his ugliness and awkwardness would prevent him finding a buyer. Nothing of the sort.

Toward the end of the market, a little one-eyed man with a face pitted by smallpox scars, who walked with a limp, approached Grison. I knew him by virtue of seeing him every year with his caravan camping near our house for a few days.

My most distant memories recalled each of his regular migrations. I knew the probable epoch of his arrival, the duration of his stay and the peripeties of his life. His wife was of giant stature and every year there was one child more in the rolling gipsy house. This time the number was six. The latest one slept with the dog under the vehicle in a box filled with straw, which swung as it progressed.

The bad character of that runt was proverbial. Scarcely had the vehicle stopped in the shade of the great lindens than the children poured out like a litter of kittens. Immediately, he struck them furiously. He also struck the dog, an enormous mastiff, which could have killed him with a bite like a malevolent beast. Finally, he beat his wife, and no words can describe my indignation against the man for striking those inoffensive beings, and against the gigantic female for not avenging them all by crushing the venomous little monster with her fist.

The one-eyed man bargained for Grison ardently. He struck the ground with his stick, poured out a flood of words, felt the colt's ribs and legs, pulled his tail, lifted up his mane and interrogated his jaws.

The fat impassive peasant maintained his price, sniggered, spat in his hands, spying with a sly gaze on the lassitude of his adversary.

Finally, he suddenly lowered it by ten francs and said, with tranquil scorn: "That's twenty pistoles now, I tell you. You heard me, wretched galu,[1] and get a move on if you want it, for, you see, it chagrins me to quit my horse to a vagabond."

Grison was taken away by his new master. Our adieux were heart-rending. I sobbed on seeing him harnessed to the caravan, and I followed the nomads to the edge of the village.

The desolate meadow appeared to me to attain the melancholy of a cemetery. My comrade came to haunt my dreams. His memory obsessed me like that of a dear person departed forever. My thought followed him desperately along the dusty roads, climbing the slopes whinnying; in the corner of a wood in the shade of hazel trees; or, on the bank of a river, savoring obscurely the magic of great flowing waters. And I wondered whether, in return, the vague reminiscence of my tenderness remained in his tardy skull . . .

Five years went by. I did not see Grison again, drawn with the one-eyed man and his family in a new cycle of peregrinations.

I had quit the paternal house and I had no desire to see it again, nor the tall pear tree shaking its rugged fruits, nor the hayricks capped with gold, tottering in the shaven plain, drunk on summer, not the wild grass with its poppies, cornflowers and its ephemeral plumes, the sight of which communicates a mild herbivorous peace to the soul. I was subject impatiently to the malady of *being*, the denouement of which is death. In spite of my fear of the profusion of life and the richness of incidents, I loved the somber cities, the

---

1 Author's note: "One-eyed man."

tangled thoroughfares; I loved the street, not for itself, but for love of the dolors of the crowd, which I wanted to share.

In vain a voice said to me: *Trace a wide and deserted path, where you can walk at an assured pace.*

I responded in a whisper: *My heart, what will I make of it?*

It will become your own conquest, affirmed the voice.

I shrugged my shoulders, knowing full well that it would never belong to me, that when I wanted to ripen it, it would slip away from my thoughts and escape outside through all the issues.

Thus having wearied of giving it, I communicated in silence with the soul of the weak and the soul of the strong; my pity fell uniformly on the criminal and the just, the old man and the child.

One day, radiant for the fields and heavy for the city, I was strolling through a populous outlying district of Paris. I was walking alone, plunged in my altruistic dreams. In front of me an old horse was advancing painfully. The sun, a glory for beauty and juvenile forms, cast upon its poor peeled carcass, its wounds and its scars, the raw irony of truth, and the ardent light irradiated its sparse gray coat and plastered it with a strange pink tint that made me shudder.

A hideous little old man was leading the animal, and as we were in Villette I divined that he was taking it to the abattoir.

In an indefinite awakening of the past, a direct memory, a blow to the heart, I recognized them: it was Grison and his torturer.

We had already crossed a barrier. We advanced into an immense courtyard where one respired the odor of a cowshed, mingled with that of carnage. It was the hour of the daily massacre. Paris was waiting for its fodder. We encountered carts overflowing with horns and bloody remains, soiled hides. The feet of cattle, skinned with the sinews dangling, were heaped up outside the doors. Masked cows were shivering with fear as they respired the warm mist of blood that rose to their nostrils. As far as the eye could see, in immense market halls, animals were lying, their flesh trembling, extended on trestles; on the ground there was a red sea carrying ripped-out oesophagi.

Terrified bellowing added a further desolation to the ambient horror.

In spite of that lugubrious apparatus I thought that death was kind for Grison. He had red eyes like an old pauper who has been weeping, and lashes fell in tufts over his semi-extinct pupils. His skull had that strange hole above the eyes, which was sufficient for me to identify him among a thousand.

The slaughterer was full of pity; he offered him a lump of bread before felling him with the fatal blow.

Old caravan horse, who will relate your exodus?

Grison, lying at my feet, had become as different from the ugly little frolicsome colt of old as I was different from the pensive little girl who had given her heart, overflowing with tenderness, to the disgraced animal.

O youth, old paternal farm, prolific pear tree, meadow filled with horsetails, green ladies dancing on the edge of the pond.

Honest Grison, is that you?

THE FESTIVAL OF SIDI-SELIMAN
(*La Fronde*, 13 September 1898)

HAVE I dreamed those beautiful days passed under the unalterable sun of Africa? Have I nursed the hope of a happiness to come hidden behind the veils of the future on that dormant sea, and are the memories of the Orient that fall back upon my heart like the strophes of poems true recollections drawn from the rich reliquary of remembrance, or do they emerge from a slumber filled with inflamed visions? A name of a village, an echo in the peaceful night, a scrap of embroidered cloth hung from the door of a bazaar causes them to rise. Some have the movement, the vivacity and the color of paintings by Delacroix; others, landscapes scarcely animated by humans, float in mists like those that the sun rips up on the superb slopes of the Atlas mountains.

I have not dreamed; no reality could be more delectable and more regretted. My cob house is all alone high in the mountains. It possesses a terrace lost in the azure, open over the emptiest and most marvelous horizon. From that place the soul takes flight every evening with the untiring wings of a petrel, while the body, its indolent prison, remains inert in cold tranquility, drunk on the perfumes of the orchard.

In front of me, severe mountain ridges, the Atlas; at my feet, a valley, the blue morning, mists rolling like the water of a river; bathed in the middle of the day by a light with infinite reflections and drowned at dusk by a shadow still azure-tinted; its name is the Oued-Djer.

Two placid and silent colossi guard the defile: the Zaccar-el-Gharbi and the Zaccar Chergui. On their summits live pastors, many of whom never descend into the plain; I would like to live thus without ever descending from my dream toward the human valleys where reality grips.

I cannot take account of what it is, in that bizarre life and in that severe place, that delights me so profoundly, what philter of solitude intoxicates me and enchains me. I would like an Arab soul to be revealed within me; I await it motionlessly. I have rubbed shoulders with more impenetrable strangers in the streets of Constantinople and Algiers than in the mountains, along the abandoned Roman roads; that is because the indigenous life in more accessible here, less walled in, and the year will not have completed its revolution before I know everything that there is to know about this plateau, from the Djebel Hammam all the way to the region where the Sahel expires.

From the village—some twenty fires—one climbs to my house via a large staircase half beaten earth and half stones, skirting my garden, near which a fresh ferruginous spring provides an inappreciable pure and gaseous water. All day long there is a strange file of laborers in short shepherd's tunics and light women under their superb muchachos veils, water-jugs in hand. Mozabites, Spaniards and French colonists come. Some days there are Jews, worthy to teach their children to read the Pentateuch, accompanied by their wives; the bodies of the latter are confined in tight robes, their feet in sandals, their manner nonchalant, their hair braided, with headbands. Some, of a finished beauty, evoke the living and poetic memory of Rebecca, and thus a forgotten Bible lives again, in a décor that adds to the illusion all the expected precision. Those pilgrims come from the thermal establishment that is reserved for them a kilometer away; their arrival announces to me that the season of the Waters is open.

With regard to those Waters there is a legend extremely famous among Arabs throughout the Magreb. I remember having heard it recounted by an old marabout attached to a little koubba lost on the mountain dedicated to Sidi-Seliman. Pitchers and alcarazas were hanging up inside and all around the narrow white dome: ex-votos of Arabs cured by the Djinni of the Waters, of whom the old man who was speaking appeared to be the last minister. It was a delightful fiction that fit well with the winged and delicate imagination of the Arab mind, which lifts those people up toward I know not what poetic cloud, far from habitudes that are, in sum, rather base, and trivialities that are shocking, as if paradoxical.

The place had an excessively austere gravity, the details of the scene too carefully selected not to become easily memorable. What was said to me in that place, to the indefatigable murmur of noisy and fuming waters, had no other witnesses but an ancient cedar planted in the middle of an ancient abandoned cemetery, similar at dusk to a shepherd guarding a flock of shades, and a woman a short distance away, who was modeling tall clay amphorae destined to contain wheat.

Sidi-Seliman is the Jinni of the Waters. He lives, along with his angels, in the grottos of the mountain. His palace is in the very heart of the Zaccar-el-Gharbi, varied in the deposits of statuary marble it contains, which the Romans quarried. His angels are occupied in warming, with the wood of the forests, the springs that gush from the ground eighteen times. Belated travelers have seen them in the pine-woods and olive groves, in the moonlight, performing that charitable service. The saint purifies the bodies, cures maladies, renders sterile wives fecund and protects fidelity. He is only rendered a worship of complete purity by plunging into the marble baths, taking advantage of his gifts, and as it is thought that he loves light and perfumes, candles are lit for the bath and essences burned in his honor.

The old man spoke French with perfection, measure and nuanced choice; such a place had surely not heard a similar feast of poetic and rhythmic prose since the time of the Antonines.

Those sixty leagues of free air, mountains with strange gibbosities, volcanic rocks strewn with nameless villages, gourbis shaven close to the ground like larks' nests, around which human labor is distinguished from uncultivated soil, accustomed to long slumber, by little green and blond squares; that entire fertile valley, sheltered by the legendary Atlas, was, for that marabout with fine and powerful ideas but an almost infantile imagination, under the fortunate domination of a superb jinni, the master of the pure waters, pouring the urns of torrents, eternally invisible and present, toiling relentlessly for the prosperity of that Atlantis.

"Does this jinni not have a daughter?" I wondered aloud, dreaming a little.

My interlocutor replied negatively with a rather scornful condescension.

I shut up. While he was speaking I had had before my eyes, luminous and steaming, Ingres' spring.

I also learned that once a year, the local populations openly celebrated, and not without pomp, the good jinni of the place.

"Look carefully on that day," the old hermit said to me, with a glint of national pride in this eagle eyes, "and you will see the Hadjout."

I promised not to miss that spectacle, and I did indeed witness it some time afterwards.

It was before the heavy midday, on a morning when a light sirocco was blowing, spreading a subtle amber flame in the ordinarily-dry air. At the majestic pace of a procession, making its regal entry into a subjugated city, an imposing cavalcade advanced toward us, composed of a hundred horsemen armed for war, the sight of whom transported the mind to the times of Omar and Saladin, worthy to glorify any jinni of the Orient whatsoever. Emerging from the forest of cork-oaks and arbutus trees, trampling under the feet of the horses the glorious remnants of the ancients' Aquae Calidae, it arrived, after having honored the springs with a libation, on the slope where the sun rises over the somber masses of the woods, as if emerging from the gate of the dawn.

I experienced a sudden dazzle, an admiration without mixture, for that perfect equestrian scene.

The procession emerged from a cloud of dust, advancing religiously to the tune of a bizarre march, over the unique road that overlooks the immense panorama of the mountains and turns slightly, so that each line of horsemen was outlined momentarily like a cut-out over the void of the sky.

Musicians, players of oboes, fifes and derboukas, opened the cortege in serried ranks, preceded by an indefatigable marabout who danced all alone in front as if intoxicated by a holy transport.

The silk standards of the caïds, glorious rags exhumed from the reliquary of each douar, red, green and yellow, surmounted by copper balls and crescents, were shivering, lifted up by the breeze of the Atlas, and the clinking of stirrups, the ringing of little bells hanging from velvet horse-blankets, and the whinnying of mares, served to accompany the sacred chant magnifying the prophet, which was inflated as it drew closer.

The humble village of the victors, with its tiny cottages of miserable colonists and Spanish charcoal-burners, felt its peaceful ground tremble under the horses' hooves in a tempest of noise, and its silent air vibrate with the canticle emerging from breasts inflated as if by cries of triumph, before resounding with the detonations of the fantasia.

I think that the few spectators of that imperial procession—field-workers from the south of France in laborers' smocks—had obscurely, as I had, sharp to the point of dolor, the sentiment of a physical inferiority and an immediate irrational humiliation that spring over an entire race.

Whoever has not seen an Aarab fantasia does not know what a costly weapon, a thoroughbred horse and an elite horseman can produce of superb movements when the animal and the man are lifted up by that joyful union that makes a centaur. The old marabout had told me that I would see the Hadjout. I did, indeed, see the most admirable and the most aristocratic horsemen, reproducing the Moorish type in all its purity, such as Granada had doubtless once admired emerging from the gates of the Generalife or the Alhambra.

Through the dry and blonde atmosphere of the sirocco there was a tumultuous action, a warrior intoxication, a hectic flight of dazzling fabrics in the midst of a cloud of dust; a blinding sparkle of sunlight over the metallic decorations of harness; the fire of diamonds in hands juggling with damascened rifles, and profound cries tearing one another in raucous clamors, doubtless made to be heard by Sidi-Seliman, sitting in his marble palace in the heart of the old volcanic mountain.

In fact, the Saint manifested himself to his faithful in an unexpected manner, which cut short the festival and gave rise to a superstitious presage. There was a sudden rumble of subterranean thunder and the earth began to tremble in a series of convulsive movements; for a moment; one might have thought that one was hearing the powerful respiration of the prodigious being enclosed in the soul of the mountain.

The earthquake had chased away the Arab horsemen. That magical vision seemed to have been borne away by the desert wind in a tornado of sand.

In the evening, when there were no longer any customary sounds or lights, and the valley rolled I know not what mystery in its waves of shadow, I went up on to my terrace and I turned toward the Roman town asleep in the dust near the forest of cork-oaks and arbutus trees.

At such hours is it not laudable to imagine a mind intoxicated by dreams? Eighteen centuries were effaced. Nothing had changed in that prodigious décor since the reigns of Tiberius and Hadrian; in my thought, the recumbent statues recovered their pedestals, the temples and the houses stood up with their courtyards, their baths paved with mosaics, their banqueting halls and their terraces open to the same horizon before which I was thinking, before which the Roman soul thought.

Accompanied by a harp, upright, facing the incomparable starry tent that is the Oriental firmament, the elegant Romans declaimed verses by Horace. I seemed to hear this one:

"The rapid seasons find their renewal in the heavens; for us, as soon as we descend from where the pious Aeneas reposes, we are no more than shadow and dust. Do not hope for anything durable . . ."

On that melancholy affirmation of destructive annihilation, all the enchanted constructions of the dreams suddenly collapsed. I saw that nothing remained in their place but recumbent marbles, attesting a finished reign, an almost menacing solitude, in which the eighteen springs of Sidi-Seliman were whispering I know not what crystalline litanies, without paying any heed to the yapping of the hyena and the mewling of the jackal.

RUSTIC IMAGES 4
(*La Fronde*, 28 September 1898)

ROGATIONS

"LORD, bless the fields and watch over the thatch groves. Nights, pour forth freshness; Mornings, bring back the sun. May the grain prosper in the furrow and the hail spare the fruit. May the grass cover the meadows and draw inebriating juice from the earth. In autumn, may the flourishing trees be enameled by apples as brilliant as golden stars, and let your gifts be harvested in peace."

The old priest, like a haymaker lifting a sheaf and suddenly scattering it, his arms extended and tremulous, spread his prayers and benedictions over the fields.

The faithful followed him along the narrow path, chanting the litanies of rogations.[1]

The sanctuary toward which the procession was directing its march that day was an abandoned chapel near a wood, dedicated to Saint Roch. It had for adornment a roof of green and plushy moss, and an old bell with a woman's voice.

A delightful humidity impregnated the earth like an essence.

---

1 Rogation days [i.e. beseeching days] are held in Christian communities on April 25 and the three days preceding Ascension Thursday. They were often traditionally associated with a ceremony like the one described here, known in England as "beating the bounds" of a parish.

The dew on the corollas resembled tears that had scarcely dried up on the cheek of a child, terminating in a smile.

Over a sky of the most tender blue soared white undulating scarves; on the horizon there was a bank of small clouds the color of amethyst, gilded in places by light. The sun was shining like a diamond.

Solemn weddings were being celebrated everywhere. Some believed in betrothals between the spring and daybreak, others in a hymen between amour and death. Something candid spread in the air softened the heart. Flakes and feathers fluttered. The country was ornamented like an altar, as white as a young woman's shroud. The slightest breath of air made the grain shudder, the crazy oats shaking their empty ears in the tremulous breeze, hearts suspended, bromes sterile, stems bronzed and sweet grass odorous, its wild plumes more perfumed than vanilla.

"Saint Barnabe, pray for us!"

"*Ora pro nobis.*"

The cantor marched at the head of the cortege, letting an invocation fall upon the crowd at short intervals, agitating his white cope.

The choirboy took up the litany in a pure and high-pitched voice. Then the song snaked, dragging, devoid of measure, all the way to the most distant of the faithful; and, without waiting for the last echo of his rearguard, the cantor was already resuming, with even more majesty:

"Saint Joachim, pray for us!"

"*Ora pro nobis.*"

Something worthy of notice: in celebrating this fête of nature, hardly anyone was to be seen except children and old people.

The children laughed, trying to disband, or bent down to tear up rushes. The boldest emerged from the ranks to shake their clogs, and others ate hunks of bread without thinking about anything.

Then, commencing the file, old peasant women with extinct eyes and callused hands, whose jaundiced profiles were confused with the light brown headscarves; faces whose skin, tanned by the August sun, was now stuck on the cheeks as if to the bones of mummies; labored foreheads in which poverty, hunger, the cares of the household and the exhaustion of labor were legible: sixty years under the yoke of life!

They passed by like phantoms, the old peasant women, muttering psalms with their parted lips.

They reached the chapel.

A huge rusty key was introduced into the lock, but the old door resisted efforts resentfully, like that of a neglected cottage. When the latch ceded, the light spread into the nave in floods, leaving the pillars in shadow. Immediately, blue smoke exhaled by the censer rose all the way to the vault, and the priest inclined over the flagstones.

The church was bare; one could not sit down there. The forgetfulness of souls had chilled it, abandonment rendered it more austere. It seemed consecrated to a dead cult, like a barbarian temple built by barbarians to some primitive genius. A virgin occupied the altar; her body, scarcely outlined in the wood, was covered in gilt; the expression of her features presented something grim, idolatrous, mysterious and familiar; she was like one of those generic figures that are found in hypogea or among druidic ruins.

After the mass had been said, the bell was agitated one last time. A woman at the door sold brioches contained in a basket wrapped in linen, and everyone dispersed. The church remained wide open, the care of the key having been confided to the wife of a local farmer.

In traversing the windows the sunlight designed violet diamond-shapes on the flagstones. Alone now, the virgin had an expression as cruel as the science of evil. She seemed to be saying:

162

"The innocence that circulates everywhere is a trap, and a trap any promise of wellbeing signed by the spring. Dolor is an endless apprenticeship, experience a disenchantment, the truth a skeleton, death a benefit; when a man has desired everything, possessed everything, lost everything and cursed everything he no longer finds anything on his route to guide him toward the unknown terminus of his pilgrimage but bleak resignation."

Outside, however, the earth lied audaciously, contradicting the grim virgin; to hear it, there seemed to be a little joy for everyone, a petty share for everyone of the superb heritage of humankind.

No flora more extravagant and bolder had ever streamed over the Breton glebe. In the wood, no path had been traced among the flowers. Here, a sheet of wild hyacinths undulated on stems as brittle as Venetian glass; there was a plain of anemone Sylvias[1] with trembling corollas and lanceolate foliage, the bitter almost perfume of which intoxicated the soil; lilies of the valley followed the course of an uncertain little stream, which filled the hollow of a round stone with its waters, giving the impression of a nymph's bath.

The primroses were gathered in clusters, the hawthorn was still in flower, the grass escaping the meadows rose up the bank and clumped in the ruts. At every bend in the path, one thought one saw spring advancing in the guise of a handsome youth with rosy garments, escorted by a host of birds.

In the depths of the sanctuary, the virgin with the face of Cybele inhaled all day long the perfume of the woods and fields, but neither the cascades of flowers respiring in the vicinity, nor the orchestra of hectic birds celebrating with a thousand joyful cries the softness of nests, the embalmed freshness and the blos-

---

1 "George Sand" was among the notable French horticulturalists who contrived to adapt the woodland species then known as the "anemone Sylvia" to grow in their gardens.

somings in the lush valley enabled her to share the delirium of humans, animals, trees and the humblest sprigs of moss.

The ancient statue, the robe of which scintillated in the mystical shade of the altar, remained impassive, fixed in its age-old experience in the midst of the silence full of life.

Until the evening, the burning lamp swung its golden eye before her.

THE EXORCISM OF THE ORCHARD

PIARIK'S cabin is covered in broom.

A large hungry dog, which is yapping angrily to distract his hunger, is guarding it. Little children are rolling on the threshold with the pig, near their empty bowls. In the depths of the house there is an old woman who spins from morning until evening and makes broth.

Piarik has nothing but an orchard, with the hemp he grows there to dress himself and the grass with which he nourishes his cow. The enclosure is so narrow that the two old apple trees that are interlaced there cover it almost entirely. When Piarik was small he sat underneath them and played with the sow and her piglets.

As over all things, spring has risen over Piarik's orchard, and has ornamented it with new grass, daisies and hyacinths. The breeze blowing in long, warm gusts, the old apple trees have woken up and their twisted branches are covered with radiant snowy flowers. One is all white, the other all pink.

Piarik is drunk with joy on seeing them rejuvenated. When he comes back from work, soiled with earth, he raises his ecstatic gaze to them. They are the poetry of his hard life, and the veneration with which he surrounds them does not suffer sensibly from the worship that his pagan ancestors rendered to those trees.

Now, one morning, Piarik gets up and runs to the orchard. Disaster! A swarm of insects with large wings of mourning is covering the snowy clusters and rosy garlands, promises of golden and crimson fruits; they can no longer be seen through an immense crepe.

Bewildered, the old woman goes to fetch the priest; the children cry. The impotent Piarik sobs and blasphemes. Soon, nothing more will remain but bare branches. Adieu the sweet apples and the clear cider.

The sun shines, the priest reads the daily gospel, and the eternal Maia laughs at their trouble.

Piarik's beautiful flowers have been devoured to the very last one by the intoxicated flies; evil fatality has wished it. However, the next day, the old woman, her eyes red with tears, goes to the priest's house and, without saying a word, pours a measure of oats into the flour-coffer.

As the servant protests, she says, not without nobility, with a despairing shrug of the shoulders:

"Leave it be; Piarik is proud; we still have enough black bread, broth and fresh water to await the day of necessity."

THE LOTTERY
(*La Fronde*, 18 October 1898)

FOR a fortnight it has been icy enough to split stone in the Bessin. Thick, solidified and shiny, the snow pads the polders as far as the eye can see, doubling the silence, broadening the horizon. The river flows through the middle, the only thing seemingly alive, rolling its full waters all the way to the sea, which is growling without anger, beating the shore more sonorously than a profound crystal chime. An Arctic splendor extends over the mute glebe, no sigh emerges from the buried grass, no plaint from the subterranean roots, no tear from the black branches; the earth has a rigid beauty that disengages, at length, a bleak stupidity.

Then the thaw begins, and the following night, a recrudescence of the cold renders the great meadows similar to mirrors broken in a thousand places by meager tufts of brittle diamantine grass, which the cows brush sadly with their quivering nostrils and the tips of their pink tongues.

After the belated and icy daybreak the sun rises, red and devoid of warmth, an opaque globe with a cold stony glare, resembling an enormous ruby.

On the road, at long intervals, footsteps resound. They are sometimes those of hunters of water-fowl, equipped as if for a polar expedition, with snowshoes, over the grass of the Grouin, returning from the nocturnal ambush, sometimes of boys on their way to the distant school, wrapped in faded mufflers, stopping at every frozen puddle in order to go around it.

A red-faced and red-haired fellow emerged from Master Pierre Poincheval's farm, known as Chapelle Gauthier Farm, walking with a heavy tread, the tread of an ox that no human power, it seemed, could hasten or slow down. It was the day of the lottery in the canton of Cricqueville and he had dressed up in order to take part, clad almost like a master in his capacity as a grand valet.

He stopped and listened. The entire country was deployed before him; fields of all forms—large and small, square and triangular—framed by high banks made by human hands, cut by an infinity of streams: water, water everywhere, arrested by the winter in the icy veins of the dormant humus.

A faint sound of bells could be heard in the distance on the road, and a little cart appeared, drawn by a nag with a short trot, bringing back the farm girl charged with milking the cows on the far side of the farmland.

She was very young, clad in a cotton bonnet, with wisps of tawny hair fluttering around her forehead.

She got down awkwardly while he smiled, constrained, saying: "How are your cows?"

"Coughing, badly. Ice after the rain that I've had is enough to reckon with them!"

"Yes, and no hay, because the spring was rigorous. Master Poincheval says so. Milk cows can't do anything in a dearth; beef castle yes, sheep yes, colts I can't say."

He spoke with assurance, Aimable Gancel, the grand valet, about matters of the soil, the only ones that had any interest for him; but the girl had something else to say, a subject of more urgent speech. A pregnancy, not far advanced, deformed her slender body, and over her young face, where youth had left pads of baby-fat, a pale complexion extended, a sign that makes aged country matrons say: "It'll be a girl."

168

While listening she had felt a physical torture in the heart, a cramp of fear, the intimate abandonment that makes humans tremble before death, which they must enter alone.

"Well, it's tonight, the draw,"

And as he remained mute, not finding a gesture that meant: "I can't do anything about it," she put her fists in her eyes and lamented.

"What's going to happen then? What will become of me? Alas!"

"Having no one but you," replied the man, "you have no one who can reproach you."

"That's sure," she said. "No mother, no father, nothing."

Her name was Armandine Mandeville. Her father, whom wine made morose, had hanged himself after drinking, in a hollow hidden between two fields near Master Poincheval's farm, from a tree that she knew well—an old oak of which the crows were fond—in the wan twilight. Her mother had died of the disease of poverty and chagrin, which spoils the lungs. That heredity had given her a melancholy delicacy, foreign to the lush Norman race. Formless, all that past sadness invaded her, pouring ennui into her in floods—ennui being the expression that replaces, in this region, your grand words: chagrin, dolor and despair.

She went on:

"It's not so much that all that chagrins me, but lack of bread for a kid. If I were older I'd win, for sure, but at my age, is that credible?"

He remained silent, seeking expedients. Finally, he murmured: "Cristi, I know what you're going to do; I know. You're going to pledge yourself to Saint Claire . . ."[1]

But in the farm, an hour chimed. They suddenly heard:

---

1 The Saint Claire to whom Aimable is referring was the follower of Francis of Assisi who founded the monastic order often known as the "Poor Clares" by virtue of its devotion to poverty.

"Cuckoo, cuckoo." The mechanical bird emerged abruptly from the clock, and launched its ironic appeal eight times.

Then the fellow said: "I have to go to find the others now. You look after the calves; beasts don't need hope. You don't have the temperament. Come to Cricqueville. Wish the mistress well."

He set forth heavily, glad to flee, going round the bushes.

Timidly, she asked: "Is it you who's holding the flag?"

"It's me," the man replied, without turning his head.

✳

She set out on foot for Cricqueville, the chief place of the canton. There were many others on the Norman roads at the same time, milkmaids fearful of losing their amours. In flat shoes, white stockings and black slippers, brocade skirts the color of rust, like autumn leaves, the dark red of Avonie plums or the gray-green of Crassane pears . . . skirts that were too short and lifted further over petticoats of coarse white wool.

Although the lottery is not a fête, the depths of the region are agitated by the announcement of that formality. The farms are deserted.

The conscripts arrive from all directions. That is because Cricqueville is a place of consequence, the chief place of a canton that contains seventeen parishes, large villages of herdsmen set in the green fields.

The crowd augments in the streets, and then suddenly flows into the square. At eleven o'clock the gathering is complete. The prefect has just arrived. He installs himself in the drawing room of the Mairie, approaches the large fireplace, in which a big fire is blazing, and then comes to show himself behind the window momentarily to the peasants, tightly bunched down below.

The conscripts of all the communes file past, flags at the head: fine stout lads in shiny blouses and rolled-up trousers, over which particles of frost shone and crackle; clerks and employees returned from Bayeux, Caen and Paris for the occasion, dressed as on the prospectus with flamboyant cravats splashing the heavy cloth of their shorts. And all those young men, risen before dawn, are excited, already a little intoxicated with a cowardly bravery.

The parents huddled in stairways and on the lawns wait anxiously, without turning their heads. Every time a youth appears, his eyes still haggard, there is a clamor, and numbers are returned.

The good folk jostle in order to be the first to see the number, over the hall black hats of the peasants as well as over brand new cloth caps, which is repeated from group to group as if reverberated by the echo of a thousand voices, toward the drawing room where the Maire, a butter merchant, continues stammering the summons to the conscripts confusedly.

Now it was the turn of the men of Osmanville. As he had announced, Aimable Gancel, holding the flag, was marching at the head. He recognized Armandine, who smiled, happy in spite of everything to see him so proud; he said bonjour to her in passing, and was engulfed with his troop in the communal building.

As destiny was pronounced, the young men came together on the trampled lawns and formed into groups, arm in arm, in limping pairs; then they set forth again, suppressing grievances in order better to stun themselves, excited, feverish and even cheerful, singing through the streets of the little town.

> *Forward Normandy!*
> *Let's march heads high, my lads;*
> *It isn't sluggish,*
> *The race of Norman folk.*

Armandine waited, shivering, strangled by anguish, her eyes riveted to the door from which Aimable would emerge.

He finally appeared; it was impossible to tell whether what was shining in his cunning eyes was displeasure or joy.

His cap bore the number three.

The young woman ran toward him, arms open, regardless of other people. Was he not her family, that man who, alone, had pressed her to his heart?

Large tears rolled over her round child-like cheeks; she murmured through her sobs; "Oh! what woe, Jesus, what woe! I'll hope for you, Aimable, I'll hope for you."

He stayed there without budging, having something to express that did not emerge, which remained in his arid throat and dried out his tongue, words hidden in the depths of his consciousness with a heaviness of stone, murderous words that were about to lodge like bullets in Armandine's breast, and which, until then, only his silences and his gazes had allowed the divination.

"No," he said, almost gently. "I have it for three years, it's necessary not to hope for me Armandine, necessary not to hope for me, you hear."

She loosened her embrace, weary, consenting to the abandonment, finally conscious of the death of amour, certain of her doom."

Somber, shrugging her shoulders. She said: "That's all right; I knew that I'd have to face up to it. Good luck, Aimable."

Everything whirling in her head now, she repeated: "A kid, I'm going to have a kind. It's incredible! At my age, at my age!"

As if in a dream, however, she did what the others did, drew in the lottery on the square and won a drink, shared the stew with the other girls who had come to see the draw, shouted, sang, carried out the commissions given to her by her mistress, and when night came and "ennui" filled her heart she took the road all alone to Master Poincheval's farm.

She marched and marched, and her beech-wood clogs clicked dryly on the road. To begin with, at intervals, she had heard crackling in the ice, the trees seemed to be stretching, lifting their shrouds with a need to respire and live. Now that the cold was intensifying, nothing was palpitating any longer, all the ferments were dormant under the rigid cope; the frightening immobility and the pure whiteness of things invited Armandine to become as white and motionless, delivered to the burn in her heart . . .

All the branches summoned her, extending their arms toward her. Soon, her little clogs were no longer heard clicking on the road, and the diligent snow filled in the footprints with its white padding . . .

The night reigned, only troubled by the detonations of hunters of water-fowl in the grass of the Grouin and companies of drunken, half-mad conscripts returning to their villages while their parents, who could not close an eye, waited, sitting on their feather beds, their hearts constricted.

After the father whom wine made morose, on the old oak of which the crows were fond in the wan twilight, the branch extended like a gibbet bore the slender body of the child. Below was a frozen puddle, like a fragment of tinplate, where, at dawn, the hanged girl was mirrored in the midst of black nettles.

CRAZY LETTER 1
(*La Fronde*, 10 November, 1898)

Sanitarium of T***

12 October 1838

IN the course of metamorphoses, I have encountered you before and have wept before A long time ago you drank my tears with your quivering lips; you know their bitter taste. You have already killed me more than once, but you don't remember that because memory comes from dolor, which is a sign of life, and amour, which is reason, and perhaps you have neither suffered nor loved. But I have always recognized you in recognizing my dolor.

The needle with which you pierce me, the poisoned wound that you inflict on me, and from which I die, does not resemble any of the other pains with which life heaps us, for every time I have existed, chagrins have come to me from people and things that humans qualify as extreme, and from which I emerged victorious.

In whatever time it was, as soon as I saw you for the first time, I was afraid of you; I fled from you. A secret terror gripped me, and, as you perceived it, you thought: *Why is she avoiding me?*—for you didn't know . . . A fatal power threw you toward me unknown to you, certain of finding infinite pleasures in my martyrdom. You wanted to relive the ancient drama, the ancient murder, the ancient sensuality . . .

You wanted it without knowing it, beloved, and it isn't your fault if, now, your kiss alone can extract tears from me. For myself, I'm not sorry. I sleep peacefully in the depths of my tombs, without bitterness or hatred, in the cold night, far from the human din ...

I have no idea how I escaped from the realm of shadows, how I lifted up the granite of my sarcophagus ...

The first time I saw you it was in the oasis of Syouah consecrated to Jupiter-Ammon. The statue of the God was made of bronze kneaded with emeralds and precious stones, and a hundred priests were carrying it in a golden boat. You led me to the spring of the Sun, whose water is warm at sunset and boiling at midnight, and we stayed there for a long time, mute, in the shadow of palm-trees, under the palpitation of green laves. The snakes with venomous fangs hissed, impotently, in the surroundings, and the spring, like our hearts, was gradually set ablaze by a mysterious heat ...

Do you remember, then? Do you remember clearly? You were called Hemal, son of Hor. Your masters were those of Pythagoras and Plato. You were a horoscope priest, utterly absorbed in Osiris, with your head in the stars, tormented in your faith, having already overturned many idols within you, so unhappy sometimes that you envied the free and ignorant sailor and the huts of the pariahs.

Your genius enabled you to be sculpted on a bas-relief, while you were addressing a speech to an assembly. You were placed on a pulpit formed of columns and you were pressing a quill to your heart. That was also, I believe, what you loved best; you also loved a great deal, it is true, quail cooked in fennel, and eels ... which we could not eat together at a common hearth, and afterwards, peacefully, to play chess with jade and lapis pieces until the moment of slumber ...

Around the columns of that pulpit ribbons and streamers were knotted. Lotus flowers formed palms for your young sanctity, your attitude was filled with nobility, your speech suavely grave. You embalmed the Kyphi, the sacred perfume. Oh, how you took possession of my soul, my soul full of fire, softness and barbarity! Psammitique had bought me back when I was very small from the siege of Azot in Syria. As I was beautiful I had been kept among the prize booty, the exotic animals, the rare plants, the jewels and the golden vases. I had grown up in the palace, under the benevolent eye of Neros, beloved by the younger Psammit . . .

It was not him who tore apart my heart, as that of the divine Osiris had been by Typhon. I have no need to tell you what happened before the day when I was to take the lotus of burials . . . you know it. You remember the festival of Bubastis in honor of Diana, the sweetness of the flutes sighing for the goddess, the mists that fled in phantoms before the boat over the iridescent waves, the odors of stricken grass rising from the mown fields, the flocks of white birds snowing over the crimson of the evening, my lapis-lazuli clasp, which you unfastened, and no fingers other than yours ever touched.

It was buried with me; it is now in the museum of Boulacq.

In the depths of the sepulcher, however, the vigilant eye of Osiris guarded me. He prevented my dust from being dispersed; he did not want it to be employed for the base works of nature, converted into white larvae. Of my tears and my blood, of my bones and my spirit, he formed by means of his will an indispersible, persistent and conscious life. Such was the miracle of Osiris in my regard, for the dispossessed gods did not lack power before seeing their edicts weakened and their names banished from so-called veritable Pantheons. It is futile to deny it, even though there is no more shelter for them in the heavens.

※

I was born again. It was in the depths of Cornouaille, on the shore of a sea the color of eucalyptus leaves, with green opacities mingled with a washed and transparent lapis. My nurse had very soft songs for me. For cradle-songs are written for the chagrins of children, puerile songs to console them for their great chagrins of another life. What terrible chagrin my ulcerated heart already contained. I grew up strong and sincere, and with all my power I loved the sea, as the gulls and the great white swans love it. It did not hide any of its mysteries from me; it showed me its flowers, its prairies, its marine vines; its herds of mollusks, its lakes, its shells, its pink ferns, its tresses of dead undines, its treasures, its veils, its poor. I penetrated all of it. It retained passions for me in its nacreous robe. It was all my joy and all my smiles and all my songs. Even today, although tarnished in my eyes, I do not curse nature, or death, or you, my beloved ... for your anger, your pride, your mockery, the infinite distances that your despotic will travels to flee the person who loves you, the slightest nuances of your soul, have told me how unhappy you are. When you wound me, it is for you that I weep ...

It was at the moment when Alain and Urbien, sons of Judicael were fighting for the division of their estates.[1] My father, Prince Concar, was the son of Urbien; they were defeated. We wandered from forest to forest. It was no longer the time when, in our palace, slaves brought fuming tripods before us covered in venison, and aurochs horns overflowing with mulberry wine and cervoise, when my mother Azinore ornamented herself with soft silk, furze flowers and earls from the Breton sea. She had been stabbed by our enemy, by Alain himself. Tuirwal, one

---

1 Judicael is now thought to have been the king of Domnonia, one of the Breton realms, in the early seventh century, but he is named as King of the Bretons in the Frankish *Chronicle of Fredegar*, one of the most important sources of information about the history of Gaul prior to the mid-seventh century. He was succeeded by Alain II but his relationship to Urbien Meriadoc of Cournouaille, also known as Gradlon Flam, the father of Concar, is less certain.

of his officers, followed him, sword in hand; as he was about to pierce me, pity seized him; he put me in his cloak and carried me to a fisherman who lived in an isolated habitation on the sea shore.

At the age of twenty I was sold to a lord of the court of Gradlon.[1]

It was there that you appeared to me, on a peaceful evening, in a sacred landscape. The soul was lost in an infinite horizon. A supreme verity emerged from the tenebrous woods of wild laurels; and from the tumultuous sea, from the sky traveled by noble and inflamed clouds, a supreme beauty.

You preached Jesus the new God; you no longer remembered Osiris. Your eyes, which scorn for amour and pride rendered timid, encountered mine, which the terror of loving made grim.

You considered in silence my lips, my forehead, my hair and my hands; I enveloped you with my astonished gaze; I sensed the soul of Velleda palpitating within me. I was unable to hide it from you that you had fled my heart . . .

I was afraid; I fled toward the growling wave that once came to die so gently under my bare feet. I enveloped myself in the mist of the strand, I refreshed my face with algae; I searched, in order to hide myself for the maternal hem of the glaucous robe of the sea. But the sea, the rocks and the trees, instead of speaking to me of their mute grace, only talked to me about you. Every wave adopted a low, halting and tender voice, and formed eddies of surf over the rocks softer than kisses and the crystalline collisions of earls. A need for adoration emerged from complicit things, for discreet, inextinguishable adoration bathed with tears.

---

1 The name Gralon or Gradlon crops up frequently in Breton legendry, primarily as Gradlon Mawr [Gradlon the Great], a legendary king of Armorica in the fourth of fifth century, but also as the name of the legendary king of Ys, the Breton city allegedly swallowed by the sea after defying warnings to reform issued by a Christian preacher; contemporary readers might have been tempted to assume that it is to the latter court that the letter-writer is referring.

Courage is lacking for me to narrate what followed . . .

Although Jesus was your master, a little of the poetry of the bards and the faith of the druids still inhabited your soul, and when I was dead, your dolor followed my wandering spirit involuntarily through the pools of Anguish and Bones, and from the lake of Dolor to the mouths of the Abyss. You retired among the monks of Saint-Gildas-de-Rhuys. Every evening, the sea sent you my lament, and I was loved in mourning and regret, as I had dreamed of being in life and possession. On my tomb the flower opened that I could not respire.

And now, now, no longer touch my lips, for your kiss would make me weep. My lips have turned to stone. My body itself is marble. I moan, without thinking about anything. In my heart is a crystallized spring, like water under frost, which sleeps and dreams, but if you touched my lips, if your cruel lips brushed them, the hidden spring, the profound spring, would bleed again.

Oh, why does the dusk have such a bleak face? It is not the first time that I have found the earth gray, over which the evening parades its crepes with such a lugubrious swelling of tombs . . .

It is not the first time that the setting sun, bleeding over the woods like a divine heart, changing its flames into red rain, sprinkling the foliage with its burning drops, has represented my own heart to me, my poor incandescent heart weeping its last crimson . . .

I tell you this: Later, my beloved, after . . . the centuries will keep me for you; time is nothing, compared with time. Prodigious duration leaves me the terror of hope . . . But the goal to which we are marching through it . . . I don't know; it remains with God.

Copied verbatim.

TALES OF THE PRESENT
AND THE PAST 1
(*La Fronde*, 8 December 1898)

Eighteen tailors had made the young woman's dress,
in which twelve stars shone.

THE shepherd had already put on his cloak in order to take
the sheep to the heath. In the wood of chestnut trees, where
the yellow leaves were falling day by day, the lilies of the valley
bore red seeds and the colchicums were deflowered. There were
balls of mistletoe in the aspens, starred with mat-white pearls.
Sometimes, the wind in the northern corner of the farm resembled a pack of howling dogs, imitating the thousand speeches
of a crowd, among which one profound voice appeared to be
calling for help; sometimes, too, it sang with the low and sad
tone of an old cantilena.

All the grain was threshed and stored, the best fields sown
with cereals, and the other pieces of land reserved for spring
oats; the seed wheat was sold. A period of repose was beginning,
a truce in the incessantly-renewed preoccupations of the laborer. No one was asking any longer whether the wheat was bright,
whether the fields could be harrowed, the seeds sown in time,
whether it was necessary to fear a penury of hay or the high cost
of reapers, and whether the alternations of rain and sun would
do much harm to the newly-shorn ewes ... No, now it was nec-

essary to think of clothing oneself, and kemeners—tailors—had been summoned to Resporden who were fine embroiderers, for it was a matter of wedding costumes. Mannnaïk, the heiress of Kéranfurus, was marrying Jean-Louis Prima, the master of Izella farm in Port Manech.

The domains of Kéranfurus and Izella were facing one another on either side of the mouth of the Belon and the Aven, separated by a tumultuous arm of the sea, the foam of a bore terrible to cross and as frightening as a fabulous monster. The parents were dead and there was need of a woman in the farmhouse, so the marriage was not put off until the spring, as was customary, May, the month of flowers being the season of Breton espousals. For the domain was waiting on the edge of the waves, with its fields fertilized with wrack cut into strips, in red silky ribbons and tufts of amaranth plumes; with its long swollen furrows sown with seashells as shiny as a woman's fingernails; with its chestnut-trees, its heaths, its centenarian rushes, its mosses of mingled land and sea, its orchards of apple trees rising up the blue hill where the sun rose. And the cold oven was waiting, widowed of loaves of rye and odors of flour, the venerable oven florid with snapdragons and long grass. The well, the bride's matinal mirror, was waiting with its black and profound water, its proud hart's-tongues, its granite with sculptures corroded by the dampness of the moon. Inside, under the thatched roof, enclosed in its decorated coffin, the clock was waiting, weary of not measuring the hours of a new life. And the closed bed, in wood perforated like the grille of a Moorish cloister, was also waiting, very mysterious for having enclosed so many accomplished destinies.

Something religious floated in the deserted house, the light there poured out a gold and azure smoke similar to a mobile swirl of incense. The heir only went in there in his slippers, his felt hat in his hand, and he lay down in the cowshed for fear of solitude. The master, the animals in the crèche, the unquiet

181

poultry and the silent fields were all requesting imperiously the young wife with the joyful laughter.

She would soon come, to the sound of bombards, in a boat, like a distant queen, to the severe house of Izella.

The tailors had been installed at Kéranfurus since Saint Hilarion.[1] They had arrived with their provisions of gold and silver thread, spangles and sequins, their pincushions, their scissors and their thimbles, with sacks full of bobbins of crimson, green and blue silks, memories full of tales and songs. Sitting in a circle, they worked in the barn, for tailors cannot enter Breton houses without attracting great misfortune, and the belief is one of those that remain inviolable in popular consciousness. They plied the needle incessantly, chatting with the lads who were removing the hemp from the oven, with the valet who piled up the fodder for the horses, and with the bride herself, as supple as a strap and as light as a rope-dancer, who gazed at them for a long time with a pensive expression, handling the garments stiff with embroideries, the fine garments of her wedding.

Only one, the most skillful, Alain Joa, said nothing, and kept his large dark eyes lowered. He was a slim and handsome fellow. He came from two leagues away, from the forest of Coat-an-Noz, the Land of Woods, a country of harsh mores, the last refuge of the minstrels and bards, where there was often a shortage of black bread, but never of bagpipes and dreams. He had often composed roundelays to rejoice the local lads, songs of amour to make them weep, in which images sparkled like embedded jewels. Innate poetry flourished in his ignorant soul, cradling it in a paradise of mysterious floating dreams. And now the amour that did not choose, the amour that knew no reason, had gripped him with treacherous violence while sewing that wedding dress for the daughter of Kéranfurus.

To begin with, it had been a pure devotion for her blonde beauty, a radiant enjoyment in seeing her walk around the barn,

---

1 i.e., October 21.

respiring like him the air charged with the perfume of flour, honey, cider and bruised apples; and then there were singular tremors, lurches of the heart and causeless fits of sadness, a vertigo and a mortal chill in thinking about her wedding, and then a jealousy, increasing every day, at the sight of Louis Prima.

A hatred also took hold of him against his métier. Strong and nimble as he was, would it not have been better, rather than ply a needle like a woman, to become a mariner? Then, instead of gnawing away his soul with the same idea, as stone wears away a cart, perhaps he would be three hundred leagues away, or cast into the great sea as fodder for the fish. No one would know in his homeland whether he were still alive.

Oh, how heavy it became in his fingers, that dress decorated with gold and silver, on which he had worked with so much ardor! Golden stars blossomed there as in a nocturnal sky, pale images of those he considered from the heaths of Argouat in the unfathomable immensity. And only twelve remained to be embroidered!

Except for that, everything was ready, the companions had gone and the marriage was the following day. Jean-Louis Prima had brought a torch himself to the tailor to illuminate the ultimate task, and he invited him to drink a bowl of old cider with him.

His silhouette, powerful and massive, was outlined in shadow on the wall, where seeds hung on their desiccated plants between the cobwebs.

"Let's go, Kemener. Finish soon so that we can drink to the happiness of Mannaïk."

Very pale the artisan had replied: "You're impatient, Master. There still remains another star to make, only one more star . . ."

"Well, hurry up," said the jovial fiancé. "I'm taking you with me to Izella; you'll sleep in the barn."

A troubled gleam in his wild eyes, the young man said: "That's good, Master Prima; wait for me and we'll cross the water together."

The wind was weeping in the corner of the farm, as if it were Saint John's Day in autumn; the fragile apple trees were creaking in the enclosure, there was a riot of black clouds in the sky.

Singular ideas were colliding in Joa's head; his head felt heavy and his soul was dull with fear. When he had finished, a maidservant took away the dress, and then threw woodchips on the fire and a few roots from the heath, reanimating the resin, and went toward the cowshed.

The bride was seeking absolution in the village; the house was deserted. The kemener approached the window. A profound pain filled his heart. Images of sanctity were pinned to the colonnettes of Mannaïk's bed; a polychromatic Virgin gleamed on high on the reliquary; a little calfskin haversack hanging from the bed-head contained the ashes of fires lit in honor of Saint John, and the golden stars of the dress radiated a mystical glow.

To enter, to enter there weeping, to say adieu to those things; that was what he wanted. But age-old belief stopped him, raising before him the obstacles of ancestral superstitions, nailing his feet to the floor. However, he could not tear himself away from that scene, or cease to meditate that crime: to enter, him, the pariah, whose presence caries ruination under the roof of men . . .

But the culpable desire, stronger than circumstance, invested with an unknown power, formulated in his heart the eternal and ferocious determination of amour before the impossible realization . . .

※

An appeal rang out through the unchained wind.

"Where are you, Alain Joa? Where are you, Kemener?"

Side by side, in the night, the two men went down to the shore. The ferryman was already asleep in his hut. He was a mute old man, his head crowned with white hair, who lived as a hermit. No tempest stopped him. His boat crossed the formidable bore at a single stroke. With a broad gesture, he showed them the sea, the "white mare," bounding and howling, spitting its drool at the stars.

The bore, gigantic, like a fantastic dragon, twisted its foaming green spiral from one bank to the other. In the distance, the bleak roof of the domain was outlined in the moonlight.

A miracle survives weakening faith. Legend describes a parabola in time, and we do not know when it dies, when it loses the suggestive power that it had in the past. They did not arrive in Izella. The tempest wanted the age-old triumph of the idea. Only the petrels and the gulls, rising over the volute of the wave and the silent heavenly disk know how the sea vanquished the fatalistic old ferryman.

At dawn, only the body of Louis Prima was found on his own shore, on the threshold of the fields with swollen furrows sown with seashells. He was asleep on a bed of shiny tangled green algae. The shore resembled a spring meadow, exhaling a delightful freshness of new grass, as if the deep pastures of the Ocean had been mown by night, by nimble naiads. A weary murmur emerged from the sated sea, half dead, displaying on its dull face the gray pallor of supreme fatigue . . .

In the meantime, the thoughtful Mannaïk put on her wedding dress on which twelve stars shone. As she put on her delicate shoes she found, near the bed, the ivory thimble of the young kemener from the Land of Woods, the ancient forest of Coat-an-Noz, the last refuge of inviolate myths.

IMAGES IN THE STREET
(*La Fronde*, 17 January 1899)

UNKNOWN SOULS

HE descended the boulevard every evening, thinking about her, at lighting-up time, when a blue mist descends into the trees with an appeasing freshness. The dust settles then, although an atmosphere of overheated life still lingers over the pavements, and ground level, and burns the swollen feet of passers-by. There is still an agitation of the crowd, but the noisy activity of the day has decreased, melting into bewildered lassitude.

He did not cast a glance around him. Allowing himself to be borne unconsciously by the human swell, he advanced as if in the midst of a herd of uniform beings. The mystery of varieties did not affect him and he doubtless did not experience the sensation of vertigo that one feels in rubbing shoulders with so many impenetrable consciousnesses.

Would she be glad to see me again? he wondered, as he plunged into the tumultuous streets. And, remembering all her gazes, her intonations, and the least of her words: *Yes*, he said to himself, yes, *there's no doubt about it, for I've seen in her eyes that she might have been able to love me, but to love me before, before having a broken heart. Amour is incompatible with the state of resignation that she appears to have attained; her accepted unhappiness seems to her to be irreparable. But perhaps I'm mistaken*, he thought then, pleading in contradiction to his own reasoning, *perhaps the heavy yoke that that man made her bear has left the faculty of loving intact within her heart.*

I ought to expect, he reflected, *the noblest scruples. The senses don't exist for that being, so evidently passionate. Well, I won't seek to vanquish them, I'll remain her friend, I won't add to her torment; that will still be a felicity.*

The beloved woman appeared out there, outlining her svelte phantom with an aureoled head, against the vast Norman plains, refreshing to see, covered in their robe of thick grass, where he had encountered her, and a burning desire launched him toward her; then the reality of things seized him to the point of evidence . . .

I'll never be able to see her; is she not a prisoner?

He fled, without fatigue, along the broad roads filled again by the world of pleasure, similar to a man traversing a forest in haste, by various paths, in order to reach shelter before a storm. And the image that he bore in his heart, interrogated and scrutinized incessantly, an apparition made of gracious mutism and prudence retrenched in vague mystery, instead of opening to him, seemed then gradually to fade away before the violence he had employed in order that she might reveal herself.

After a thousand circuits he went home, having completely lost the image, and tried obstinately to resuscitate it again, until nightfall, his forehead on the marble of his table and his eyes closed.

He had never experienced anything similar; he was tormented, above all, by the desire to know more, to penetrate that soul entirely, where he sensed that so many sweet splendors were contained. He would have liked portraits of her as a child, to imagine her was a young woman; the peripeties of that destiny would have appeared to him more moving and more sympathetic, on learning that the combination of all the human calamities that had reached her acquaintance prior to today.

On rereading the bitter pages that emerged red hot from his imagination and were presented to him as a series of hideous frescoes, in which humanity, tortured by misfortune, agonized on the rack, or prey to the cruelest tortures, he had once arrived at interrupting himself in order to ask himself, ironically: "Of what is my pessimism made?"

"Of lost illusions," replied another voice.

"Oh!" he said, then, imploring the fate that holds in reserve for us so many different fruits, "If you could still give me one of them, or more than one, would I lose it again, and bemoan it?"

And the genius, which becomes, for certain people, so jealously miserly with its treasures, had detached a golden apple from the tree of chimeras in order to feed him once more.

Spring came to stir and soften him.

The oaks, the aspens and the elms were already putting out their first leaves in the parks, and the breath of the forest depths was exhaled by boxes of lilies of the valley carried along the sidewalks, giving the dusty passers-by a taste for reminiscences.

It was necessary for him to go toward nature, like a thirsty traveler searching for a spring. The forest of Sénart offered him its enchantments. He admitted everything with an abundance of inexhaustible sentiment, which he had not known for many years of sterile struggles, in the blind prostration of dead ends. Hours of complete insouciance had offered him a kind of second helping of rediscovered adolescence, savings set aside by his good angel in days of fever and shame.

Delighted, he went into the green shade falling from the high branches; all the foliage seemed exquisite to him, of such a young hue: that of the elm, scarcely open, more delicate than capillaries; that of the aspen, white and quivering, which made the tree that bore it resemble a poetic specter appearing in the depths of a clearing.

The air was pure and odorous. He sat down, sensing his heart swell with the joy of loving. An infinite gratitude came to him for the woman, the sight of whom and the mysterious attachment of the soul to her had regenerated him. He nourished himself on that sentiment as on a delicate aliment in which exhausted youth rediscovered fierce flame and vital spirit.

Who could have told me that I would have remembered her like this? That she might have saved me from moral death? A strange power! A mysterious magnetism, the force of which one senses, where one had never expected to encounter it! So many women traversing my youth, he thought, *have fallen into forgetfulness, for whom I only feel coldness in my heart. So many others, beautiful, free, exhausted in seductions by an enviable fate, glimpsed like this one, who, once absent, have never presented themselves to my desire.*

He imagined the state of detachment that absence makes us experience for certain beings, by means of an ingenious comparison: an aerostat rises, a man is suspended from the nacelle by one hand; terror takes possession of the witnesses and they shudder; but as distance separates the man from the crowd, shrinking him in their eyes, they become detached from him; he no longer offers the same terrible interest; they become indifferent to his fate, even his death. Everyone reenters into himself, and there is no longer any question of the stranger.

He felt full of pride at being able to experience amour again, to see it flowering once more in the midst of his life made of bleak privations and devouring struggles, as a magnolia plant, transplanted and sterile for a long time, opens its alabaster bud on the first day of summer, unfolds its smooth and fleshy petals and pours the inebriation of its perfume over the culinary plants ripened at its feet. Noble preoccupations and subtle sufferings confining delicate sensuality were not, therefore, the exclusive prerogative of the idle, as a number of writers tend to believe who imagine that it is necessary to dispose of leisure in order to be susceptible of experiencing passions and that the fact of having to defend oneself against hunger closes the golden gates of dream forever.

It was, therefore, possible to transport one's paradise to a hovel, to build enchanted palaces, tottering in the mist, when one has cold feet, a head on fire, and a problematic supper. It was not indispensable to repose one's eyes on a suggestive milieu, and the mildness of material impressions did not have the decisive influence one might believe on the fashion of envisaging and feeling amour.

It seemed to him, therefore, that a redoubtable chilly infant with his feet posed on bare ground, or the dusty floorboards of a mansard, was as beautiful in his pure nudity as one treading carpets in a hothouse atmosphere, outlined by light filtered through lace windows.

O splendor of divine Equality! The poor man also had his share of the royal cake, as in the days of the Epiphany, in his childhood, a fragment of the embalmed crown was offered by his mother to the most wretched passer-by. He sat down at the brilliant table and could aspire to the bean baked into the cake; his eyes sparkled with joy in his wan face and no one in the house was happier than him.

No, the pathetic in human destiny was not banished by poverty; it did not soften the finesse of the senses; it did not put the faculties to sleep; it was, after all, only a hindrance that hobbled the limbs, a cannonball that retained a foot ready to leap forward. But by envisaging it without resentment, what an admirable moral discipline, what a superior instrument of perfection it became in certain hands. How much self-knowledge one owes to being tested, like elite weapons whose temper is never known if they have not been hurled into combat; with grave hands, it removes the blindfold of individual egotism, it cures the blindness; as soon as it is pressed to the meager breast, the man reads real things in its profound and clear eyes, not as they ought to be or as one would like them to be.

On returning to the great city, his thoughts were confused, like the flowers that he had picked in the woods in the shade of centenarian trees: humble flowers with calices as pale as anemic faces, exhaling a sweet wild odor that the fatigue of the road and the warm pressure of his hand had caused to fall back, half-fainted, mingling their delicate corollas.

⁂

At the same time, she often came to lean on the rural fence that separated the narrow orchard from the flat countryside.

Her elegant stature was outlined against the Norman meadows. Before her unfurled a vast array of varied and lush green fields, which the distant sea bordered with a dark blue edge; and brought odors of tar, hemp and resinous wood from the port; she perceived masts leaning over sails folded like mantles or inflated by the breeze, rope ladders rising toward the summits of masts, mingling with confused topsails. Light skiffs spoke to the soul of unexpected flights toward new, gentler fatherlands, and the rejuvenation of the heart in the forgetfulness of present struggles.

That horizon seemed still to reserve new mysteries for her. She forgot herself there in the state of abstraction that is the removal of the soul from its persistent wounds: a strange flight into the ether, a dispersion of all our being in the impersonality of things, which re-tempers us for the proof by snatching us away for a moment from all our bonds and all our tyrannies.

But she considered the distance with calm, motionless, without the impatient desire to attain them. She had had a dream that she did not want to live, and whispered to herself:

"I shan't see him again!"

TALES OF THE PRESENT
AND THE PAST 2
(*La Fronde*, 23 February 1899)

TOWARD the end of the month of March in the year 700 Saint Aubert sent Scubilion, Gautier and Jehan d'Argouges, clerks in his abbey on Mont Tombaë to Mont Gargan, in order to obtain from the monks the relics of Saint Michel des Loups. The archangel had appeared to him, sword in hand, with the result that, seeing evidence of his will, he had dedicated the monastery to him that he had just constructed on the summit of Mont Tombaë, a somber and terrible granite cone six hundred meters high looming up in the middle of the forests of Seyssi and Koquelonde, the refuge of the last druid spared by the Romans and a lair of wild beasts.

They set forth at dawn, equipped with their psalter and a pilgrim's staff. Scubilion was all pride and sanctity, Gautier modest fervor and d'Argouges poetry.

It was the Golden Age of the cenobitic life. Saints were sprouting in Gaul, as hard and vigorous as plants of the woods felled by Tiberius after the massacre of the druids.

Our clerks were walking gravely, like young men who can already sense the circle of a nimbus around their heads. The forest opened before them immense and mild. The sky was pale and gray with blue depths. To the right and the left there was a uniform sea of motionless ferns and slender trunks, a calm and profound underwood.

When they climbed an eminence they saw the treetops in

the distance forming undulations, a broad swell extending and swaying toward mauve hills with smoothed angles. They breathed more easily on plateaux open to the sky than when descending into the mossy depths.

The perfume of violets filled the pagan forest of scarcely-fallen idols. It penetrated the coarse robes, and clung to the hands and nostrils, as if it were the dying respiration of Sessia, the vanquished goddess.[1]

Scubilion, a punctilious man, the son of a Jersey fisherman, reminded his brothers severely that it was the time when the monks of the forest, wearing cilices under their goatskins, were saying their prayers in their hermitages of Mabdanum and Kenfrith, and that it was appropriate to do likewise. He praised the good fortune of monasteries situated on the edge of the sea, which had the right to catch fish, collect wrack and finds, the right to take royal and fatty fish, sturgeon, baleen whales and cachalots. Above all, he loved shores and little osier boats lined with leather bobbing gently on the waves.

Gautier, with the profound eyes of seers, declared that he asked God incessantly to be able to domesticate ferocious animals, and that he hooped to encounter on his route the monstrous idol of Mendès that the faithful had recently cast down, in order to exorcize it . . .[2]

---

1 The name Sessia is found in the writings of Tertullian as a Roman goddess of crop-sowing, but her invocation in connection with Bretagne is idiosyncratic, its relation to Sesiacum, Seyssi or Scissy, the name of a mythical forest that supposedly once connected northern France with the island of Britain before being submerged in the early eighth century, apparently being a whim of the present author. The story of the sunken forest forms a significant part of the legend of Mont Saint-Michel and was elaborately developed in Leopold Quenault's scholarly fantasy *Les Mouvements de la mer, ses invasions et ses relais sur les côtes de l'Océan Atlantique, del a Méditerranée, de la Mer du Nord, de la Manche, de la Baltique, et en prticulier sur celles de la Bretagne et de la Normandie* (1869). Alice Télot would have taken a strong interest in the story because the supposed point of connection of the vanished forest to the surviving coastline was the area surrounding Granville, where she surely spent at least part of her childhood

2 The reference to an "idol of Mendès" presumably has in mind the "goat

193

D'Argouges, smoothing his long blond beard, opening large eyes misted by dreams, said that he would love to see the goddess Sessia . . .

Sessia had given her name to the forest, then Sesiacum; she presided over the sowing of seed and had care of wheat.

The new-born spring shook its perfumes in the branches. The sweet songs of little birds fell from the treetops. An invisible spirit spoke in the murmur of the wind with a mysterious accent, and green plants with flexible stems swayed soundlessly.

"Be careful, d'Argouges," Scubilion fulminated. "These woods are fertile in ambushes. Saints need sands devoid of shelter, arid deserts with meager rosemary and desolate promontories. You are of a proud race that claims to be descended from a fay,[1] from some priestess infidel to temeritous vows. Remember that! You are a good monk, but paganism is in the depths of your veins, like dregs. A villein like me is less at risk. Be careful, d'Argouges!"

D'Argouges lowered his eyes. A pink flame shone on his cheeks, and a sigh inflated his breast. He said: "It isn't my faith that is vacillating, Scubilion, but I can't help loving the souls doomed by idols and admiring all faith, even in error. So, when

---

of Mendes" employed as a symbol by the occultist Eliphas Lévi, borrowed from a mistaken passage in Herodotus (the deity of the Egyptian city of Mendes actually had the head of a ram, not a goat). Lévi's illustration was very frequently reprinted and was belatedly associated by nineteenth-century occultists with the "Baphomet" allegedly worshiped by heretical Knights Templar, whereby it entered the lexicon of modern Satanism. It is conceivable, however, that the author of the present tale also had in mind Catulle Mendès, the great pioneer and exemplar of the kind of newspaper short fiction that *La Fronde* was carrying forward and feminizing.

1 The well-known legend of Mélusine had a Norman parallel in which Robert d'Argouges, a member of a notable family of the region, married a magical woman encountered by a spring, who imposed the condition on him that he must never pronounce the name of Death before her; when the proscription is eventually broken the enchantress disappears but subsequently makes ghostly returns, crying the fatal word. The best known of several literary versions is *La Fée d'Argouges, légende du XIVe siècle* (1838) by Alfred Castel.

we meditate in the Cloister, I think about the times when Mont Tombaë, newly dedicated to the Archangel, was called Belenos, and when that gigantic rock served as a shelter for a college of new druidesses, suspended there like a nest of doves, but doves with the hearts of eagles. Is it not true that they were pure and that their prayers rose toward the Sun as ours rise toward God?"

A sarcastic expression passed over Gautier's lips. He responded, coldly: "It's difficult to belie one's blood. The harp of the bard and the burning fusions of poetry suit your spirit, more young than mortified. Human love attracts you and the very thought of woman has a dangerous sweetness for you. You have not put on that robe to love the grace of creatures.

D'Argouges had a charming smile. "I can only love that of Jesus," he said.

Scubilion commenced an interminable orison, until fatigue and hunger took possession of the ingenuous travelers. They searched for a propitious place in order to take their frugal meal and their siesta under the protection of God.

One did not take long to offer itself to them, where tall beech trees guarded a little spring. Russet leaves formed a noisy carpet; three mossy stones served as seats and a rock as a table. They took bread and cheese out of their satchels, sated their hunger, and, pulling their cowls down over their heads, they went to sleep on the moss without paying any heed to the wild beasts that were roaming the woods.

Scubilion dreamed that he was walking barefoot without wounding himself through madrepores, stones, shells and marine plants. He laughed on seeing the armored crabs, the silvery lepas and shells in the form of oval cups. He imagined that he could hear the voice of the rising Ocean, a grave, swelling song, the immense sigh of the wave, gliding over distant beaches.

Gautier imagined that he had replaced the idol of Mendès, and received the gift of miracles and transformations. Jesus had given him a wand, and he touched wolves on the head, and they sang the praises of God, following him in solitude. He also read the future and made peoples tremble, frightened by his revelations.

D'Argouges was filled with the charm of the forest. He heard the songs of birds in a celestial harmony. The perfume of flowers intoxicated him like aromatic smoke. He could not sleep and thought he saw shadows gliding through the tangle of willow branches. But a light step made the leaves crackle and, opening his eyes, he perceived an admirably beautiful woman a few paces away from him, who was cutting the bark of a beech with the point of a dagger.

"Ah!" said the poor monk, rubbing his eyes. "Am I dreaming?" And he uttered the war cry of his race, which was: "To the fay!"

She did not turn her head until she had finished her task, immobile in her white tunic, and he soon read with stupor on the trunk of the tree the name of Belenos, which means Sun.

She finally showed him her snowy face, in which an eternal youth shone; then, smiling softly, she said: "I am Sessia."

The forest quivered on hearing her name; the treetops inclined; multiple distant crystalline voices murmured: "Sessia! Sessia!"

"Come," she said to d'Argouges, "my forest no longer contains a fugitive Celt, a proscribed bard, a druidess without an altar, or a servant of Theut;[1] my forest no longer wants to live, and you are seeing its last day. Follow me!"

Devoid of will, with an automatic tread, Jehan stood up and marched in the wake of the white robe. His pale lips murmured a vain prayer.

---

1 The name Theut is deliberately ambiguous, probably uniting a variant of the name of the Egyptian god Thoth, important in French Occultist tradition as "Hermes Trismegistus" and the hypothetical god of the Teutons, patron of the Germanic peoples.

The goddess said: "I protected the crops; by my cares the wheat germinated healthy and strong; the furrows owed their verdure to me; in summer I lost myself in the ears, I crowned my head with cornflowers; the granaries of the farms were overflowing and the laborer, baking his bread, blessed Sessia. I was good, little children knew my name; even the men of the sea bought me presents to their moorings and I consecrated the arrows of warriors; my power was known."

She put her hand to her forehead, where vervain was wilting.

"I had even renounced amour, so much did the benefits I could distribute satisfy my heart. Monks like you came and hunted my druids and my priestesses, the laborers misunderstood my gifts. So, I am going to take them away from the earth where the most beautiful wheat in the world germinates, and draw the green waves to me in order to make a shroud for myself. Where we are, there will be nothing more tomorrow than the sea and the sky."

She cocked an ear, with a distracted expression.

"Can you hear? Can you hear my trees, my grottoes, my rocks, my reeds, my blades of grass and my first flowers, sighing before being annihilated?"

Sessia became pale and began to weep, and d'Argouges remarked that the tears rendered her beauty more striking than her smile, as if divine. He sensed his heart melting, and marched more resolutely behind her.

A signpost suspended by the roadside bore the legend: *Crossroads of the Precipice*, and another, a little further on: *Road to the Abyss*. The monk read those indications, but they did not stop him.

Scubilion and Gautier woke up shortly afterwards; they no longer found their companion. Before them, flamboyantly incrusted in the bleeding bark of the tree, was the hated name of Belenos, the last challenge of the druidess.

They resumed their march, sadly.

Already, a furious storm was tearing clumps of ivy and moss from the trunks of the trees; the branches were colliding like Frankish bucklers, with a sinister sound. The wind started to blow tempestuously, a prelude to the imminent equinoctial tide. The frightened woodland birds, warned by their instinct, quit their shelters, flew away in a confused cloud with sinister cries, and came to settle in the mountains; packs of wolves, foxes and wild boar ran hither and yon, as if mad with terror.

The tide rose, immense, green and glaucous, breaking everything, crushing everything, rolling enormous blocks of stone over the largest trees, which it reduced to thin twigs. The sea advanced incessantly, casting down all obstacles. The wave rushed over the mountains, coiling and writhing like a gigantic serpent that was raising the tempest. Finally forced to obey the ebb, it withdrew, growling, full of menace for the next tide.

The sunlight, traversing the somber clouds, came to illuminate the desolate spectacle. Of all the immense forest of Seyssi, nothing subsisted but a group of islets, which conserved the name of Chausey, a few rocks here and there that the sea had not been able to uproot, marshes and ponds, in the middle of which Mont Tombaë raised its beautiful and severe structure, still streaming with frost.

On returning from Mont Gargan, Scubilion and Gautier, who were carrying devotedly the relics of Saint Michel des Loups in a precious enameled casket, believed that they had been transported into another universe when they no longer saw the spacious forest that the sea had invaded.

On the hillock of Lihou the body of Jehan d'Argouges was found, clutching in his arms the cadaver of a druidess in a white robe. At that spectacle the two clerks turned their eyes away, making the sign of the cross.

At sea, a black line designed in the north-west the new islands already covered in algae protruding from the water in the midst of long fleecy waves.

Thousands of sea-birds and storm-birds were circling over the reefs. The cries of curlews and sandpipers had replaced the chirping of the blackbird and the nightingale.

LAST DIALOGUES 1
(*La Fronde*, 20 March 1899)

IT was during the calm decline of one of those days divided between sunlight and rain, when so much perfumed warmth floats in the air, that Frédéric decided to penetrate like a thief into the garden of the Calipel house.

Birds were still chattering in the branches, in spite of the late hour, and a residue of light was allowing a soft gray clarity to filter over the countryside.

How that evening recalled others in his memory! All the savor of the past rose from his heart to his lips, with the profound charm of things that we have had and lost before, which have expressed the last drop of juice from the possession and the happiness.

It was the same horizon, the same black and florid river, strewn with stars, the same warm odor of cowshed, the same divine freshness of dew, the same woman. A kind of intoxication drowned that uncertain soul in detailing all her charms, her intelligence, and now her money, the sole superiority that he had possessed before over her, which gave him a little aplomb and advantage.

His hands were trembling; he had to sit down for a moment on the edge of the lawn, until he recovered confidence by thinking of the intimacy of their former relationship.

To confront her point-blank with a sharp sentiment of her past wrongs and the consciousness of a perfect social equality that had arrived between them by virtue of a caprice of chance, did not seem an easy thing to the scantly valorous Frédéric.

He started walking, and then circling slowly around the patch of grass where two statues were moldering.

Finally, Clara appeared. He saw her emerge through a glazed door and advance toward him. Nailed to the ground, she seemed to him to have an imperial pride in the noble sway of her shoulders, her air of virile boldness, her beautiful, imperious and slightly somber face, crowned by chestnut hair with profound veins of gold.

Although half-submerged by the invading shadow, the young woman recognized her former lover immediately.

She had been expecting this moment for a long time, knowing full well that it would come; she was calm and firm.

However, when they were before one another and the features of their amour, covered with the dust of the past, were suddenly illuminated and animated, they experienced the same dolorous internal shock for a few seconds. Their souls were battered and disconcerted by the magic of memories, like boats delivered to waves whipped up by the wind.

After a rapid and anxious examination, Clara suddenly turned her face away, as if she mistrusted her eyes, ready to soften; her cheeks were covered by a severe redness and she said in a grave and tranquil voice:

"What are you doing here, Frédéric?"

He was happily surprised by that familiar tone, and he took a good augury from it for the return of her tenderness.

"How can you ask that?" he exclaimed, taking her beautiful hands with transport. "I've come to tell you that I've never ceased to adore you, that I've been suffering mortally for three years, and that now, if you want, we can be very happy."

"Speak, then," said Clara, in an impassive voice, with a direct gaze from which all weakness had been banished. "I'm in haste to know how you propose to make my happiness. There was a time when you could have, if you had had a heart similar to mine . . . and if you had found me worthy of it."

"Let's not talk about the past, since the present is smiling on us."

"Undoubtedly, let's not talk any longer about the past," she said, shaking her head slowly. "But a few more words: tell me what has caused this fortunate change in a will that was once inflexible."

"Please, don't remind me of those unjust rigors. Don't put my mother on trial; she consents today, let's not talk about it any more. It's only a matter of the two of us, of my amour thwarted by events stronger than me, but so ardent, so sincere!"

The impenetrable gaze that Clara attached to Frédéric oppressed him; a vague dread invaded him gradually, chilling his audacity of command. In vain he tried to reassemble his weakening forces; he sensed in advance that the victory belonged to his adversary.

"Yes, yes, let's not talk about it any more," she replied, with an air of ironic concession. "You're right, we only answer for our faults when we succumb to them; success is everything. Let's applaud ourselves. But it's necessary that I confess my scruples. I fear no longer being able to love you as much as I did in the past. The memory of the man who saved me from opprobrium is crushing for you. As gratitude took possession of my soul, you recoiled and shrank into the past. I see him in dreams every night . . . perhaps you will also dream about him later . . . but if his shade embarrasses us, we'll expel him, won't we?"

A confused murmur descended from obscure foliage, a sad whisper of leaves; imperceptible creaks were audible in the bushes, the branches of which were stirred by a slight wind, suggestive of the anxiety of an indiscreet witness betrayed in his espionage.

"Dear Clara," he said, in a low and suppliant tone, "chase away those visions, your heart is becoming ill in this solitude; one cannot live with the dead."

202

"You think me mad," she replied, in a somber tone full of contained force. "You can't support the impact of the truth, wanting at any price to shore up your happiness with the customary lie; I would rather confront without false light the picture of my life. Perhaps you don't know that I had a child. Learn it, then . . ."

"We'll have others!"

"But the first child to emerge from the entrails of a woman, you don't know, Frédéric; no, you don't know how one loves him!"

He imagined the frightful thing that the old man's child would have been, monstrous proof that she had belonged to him. Oh, the cruel woman! How easy it would have been to let him forget those atrocious details in the midst of felicity!

"Come on, these aren't things that are good to recall. Don't torture yourself thus; we'll forget all that."

"Yes, yes, we'll say: that never happened—as all men do, we'll kill the past."

The sour philosophy that flowed from Clara's lips like a bitter liqueur had the merit of emerging fully armed from her primitive brain and owed nothing to her memory; it was the fruit of misfortune, keenly felt and turned in every sense before clairvoyant and pitiless eyes.

Frédéric sensed that the game was lost, but he clung to the vague hope of an unexpected reversal. He told himself that in testing him thus, perhaps she wanted to double the price of her defeat.

"Certainly," he replied, "it is only the unhinged and those who are their own enemies who torment themselves with phantoms."

She suddenly struck a seductive attitude, and her face became young and soft, with a brilliant gleam of illusion in her bright eyes, in which hope seemed to float.

"And will you love me as much, Frédéric, tell me? As much as you did before, in my hovel decorated with flowers, when I put on my pink dress?"

He thought that she was finally capitulating; a flood of lust invaded his heart, his legs flexed, and he fell to his knees.

"I will love you as much and a thousand times more," he said, trying to seize the hem of her dress.

But she pulled away from him.

"Oh, truly? Even more!" she said. And the shadow of branches, in which she had taken refuge, hid from the lover's gaze the amorous face that he believed to have softened and to have been steeped again by the wellspring of passion that had become somnolent in the past.

"Enough," she continued, in a low voice vibrant with indignation, extending her hand over him imperiously; "enough lies, I despise you! You would bring me a realm that I would not want from you. How can you have the audacity to hope to be forgiven? Do you think that I have descended to your level in becoming rich? There would never be anything in common between those bourgeois and me. Happiness via amour is no longer the goal of my life."

Frédéric remained speechless before her. Anxiety and disappointment put wrinkles on his forehead and around his eyes. Suddenly, he launched himself forward to take her in his arms, as if to melt hatred and amour with his kisses in a desperate embrace.

"Back!" cried Clara, pushing him away forcefully. "You're seeking a lost heart. I no longer love you; go away, cease importuning me, and never appear before me again."

And she disappeared in the direction of the house.

He heard a bolt pushed, and sensed that it was finished forever. A simple perfume of vervain floated over the path in the wake of air that the young woman had traced in fleeing.

A tear ran down Frédéric's cheek.

RUSTIC IMAGES 5
(*La Fronde*, 2 April 1899)

THE SORCERER

HE was not known to have any family; his origins were lost in a discreet shadow. Even the epoch in which he had established himself in Saint-Saveur, in his house on the water's edge at the extremity of the quarter remained unknown to everyone. The beginning of his career were the humblest, the pettiest operations seemed to frighten him; he proceeded by fearful groping, as if surprised by his impunity; then he became gradually bolder, relying increasingly on dread and credulity, on the profound and ineffable impulsion of people toward the miraculous. His clientele increased without him apparently having done anything to attract it to him, and at the moment when his reputation as a sorcerer began to run around the region, it was learned that he was very old and spoke in a hoarse voice, like a very old woman.

He must always have been feeble, even when the blood of youth warmed his desiccated veins. It seemed that his body had been stopped in its development by an excessively strong soul, in which indomitable desire had held in suspense all the expansions of nature. Doubtless he had long endured scorn, without weapons, on the part of individuals worth less than him. He had not found pity; that was visible in his sealed lips, the sly and ironic mildness of his eyes, the eyes of a slave of genius led by that brutal master, destiny.

He did not say much, and when he was obliged to exchange a few words with his clients, he borrowed the gross low-Norman dialect commonly used in La Houle, but it was not in that rude language that the strange spirits inhabiting him held their interminable colloquia; they made use of a pure speech and chosen terms; they emitted ideas of philosophy, of the naturalist and the alchemist. And the sorcerer was all of those things as well as a wretched bone-setter.

The old man had seen austere, laborious days go by; he had only one vice; only one demon tormented him, that of money; he was a miser.

The sorcerer's dwelling, solid and very ancient in form, was decorated externally by a projecting roof of stone corroded by damp, advancing over the windows, the small green-tinted panes of which the daylight had difficulty penetrating. Two granite benches placed near the door only served for the gamins of La Houle who came in the evening in gangs to climb on them in order to enrage the sorcerer.

On darker nights, however, the old benches had other visitors: lovers in escapade, two mute shadows enlaced and immobile, two bodies numbed by a quietude still innocent and voluptuous. At intervals, kisses were exchanged, the young man leaning them over his friend's head, the hair of which, unshielded by any hat, had the sweet freshness of damp grass. They did not say much, having almost nothing to say to one another, too far apart in education, fortune and future for a perfect accord ever to exist in their young amour. The heredity carried in the veins of the young man a scorn for poverty; generations of ancestors had bequeathed to the young woman, along with poverty and the heart-rending traditions it engenders, a passionate hatred of the rich.

When ten o'clock chimed on the nearby clock, the lover drew away, hastily returning to his rich dwelling and his bourgeois wellbeing; the young woman remained there, leaning on the wall, her heart pounding. She watched him disappear through the sheets of curbed grass, under the cope of the sky extended over vague nature.

But one evening, when their rendezvous was prolonged, she remained thus until midnight, staring toward the town at the point where the silhouette of the handsome young man was confounded with the houses of La Houle. Each of the twelve strokes seemed a palpable body escaped from the bell and falling very close to her in the profound sonority of the great torpid meadows.

When the last vibration died away in the quivering air, the attention of the dreamer was attracted by a sort of stifled whistle, similar to the hoarse whistle of an owl, and, turning round abruptly, she recognized the sorcerer immobile beside her.

She fixed him boldly with her hard eyes and folded her arms in a challenging manner.

"Well?" she said, tapping her foot.

Then she noticed for the first time the expression of magnetic softness that he could give to his night-bird face. His accoutrement, composed of old peasant garments, patched-up fragments of cloth in various colors, equally tarnished, was rendered more bizarre by a black bonnet, clogs and an old brocade apron with which he covered his arched back.

"You weren't expecting me, girl?" he commenced, in his hoarse voice. "You're surprised to see me here all of a sudden? Don't be afraid of me, I don't mean you any harm. After those moments that you find so sweet, the apparition of an old man like me makes a somber contrast with amour ... I understand that ... heu! heu! heu!" the old man continued, seized by a sudden fit of coughing. "I understand that," he repeated, in a shrill voice.

There was a pause, during which the distant croaking of a frog was distinctly audible.

"I know everything," he went on. "I hear everything. Your turtle-dove fumblings under my window make an icy frisson run over my body. Poor girl! You're blinded by your hope; your will is so strong that you believe it capable of breaking anything. I admire your vehemence; your belief that will is all there is. Poor girl!"

"Have I asked for your pity, old thief, old wretch?" the young woman vociferated.

But he went on, with even more mildness, as if he had not heard the insult: "The man you love and to whom you are going to deliver yourself is your cruelest enemy. You have nothing in common; remember your suffering, your poverty; do you believe that he will forgive you your poverty? Come on, speak."

"No," she said, dully.

Then she had a revolt, and threw herself sideways as if bitten by a viper: "Why are you occupying yourself with me? Why say all that? You'd like to make me believe that you can read my heart, but don't play the sorcerer with me."

"Why? I'm asking myself the same question," he replied, with a strangely pensive expression. "I've interrogated myself a thousand times to discover whence comes the interest you inspire in me. It's doubtless your proud attitude . . . unless it's only your beauty. My torture is hearing you so close to me. Don't come here any more with him! He doesn't matter to you."

"What are you saying?" cried the young woman, utterly astonished.

"The amour that you have is that of revenge," he went on, with a somber hesitation. "It's the joy of getting closer to an envied and hated class. If that man were poor, like you, you wouldn't love him. Money, that's what you desire, that's the foundation of your ambition. Well, I have lots of it, the wherewithal to buy land, woods, a château, men . . . Come with me; I'll show it to you, you'll understand how beautiful it is."

He seized her by the hand; she resisted.

"I don't want to look at your money, you old skinflint. It's the Devil's money."

"The Devil?" said the old man, with a thin smile. "Where is he, the Devil? Every man carries him within him, there's no need to look for him elsewhere. Come on, let's go."

They went into the little house on the water's edge. The daughter of the people wanted to go on ahead to show the bone-setter that she wasn't afraid of anything. The old man lit his lamp, the glare of which suddenly illuminated the flanks of copper pots arranged along the walls, and he looked at the child with an inexpressible joy.

"How beautiful you are!" he said, putting his hands together. "My money, that money so hard won, will be yours. Although you're a woman, I've chosen you."

"Me! Me?" she said, stupefied.

"Yes, you," he replied, nodding his head. "I need someone to succeed me, who will continue my dream. I need someone like you, who knows misfortune, infamy, hunger, whom the injustice of others has flagellated repeatedly, someone that all humankind has rejected . . . but if I've cast my eyes upon you, there's also another reason."

The young woman's attention increased.

"You don't suspect it . . . naturally. However, if you wanted, I'd be your slave . . . and you'd be happy, happy! It only depends on you."

He had shouted that all in one breath, trembling in every limb.

And as she remained mute, darting her large staring eyes at him, he said, twisting his fingers: "Well, do you want to? Understand me well . . . do you want to marry me?"

She started, opening her lips to respond, but he made a violent and imperative gesture to make her shut up.

"Eh! What is his amour compared to mine? You'll be queen here, adulated and adorned! Simply to have you around me would be an ineffable joy for me. Consent, I beg you. What can that one do for you? He's a coward; he'll say that you seduced him, and everyone will curse you; you'll become an object of horror, your beauty will be lost, you'll wither; whereas, with me, you'll blossom!"

"Marry you! Me? Is that possible?" she said, her lips pale. "You're asking me that? Never!"

"What does it matter? Look at the rivers; they go less quickly than the forgetfulness of men before prosperity."

"Let me alone, shut up; you truly are the Devil," the child murmured, extending her hands before her as if to repel a phantom. "You're joking, you're making fun of me, old owl!"

"Don't you believe me? Is that possible?" He was suffocating. "Look at me, then!"

A mortal pallor covered his face.

"Once again," she cried, "what are you thinking? Have I asked you for your money, your affection? I don't want them. Adieu."

"Proud, proud! You're proud," he said, without paying any heed to her scorn. "That's why it's necessary for you to be rich. Understand then—how can you be both proud and poor at the same time? One dies of that."

But the child left without any response, walking backwards, her arms extended, with the tragic expression of an Erinnye.

A DUEL OF MARSOUINS[1]
(*La Nouvelle Revue*, 1 April 1899)

RETURNING from a three-year campaign in the Marquesas, Mathieu Mahaut descended on land for the first time. Brest opened before him like an Eden. With a lithe step he advanced through the gray streets. His pocket full of gold weighed upon his side and burned it. Although a simple matelot, he possessed a round enough sum, the custody of which embarrassed him and made him proud. That metal, so hard-won, counted for nothing in his thought but to serve for a brief feast of Sardanapalus. He dreamed of a superb role of a prince in the Thousand-and-One Nights, the dazzle of a café concert star subjugated by his Oriental sumptuousness, whom he would love royally for a week. It would be some young woman faded by nocturnal fêtes but sparkling with make-up, fake jewelry and flashy clothes, representing a sort of queen coveted by an envious crowd.

He had done his duty and had the right to amuse himself. His sisters were big girls who had no need of his aid. A delegation of twelve francs a month to the aged mother to pay for treats was not too bad for a kid who had been thrown out at the age of twelve to naval school, to learn morality from blows of

1 The literal translation of *marsouin* is "porpoise," but the term was much more familiar during the era of French colonialism as a slang term for an expeditionary soldier.

211

the cat-o'-nine-tails. Oh, he would remember for a long time the whip with the tarred thongs called Tricolor, which the corporal employed with a masterly hand. At present, the gold in his purse was for enjoyment. Short and sweet! One day he would moor his boat for good, of course, like so many others. Cholera, yellow fever, who knows? Or the big boat would go to the bottom. Life at sea was no farce, damn it! Oh yes, short and sweet. At twenty-one, one doesn't want heirs; he bequeathed his carcass to the sharks, his soul to God and his memory to the old woman.

The fête was about to commence, but with whom?

He would have liked to find a comrade, to encounter men like him who no longer wanted to know how long their halt on *terra firma* would be, as in the bewilderment of long voyages over infinite seas they no longer wanted to count the days of ennui. How long would these fabulous days of good cheer, amour and repose last? Not long enough not to be regretted, but enough to render to the troubled and restless sea its magnetic power over their souls, to the wind in the rigging its rude poetry, and to distant shores their mystical attraction.

All the married men in the crew had returned to their hearths—they were Bretons anyway, with whom he had little sympathy. He had fought with the others over a parrot and had nearly felled several. Suddenly, he remembered a tavern where lads from the homeland met up: Au Rendezvous des Grandvillais, and he started to march with a new haste.

It was March, a big wind was blowing, one of those Breton coastal winds, lukewarm, with a special moisture that soaked the hair and wet the skin. He did not take long to find the place for which he was searching. With the storm menacing, the door was closed. When it was opened, cries, laughter and oaths emerged. The light penetrated it abruptly then, blue-tinting the thick pipe-smoke, in which one could scarcely distinguish a brother at two paces; but Mathieu had eagle eyes, and he took in the room at a glance. Some were playing cards, others were telling stories with voices as resounding as the roar of the waves; of those who were drunk, some had the sad drunkenness and were drinking and drinking, shaking their heads, thinking of sinister things that made them weep, others were singing as loudly as they could, and there were some who remained before their empty glasses, their heads leaning on the wall, thinking about their lost mistresses, their village, or nothing at all, their heads empty and a fog in the soul.

He was quickly recognized by all that youth. "Mercy!" cried one of them, looking at him with round dilated eyes. "But it's Mahaut! Over there, lads, do you recognize him?"

"Not possible, but yes! Ah, twenty gods, he's profited rudely, the kid!"

They had got up noisily, tipping over the benches, and the noise they made drowned out their rude words. All hands were extended; there were forceful accolades.

"Well, you others," he said in a sonorous voice, "I hope that you're here in number. Delalande, Montsurvent, Carrouges, Servan; All the friends."

They pressed around the good fellow with a special consideration because of his ungovernable head: a simple matelot, like the majority of them, but belonging to a race of heroes.

They did not think him a failure for not having wanted to join the navy. He thought himself that going several generations back, his forefathers had not done any different from him, mariners all until the remote times of ships constructed entirely in oak with high poops, thick timbers and sails made of soft hides.

He sat down next to some domino players. Scarcely had he done so than the door opened again and a man came in, rather puny, pushed by the squall, his collar turned up. He had blue, slightly stupid eyes, and something ridiculous about his person that no one could quite define.

He was greeted by an ovation, as one those who are habitually found amusing.

"Hurrah, hurrah, it's Gaud Pylvestre, Bavoux Pylvestre . . . Pylvestre, eh! Pylvestre!"

He was acclaimed furiously, and stood there, laughing good-humoredly at that ovation, the irony of which was devoid of malice, not proud of his rank of leading seaman, not playing the superior.

"Well, what?" he said, in a high-pitched and stammering voice. "Here I am; have you finished?"

"Shut up, you lot," clamored a voice from the back of the room. "Let's have news of Granville!"

All woken up, they were ready to laugh and joke. The fault of pronunciation to which he owed his nickname of Bavoux made Pylvestre a celebrity.[1]

"Come on, talk. What's new?"

First of all, the leading seaman articulated, with difficulty, there was Master Christofle's boy, who was to embark at Le Havre for a long haul before entering the service, and the Alexandre son who had anticipated the call by engaging in the fleet. He also talked about other young men that conscription had taken away that year for the land army, about the oyster fishing, which had been fruitful, the carnival, of a folly more delirious than ever, a few old men who had died and a few old women who had followed them.

Then one of the others intoned the last four lines of a roundelay well known to Granvillais mariners:

Friends, don't be afflicted,
The poor old darling
Hasn't stolen her grave;
One sleeps well when one is weary.

---

1 An approximate English equivalent of Bavoux would be Dribbler; it means that Pylvestre has a stutter.

"That's all well and good," mocked a youth of scarcely seventeen, "but you're not telling us anything about amours."

A silence followed, and then someone shouted: "Aren't there any more amours, then?"

Pylvestre paled and uttered a vague and bitter laugh. The room spun, so contracted was his heart; his saliva contained a drop of blood, and he sensed his ears filling with a muted and violent hum. Nevertheless, rubbing his hands and sniggering, he said: "Yes, yes, there are . . . there's Vincente Mahaut, who's going to marry a Breton . . ."

They did not have time to hear any more. Mathieu had bounded toward him. Everyone recognized him and whispered:

"That's the brother!"

"Oh la la, a bad business."

"And the bavoux is in love with Vincente . . ."

It would be necessary to have been born in the region of the Manche and to have mingled with those bellicose races who fish for cod to understand the local value of that strange insult. On the eve of embarkations for Newfoundland, the port of Granville is invaded by an army of poor Bretons destined to serve as manual laborers out there. They are derisively known as "Saint Peter's horses." They are almost all children expelled from their hearths by poverty, and who, clad in sordid rags, are heaped up in the depths of the hold. Nothing can render the scorn of the Granvillais mariner for those miserable passengers.

Fifty years ago, if the registers of civil estate can be trusted, all the Granvillais were relatives or allied; social rank did not exist, the glorious past of the old town belonged to all. Foreign alliances were not tolerated. The prejudice still exists forcefully in a few old families. In thinking about the pleiad of Granvillais heroes that the Revolution had brought to the forefront, whom the Empire had ennobled, perhaps an excessive pride animates their grandsons and nephews. They esteem their blood so highly that they do not want it mixed.

Doubtless Mathieu knew full well that the age-old insult was valueless, but he was from a region where people fight to the death for a local feud and commit suicide for a saying.

There was a brief pause. The young matelot enjoyed the renown of his family. His father was an old sea dog, a master helmsman, and his grandfather had been killed at his post defending the entrance to the port of Granville against the English. He had the bravery of a hero, the strength of a young triton and such a hot head that he agreed himself that he would end up receiving a dozen bullets "in the beak." His black eyes launched terrible or joyous flames depending on his humor, and his proudly-camped head was thrown backwards with a natural and superb movement common to all those who have the gift of confronting danger and leading others into it, particular to sons of races pure of all mercantilism.

"Tell me, Bavoux Pylvestre, who you're talking about like that? Is it my sister? It's necessary that you express yourself more politely, because, if you continue, I'll give you a slap with one hand"—at the same time, he slapped him vigorously—"and lift you up with the other." A formidable shove restored the unfortunate leading seaman to an upright position.

People leapt forward to separate them. Pylvestre, utterly pale, was bleeding from the nose and dabbing it with his handkerchief. Anger stifled him. He was no longer able to talk, but he waved his arms in the air like a drowning man.

A deathly silence was established. Mathieu had just struck a superior officer; he was at Pylvestre's mercy. The latter went out without giving any explanation.

The next day, the young man was expecting the gendarmes when the post corporal handed him a letter. This is what it contained:

Monsieur,

The insult you have made me is too considerable for me to be able to forget it. I shall therefore send you two witnesses, who will confer with yours. If you have difficulty finding any for your part, there is Daireaux, who spends his life in the tavern. You could also ask the Twenty-fifth of December, whom you know—Noël Dagueret, whose face is badly scarred by smallpox; he is in Brest.

I have the honor of saluting you.

Pylvestre.

Pale, slightly emotional and softened, he turned the paper over in his fingers.

There's one who isn't a coward, he thought. *He could have sent me to a court-martial. A good devil, in spite of everything.*

He put on his boots and, following the advice of his adversary, went to look for Daireaux and the Twenty-fifth of December, whom he found in an inn frequented by merchant mariners, where everything reeked of the sea, hake, pitch and tar. After having traced the line of conduct that he had to follow, he returned to his ship.

The four witnesses met at the Rendezvous des Granvillais, the site of the quarrel. The officers sat down at a table in the places of honor, backs to the wall; the matelots were facing them on rickety stools, stiffly, a trifle formal, and mute.

One of Pylvestre's seconds spoke severely; the leading seaman had been insulted, he had the choice of weapons. They would fight with naval sabers. That was it.

"Agreed," said Daireaux.

"Agreed," repeated the Twenty-fifth of December.

The same officer continued: the encounter would take place the following day, at daybreak, in the most deserted part of the Cours Dajot, save for obstacles.

"Agreed," said Daireaux.

"Agreed," repeated the Twenty-fifth of December, meekly.

Being in accord, they separated, full of dignity, without offering to clink glasses.

The two matelots hastened to find Mathieu. He was waiting for them on the Cours Dajot, where they were to fight, at the foot of the statue of Neptune.

"Well?" he shouted to them from a distance. "Have you settled it?"

Having recovered their loquacity, they told the story of their conversation with Pylvestre's witnesses, amplifying it considerably.

"Ah!" said Mathieu, marching back and forth with great strides. "He has the choice of weapons, but I'll fight him any way he wishes, with cannon if he wants to."

And he quit them in order to go and bring his saber ashore.

At dawn, Mathieu set forth with his friends. He found that his adversary had preceded him to the terrain and was stamping his feet to warm himself, as were the other two leading seamen.

The weather was fresh; the combatants took off their coats, and a cold wind stung their bare shoulders.

Mathieu displayed his vigorously framed body of a sturdy fellow, his broad chest and his bronze biceps, before Pylvestre, who, slightly stooped and hollow-chested, nevertheless received his weapon with an assured hand. The young mariner had seized his with the tranquil assurance that is already half the victory, and he considered his adversary, pale but resolved to leave his skin if he had to do so.

As he put himself *en garde*, Mathieu said: "Pylvestre, my lad, you're holding your saber like a ladle. I'll run you through for sure."

"Sacred thunder," replied the Bavoux. "Get on with it, I'm waiting."

There were a few passes, during which Mathieu had great difficulty preventing the other from skewering himself. Sensing that he was at his mercy, he cried: "Your life is in my hands; you're a dead man. I don't want to kill you, poor fellow; I'll simply give you a little cut in the wrist—there, on the arm, for honor's sake."

He pricked him with the point of his saber, and blood appeared immediately, They were reconciled. A café received them—not the same one, in order not to remind them of the quarrel. When the witnesses had gone they remained together very fraternally.

The morning wore on; they drank slowly, punctuating the glasses with long silences, which filled their thoughts, and speeches in which they could only succeed in expressing superficialities in simple, slightly naïve words.

At one moment. Pylvestre asked, timidly: "It's all right with you, then, that your sister is marrying a Breton?"

The giant reddened, but a philosophical calm had descended upon him.

"What do you expect, old chap?" he said, pensively. "I've been away for three years."

He reflected that he had become a stranger to things, that he had lived fully a parcel of time removed from the preoccupations of his races, and that such pettinesses could not afflict him. His memory filled with the décor of the Marquesas, like a gust of strong perfume, and before him surged the woman from out there, Topé-Wainé, and her son Pou-Naï; her hair inundated her delicate body, modeled for amour; the child, truly adorable, had something new in his eyes, a flame unknown in Polynesia, and a willful crease in his forehead, the birth of which was lost in the ages, hollowed out by the effort of progressive races: lost delights for which the heart of the barbaric young man still had frissons. The joyful Polynesian woman clasped to her heart the child conquered from the European race, having added new elements to her blood. Old Europe would not have welcomed as an equal the child of the enchanting isle; it had its laws, which protected the pale products of its marriages from contact with the sons of youth and amour.

But Pylvestre was waiting for his response, and with mild obstinacy he repeated: "Then it's all right with you, Mathieu, that your sister is marrying a Breton?"

"Breton or otherwise," said the mariner, gazing into the depths of his glass with his soul still absent, "if he's the man of her choice, what do you want me to do about it? Don't get upset. If not her, you'll have another."

But Pylvestre, utterly downcast, with tears in his eyes, replied: "It's her that I wanted; I'll never find one like her. There are none."

His sister Vincente! It was that little scamp who was already being disputed by the covetousness of men. Sweet blonde prey! She escaped his memory, which summoned her. She was a fugitive apparition, which toyed with his effort; he could not see her entirely. The singular phenomenon of forgetfulness that long absences in foreign regions produces stabbed him dolorously. But his thought drifted toward accessories, and he saw everything. A calm tableau was composed in the half-light of the low room in which the family came together, and when he evoked the maidservant Rénotte cooking the smoked fish on the embers, everything appeared to him: the old mother maintaining a grand air in the midst of decent hindrance, the numerous sisters, as beautiful as Jean Goujon nymphs, ornamenting the hearth from which the wealth had departed.

His thought went along the streets, into the church; he saw himself there distinctly on the day of his first communion, and then baptisms, and weddings; finally, it stopped in the square that surrounds the church Notre-Dame, and his native land was offered to him.

The town was staged before him, as gray as the sky that crowned it, as if carved in a single block of granite, mined and vaguely gilded by light lichens. A road climbed steeply between the superimposed houses, straight and the color of freshly-cut wood. Prolonged appeals had just expired on the ramparts; shrill voices, singing and profound voices made for piercing the mists responded in the distance. The boats came back, seeming minuscule from the height of the cape, as fragile as children's toys, and the sea, where a veiled light floated, extended out there to be confounded with the sky toward the horizon, beyond a broad violet strip. He took pleasure in prolonging his dream, in giving it the movement of reality and the unexpected changes of the atmosphere. It was thus that he imagined the sun suddenly emerging from white clouds, and showing, in a rapid projection to the north-west, the archipelago of Chausey, fifty-two islets covered with green algae and lichens, heads emerging like a herd of monsters from the milieu of long fleecy waves, while a sector of blue sky azured the salty green of the waves.

Nevertheless, he said to his companion: "Don't make bile like that; it's necessary not to undermine the temperament. Leave it there, old man, for you're upsetting me with your story."

They shook hands to make the bones creak, and emptied their glasses in a single draught.

"It makes no difference," said Pylvestre, obstinately. "There are fellows worth as much as Bretons on the old rock; she had no need to choose an outsider. One day, I tell you, she'll see the family of her man landing, a bagpipe on the back or begging in a port; she'll weep, for she's proud, and she'll end up singing the *Granvillaise*:

> *But she's proud, and not to displease you*
> *That pride befits her, one can't do better*
> *For, better than a duc and peer, the Granvillaise*
> *With pride can count her ancestors.*

It's her who keeps the memory
Of what the old rock was
It was Grand-Ville-la-Victoire
Noble blood can't lower itself."

Mathieu made the glasses jump with a blow of his fist. "Don't say that to me, Pylvestre, don't say that to me; I'll see red."

"Oh, I would have suited her," the leading seaman continued, "because in your house, as in mine, no one has ever quit the land; your name is marked in the stones in the church and mine in the cemetery, one walks over them. Do you remember when we went to school at old Père Quinette's, who made us bring bundles of wood in winter?"

Then they became sentimental in remembering their childhood. "Of course you're a worthy fellow," said Mathieu, "and if it weren't for my sister I'd gladly strangle that lover. There's one whose bones I'd break."

"Right," said the other, in a soft voice. "I know you, you couldn't help it." The conversation, punctuated by alcohol, had uplifted him singularly, and he had hope in his heart again. If the giant Mathieu decided to get rid of the suitor, he could still hope to possess the beautiful slender girl with wrack-blonde hair and changing eyes, who draped the black *capot* with sharp creases so beautifully over her round hips.

"I'd throw him down to the shore from the top of the cliff," said the one.

"I'd drown him in the bottomless pool that swimmers dread," said the other.

They invented endless tortures and a hundred fashions of getting rid of the intruder. They were no longer thinking about their grievances and the cause of Pylvestre the bavoux had become the cause of Vincente's brother. They lamented mutually: "Poor old chap, my poor old chap!"

But Mathieu had a mobile mind, especially when he had been drinking. Suddenly, he straightened up and said, as if at the beginning of a conversation: "You see, my poor fellow, that's all well and good, but it was written, as the Arab Indians say. There's nothing to be done, because he's the man of her choice."

He squared his shoulders, shifted his head, looked down at the crestfallen Pylvestre, who made no movement, like a man felled by the blow of a tomahawk. A sentence had been pronounced, which annihilated the leading seaman. His companion plunged his gaze into the distance as if he glimpsed, confusedly, the mysterious laws that regulated amours and the absurdity of trying to struggle against them.

There was a long mute pause. The wind was raging outside, agitating the trees still stripped of leaves. A heavy sadness falling from the sky drowned their weary thoughts in an infinite mist. Melancholy, they sang in low voices to give themselves countenance. Time passed without dissipating the embarrassment and ennui that had descended slyly between them.

They searched for words to give birth to a new discourse in which nothing of the other—exhausted, importunate and inapt—would subsist.

Finally, Mathieu got up and said, laughing: "Necessary not to drop anchor here; I have piastres." He slapped his pocket with a sonorous blow. "Let's put all sail aloft and cast off."

They went out. The evening found them at the home of a female friend of Pylvestre's. They were laughing and singing, without thinking any longer about the duel, nor of Vincente's marriage. The leading seaman's acquaintance had bright eyes devoid of thought and a watery tint; her entire face was like a pale corolla. In the evenings she sang falsely ingenuous songs in a few taverns; Mathieu found her to his taste and resolved to have her. Pylvestre was very proud of her, he gave her all his money, and although he was ugly and stammered he believed that she was faithful. He did not perceive that the girl's gray eyes were looking with a furtive pleasure into Mathieur's dark eyes, or that the latter was playing the fine talker. Furthermore, in order to dispel any suspicion, she proposed to the young mariner to go in search of one of her friends—also an artiste, she said, with a comical seriousness—who would be charmed to see him, but he was able to make her understand his desire in a madrigal, and she stayed with him, drinking his words with security.

Mathieu was now laughing in an odd manner when he looked at Pylvestre, and looking in all directions with savage eyes, searching for some bold move with which to get rid of him; he almost regretted not having given him, that morning, a solid saber-thrust, and he no longer felt any amity for the comrade who had become a hindrance; he was a loser. He had left him his life, undoubtedly, but the desired woman, never.

However, the leading seaman looked at the two of them with benevolence and admiration, and when a nocturnal round summoned him back to his ship he left them together, promising to return soon.

When he reappeared, the door was closed, the blinds lowered, and no light was filtering through. Disappointed and perplexed, he thought that they had got tired of waiting for him and he set out to search for them in the places that he frequented with her; but he explored them in vain. His soul forlorn, he came back to the beauty's lodgings, firmly convinced that they would now have returned. He started running in the fear of rendering them impatient. On the threshold, the landlady laughed on seeing him, and, without being able to discern the cause very well, a suspicion bit him. Out of breath, sweating, he ran up the stairs and banged on the door, striking it with both fists.

The laughter of the woman rose up from below, increasing his fury. He vomited invectives and mariner's oaths, punctuated by long stammers escaping painfully from his strangled throat.

"Oh, the dirty dog," he said, "the dirty dog. I'm going to be cast off again!"

And the leading seaman, who had drunk a great deal, thought again about his duel, the lost Vincente, and the last and most sensible defeat. Sitting on the first step, he thought that he wished he had swallowed his gaffe, as his sailor's language had it, a long time ago, and when his anger declined, with his head in his hands, he began to weep . . .

MISTRESS OLAF
(*La Fronde*, 9 May 1899)

What is the last word of things, which nature
pronounces when she is entirely awake?
A. Fouillée[1]

SHE arrived toward evening, a little later than the hour announced. A timid stroke of the bell, light footsteps, and we saw
on the threshold of the drawing room a pale young woman with
short curly hair, who looked like of a child of fifteen, a charming
young boy. Her voice and her gaze made a strange impression on us,
which we did not seek to analyze immediately, and which I would
try in vain to translate today other than by the words: resounding
interior, mysterious astonishment.

An indefinable androgynous grace, a boldness of adornment,
the outré originality of which did not, however, succeeding in at-
taining ridicule, had to attract unhealthy curiosities on that young
woman's route.

She was made to impress the coldest imagination, but not, I
believe, to inspire amour. She personified to the highest degree the
foreigner at whom one does not laugh, whose homeland one cannot
divine, who attracts less as a woman than as a confused problem.

---

1 Presumably the philosopher Alfred Fouillée (1838-1912), although his
wife Augustine, a writer for children, was more likely to have been acquainted
with Alice Télot.

Her pallor struck us first, contrasted with the flamboyance of her red hair, and then her splendid green eyes, wide open and impenetrable. Those enormous eyes are the indication, among those who possess them, of a threat of mental disorder and, doubtless because of that, the mark of a stormy destiny.

By way of the open bay windows the sound of the city rose, whispering, through the dying curtain of virgin vines that reddened the veranda. Without definite accents, without discernible words, Paris murmured in the foreigner's ear the weary hymn of dusk. The setting sun rolled moist spangles in the river of gold; the sky, fantastic and fiery, seemed to have emerged from the victorious brush of Poussin; the edifices, heavy or light, with domes or steeples, lost nothing of their eloquence; the evening put a crepe over them that veiled them with a more arrogant mystery.

"Oh! Splendidful," she said.

And the word, flying from her lips, seemed to roll along the river like a distant caress.

That evening she informed us gravely of everything concerning her, events of her life that we only knew vaguely. She was an orphan, and had a brother still at Oxford. Their patrimony, exceedingly modest, could not provide them with a decent income, but they had no need of one, she said, before dying young! Their parents had succumbed at an early age to afflictions of the lungs, and their more distant ancestors had died prematurely of various unknown and often mysterious causes. None, to her knowledge, had surpassed thirty years— with the consequence that the two orphans, conscious of their destiny, had decided not to marry and to draw on their capital to supply their needs. All of that was said with a smile, without melancholy, as if it were a matter of an ineluctable law that could not be avoided.

She was modern, and sporty, having traveled the banks of the Rhine and the Tyrol alone, on foot or by bicycle. She was literate and mystical, her mind somewhat illuminated by the assiduous reading of Swedenborg. The cult of the strange that she had drew her northwards and she would only quit us for the Scandinavian peninsula.

She was quickly sated by Paris. She wearied quickly of admiration! Her vagabond soul liked indefinite, somewhat deserted, routes, the rude caress of the free wind, the sea and the mountain.

She quit us, leaving us with a little emptiness and sadness, and also a little relief, because of the anxiety of her eyes and her presentiment of death.

Subsequently, we obtained news of her incidentally, and, at the end of a year, a laconic note informed us of her marriage to a Swede named Olaf.

Fortunately, her presumptuous vows of celibacy had yielded before amour, and henceforth, it was with a heart almost entirely tranquil that we thought about the bizarre child with the indecisive graces. But if we had no more fears, a curiosity remained in her regard, and often, in talking about her, we asked questions without response.

Mistress Olaf—a singular legendary name. A puerile association of ideas made me remember, in pronouncing it, a ballad sung in Denmark and Sweden entitled "Sir Olaf in the Dance of the Elves."[1] That was one of those strange obsessions devoid of any link with cause and effect.

Sir Olaf mounts his horse, and encounters on his route a brilliant dance, the splendid ball of the Elves. The Elves try to draw him into the dance but he does not want that. "No," he says, "for tomorrow is my wedding day."

From the temptation of Olaf by the Elves one passes abruptly to the tragic end of the ballad. The bride says that day: "Tell me, why are the bells ringing like that?"

---

1 The story in question, known in numerous variants, is the most popular Medieval Scandinavian ballad, and has analogues in many other European languages.

"It's the custom of our island that every young lover rings in honor of his fiancée, but we dare not hide it from you: your fiancé, Sir Olaf, is dead. We have just brought back his cadaver."

The Elves had wanted the handsome fiancé for themselves, traveling over the snow-fields, and as he resisted, thinking about his fiancée of flesh who was waiting in her chamber painted all the way to the joists with black and red arabesques, they had drowned him in a furious torrent while he launched a desperate cry for help to the heavens.

※

Two years went by, and a veil of forgetfulness extended over the fate of young Mistress Olaf.

One sad evening, there was a misty dusk and a bitter north wind; outside there was snow, no longer crackling and virgin, but collapsed and soiled, allowing the sight in places of the ugly earth, in puddles of black mud.

The river, jaundiced under the dirty sky, darkened, and sometimes, the shining red eye of a bateau-mouche bloodied the turgid waves.

A light stroke of the bell, timid footsteps in the vestibule, and I stood up, urged by I know not what anxiety. A slender form was outlined in the semi-darkness, and a name fearfully anticipated, flew toward me, brushing my soul like the wings of a night-bird.

Mistress Olaf!

I repeated, aloud: "Mistress Olaf!"

And another voice, as if broken in its timbre, responded: "Dear Madame!"

Two icy little hands squeezed mine and I drew my visitor toward the clarity of the lamps, and the flames of the hearth.

I had before me a being as light as a shadow, a veritable specter of the one I had known. A world of thought agitated over her marble features, and among those thoughts, a disorder was divined that we had once read in the large green eyes, an unspecifiable symptom.

She was wearing a vividly striped mantle, in which red was dominant, and her saffroned crimson dress augmented her pallor, making her resemble a tragic Henner.[1]

As she remained mute and shivering, I articulated painfully: "Sir Olaf?"

"Dead," she replied, with an infinite despair and a torn voice.

She almost fainted; I had some difficulty reanimating her. A cup of tea with a dash of rum calmed her frissons, and after a moment, she said: "I want to confide in you; I want you to know the horror of what has happened to me."

I assured her of my sympathy and received her mangled, often incomprehensible, confidences

"I'm pregnant," she said, "And . . . it isn't Olaf's child!"

"Oh, wretch!" I said. "You've deceived him, and now the remorse . . . ?"

She shook her head disdainfully.

"No," she said. "Me, deceive Olaf? How could I have done that? We didn't quit one another for a minute from the day of our marriage until the fatal moment when he boarded a boat without me, to perish before my eyes in the depths of the fjord. I cherished him; furthermore," she added, volubly, "do you remember my vow of celibacy, do you remember? Well, I've never broken it."

She stood up, shivering.

"No, this child is not the child of Olaf's will. He didn't want his life, and I don't want it. It has to be destroyed!"

I darted a gaze at the young woman full of astonishment and terror. Her thin figure still had the same frail grace; there was no evidence of an imminent maternity.

---

1 Jean-Jacques Henner (1829-1905), a prolific painter of pensive women, many of them nudes.

I thought immediately of a Swedenborgian marriage, which only inspires spiritual pleasures, a union that does not produce children.

She wept, mingling her ardent words with sobs. "We lived as brothers, we had become the same spirit, our celestial joys were realities, our enjoyments infinite . . . Our happiness would have killed beings submissive to natural laws . . . We had broken our chains, we had escaped into the divine . . ."

For myself, I thought about their youth, their amour, such temeritous oaths; about the moments of delirium and dream that bring down the most hardened, the most determined . . .

I took the hand of the child who had rejected nature and exalted her life in a sort of intoxication as far as the cold summit of Platonic love. I tried to rehabilitate in her eyes the terrestrial work of woman, to reattach her to the enigmatic human flower that would soon bloom beside her, material testimony of human amour. All my efforts were in vain.

"It's necessary," she said, pressing her abdomen, "that this strange creature perish, or I shall never, never be able to rejoin Olaf, who is waiting for me, clad in his robe of light!"

I had vertigo; with that tormented spirit I fell into bottomless gulfs. My soul was saturated with fantastic images . . .

A fortnight later, the drama reached its denouement in a great Parisian operating theater.

Mistress Olaf perished under the impotent scalpel of the most skillful surgeon. Nature, betrayed in her secret and imperious will, had taken a ferocious revenge on the infecund organs

The manifestations of the young woman's internal malady had caused the error that had driven her mad. When she learned the true and mortal cause of the phenomena that she had observed, she became suddenly calm and happy. It was impossible to make her emerge from her memories and cataleptic visions.

In the midst of light and melodies, crystal waves and rocks covered with moss, the beloved summoned her, promising delights toward which her ardent lips were extended.

One evening, her soul flew toward the land of Norway, through the avenues of the fjords, sliding between the rocks and the parabolas of cataracts, soaring over the islets and the gentle emerald prairies, turned to the south.

Her throbbing body gaped in the amphitheater, her blood coagulated under the blade of the scalpel.

As virginal as the mountain snow, in the unknown world of eternal vows, in the regions of infinite hope where one rediscovers one's beloved, the young woman was able to rejoin Olaf, who was waiting for her, clad in his robe of light.

LAST DIALOGUES 2
(*La Fronde*, 11 June 1899)

IN the fifth century, imitating the example of his elders, Saint Hyvarnion[1] resolved to flee Saxon domination and seek a new fatherland on the coasts of Armorica. He quit Great Britain on a tempestuous day in a stone trough, which was very fashionable among the saints of those days. The deep ocean did not frighten him. A flotilla of the intrepid faithful followed his example, emigrating with their wives and children.

At the beginning of the crossing they sang the psalm of the Hebrews, translated into Breton, accompanied on the harp, and did their best to followed Hyvarnion's trough, which flew over the waves. Toward evening, however, a frightful wind came to assail them. A big wave took away one of the passengers, a father of several children; the masts were demolished by the sea, which swept over the ship to the height of the masts. In view of the coast, one boat sank without anyone being able to bring help, and it was a spectacle worthy of pity to see that little flotilla, disabled by broken masts and torn sails.

At the moment of peril the Bretons had made a vow to erect a commemorative chapel if they landed safe and sound on the

---

1 Hyvarnion was the name of a British bard said to be the father of the popular Breton Saint Hervé, who lived in the early sixth century, but the present character is evidently a hypothetical predecessor in an entirely imaginary past.

shore. In fact those who reached land set about constructing it without preoccupying themselves with those who had remained on the sea-bed.

The people of the faithful did not take long to find a superb place to establish themselves, in the shelter of secular trees. Huts were constructed, of which one was built slightly apart for the saint.

The soul of that new fatherland was wild and mild; it was good to ply the plow there under the serene gray sky.

The furrows yielded wheat and millet, and the emigrants' days passed smoothly, like water flowing over diaphanous stones. They worked for Hyvarnion and nourished him, for his profession was to watch them live.

And they lived happily, surrounded by women and children, while the solitary only had domesticated wolves for society and a young boar that grunted incessantly.

In his quality as a saint, he had temptations of which his flock, possessed of simple hearts, were unaware, with the result that they had pure hearts while he, without committing any sin, had an imagination incessantly soiled.

He knew that his austerity was only external, which made him despair, and he would have liked to change by mortification; but the more he multiplied fasts and vigils, the weaker in body he became, and the more he fell prey to dreams. He wondered incessantly whether Jesus Christ was aware of his struggles, and sensed that his soul was lost in desolation.

When he went out, however, the men in the fields prostrated themselves at his feet, kissing his sandals, reminding one another of the miracles he had accomplished, and he forgot his infinite misery and his solitude for a few moments. Then he wanted once again, and more forcefully, to be a saint!

He folded his arms over his hollow chest full of sobs, walking with his head bowed, and his flock said: "He's thinking about

God!" but he was thinking about his enemy, whom he called "the Demon."

Often, in the evening, he delivered himself to meditation beside the sea. The rocks, assailed by the waves, seemed to him to be as sad as his soul, combated by doubt. He thought about the initial pleasures of his estate, about the prompt appeal of his vocation.

One day, when he had been playing with his brothers in his father's gardens, he had heard sounds of music outside, mingled with songs. It was a company of monks, with white robes with seraphic faces. An abbé was marching at their head, harp in hand, singing the praises of God—with the result that he had said to his brothers: "Return to your games, you others; for myself, I'm going with these persons."

And he had quit the paternal house joyfully, intoxicated by the beauty of hymns and the sound of the harp.

One morning in spring, when he was climbing the mountain, thus plunged in returns to the past, he rested his eyes on a village of smiling grace established in the valley. A blue mist enveloped it with a veil as light as gauze placed on the ruddy face of a young woman.

The apple trees, sacred trees cherished by Bretons in the joyful days of flowering, were snowing white and pink, extracting admiration and smiles from the most indifferent. The blue sky protected them, the sun made their crowns shine, the grass wept with joy in being in their shade, with all the drops of dew; the somber and profound oak-wood gave the impression, in the distance, of a crowd of grave people who had come to admire the apple trees. The laurels lamented being so severe and not being able to soften with tender emotion.

Oh, Hyvarnion had never heard mention of similar apple trees. So old and so virginal, so pagan and so religious—as religious as the bouquets offered by nature to God, so full of intoxication and so pure.

Village of idolatry, the apostle said to himself, and the imperious desire to convert souls filled his heart again.

He seized a dogwood staff and put a dried galette as hard as a pebble in his satchel; then he headed toward the joyful village that the flowering apple trees ornamented with such a pagan triumph.

He arrived there at the hour when the sun was commencing to burn; the soil there was prosperous that year because of numerous rose-bushes, presaged by the arrival of brilliant scarabs. The hemp was shining gaily in the enclosures, the flax gazing at the sky by way of all its flowers, as blue as innocent eyes.

On the threshold of a thatched cottage he found a laborer with a bronzed face, and before saying anything else to him, he asked him why the apple trees in that valley were so beautiful, more beautiful than all those he had seen in flower.

The man, full of assurance and very noble, replied:

"They're Merlin's apple trees; it's in their shade that he plays the harp, dreams and prays. In their shade, he loved a woman, was happy, and then wept. Can you compare Merlin's apple trees to others? The old bard has more influence on the plants than the full moon on the furrows in the black months that follow the sowing. Where have you come from, ignorant barbarian, that you do not know about Merlin's power?"

The ascetic replied, severely: "I don't believe it. Fable and lie! Outside of God there is no diviner; now, I order you to take me to this fake enchanter."

"Come," replied the laborer, disdainfully.

Hyvarnion found Merlin in the wood where he had lived with the magicienne, in the shelter of two apple trees larger, rounder and more perfumed than all the rest. He was strong and superb, more majestic than a king; his beard was as white as the wool on a bush on the heath; his harp reposed by his side, suspended by four chains of fine gold. He wore the bardic ring on his finger, more glorious than a scepter; his eyes shone like water in a basin over a fire. He was lying on the moss among new flowers; a bouquet of willowherb, propitious to enchantments, which he had picked, reposed near his long, wrinkled hand. He watched the ascetic and the man of the glebe coming with his haughty and immutable gaze.

Hyvarnion stopped, intimidated by the arrogant appearance of the bard, and the laborer said to him, ironically: "Dare to interrogate him." Then he left him alone.

The saint remained nonplussed before the diviner versed in the magical sciences. Breaking the heavy silence, however, the old bard addressed the first *Ave* to the priest of Christ.

"I salute you," he said, "O man of future errors, you who pretend to replace me and who continue me."

"And I," said the ascetic, "salute you in the name of the unique God, who has conferred the gift of miracles upon me."

An indulgent smile passed like a gleam over Merlin's discolored lips.

"I have told you that he is several. As for miracles, listen! Merlin has fled the court of the chiefs; he has fled the people who uttered cries of joy on seeing him appear; he marches bare-headed, he is a man, but see!"

As he spoke, the bard seized his harp and drew penetrating sounds from it. All the flowers of the apple trees were detached from the branches and began to rain down on Hyvarnion's head, while Merlin recited the poem that he had consecrated to the tree.

"O apple tree," he said, "mild and dear tree, I am anxious for you; I tremble that the woodcutters might come, might hollow out around your root and corrupt your sap, and that you will no longer be able to bear fruit in future."

And he took his harp between his emaciated fingers again and made a victorious song burst forth. Immediately, odorous crimson and golden apples covered the branches, which leaned over, weighed down all the way to the green grass.

Then the wonderstruck saint sat down next to the bard and they conversed at length. When night fell they emerged from the wood, the tall old man leaning on the fleshless ascetic; they talked to one another with serenity, letting their words float like a shroud devoid of sadness, and their frozen hearts were reanimated under the impact of their hopes, as burning as a rain of fire.

Death smiled at them, promising eternal renaissances of spring.

Merlin said: "The task is finished; we have wanted, we have thought, and our wills and our thoughts will reverberate in the future all the way to the confines of infinity."

Bats collided with their heads. Life seemed to them to be akin to a book trampled in the mud, spelled out long ago; and the future of their souls, beyond the tomb, a fatherland overflowing with unknown treasures . . .

In the darkness, they both embarked on the howling sea, and the ocean of the Earth, in drawing them into its gulfs, led them toward the unfathomable ocean of Time, whose waters, like ours, are briny with the bitter salt of human tears.

RUSTIC IMAGES 6
(*La Fronde*, 27 July 1899)

IT was a poor country church, which one reached by old abandoned roads, sunken roads like the beds of streams, where the
roots of old oaks extended the menacing gesture of tortuous
arms at head height, their black claws open.

Time had embellished it by ruining it. Half-buried in the
earth, it was necessary to duck in order to pass through the low
arched portal. The stone of the pillars was so worn that it had
metallic gleams. A great silence reigned there in the meditative
obscurity.

It was scarcely frequented any longer except by souls in pain
whispering their dolors there—it is for that reason that it was
sad—or by lovers who came there to shed tears; it is for that reason that it was damp and warm. So much melancholy proffered
or retained created an atmosphere around that divine abode of
suffering, the poetry of which, as ungraspable as the notes of a
nightingale, was respired with tremulous delight.

Around it, the ancient cemetery had become a meadow
brilliant with flowers, superabundant with life, devoid of sym-
bols and memories, where insects cried, burned by the sun and
intoxicated by the azure. Poppies burst forth there in long flamboyant streaks; daisies loomed up, pale and proud; foxgloves
launched forth in jets, letting their striped mouths, heavy with
venom, hang down with a noble languor.

And all those flowers resembled the thoughts of the dead, for death flourished and fructified the insatiable earth. The evil of souls, disaggregated atoms, emerges in poisons in plants, and the good, doubtless, in beneficent perfumes and medicinal virtues.

An old Breton woman entered, who was weeping. She was so small and so curbed by age and labor that the low arched portal was high above her, crowned with the gold of wallflowers.

She was weeping. Her cheeks were like walls washed by rain; because of infinite sobs her mouth made a sad grimace that resembled the smile of a wan and ironic corpse; her neck was like a thick, slack and distressed rope; her short torso was contained in a meager bodice as narrow as that of a ten-year-old girl. Her hands were as hard as metal, eloquently sculpted by labor. Her white woolen capeline bordered in black—a mourning capeline—striped her forehead, wrinkled like a plowed field, diagonally.

From beneath her mantle she took a pair of dainty clogs—clogs sculpted patiently with daisies, arched clogs, as if for the high and slender foot of an Oriental woman, with a crimson strap and tapered heels—and she sought the Virgin in order to offer them to her.

Alas, the Mother of God, the venerated Black Madonna corroded by damp and the centuries, had crumbled away. Her poor child was all alone in the empty niche, as pitiful as an orphan. Nothing was more lamentable than that image in dust, a dust that had a human air ...

In the sanctuary, Saint Cornely could still be seen in a Persian tiara, the head of an ox at his feet. Saint Laurent, with his grill, was facing an individual with thick lips holding a decapitated head with a long blonde beard. Saint John was gazing at the Magdalen.

The last-named was extremely beautiful and admirably well-conserved. The ancient Breton sculptor had exhausted his art, still primitive, but respiring a pagan love of beauty, in draping wood over the suave limbs. One of the legs, very long, was designed under the robe with the most voluptuous concern for the line; the small and youthful bosom swelled the corselet than contained it without gripping it; the neck had the singular grace of a lily stem; the mouth, a carnal flower kneaded for a kiss, parted its lips for repentance; and the eyes were looking at you with a wide, bewildered gaze: the bewildered gaze of beings replete with errors, who have suffered immensely.

The old clog-maker approached the beautiful saint and placed the little cogs before her.

"They were not for you, sinner," she said, fixing her with a sort of admiring hatred. "They were not for you. I have shaped, emptied and sculpted them for the Mother of God, who has lost her son. You had no son," the artisan continued, with a somber snigger, "and perhaps you would not understand my pain."

She paused, raised her shoulders, and stared at the statue of the woman, too beautiful not to have sinned. Finally, she continued, her voice whistling in her toothless mouth, and she shook her head, in the impotence to render her grief.

"Magdalen," she said, "listen anyway. I have such a sick heart that it is necessary for me to speak. I'm a poor maker of wooden clogs, a clog-maker without a hut or a hearth. I eat black bread, myrtle seeds and mushrooms. For you know that the Breton prophets lied. Always we were told: 'The poorest earth will yield the best wheat' and 'Brilliant gold will fall from the trees.' We were deceived; the earth is bad and nothing falls from the trees but dry leaves, as yellow as gold, to make the beds of poor folk.

"Often, I beg on the roads, but that is nothing. Say, Magdalen, do you know how to live without love? I had eleven children, though, all raised in the same cradle: what a fine open cradle, ornamented with golden and sculpted silver nails! I would have been with my little children, with the sons of my sons, making a great noise in the house, if there had been any justice!"

241

She stood up, and continued, seeking the causes of her abandonment.

"As they grew up, they departed for the cities in order to earn their living; and their letters, if they wrote any to me, did not arrive in our forests; and the messengers they sent me, if their hearts turned toward me, never brought me anything.

"Now, I am lost. I do not even know the name of the woods where I live; my eyes are dying, I'm as mad as the moon up above; my carcass is as rotten as yours, O Mother of God; I'm entirely . . . entirely . . . dead, except for the heart!"

She slid to her knees, begging, and her voice became soft and plaintive; she raised her fleshless arms toward the idol.

"Render me one of them, Magdalen, make use of your witch's eyes to seduce God; wipe the feet of the angels with your beautiful blonde hair. Pray, beg! Who can resist your charms? Listen! Render me the last, Loïez Kam, that's his name. Lean over the earth, my little white dove, see whether my benjamin is still alive, and bring him to me. You'll have my sculpted clogs, emerged from the finest beech in Broceliande; and look, here is the very ribbon of my wedding, white, pink and black, the color of sweet pea. I won't have any need for it in my tomb. It's no longer fresh; it's old, like my face and my dreams. Take it, and return my son to me."

But in the shadow, through her tears, she thought she saw the saint laugh. A great fury invaded her, and she clenched her fists.

"Ah, you're laughing!" she cried. "You're laughing, woman without faith, false saint. Well, if you don't help me, I'll take my hatchet and I'll cut off your head; I'll make your body a formless log."

Having spoken the sacrilegious words, the madwoman fell to the ground, and then remained motionless, as if dead. Her lips gasped: "Pardon, pardon . . . !"

A young man came into the sanctuary, and he threw himself into the middle, with a rude shock of the knees on the stone. He brought in his long hair the perfumed odor of hedges, and his tears, suspended from long lashes, sparkled like diamonds over his dark eyes. He was about to pronounce his amorous trouble, his profound, infantile pain, when a voice cried:

"It's him, my son, it's Loïez Kam!"

And the old clog-maker, on her knees, kissed the feet of the stranger.

With volubility, she told him her story: how she had sculpted the clogs for the crumbled Madonna, and that it was the Magdalen who had had them, with her prayers; that she had even threatened her with her hatchet, insensate, madder than the moon up above, and that her prayer was granted now. She laughed and she cried, kissing the young man's hands

Deceived by amour, and orphaned of birth, he thought: *It must be good to have a mother!*

Then, very handsome, his eyes brilliant, full of mercy, he leaned toward the delirious clog-maker and said to her:

"Get up, Mother, and come to my house, for I truly am Loïez Kam."

DREAM OF ANTIQUITY
(*La Fronde*, 24 July 1899)

ON a high plateau of the Djebel-Hammam, in the time of
Tiberius, the marvelous city of Aquae-Calidae rose. The
warm waters, springing from the ground eighteen times over,
had been collected in basins of white marble. A temple to Venus
had been constructed there.

A palace was built there, soon surrounded by immense gardens in which orange-trees flowered above roses; where almond
trees shed their snowy petals in the breath of the wind over the
odorous heads of vervain; where pomegranates lit their red
lanterns in the bushes near the evergreen tree whose branches
faithfully escorted the lyre accompanying verses in honor of
Eros; where the jovial vines were suspended and rose toward the
crowns of fig trees, as if for a caress; and where the generative
warm water circulated in asphalt channels, pouring life into the
flowers and fruits of that Eden, intersecting with science over
the bosom of the earth, as a network of veins enlaces the breasts
of a young mother swollen with milk.

People came there from all parts: from Icosium, from Tenes,
from Julia Cesarea, the capital of Mauritania, situated on the
skeleton devoid of history of dusty Yol, from Tebesse at the foot
of the mountains that prolong the Aures, from Greek Cirtha,
which watches the furious Rhummel swirling in the depths of a

gulf between two walls of sheer rock, and from Lambese by the road that the legion of Augustus constructed between Carthage and Tipaza.

It was a place of pleasure. Patricians and young barbarians flocked there. The spiral road that led to the Thermes, as it wound around the flank of the mountain, was covered with carts, white mules with silver irons, fine desert stallions with fiery eyes and feminine ankles, and elephants from Numidia.

King Ptolemy, the grandson of Cleopatra, was seen there, as sovereignly beautiful as his ancestor, bearing a bitter crease in his pure features of a young pontiff, looking at his shadow before departing for Rome, where Caligula would have him strangled.

The Roman patricians, the new masters of Africa, found all delights there in repose, and the elements of the softest sensuality: luxurious baths where hasty slaves agitated like a black swarm, massaging refreshed limbs, crushing perfumes, pouring essences, applying make-up with a refined art that one still discovers today in the secrecy of the seraglio of some rich Moor; mute gods in the depths of their temples, draped in porphyry, marble and agate. And what gods! The most joyful, Bacchus, who guides to intoxication; Venus, who invites to amour.

One drank there, from full bowls, the fresh water saturated with iron and gas, which can be seen springing from the black shadow on a clump of carob trees and green oaks, and from full cups, a golden wine rivaling Falernian.

All species of birds were found there in abundance, and appeared at the festivals. The innumerable family of shellfish with strangely contorted forms and fish from the corals of the coast of the great blue sea were brought there, still alive, after a three-hour journey.

Sylphium, white truffles and asafetida came from Cyrene, and lemonwood trays with pantherine veins sustained, on the back of an immense ivory leopard, the strange fruits that grew in the oases, mingled with all those that ripened along the

245

Mediterranean shores, piled in pyramids crowned with clusters of Berber grapes, or crumbling in the midst of flowers separated from their stems and spread in multicolored sheets.

A gilded light, of a light and pure transparency, bathed the entire region, enveloping the monuments, playing upon the marbles and the flowers, bringing out the delicate line of a capital garlanded with acanthia, the grooves of a column, the rustic grace of a sylvan or the harmonious contour of a caryatid, brightening the colors of birds, rendering clearer and more vibrant the elegant slenderness of palm trees.

The candor of the dawn there made a dream of the first mornings of the world. Mists rose in the valley enclosed between the Djebel-Hammam and the narrow isthmus of the heights of the Gontas and filled it with their gray webs; at first it was like a river flowing between two banks. Some thought they could see a placid pond there, others curiosities brought from the depths of Armorica, bearing the Roman yoke, in vain reflection of the waves that blanched their deserted strands, at the feet of oaks and chestnut trees.

Then, suddenly, the sun unleashed its sheaf of luminous rays and drank in an instant the dew suspended from the summits of young wheat and heavy grass; the mists were torn apart, floating and trailing in the matinal air like shreds of gauze the color of hyacinth, ocher or crimson. Vultures soared above the tormented mountains and the flocks climbing the hills pressed tremulously around their shepherds on perceiving the shadow of their great wings.

In the depths of the gorge between the Djebel-Hammam and the mountains of the Sahel, a river flowed in the fashion of a petty torrent in a bed that was too large, strewn with rocks polished by the water, where its course was always lost and found again.

Impenetrable clumps of lentisks, myrtles and oleanders joined up above its silvery thread, and already the hyena, the jackal and the lynx, anticipating the twilight, were lying down on returning from their nocturnal hunt.

It was the hour when iron was heard resounding on anvils in the forges of swords established on the slopes of the Zaccar-el-Gharbi, under the immense plane trees, pouring their green shade over the little town of Miliana; when the hunter disappeared into the depths of the forest to take up his traps or, armed with a pike with a hardened point, to surprise a sated wild boar in its den, pierce it, and, when death closed its grim eyes, cut off the head of the beast and bring it back as a trophy; when the bees, whose blonde treasure was sheltered in fissures in the rock, sent their young companions to collect the sweet harvest; and the latter spread out over the florid fields, the orange trees, amid the calices of roses, jasmines and myrtles, suspended with a joyful buzz from leaves of lettuces, lavender, fennel and sage, collecting a honey sweeter than that of Mount Hymetta.

On tripods in the temples paved with mosaics, the pure incense of Cyrene was burning; a priest bore to his lips a sculpted cup full of salutary spring water and rendered thanks to Aesculapius. The sick, lying on beds of thuya under the florid porticoes of their dwellings, and elegant young Romans, contemplated the splendor of that Oriental isle, where the Latin life, in a sublime exchange, spread its civilization, its arts, its intellectual impetus, and received in return the tributes of Ceres, for the mountains, the valleys and the plateaux were clad in a changing robe, emerald in spring or brown in summer: wheat growing everywhere, everywhere the welcome of that land of grain; its sheets undulating in the breath of the sea breeze; the Berber crops displacing the goats of Getulia, and the Atlas oppressed by the weight of sheaves.

For several centuries Rome, impoverished, received its bread from the pacified shores of Africa, a source of inexhaustible riches.

But while prosperity is at its height and overflowing in the pomp of inscriptions, there is an unexpected scourge ready to fall upon the imperial colony. The Vandals ravage the Occidental isle, and silence returns to hover over the crumbled cities. Old Libya, beautiful with its solitary charms and precious ruins, the soil of which shelters the debris, reappeared then in primitive austerity, exhausted by the uninterrupted labor of its glebe accustomed to long slumbers.

And now, who will reawaken it? What people will return its prosperity? Is it you, ephemeral Byzantines? You are scarcely able to shore up the ruins! Will it be the flood of Arabs drawn by Mohammed, the Fatimids of Egypt, Barbarossa, or the reign of the Deys?

No, a period of eighteen centuries is not too long for another people to appear in the Maghreb worthy to succeed Rome in this land devoted to conquests. France, spiritual heir of the Latins, it is for you that it is appropriate to surpass Rome.

All that humans have edified, time has felled and the earth has reclaimed.

Nothing any longer remains of the brilliant city of pleasures but the marble tombs where the rain has accumulated, where Arab shepherds mirror themselves, and statues of gods; the ashes of the dead have flown away and the ignorant colonist does not know the divine effigies. What cannot change is the suave line of those beautiful hills, streaming with an ineffable light . . .

KEMP OWYNE[1]
(*La Fronde*, 3 October 1899)

Prelude

CAN you see the scene again? Is the past hour present in its poetic rhythm? Is the light of our dreaming still shining in your soul?

. . . A golden evening in the Jardin des Plantes, the expressive language of strange animals; a continuous strident quarrel of winged beings; rare and superb trees, a beech with crimson leaves, higher up, a cedar extending its branches toward the city like noble prophetic arms. A slow ascension of the Belvedere: before us, Paris, like an immense gray canvas with dull bulges, a leprosy of banal houses; a few slender bell-towers, a few proud spires standing up like free individualities, rigid thinkers dominating sordid appetites with their arrogant will and vengeful scorn.

---

1 "Kemp Owyne" is one of a set of English and Scottish ballads assembled by Francis James Child in the late nineteenth century, which attracted attention from fashionable Celtomaniacs. It tells the story of a young woman changed into a "worm"—i.e., a dragon—by her nasty stepmother, cursed to remain so until the king's son kisses her three times; different variants offer contrasted denouements. The ballad refers to the location of her torment as "Craigy's sea," perhaps a bay in the ancient district of Kyle where the modern parish of Craigie is located. The name of the male hero remains deeply enigmatic, although some speculators suggest that he is a borrowing of the Yvain of Arthurian legend. Adaptations of the ballad have been recorded by several modern "folk singers."

One divines the buzz of blind words and dolorous songs ... A narrower enlacement brings us closer together. Our hands talk to our hearts; then one of us, with a smile: "Are we not contemplating that with the soul of a Rastignac?"[1]

"No, we're not experiencing any covetousness."

Over that height, the summits of our ideal shine with joy. What there is of the most noble in our minds combines.

You say to me: "Eve, magnified by dolor, incessantly chased from the paradise of thought by obscure torments, why are you weeping? Become devoid of sighs and tears. Do you not know that the spectacle of beauty is insupportable to ugliness and that the art of nature is creating monsters? What jealous furies would ignite inextinguishably if the human eye could contemplate the splendor of a heroic soul, that interior sky vibrant with stars of fire!

"Our soul, child, always encounters its cruel mother, the terror and despair of our uncertain wails. The torture is necessary, and also the wait for the one who will save us from the torture; persecutions and crimes border the route by which beauty rises from the flesh to the spirit!

"Do you know Ribera's *Prometheus*?[2] To become strong and sublime it is necessary to have been enchained. It is thus that wings are earned. Deliver, O deliver your captive deity."

But, puerile by virtue of amour, I said: "Next to yours, my soul is that of a child. If you want me to understand and accept, speak, speak again about liberating dolor."

"The repose of the day's end numbers the senses and throws a veil over real life. Listen; I shall search in legend, which describes its parabola through the centuries, for the profound symbol."

1 The ambitious social climber Eugène de Rastignac is one of the key characters in Balzac's *Comédie humaine*.
2 The striking painting by Jusepe de Ribera (1591-1652).

Once, on the coast of Scotland, there was a poor fisherman whose wife had just died. He had a daughter as beautiful as a nascent flower: the rosebud in her cheek had just opened; her face resembled an April morning.

When the dead woman was buried, the fisherman and his daughter remained alone, mourning the defunct. Moons succeeded moons, the eyes of the widower dried. Soon, he brought another woman into the cottage, the Megaera Margaret.

Isabel's beauty infuriated the new wife. When she spoke to her, it was as if one were seeing a dragon with flaming eyes crouching on her shoulders. As the soiled earth implores the rain of heaven, her hands needed to be washed in blood. Kill her! Kill her!

In sum, death appeared too mild an expiation for the crime of beauty, and one furious day, she dragged the child by her long hair to the sheer rocks of the shore and threw her into the savage sea of Craigy, saying: "Stay there, dove Isabel, and let all my ennuis remain with you, until Kemp Owyne comes, traversing the sea, and redeems you with three kisses. But the world might elapse . . . oh, you'll never be delivered!"

The girl uttered plaints so resounding and sobs so profound that the seabirds, gulls, gannets and cormorants assembled, trying to console her, circling around her with compassionate cries; the sea serpents, like domesticated animals, licked her feet and enlaced her tenderly, but in a short time, her enchanting voice became loud and hoarse, and then frightful, like the bellowing of a savage monster.

The friendly birds were alarmed, crazed by fear, and then fled, and the inhabitants of the shore ran away. Their fearful stories reached all the way to Kemp Owyne, the hero who lived far away, beyond the seas.

His great black vessel arrived on the shores of Craigy at the solemn and mysterious hour when the night and the morning meet. The sandpiper began to sing and a smiling dawn was born, illuminated by rosy radiance.

The sun rose, setting the rippled nacre of the waters ablaze with crimson fire.

What became of Kemp Owyne when, instead of the savage beast that he was ready to combat, he saw, floating on the green mirror of the waves, a woman as beautiful as the agonizing Medusa, magnified by horror?

Her hair was undulating around her, tangled in curls; two of her long tresses wound three times around a tree. Her body like those of mermaids, was terminated by a fish's tail with ruby scales.

Isabel recognized the liberating hero and raising suppliant hands toward him.

"Save me," she said. "I can no longer live except in hope of you. Toward you I cried, like an eagle desperate at being unable to rise into the sky. Here you are! My God, how handsome you are! You seem to inhale light and spread it, O Kemp Owyne. Save me! I want to tread the land again with human feet and respire perfumed breezes. Will you enter into the sea of Craigy and give me a kiss?"

"I cannot obey you at the moment," replied Kemp. "I have my mission and cannot squander my actions. Perhaps I am separated from you by an insurmountable abyss. You do not know me, you do not know what I want. Your beautiful eyes contain the lightning of the soul or the vain intelligence of terrestrial desires. Speak! What have you to offer me? I am afraid of finding in you the stone that causes one to fall . . ."

Isabel replied, tremulously: "O Kemp Owyne, no gift is worthy of your celestial beauty and your power, but from the depths of the sapphire waves, the serpents have brought me for you a few of the treasures of the sea, which does not render any. Here is a royal ring in which a pearl radiates; so long as you wear it, you will be loved."

"I don't want a blind love obtained by magic," said Kemp Owyne.

"Accept, then," the child went on, "this royal baldric. So long as you wear it, you will reign over peoples."

"I have already reigned," pronounced Kemp Owyne.

"For pity's sake," begged Isabel, "don't disdain this sword enriched with diamonds; it renders one redoubtable to death; as long as you bear it on your thigh, you will live."

But Kemp Owyne said, not without disdain: "Gems are devoid of value, and I do not believe in death."

Then the girl threw the useless talismans back into the waves and started to weep.

And like a great black swan, the hero's vessel drew away.

With despair, her arms extended, Isabel saw it disappearing into the red sunset, and she said: "A kiss from you, Kemp Owyne! Ah, only one kiss from you and to remain enchained forever!"

That amorous thought loosened one of the long blonde tresses that attached her to the trunk of the tree near the shore of Craigy.

"Ah!" she said, again. "I can suffer now, resigned; I have seen you and I can think about you."

The acceptance of injustice and dolor untied another imprisoning tress.

She floated freely on the water.

"Let us stay," she said, "in the place to which the liberator came."

And, rocked by the waves, she went to sleep profoundly.

At the solemn hour when the night and the morning meet, the vessel bearing Kemp Owyne reappeared.

As soon as he could hear her, Isabel cried: "O beloved hero, don't abandon me today. Hear me, I sense that clarity is near. In me, a choir of immobile spirits is singing the ascension. Like a frail piece of wreckage I have been tossed by the waves, dragged into the torment, torn apart by the winds. Haggard, I have sunk into the gulf. Never has my life been so powerful as since it has communed with the abyss. Today I have thoughts as burning as veritable flames of dolor."

"They are what has liberated you, O beautiful infant soul," murmured the hero, pensively. "Peaceful, you can now quit the savage sea of Craigy."

Veiling her face with her long hair, Isabel sighed.

"Can I depart, O hero, without receiving the three kisses from you?"

"I'm beginning to understand," said Kemp Owyne. "Suffering has been for you victory; your feeble eyes are beginning to conceive the invisible. I will give you, with my amour, the kisses that deliver."

He took her in his arms, weak with joy, and carried her away in his black vessel, far beyond the seas.

THE NEW AREA
(*La Fronde*, 21 October 1899)

IN a lost, wild corner, a little manor is flanked by two stout towers. The farm adjacent to the fresh orchard is filled with tangled bushes. The old master and the young farmer lead almost the same rustic life. Mute, with the sadness of an ancient weeper, an old woman, a widow in a black headscarf, serves them. Manor and farm alike have forgotten beauty and young voices.

The peasant is rough-hewn by dint of living in proximity with the old seigneur. His brown, emaciated face with lines of superb violence rivals in noble beauty the scornful raptorial face of the master. They speak little and their shadows rarely ask together. A gesture suffices for them to understand one another. Often, their arms folded, heavy with melancholy, they consider one another from a distance, their souls soaked by the merciful grace of the morning, listening, through the sound of the waves, the sound of bells or the faint music of the wind in the rushes, to the formidable struggle of their souls between the request that rises eternally from the lips of the young man and the confession that the pale proud mouth of the old man does not want to let escape.

However, the young man loves the old man. Oh, the insurmountable wall that is raised between them, behind which they are suffering. How has it come about that they are separated thus? What is the unappeasable dolor that barks like a lost dog in his once-peaceful heart? And those errant thoughts of Cain? What has become of the evenings of his childhood, when, next to the seigneurial hearth, he extended his pink cheek to the master to kiss, where the pale proud mouth found paternal smiles for him, which filled him with joy?

Paternal? Yes. Marquis de Kimmerch, the farmer Gildas Guivar, as proud as a gentleman, knows full well that he is your son.

Through circles of shadow and light, at the age when life seems to be a game, he has wandered in the forest of distant memories with tangled branches. On certain days his memory becomes as transparent as a sea scarcely striped by the rare passage of ships. He sees you, Marquis de Kimmerch, with his mother Morised, the beautiful and gentle Morised, dead so soon, who enlaced your smitten fingers.

Oh, the bitter enjoyment of remembering, of having kept in I know not what receptive frame, that image in which you are caught, in a moment of intimacy, or the loftiest abandonment.

Many other clues, indications of old people in the village, and mockeries, and the certainty is elaborated, including the resemblance between him, Gildas, and the portraits of ancestors in the manor, suddenly struck and thrown into evidence . . .

And the marquis, at the fiery gazes of his son, senses himself divined . . .

On sapphire mornings, in the dust of the sunlight, in spite of the summer lightning striping the heavy sky with fiery serpents, the harvest is completed. With broad, regular strokes of the scythe, shirts stuck to backs, making great efforts, the men and women have felled the wheat, the barley and the rye with pale blue ears.

Nothing any loner remains in the fields but the vain and de-flowered plants that no one cuts, and whose white down snows over the bushes.

The area has been examined before abandoning it to the threshers, but the surface is no longer even and the marquis has had a new area published. Fête at the manor: cries, games, wrestling, dances and poetic challenges follow the rites from which no one is liberated.

From plunging sunken roads, teams of oxen rise in the night, and heavy carts in the form of boats or coffins, filled with potter's clay. The men who lead them to the château sign themselves, because, for a long time, a phantom woman has been seen there, wandering through the pale heather around the motionless pond. The new crop embalms the air, the moon is so beautiful and so sad, she calls so clearly for passionate hymns that one would like, on gazing at her, both to sing and to weep, and before her velvet eyes, eclipsing the scintillating constellations and Arthur's Wain, everything becomes diaphanous, milky and unreal. Oh, the whiteness of the willows, scarcely quivering, the silver-pearled vapors of the valley, and that snow at the summit of the manor's towers. What mystery!

The marquis is present, and Gildas. While each peasant comes to deposit on the area the clay with which his cart is full, the old man has drawn nearer to the farmer. The night encourages him to speak; his voice trembles.

"Godson Gildas, you have been sad for a long time now; it is necessary to try to be happy. Take a wife; solitude is bad. You are too sage and too somber, godson Gildas. Amour has changed brambles into roses and bitter bile into sweetness."

Grimly, the young man responds: "The proud peacock cannot nest with a domestic fowl, nor the falcon with the turtle-dove. There is no wife for me in the village . . ."

"How do you know?" responds the marquis, striving for assurance "Oh, how quickly the heart is caught! What tells you that tomorrow, at the dance, a single glance will not change your determination?"

But the young man extends his arm toward the towers with mad laughter.

"Look at the phantom, Marquis. Look, there is Morised. An aerial form, slimmer than the body of a bird, is flying over the illuminated crenellations . . ."

A last veil of mist is tearing apart in the distance, the matinal light is streaming in liquid floods. Little birds are singing in the maples, heather is reddening the banks, osiers are rustling.

Joyous bands are passing: bagpipe players in their Sunday clothes, young woman carrying pitchers of milk on their heads and flowers, jays with blue wings are flying away. Horses with manes braided with fiery ribbons have trampled the wet clay of the area. A table is set up in the middle of the lake of mud; on the table is an armchair. And now the court of beauty opens. Where is the most beautiful? Which one will be lifted up in the arms of the master of the area and placed on the armchair, the queen of the harvest festival? Certainly she will only be delivered on the promise of a kiss. Hola, let's dance before making a choice! Ho, Gildas! What are you dreaming about?

"Make way, here's the seigneur."

The marquis advances, head high, proud, with a thin, slightly sarcastic laugh. He gives his hand to a dainty young woman whose slender waist bends, as supple as a liana in spite of the tight pleats of her richly embroidered costume. Her little feet, shod in white chamois, and her gloved hands denounce the fantasy of her peasant disguise. The lace head-dress of Celtic girls, like a butterfly on a flower, flaps its wings over her light hair. The eighteenth century laughs over her frivolous lips.

"Dainty niece Gédéone, would you like to dance, to bewilder my mountain men? Your grandmother danced here, on a new area, a famous passe-pied. Tugdual, my father's bard, a miller of Pontaro, perpetuated the memory in a famous song. What a passe-pied, my dear! Men fought over her. A man died in the evening. No new area ever went to the manor without some drama . . .

"Brrr . . . I shiver to think of it. At this end of the nineteenth century, I scarcely believe in drama. 'I also want to dance the Breton passe-pied, at the price of which,' said the delighted Sévigné, 'the violins and passe-pieds of the court make the heart hurt!'"

A large circle, silence, soft music, and Gédéone takes off, a blush in her cheeks, eyelids partly closed, she palpitates on her toes like a dragonfly on a flower.

At the first glance she has bound the soul of Gildas with a chain of ecstasy; the air that he breathes is a wave of nectar. The sounds, the colors, the forms all mingle . . .

He senses sobs within him and the flux of a tide of burning tears invades his heart.

Ah, dance, fay, dance again in the light morning air!

But the bravos burst forth, respectful and frenetic. This pagan people, madly amorous of rhythm and beauty, is conquered.

With a supple bound, Gildas is before Gédéone. Equal to equal, he proclaims her queen with a vibrant voice, and extends his arm to carry her over there, across the mud of the area to the elevated armchair.

His nostrils are dilated, his eyes burning; he is as superb as a black thoroughbred.

The marquis admires him.

"Let's go, niece Gédéone," he says. "Custom requires it; let yourself be carried by my godson."

A movement of recoil . . . of disgust.

On her lips a cruel laugh, and then a haughty expression. "Oh, no, Uncle de Kimmerch, that game is too hard."

✳

Evening has come. No one has seen Gildas again.

The fête has finished sadly. A foreign domestic harnesses the caleche that will only serve to take Gédéone home.

The horses, alarmed by the touch of an unknown hand, whinny and rear up.

"They can scent the phantom," murmurs an old maidservant, fearfully. "They're thinking about Gildas! Oh, my lady, by Notre Dame de Bon Voyage, don't touch them, don't let go of the reins, don't talk to them."

Gédéone has taken off her girlish garments. She passes through the mute drawing rooms with old wall-hangings, looking at her image in mirrors, brushing the armchairs that retain melancholy imprints in their cushions that prompt dreams, smiling at the voluptuous pastels in which grandmothers in Louis XV costumes are also smiling, flowers that perhaps bloomed in the flower-bed of the beloved, and which time seems to have revived instead of withering.

And it is a mirage of the past that envelops Gédéone with a constriction of the heart. A fear brushes her soul, a winged fear that provokes her irony . . .

The severe hall with the goffered leather hangings chills her soul. Banners, panoplies, suits of armor and lights that tremble funereally! Beyond the monumental doors, the countryside can be seen; one divines a black accumulation of woods, the placement of villages, the passionate launch of Romantic steeples. Like a somnolent serpent the river winds its dark green coils at the foot of the keep.

The horses whinny; the careful marquis given curt orders to the improvised coachman.

"Hold them firm; take the Kersabiec road. Beware of the crossroads of the Elorn meadows. Gildas is the only one who knows how to turn at the level of the parapet." And, turning to Gédéone: "Climb up, my dear. The men of our blood are as proud as Capaneus;[1] we believe ourselves to be giants made to combat the gods, but some day, we have our Phlegra . . .[2] There you go, my dear, our disdains have bloody ransoms. We have a history replete with drama provoked by the inflexible demon."

They fell silent, thinking about Gildas.

The caleche disappears along the plunging sunken road. Almost immediately it is borne by a rapid gallop, ever more rapid and crazy.

At the crossroads of the Elorn meadows, Gildas, standing on the parapet, hears the fantastic rig coming toward him.

The river is flowing noisily between the meadows.

The young man projects his great disdainful shadow over the crossroads.

All the blood of the Kimmerchs flows toward his insulted heart, choking it.

His voice tries to rise.

"Peace, Brutus Simeon!"

He is about to launch himself forward. Under the sting of outrage, however, he nurses homicidal thoughts whirling within him.

He sniggers.

"No, no, I won't touch you. Before death you'd find my embrace good, but the villein won't touch you. Aha! Here they come! Let's all perish!"

---

1 Capaneus, struck down by Zeus to punish him for his arrogance in Aeschylus' *Seven Against Thebes*, is also featured as an exemplar of irrepressible pride in Dante's *Inferno*.

2 The Macedonian peninsula of Phlegra is where Zeus overthrows the giants in the climax of the mysterious lost epic known as *Gigantomachia*.

The caleche, half broken, containing two pale individuals, en-laced, sped like an arrow through the crossroads of the Elorn meadows. The driver had disappeared. The horses were no lon-ger whinnying, the young woman was no longer screaming. The sinister silence that precedes physical and mental catastrophes weighed, fascinating . . .

With a supreme bound, the horses, mouths bloody, flecked by foam, breathing fire, crossed the granite parapet on which Gildas was standing, arms open.

A shaft entered his breast, dragging him away. There was a tumultuous din, of last profound screams and shattering glass. The moonlight sprang from the clouds; everything became mute again, with a dismal peace.

On the crenellations, the shade of Morised vanished rapidly.

And the melodious lament of the poor mad soul of the nightingale rose alone in the night.

LAST DIALOGUES 3
(*La Fronde*, 31 October 1899)

A VAST *room, very dark.*
On a low bed, the cadaver of a man clad in a black suit, still young and very handsome. A loosely-fixed bandage surrounds his jaws.

At the back of the room a door with two battens opens to a specious study with walls decked with bookshelves. All the windows are open over lowered blinds. It is a spring evening; the sun is setting.

Hélène, the dead man's widow thirty years old, pretty, with a slightly heavy figure, a beautiful complexion, scarcely paled by age, is on the threshold, a handkerchief in her hand.

Francesca, her sister, twenty-eight years old, a noble and strange beauty, is kneeling by the bed.

HÉLÈNE. What a deleterious odor is already exhaled here. It will doubtless be necessary to proceed with putting him in the bier this evening. (*A silence, then, taking her forehead in her hands:*) Francesca, the more I think about it, the more I find his reluctance to have me beside him during his last moments strange.

FRANCESCA (*oppressed and very pale*): It was the perfume, you know, that upset him.

HÉLÈNE. A perfume! I didn't have any; I'd washed my hands and my face. One might have thought . . . but it's incredible . . . one might have thought that he wanted to drive me away. It's sad for him to have died in the arms of a stranger . . . but in sum, it's necessary to obey the wishes of the dying. How did that hour pass? Speak. What did he say? It's necessary to recount the scene to me. Since the great cry of horror announcing the end, you've remained mute, petrified.

FRANCESCA, *raising her beautiful pale forehead*: Speak? Speak already? Don't you find that our voices take on a mysterious accent here? Oh, let's postpone our words until later. Low as they might be, they would still be too distinct, living a terrible life, of words . . . which . . . once spoken . . .

HÉLÈNE, *like an unconscious echo*: Which . . . once spoken . . . how you're trembling. Why that fright? What could he have said? Our life was calm and contained no drama.

FRANCESCA. No drama! Oh, please Heaven!

HÉLÈNE. Speak.

FRANCESCA, *wringing her hands*. My God! I've received a deposit; I'll render you an account of it, but I don't know whether it ought to remain between us or whether . . . (*A silence.*) He has promulgated a new law, but I don't know whether you'll understand me.

HÉLÈNE, *in a humiliated and bitter tone*. It's always been difficult for me to understand either of you. The intellectual matters that you discussed together have no interest for me. Claude and I only had in common the true life, the life of realities.

FRANCESCA. You never suspected that the life of realities didn't exist for him?

HÉLÈNE, *her eyes dry and her tone bitter*: It was necessary that it existed and that he be content with it.

FRANCESCA *gets to her feet and the two women stand face to face*: He wasn't content with it. He chose, beyond sterile noises, this infinitely silent repose. It was only in expiring, already leaning over death, that he saw the light and the law was promulgated.

HÉLÈNE, *troubled and fearful*: What law? My God, how many mysteries . . . I don't understand anything . . .

FRANCESCA, *with an explosion of despair*: How could you understand him? You didn't love him! He was nothing to you!

HÉLÈNE, *gravely*: He was my husband

FRANCESCA, *somberly, slowly shaking her head*: Your husband? Then talk to me about the sweetness of his soul, the treasures of his sensibility, the power of his intelligence, the noble combats of his conscience, the generosity of his heart! Tell me what joys you brought him.

HÉLÈNE, *docile, searching for words*: He was always melancholy and difficult to penetrate. In truth, the more I think about it, he had within him, you see, something inaccessible for me. At present, it seems to me that I've always been far, very far, away from him. It's strange—that thought has never crossed my mind with that gripping force. (*She draws nearer to the dead man.*) The more I look at him, the more he seems like a stranger. My regrets . . . even my tears . . . don't reach him.

FRANCESCA, *calmly, without triumph in her tone*: You can see that you were not his companion.

HÉLÈNE, *explosively*: How is it that it's you who is talking to me like this about Claude and me?

FRANCESCA, *mastering herself*: Because I lived his true life, witnessed his struggles and his anguish . . . and his scruples

(*A long silence, Francesca falls to her knees again, her forehead on Claude's feet. Hélène replaces the candles, the daylight having decreased. The penumbra becomes lugubrious. The face of the dead man is drowned in mystery, the lips smiling sadly at Francesca.*)

FRANCESCA, *raising her head and addressing her sister, whose back is turned to her, mutely*: Hélène? (*Claude's widow turns round, her eyes staring.*) Hélène, life is full of torturing scorn; it's in vain that one thinks that one has plumbed the depths of a heart that is not one's own. (*Anxiously.*) Tell me, whatever happened, if Claude, while he was alive, had quit you, never to return would you have forgotten him? Would you have been consoled?

HÉLÈNE: I believe so; I would also have scorned him . . .

FRANCESCA, *in a low voice*: O, my Claude, how insensate your sacrifice was! (*To her sister:*) And now he is here, icy, lost to you forever since you did not have his soul, now, Hélène, how do you envisage the days to come?

HÉLÈNE, *with surprise and coldness*: How do I envisage them? I shall enter into a severe mourning, which I shall wear with dignity, and I shall await the benefits of time.

FRANCESCA, *forcefully, her hands raised toward the dead man*: You see, adored Claude, we could have been happy without remorse. Oh, you were too late in promulgating your law.

HÉLÈNE: Again this law—what law?

FRANCESCA: *her voice rising, high and vibrant*: The law of harmony between action and sentiment, gesture and thought; the law of integral truth.

HÉLÈNE, *shivering*: But the truth is sometimes very sad; it isn't good to see what is entirely true.

FRANCESCA, *continuing without hearing her*: It's a great misfortune, my beloved, to fear the words that save. Oh, those necessary confessions that rise to the lips, and which we withhold by virtue of cowardice! There is a surgery applicable to the heart that opens the secret dungeons in which our stifled sentiments groan. The mute lie on which we had built our fragile happiness was bad. If there were still time, I would render our life innocent and beautiful. By the simple evidence of what our soul contains of amour and despair, I would have overturned the wall of our Hell, and three individuals paralyzed by the lie and dread would have resumed their rhythmic, supple and expressive movements and would be placed on the tableau of a harmonious existence on the precise plane that they ought to have occupied. False duty, false virtue, false ideal, I judged you too late. I am dying for those phantoms, young and beloved by you. The hour of agony, Francesca, in not dark, as is said but luminous. Believe like me in the sole necessity of liberating words. It is unnecessary that Hélène has regrets adequate to the transparent lie of our lives; it is necessary that she experiences exactly the sentiments in direct relationship with the truth. Enlighten her. No more dupes, Francesca. Propagate that law and thousands of beings will owe you peace and happiness; free so many slaves, dissipate the mirages of errors: infirm, inform humans of the simple and facile truth. I am expiring poisoned by the vitiated air of complaisant deception.

HÉLÈNE, *as if petrified, lifting a finger with an automatic gesture*: He was right; permit me to return to the question of a little while ago. How, without him, do you now envisage the days to come?

FRANCESCA: Claude was my entire life; I shall go to join him. Our spiritual union, moreover, will henceforth have his sanction.

HÉLÈNE, *incredulously*: You want to die?

FRANCESCA, *launching herself outside*: I can see him; he's waiting for me.

HÉLÈNE, *retaining her by the elbow*: Stay, you belong here; I'll go away. Adieu.

FRANCESCA: Adieu.

HÉLÈNE, *immobile on the threshold*: I understand why he died; he couldn't live either with the lie or with the truth.

Francesca takes a phial of poison, which she empties in a single draught; she lies down on the bed next to Claude, places her lips on his cold mouth and expires, without convulsions.

Time passes; the candles go out; it is dark.

THE RED INTOXICATION
(*La Fronde*, 14 December, 1899)

Poetry, the eloquence of which for the imagination is
irrefutable,
says nothing to crippled and solitary reason.
Edgar Poe.

STANDING next to a druid crowned with gold, the Armorican child, the barbaric child, is receiving his lesson. He says: "Three commencements and three ends, three celestial realms full of golden fruits, brilliant flowers and little children laughing."

Such is the flowery way by which the austere old man is leading the little savage to the marvelous, and enabling him to escape into the divine via the misty porticos of dream ...

The earth is virgin, almost devoid of history, and granite is king ...

Luminous and white the stones stand up in the forest like massive needles, the hopes still heavy of infant humankind.

Sometimes straight, processional and meditative, they form long roads of dream that human follow, pale with astonishment, souls suspended and tremulous, like a fascinated bird that does not know where to direct its wings.

Sometimes they are assembled in circles in the heather, leaning toward one another in I know not what quivering confidence. As dusk, the weary hunter sits down in the middle of their circle, stopped in the hasty course that is life, and within him, already desperate, the mind cannot penetrate itself.

But whether they stand motionless and tightly packed, like a herd near the cowshed, whether they are distributed over the heath, like the stars up above, without any apparent order, or whether, in grim, meditative isolation, prostrate or menacing, they guard the bones of forefathers peacefully, all of them are thoughts of amour and appeals to the light.

Melancholy stones that love the stammering of the soul, rigid consciousness of the Armorica forests and islands, the sun, the inextinguishable radiance of the ideal, is above you, red and burning, but you no longer mark out a virgin land almost devoid of history, in which granite is king.

. . . Under the branches of oaks, the long living colonnades green architraves, august and mysterious beings called druids guard the serene and imperishable beauty of the dream. Already they have added the science of the world floating from people to people like a broken thought. They have made it the basis of their wisdom, an ivory tower of the dream.

Of the individual future of the finished model of humanity that we foresee and await, they represent the prophetic image. The sea beats the mud of inviolate woods, the sun waves its golden torch joyfully over the crowns, one does not hear the clink of arms, the rumor of the night and the wind are the only sounds that traverse the parvis of moss.

Meditation, with the white wings of a gull, soars luminously, spreading its grave mildness.

But howling devastation advances, drunkenly, nailing the man of thought in the granite of its altar, soiling the white robe of the druid with its hands of a sanguinary brute.

And there were the naked Picts with painted bodies, armed with daggers and clubs, creeping through the sacred forests, violated by triumphant force. And there were the frantic hallucinations of battles; red puddles, and drops of vivid crimson on the grass, similar to new flowers. The agonies were regulated in the dusk with the death of the sun, and human flesh was seen rotting, like a vile compost heap, inviting the voracious to share the spoils.

Then, with the Romans, in spite of the antipathy of races, grating against one another on contact, like a file on steel, white maniacal hands intervene in the corruption. A curious and patient ferocity that is able to wait in order to feed, like a spectator in a circus, and to make a battlefield a spectacle of beauty!

Less meditated torture and more measure in the thirst for blood, unhealthy delectations and voluptuousness before suffering and death.

War was decorated, murder surrounded by the splendor of an apotheosis. To the sound of martial music and bellicose hymns, armies collided noisily and joyfully. Blood flowed magnificently under the hundred thousand reflections of golden helmets, behind the incessant undulation of endings, bearers of eagles, dragons wolves and minotaurs, garlanded with flowers and pine branches, agitated in the clear sky.

The barbarian, who was tracked in his deserts, became a poet in his turn. In dancing before a suspended blade, his grim soul was deflated of strident, whinnying, sonorous verses like the clink of clashing weapons.

To hymns composed in honor of Julius Caesar and Probus, and conceived in dazzling landscapes, the son of sad skies gave a burning reply, as strong and captious as vintage wine, arms in hand, on hills crimson with enemy blood.

To numb his remorse and his pain, to console him for his hard life, war had given him three poisoned talismans: pillage, drunkenness and dancing.

He pillaged, he danced, and his drunkenness became cannibalistic, wine feeding on blood and only getting drunk more easily.

He therefore sang the red intoxication:

"Wine and blood flow together, wine and blood flow!

"I have drunk blood and wine in the harsh melee, I have drunk blood and wine.

"Wine and blood nourish whoever drinks them, wine and blood nourish."

The cold ferocity of the law of talion is no longer sufficient for him. He proclaims:

"A heart for an eye! A head for an arm! And death for a wound!

"A stallion for a mare and a mule for a donkey, a captain for a soldier and a man for a child, blood for tears and flames for sweat."

The centuries are eaten away and crumble under the thin hammer of days, time is wallowed up; still the earth seems to need, and climacteric years their heavy fodder of blood.

Science raises palaces to unknown forces. The Idea flies from one to another and tries to unite them in order to enlarge and render harmonious the human brain, and, at the moment when all these Babels are about to open their doors and fuse their languages, to accumulate and classify their wealth, to disengage the ideal, to enable the true light to shine, a conquering bandit carries out an audacious theft, the powerful raises his athletic arm, made supple by futile games, against the small, and retards the peaceful cohesion of minds.

History shows us the Bretons chased beyond the sea by the insular Saxons. Seeking a fatherland they sing the psalm of the fugitive Hebrews, and that commences the misdeeds of the sanguine colossus. The end of this century teaches us that nineteen hundred years have passed over his arrogance without blunting or diminishing it. His vocation seems to be to raise, against the blind force of old Goliath, the young and irresistible courage of a David who, if he is unfortunate, will have our tears, and if he triumphs, impossibly, our admiration.

The grave Boer laborer, a religious soul, is not fighting like a barbarian of ancient times, nor a Roman.[1] He has no need of pomp or songs. He does not have the original red intoxication.

His hopeless stoicism, the superb example of courage that he deploys, which moves the most insensible, is sufficient for him to sustain himself in the haughty march toward death.

Thus, at the foot of the Celtic stones, I meditated on the eternal and fateful return of murders.

Before me, the sea rounded out in sonorous swells; a voice seemed to emerge from the glaucous waves and affirmed:

"The Druids are not dead!"

Their profound soul has come as far as us through foreign veins.

There is still a proud and free being to carry the barbarian child away over bloody roads and enable him to escape into the divine via the misty porticos of dream . . .

---

1 The Boer War, later reclassified as the Second Boer War, began on 11 October 1899; when this story was published in December the Boers appeared to have the upper hand in their attempt to take control of the Transvaal and the Orange Free State, before the British imported hundreds of thousands of soldiers and overwhelmed them by sheer numbers.

CRAZY LETTER 2
(*La Fronde*, 8 April 1900)

Sanitarium de T****

DO you remember, Maëdec, that radiant summer evening when I composed a song to cure myself? "Sing your dolor to calm yourself," you said, "open your soul." And I opened it very wide, like a window to the stars. The light from on high fell inside, rendered my specters living, and I went mad.

I sang, and as I went on I felt my tottering reason fleeing like a sick woman who sees that her bed is on fire. Like a child leaning over a well throwing stones into the water, I watched all the particles of my present consciousness falling, one by one; their fall had a sonorous and distant reverberation, like an echo of eternity; all the forces of my mind collapsed, like branches broken one after another in a tree whose wood is dead, and nothing in the world was more unspeakably anguishing.

I thought that I was being carried away toward an infernal gulf. The gulf didn't exist, Maëdec! I encountered the metamorphosis crowned with odorous flowers, like a woman of the distant islands. Her voice was as soft as the caress of her white hand. She said to me:

"Prodigy! Now the flower of the lily is going to emerge from the root of the fern. Now you are like a marine mollusk, which, stripped of its scoria, becomes a pure nacre in which the entire prism is rediscovered. From your tears and your crimes, from all your human miseries, The Poet is finally emerging, purified by divine and consoling madness."

And here are accents that you will scarcely recognize, although they are my accents, O my brother. Before my new word and my prophetic confession you will smile at the old ballads that we composed with the friendly bards on the mount of ivy-clad chapels, roofs of sky and verdure in which everyone wove his flower.

For my ideas have emerged from their misty sheath; I am employing unknown words. I am proffering them in a sort of triumphant interior liberty. I know ecstasy without limbo. I am realizing myself magnificently. I am outside the law that is hab-itude put into proverbs. I am no longer the passenger of a day. I am not longer caught in the unbreakable net of my apparent and short duration. My soul has eyes. Backwards and forwards, I can see to infinity!

For six thousand years Maëdec, I ran after myself without ever finding myself, a fugitive image, irritating and intangible. Today, in the desert padded cell, I am embracing myself for the first time. I anticipate future times fertile in metamorphoses...

Madness! Madness is the lightning flash that, through the grinding of teeth and nightmares, shows us to ourselves, which enables us to touch the phantom; it is the cohesion incessantly pursued, dolorous to the point of torture, of all our souls in one harmony.

O Maëdec, I am happy because I am mad. "But your crime?" you might say to me. My crime! I have seen all my murders again, I have killed the same woman more than once, Maëdec. I have savored her death eternally on her mouth, for I have only ever kissed her lips when cold, and I always see myself weeping and curbed over her luminous nudity. But in my imminent rebirth, the enchantment of my future, she will love me, I shall not kill her, because, from step to step and ruination to ruination, I have descended into the madness that renders one conscious forever.

✳

The first time? Listen!

The edge of the forest of Dépouilles . . . the dawn of time . . . a very barbaric squat palace . . . my face is painted; I sense myself grim and gentle. The evening is casting its ashes; I hold myself motionless, attentive to the awakening of my thought, surveying the delightful infancy of my soul, awaiting the beloved woman; our fate will be determined in this meeting.

Ah! By the twisted trees, by the owls that are gazing at us and whose eyes contain the problem of the night, by the stones as white as bones, hollowed out like the skeletons of saurians, by the path of rye-grass where I am walking firmly in order to meet her, by all the noble speechless beings that were witness to that scene, I did not want to kill her.

The secret of the future moment and the act to come was hidden in the immediate darkness. The dream of the drama had not touched me.

O radiant and unique figure of a young woman, beauty beat-ified by my dolor, body of divine grace, hands of a seraph always raised on high like enchanted doves aspiring to the azure, feet of pink marble ever ready to flee me, winged feet of a pursued nymph made to trample the white clover of happiness, soft eyes, hair like sheaves of ripe corn, velvet mouth. O radiant and unique figure of a young woman, I see you pass on my path ob-scured by mourning; I hear, from the prodigious silence of my anterior lives, the muffled voice of the embalmed and bloody past speaking to me of you!

Why regret you, since you were the empty tabernacle, the false resemblance of my eternal companion. The lying envelope of true beauty, since I have only ever had of you the kiss that thinks...

Oh, the blind transport in striking your desert heart! The dagger raised, the red rain of your blood staining the tunic!

The nothing that you were returning to dust, taken back by the mortal mud, while I weep, beg and ask for mercy...

Failed masterpiece of a weary god, I carry you within me, I want you, I have a premonition of your approach... Prisoner of nothingness, I am waiting for you to have a soul!

New voyage toward the earth.

O Maëdec, in this return of the vanished pilgrim I press with the ends of lips the overflowing mud of life. I no longer remember my dissolved form or the anguish of the sepulchral night; I am unaware of them, as the morning star is unaware of darkness.

I believe that dying means forgetting. I no longer know anything? However, a horror is within me, and, a child, under the peaceful eyes of my father the Druid, I begin to utter strange cries.

My nurse comes running and I am calmed with songs: "All beautiful, beautiful child of the druid, all beautiful!" I am brought up like a tree; I am a man. My sword has been sharpened on Merlin's stone, in order that it can cut steel and kill suddenly anyone that it touches. It never emerges from its scabbard, for my soul, in the expectation of amour, is only nourished on ecstasy... I meditate on destiny, I love Nature, I am attentive to the sidereal revolutions, I know a host of verses about the gods. Crowns are woven for me; it is claimed that I have drunk the philter guarded by the dwarfs in a golden basin, which contains universal knowledge.

But hush, Maëdec, lean over with me. Listen! We have sailed toward the isle of Mona,[1] which winter plunged in darkness for

---

1 Mona was the island of Anglesey, where, according to Tacitus, the British

thirty years. We went to witness the dances of the priestesses of Koré around the spring by the light of the full moon. I see it all again, I hear the most fugitive sounds . . . the mooring . . . the surf of the waves on the shore is like the delicate sound of breaking crystal; the numbing wait at the end of the day beneath the motionless veil of the night, until the moon is suspended from the sky like a crystalline pear.

Oh, the white temple suddenly illuminated by the stars: myriads of eternal stones—that phantasmal procession of priestesses almost liberated from the flesh! Her! Look, Maëdec—her, in that nebulous mystery! How she resembles the star! What a pearl of disputed reflections of gold and milk that consecrated virgin was!

When the dance finished she sat down on the edge of the spring. Wonderstruck, I wept without knowing why. I had kept my heart for the same beloved; nothing of what animated it in the first days of the world had been lost or distracted . . .

What are these obscure stigmata?

Why that gasp? Why are the stars sobbing? She is dead! Everything is dead on this island . . . it is her first refusal that killed her, not my blade.

I was unable to support her first refusal because it was as if it were placed in the sequence of all those she had already inflicted on me!

And now, a mad race, a mad race through the menhirs, all the way to the noisy waves, in which I drowned myself.

The fabric tears . . . everything trembles, it is no longer as clear . . . everything is obscured by mists, I can no longer see anything. The mystery closes in again.

Druids staged their last stand against the Roman invasion in 60 A.D.

Where is the profound irradiation of the past instant? I am suffering, I am broken like the ancient fallow land turned over by the plow.

Images float, a harvest scene is presented. The earth is blonde everywhere, as if sunlight were spread over the fields; nature is singing I know now what golden melody, the wheat is sounding over the area, the oats shedding their fiery robe.

Rapid incarnation of her.

Oh, that face, as florid as a wild rose, which is drawing nearer, drawing nearer . . .

Solitude. Night.

The wind is blowing, the sea is quivering, the mountain is meditating.

I am abandoned like an old dovecot by vagabond memories.

No cow or mare is wandering any longer. What anxiety is rising within me! I'm afraid! One last flash of lightning? Ah! One cadaver more . . . it's horrible!

No, no, I don't want . . . !

CRIES OF WOMEN
(*La Fronde*, 27 April 1900)

*T*O M. X***, *chief of the Bureau of Public Assistance, Penitentiary Section, Paris*

I beg you to be indulgent. Please forward this letter to my little boy. Being in La Roquette, he has written to me again. I do not want him to think that he has been abandoned completely. Knowing how he accepts his new life, I take my suffering patiently. I too am capable of putting my heart under my feet, but my mother is ill, sick in heart and mind; she will die if she does not hear any more mention of Georges, and my mother is a saint.

All this is very insignificant for you, Monsieur; I beg you to excuse me, I shall not importune you any further, but allow me to defend myself . . .

Well, I had engaged my life badly; I was in an impasse; it was necessary for me to make an effort to get out of it. I couldn't do it alone. Certainly, I wouldn't win the rosette for the most virtuous girl in my village; the life of a woman when she has nothing but her work, isn't always droll. How to subsist on forty or fifty sous every two or three days. And the dead season! And illness!

When I had my son I was scarcely nineteen years old, his father twenty.

He was a boy with whom I had been at school. He thought that he was too young to be a papa and left me.

My parents were old and poor.

I came to Paris to work. At twenty, one isn't made of wood. I had a heart then. I had had a shared passion for a childhood friend. Unfortunately, he was married; his wife found out about it; there were scenes every day. I left my friend to his wife and his children.

Alone, unable to raise my little boy on my work, I took another friend. This time, my lover was from a good family, he was an heir, a dowry was sought for him, I let him go to it. With the charge I had it was necessary for me to work night and day, my son had not forgotten him. Until then I had made matches. It was necessary for me to take a lover to pay the rent. Then the disaster happened, my health was demolished. Oh, I was weary, discouraged, heartsick. Think about it: returning from the workshop, going back to work, then running from rendezvous to rendezvous, to which I often brought more appetite than amour.

At that time my lover was the director of a great administration, earning a lot of money. His generosity consisted of paying my rent of three hundred francs. For that he had me at his disposal twice a week, to submit to his caresses when I wanted to spit in his face.

That's how I had lovers: my heart lurched when I was treated as a *fille de joie*, me who did not know what joy was.

I never had fine excursions or good dinners. A walk in the Meudon woods, and then . . . not often.

Oh, a woman is scorned. Men put on airs to throw it in her face that she has had lovers. Men are most despicable who profit from her youth or her poverty. Not one will extend a hand for her to try to raise herself up. They throw gold into the alcoves of prominent courtesans and prostrate themselves before them like lackeys, but a worker . . . get away! She's a slut . . .

Now, Monsieur, I get by; I have work, a few savings. I'm not old, I've learned to live on my income. If my son were returned to me, I wouldn't be a bad guide; I'd have a firm hand. With a good trade, he'd have a future. He's very intelligent but of a vagabond humor, I'd make him someone. When very young, he wanted to be a mechanic. He often missed school and spent entire days watching machines from the height of bridges. That would be better than being a burglar, as on emerging from correction. Oh, don't worry, the lesson will serve both of us. Believe me, I'd only have a heart for my little boy. During the week I'd work, on Sunday we'd go for a walk. I'd make him a comfortable life, I'd have courage, I'd take my mother with me and the three of us would be happy.

At least, Monsieur, give me news of him and leave me hope, for continuing such a life will be impossible for me; I'd rather throw myself in the water. People weep for the dead, I'm weeping for someone alive. Don't let it be said that it's all the same to you whether mothers fall into the mud or into the Seine, whether grandmothers die of chagrin, because women of the people are worthless.

I'm putting myself on my knees to ask you to return my child. I'll reimburse you what's necessary. I await your good reply. You have no reason to refuse me. You told me that if I lived alone, and worked, you'd return my son to me. I've done that. I'm counting on your word.

Copied verbatim.

SERVANTS OF HATHOR
(*La Nouvelle Revue*, 15 October, 1901)

I WAS in the land of Isis. A dream had taken me there, one of those light pilgrimages of the soul, the mysterious attraction of which leaves the most precise reality far behind. It was night. Leaning on a pyramid, I was waiting for daybreak. The cold of the stone chilled my shoulders; a shadow of prodigy fell upon me from an enormous height, enclosing me in a rectilinear limbo; I could hear the broad and peaceful rhythmic respiration of the Nile. The mausolea of the Pharaohs reigned over the delta, heavy poems dedicated to Eternity. I waited, my heart prey to the fearful hope of some apparition. Cheops himself could have loomed up before me without surprising my expectation. But the landscape remained plunged in a silence that indistinct palpitations caused to live without troubling it; it was like the muted beating of millions of hearts, dormant and frozen hearts, which had woken up within my own heart.

Whispered very softly, the names of human beings brushed my ears, rolled in dull waves, and the illusion of names filled the desert, as if the ferryman who carries the dead across the lake of Acheron had unloaded his cargo of illustrious souls close by.

From the Valley of Tombs came a light wind borne on innumerable wings with a silken rustle. Deep sighs reached me. Coming from the distance, coming from the past, those sighs traversed the divine silence of the night still solemnized by the religious tremors of the trees and the slow rhythms of unknown things that swayed in the uncertain darkness. Then the stars were eclipsed; I saw their eyes extinguished one after another. The sky became white. Impalpable fabrics, the linen of the nascent day floated, palely blue, at the zenith.

My soul was increasingly excited by the expectation of some prodigious spectacle. Now, I only saw this: the Nile, flowing wide and beautiful before me; its pale waters enlivened at that moment by singular crimsons, like mingled blood and wine; lotuses flowered thus in prosperous days, but a drowned young woman was floating in the water. She was delectably adorned, beautiful and fragile, with flowers in her hair.

My thought, overwhelmed by majestic visions, was attached to that child; I forgot the Pharaohs in contemplating her. The waves rocked her, close to the bank; she seemed to be asleep, but when I had fetched her out of the water she woke up, with a lovely smile. I remembered at the same time the custom the Egyptians had of throwing a beautiful girl to the Nile when the river flooded, promising richness to the plain.

Curiously, I asked her: "Are you not one of the virgins sacrificed on the night of Drops . . . ?"

But she interrupted me with slightly scornful laughter.

"Virgin, me? No, I'm a courtesan."

"A courtesan?" I said, and nothing could equal my delight, for I had heard numerous stories about matrons, wives and concubines, but I had heard nothing very precise about voluptuous creatures. And I repeated: "Courtesan, courtesan!"

The sun rose; she took off her tunic of pearls, which she draped over the reeds to dry. She took off her narrow robe of striped silk and remained as naked as an amphora.

Questions pressed upon my lips. Who are you? How did you come to be exposed on the river? In what epoch did you live? What was your story?

And I got ready to listen as religiously as the prophetess of Dodona must have listened when the black dove ordered her in human language to found an oracle; but the Egyptian woman appeared to have little regard for my haste.

There was a singular grace in her gestures. She uncovered a mirror, looked at herself therein for a long time, collected blue lilies on the bank, suspended them in her bushy black hair, got dressed, and was astonished to have lost her tablets and to be unable to write to her friend. Finally, she appeared to remember me, and said, in a very soft voice: "My name is Archidice . . ."[1]

"What!" I cried. "You are the Archidice who flourished in Naucratis and was able to render her name famous where the slave of Jadmon, the companion of Aesop, the divine Rhodopis had lived and reigned?"

She smiled and said: "I'm surprised that you know me; I thought that people only remembered the names of their oppressors and a few dates of hecatombs!"

"Oh," I replied, "nor does tradition forget those who dispense much joy . . ."

"Alas," sighed Archidice, "every man we love carries a little of our life into his tomb. All those shreds rot, dispersed, and how can they be brought together again?"

But I affirmed: "Tradition knows you, O Archidice, or at least it mentions you; for when it is ignorant it would rather lie than keep quiet . . ."

She smiled, charmed hat lips still rounded out in her praise, since no lips had been able to stir to her kiss for a long time.

"Come to my house," she said. "We'll be able to chat more at our ease."

---

1 This name, which the author renders Achédice (it is Archidike in some translations), is taken from a passage from Herodotus, which forms the basic substance of the present story, although Fréhel modifies Archidice's story and that of Rhodopis (which he renders as Rhodope) in accordance with a subtle feminism.

"Tradition, you see, is a woman's mouth that incessantly changes form: fleshy, sinuous, thin, pale, red, toothless. It comes to us from the depths of time, perfumed with light aromas. It is a lamp always ready to go out, on a boat threatened with shipwreck, which hands reignite even in a tempest. Your story, courtesan, has passed through that long garlands of lips, and, as you know, the daughters of earth do not care to remain mute ..."

Hellenium and the radiant temple of Jupiter, elevated for foreigners, were behind us, the port at our feet; then a sea with motionless waves open to infinity formed a blue plain spangled with whitenesses that resembled thoughts of joy; over our heads the most beautiful sky extended.

Brilliant things were radiant in the corners of the palace; scents of the sea rose from triremes with dazzling sails; fishermen's nets hung their light mesh from one mast to another, seeds of aromatics, lost on the decks of ships, burning in the sunlight, glorified the forests where they had ripened, and exhaled toward us the peppery breath of the Orient.

I recognized Naucratis, the city of navigators. It seemed that the courtesan's powerful smile had rebuilt the city and reconstructed the past.

Archidice took me to her house. A crowd of men who were waiting in the vestibule ran forward to see her and to make themselves heard, for those young men knew that she had lost her lover. It was even thought that she had wanted to die, but as each of them knew Archidice's character, that her sobs quickly gave way to smiles, that she emerged from affliction rejuvenated by joy, and that she made tears into a bath of roses for her beauty, hope flourished in the hearts of her friends. Each of them fainted with joy at the thought of becoming her beloved.

And the news of Archidice's return palpitated over the marine city; but, shutting herself away with me, she refused to listen to anyone.

The house of Archidice had borrowed nothing from Greek art; it was an Egyptian interior in which Hathor of the Emeralds reigned, brilliant in beauty, in the midst of figurines of other gods and a thousand charming trivia.

"You see," she said, "although I am a courtesan I have not been reduced to worshiping the foreign Venus. Furthermore, I was never a dancer or a singer, and if I lend myself to mimic games it's uniquely for my own pleasure and in memory of Rhodopis. Don't think that I'm Greek; I'm Egyptian. The proof is that I never ask others what happens in their country and I gladly teach them the customs of mine, without wanting them to emerge from our long and grave valley, like a promenade of the gods. But it isn't about me that I want to talk to you. What good would it do you to know that I was obliged to sustain the old age of my parents and bear the cost of their funerals alone; you'd believe that I was excusing myself for being a courtesan, whereas I praise the gods every day for having conducted me to that destiny, for the wisdom and the strength of soul that it has given me."

I listened with surprise.

"Archidice, you don't resemble your peers if you aren't nonchalant, capricious, rapacious and prodigal."

"Why would I be all that? I have nothing to desire . . . and I find myself as innocent as the souls of the fifth hour, destined for the celestial harvest. I march toward a purity that nothing can take away from me, and the gentle daughter of Mycerinus,[1] before being violated by her father, had thoughts less chaste than mine. My knowledge is a pyramid that rises very high toward the sky; my wisdom would equal that of Solon if I were to put it in maxims. I have been shipwrecked, O unknown woman, in the sea of so many souls! All the bitterness of life is fixed on my lips, as viscous as a chilled kiss."

---

1 Nowadays known as Menhaure, a fourth dynasty pharaoh; again, the detail is from Herodotus.

"But you are so young, Archidice," I murmured. "You have the air of a dreaming child!"

"Young!" cried the courtesan. "Oh, by the blood of Isis, I find myself as old as God, the father of Always. Listen, I am the heiress of Rhodopis. She bequeathed the memoirs of her life to a courtesan who would attempt to equal her, one who would transmit them to another, who would make the deposit in her turn to one of her companions. The precious papyrus found intact in one of the caskets that served as her library are in my hands, after having passed via three heirs now dead. I shall enable you to hear them."

She got up, caused her train bordered with plums to palpitate over the silk carpet, and, unrolling papyri whose clay seals were broken, she began to read the following:

"Confession of Rhodopis.

"My homeland is Egypt, land of Sages, my favorite mirror the Blue Nile. Let no one object that I was born in Thrace; I have only lived since becoming free.

"Be praised, Charaxus, for having extracted me from the void. You were more my mother than my lover, for I owe you life and I gave you few kisses. What dream have I had? I was a slave. Aesop the Hunchback taught me to juggle with menacing ironies like swords, with words as persuasive as tears. Sappho called me Dorichus; I obeyed the pedantic and drunken Zanthus and served his capricious wife. I took part in the excellent trick that caused her to return to her stupid husband. Those were, I agree, vulgar amusements, and I blush, sometimes, at their heavy brutality. I soon knew the price of the despicable weapons that would assure me of the amour of men, but I repeat to you, that was like a dream of elsewhere, like an anterior existence, half-forgotten . . .

"I did not pass into houses of debauchery. I soon had my own palace; I no longer counted the gold rings or the precious stones; works of art cluttered my halls, my gardens and my courtyards.

"I only obeyed my fantasy, and my fantasy was only to have near me poets, philosophers and physicians. I did not like soldiers, having a profound disgust for bloody victories. And yet, I have seen coming toward me, behind the chariots of captains, Oriental marvels worthy of those that the fleets of Hatasu brought back from the lands of incense. A sculptor and a painter would exhaust themselves in sculpting and painting the most astonishing things that reached me.

"My youth was like the evergreen tree of Ammon which sees the discolored sycamores lose their leaves in autumn before its imperishable spring. Wives have envied me, and I have not envied wives, for the days of their husbands are like pitchers of insipid beer, emptied with indifference, but the instant that they give to the courtesan is as rutilant and brilliant as a cup of Granada wine from which flame emerges. As for them, tell me, can they know the amour, the life or the soul of men? The unfortunate adventure that happened to the wife of Potiphar with regard to a young Hebrew has thrown a ridiculous withering over their passions. They are children, you tell me, who are consoling their old age, but look at my daughter; is it not for her that Sappho sang: 'I have a beautiful child, whose beauty resembles chrysanthemums; I would not exchange her for all of Lydia.' And for that delectable ode, I forgive her, laughing, for the malevolent song that she made for me with regard to Charaxus.

"The daughters of the king have envied me, and I have not envied their fate. Those of Rampsinit and Cheops had strange destinies. Their fathers made prostitutes of them, one out of curiosity, the other out of self-interest. They never complained of what happened to them. The former was constrained to marry a priest that she had had the mission of discovering and who had vanquished the king in ingenuity; the latter entered a house of debauchery on the order of Cheops, who had ordered her to earn a certain sum; she obeyed. For her, as for the daughter of Rampsinit, it was the brothel, with walls painted with her-maphrodite beasts, shaken by the heavy and rhythmic tread of soldiers, with its gaming rooms, full of imprecations and cries, and an entire population of buffoons, fire-eaters, magiciennes and jugglers, destined to distract the drinkers, the libertines, the sailors and the thieves.

"My soul rose up in thinking about the boors with hideous muzzles to whom they delivered their topaz bodies. Oh, the nauseating breath, like charnel-houses, which tarnished their blushing cheeks, the stupidity of barbarian matelots waddling heavily like geese, the soldiers as dirty as crocodiles and the cun-ning faces of merchants anointed with musk, a garland of mint around the neck! Oh, how they vomited their existence, the sad daughters of kings! Barefoot, with girdles undone, they allowed the flowers of their intelligence to fade like those of their face, and only thought of immortality while yawning.

"However, the one who owed the light of day to Cheops conceived, in order to punish her father, a more savant ven-geance than the one wrought by Nitocris against the murderers of her beloved brother.

"Of each man who approached her, she asked for the gift of a stone, not one of the stones of Hathor with which the daughters of Egypt love to ornament their amber necks, but a block of granite extracted from the Arabic mountain, which sculptors clothe with figures; she soon commenced to build a pyramid, gradually raising the level of its base. The news tra-versed Egypt, like a joyous child running before her agitating a palm, and everyone wanted to know whether the strange work had been conceived by a fury in despair or whether it as a more ingenious ironic inspiration than a brand new witty saying forged on a golden anvil. People came from far away to know her thought. She would not say, and it became more celebrated in consequence. The monument that she erected to her destiny rose higher and higher, the giant blocks superimposed on one another in an immutable order. It remained indestructible, like her memory . . .

"My glory increased every day. I bore a name as radiant as a field of roses, as familiar as those of goddesses; I sensed the amour of an entire people palpitating in the distance. I was the unveiled Isis suddenly giving herself to men again, after having slept for centuries under veils more obscure than the night of the coffin and the opacity of bandages. My form was so beautiful that it was found in the most divine contours of rivers and mountains. In the evening I mounted my ship of polished wood incrusted with gold and precious stones, which dated red and green fires; its masts were gilded, the yardarms azure; the flamboyant sails, as if steeped in the blood of the gods, slapped wings similar to those of the phoenix melting on the pyre that was about to devour it.

"There, on the ivory seats, my friends were seated. I took Solon and Thales, illustrious Greeks who were traveling in Egypt, for excursions. I listened to the works of poets elevating their verses to my beauty. I engaged in dialogue with philosophers, and all music often fell silent, every voice became mute, and the courtesan's soul sank into thoughts more profound than those of men who had only lived for the idea! At other times, like a crazed Pythia, I told them things about their intelligence and mine that penetrated them with a high enthusiasm and doubled their inspirations; they threw me laurels, weeping; no lust was any longer in their thoughts.

"After having been grave enough to make them shudder, I had child-like joys and caprices that it was necessary to satisfy. All the malice of the slave taught by Aesop reappeared in me then.

"Amasis reigned, and I wanted Amasis to love me. Scarcely had I formed the project than one day, when I was bathing at Naucratis, and eagle seized one of my sandals, lifted it up into the heights of the sky and dropped it on the knees of the king, who was rendering justice at Memphis. Was that a miracle? No; I will confide to you in secret that the eagle was one of four that Aesop had trained in order to mystify Nectanebo, but do not tell the Greeks who write history!

"Now, that footwear was divine, and Amasis, curious as a Pharaoh, wanted to find the woman to whom it belonged, and I became his favorite. I wearied quickly of amusing him; he did not retain my soul for long. When he died I returned to my philosophers and allowed old age to approach, welcoming it with smiles. It said to me: You are still beautiful; and I reposed in its arms."

The papyrus, which emitted an odor of roses, was unrolled all the way to the end. The fresh and sonorous voice of Archidice had fallen silent. Her eyes were shining like the star of Sothis.[1]

I do not know what echo of our morality, gravely puerile, borrowed my mouth to plead, in confrontation with that ignorant beauty, the cause of duty and virtue.

I pronounced their names rather firmly. Archidice listened to them, stifling a discreet yawn in her bouquet. Then, all smiling, she said:

"You must have stopped for a long time, and very naïvely, before the strolling players who juggle with empty words; for if I have understood what you are saying, you really believe that there is something other than Beauty."

---

1 i.e., Sirius.

ROBBED
(*La Fronde*, 18 February 1903)

A N evening in November. It was raining terribly in the country.

At intervals, through gaps in the clouds, the moon laughed in the muddy puddles.

Over certain trees the water streamed with a dull rattle departing from the crowns; on others, with extended leaves, it had sonorous harmonies, mocking gaieties; it chattered in ditches, murmuring I know not what ironic confidence to the damp earth.

A man was marching through that desolation, swearing.

His soaked blouse was plastered over his high shoulders, the cloth lifting on his back like a flag flapping around a mast as the wind whipped it with a regular movement. Head thrust forward, he uttered blasphemies, proclaimed with fury, or words chewed and twisted by his yellow teeth, swallowed with effort and shame. He plunged into the mud without paying any heed to the malice of things, prey to some obsessive intimate preoccupation.

Suddenly, the farm was before him, with its cowsheds, into which the powerful breath of the oxen put a respiration of joy and opulence, with its hangar in which plows, harrows, root-cutters, threshers, bull's-eyes, scythes and flails were arranged, with its granaries in which precious grains were heaped heavily in opaque russet piles, new grains harvested with such ardent preoccupation and such tender care.

An odor of cabbage soup filtered through the door. Before the hearth, throwing forth high bright flames, a peasant woman, his wife, Aimée Guillotte, was standing. Master Louis Guillotte, peered at her through the window, his hand clenched on the rusty ring that served to tether the horses. His rage was blowing so forcefully that the mist-covered windows soon put a smoky veil between him and the scene. On his lips, crushed murmurs and blasphemies were confounded with hiccups of fury, and he entered abruptly, without saying anything.

He had the eyes of a wolf lying in ambush, too close to the nose in profound orbits, and his eyebrows, as long as a new-born's hair, brought together by the violent crease of the forehead, put a shadow over the ferocity of his gaze, a shadow sowing fear.

Aimée Guillotte took a brown soup tureen from the hearth and set it before Master Guillotte

On top there were many cabbages and large runner beans and underneath large slices of unsalted white bread. In the middle, a pewter ladle stood upright.

He took off his blouse and his clogs, and in large regular mouthfuls, in haste, emptied the large brown fuming pot that he held between his knees.

Slyly, a brutality in the depths of his bushy beard, he tracks his idea as a furious bull, horns lowered, crosses fields and ditches in the hope of a red adventure.

He tries to speak, recommencing in awkward phrases the scene that increases every day the suffering of the previous day.

Pale, her lips trembling, Aimée waits, and the silence is so heavy that a need to hasten the torture comes to her, maddening her; she prefers the insults and the blows.

"What's troubling you, that you're sitting there chewing blood? Are you going mad?"

"There's something new, Mistress Guillotte, there's something new," hisses the farmer—and he shrugs his shoulders all the way to his hairy ears, which resemble badly tanned leather more than living flesh. "Ah! Ah!" he exclaims, "I know all about it, good-for-nothing, and you're going to answer me, and no lies, for that's worse than mummery."

Aimée opens her frightened eyes wide large eyes in which madness is gleaming, and says: "There's nothing new, Master Guillotte."

The peasant sniggers terribly.

"I knew that you didn't want me, after three months of marriage, necessary to take you by force. But I didn't know who else didn't want you. But I learned that today at the fair under the tents. It's Master Poincheval who said it, and there were a heap of cattle-dealers from the Nord and pig-merchants from Cherbourg who were making mock of that capon Master Guillotte, who couldn't do it."

"Shut up," moaned the woman. "I can't hear you, it hurts my heart." She started to weep, her apron over her eyes, the sobs shaking her pretty young body and her face invisible under her bonnet, which two undulations of hair plastered to the temples like golden wheels.

Then he started to beat her furiously. "Good for-less-than-nothing slut."

She kept silent under the blows, curled up in a ball near the fireplace.

He suddenly stopped muttering incomprehensibly, and sat down again.

The clock measured the horrible hour with a broad golden pendulum, which displayed a sun with rays dotted with blue glass. Sated by his violence, he no longer had the strength to strike. His mouth was pulled into a rictus. He touched Aimée's shoulder gently.

She did not budge,

"Would you like to move, log that you are?"

His voice became as insinuating as an angry wind sliding into a cottage through disjointed planks,

"Come on, talk to me Aimée; I'll be more tranquil afterwards; why doesn't he want you, Léonidas—tell me?"

She replied: "I know you."

A torment gripped him more forcefully, furrowing his forehead before the complication of the problem. He thumped the table.

"Good God! What's the matter with you, that nobody wants you?"

Defeated and anxious, he looked at her again, dilating his inflamed eyes of a somber wolf with all the force of his attention.

And he said to himself: *It's something that I can't see.*

Then a strange anguish gripped him, as when he feared that he had made a bad bargain at the fair or had cruel doubts about the value of a crop to come. And as he had lived chaste for a long time, ignorant of women, he despaired of ever comprehending.

Throwing his clothes on the ground, he slid into his bed, shrugging his shoulders, without hope. But he could not go to sleep. Already he was somewhat aggrieved on seeing that his wife did not become pregnant, expecting some chubby infant with the joyous impatience that made him desire in spring the smile of the sunlight over his fecund fields.

A hatred came to him against her, whom he had taken for her delicate charm, and fury against Léonidas, the wretch, who had divined his wife's flaw. And he had not seen anything!

A profound disgust rose within him from an obscure source in his being for that sick woman having who knew what, which could not be cured, which one could not even know. He did not beat her any more, became thinner and more somber, less active in caring for his fields, indifferent to mockery.

295

One evening in December he knocked on Léonidas' door. Once inside he said, with a harsh expression, his arms trembling: "Here I am."

Léonidas, a tall, red-faced fellow, looked at him mutely, paralyzed by astonishment.

But Guillotte repeated: "Yes, here I am, it's me. Necessary that you talk to me. I don't mean you any harm."

The fellow remained inert, his gaze embarrassed, but a smile came to him, illuminating a mad anger in Master Guillotte. The farmer leapt at the peasant's throat and shook him with all his might. "Tell me why you don't want her. You take them all, all the females in the region, it's your métier, laborer." He ground his teeth as if to break them. "Tell me, tell me, why you don't want that one!"

Léonidas escaped momentarily from the farmer's grip. He launched himself to the other end of the house with a lurch, laughing loudly.

"No, but you're drunk, eh? And here you are—that's a good one! And you're not like the others, by the Good Savior, you!"

He was weeping and crying, shaken by a frantic joy. When he had calmed down, he said: "Don't get upset, you know. No, I don't want your wife. Sleep tranquil, old man. Bonsoir."

And Léonidas opened the door and threw him out into the night. He heard him muttering: "Oh, he dares to tell me that. I'm robbed, in the end."

An hour later, Leonidas went out, joyful and furtive, running to some rendezvous. He slid under a grove of large apple trees, ducking low, making haste. Suddenly, he was stopped by an impact, and also an astonishment, almost frightened already.

At first the obstacle made him think of two strange branches descending vertically, heavy and yet too supple and dangling.

In the blackness, Léonidas felt and said in a low voice: "Legs! They're legs!"

He started trembling in all his limbs; forgetful of the joy to which he was running, he returned home. And, fearfully, he murmured in a low voice:

"Is it the devil or a hanged man who kicked me in the face?"

A PARTIAL LIST OF SNUGGLY BOOKS

MAY ARMAND BLANC *The Last Rendezvous*
G. ALBERT AURIER *Elsewhere and Other Stories*
CHARLES BARBARA *My Lunatic Asylum*
S. HENRY BERTHOUD *Misanthropic Tales*
LÉON BLOY *The Tarantulas' Parlor and Other Unkind Tales*
ÉLÉMIR BOURGES *The Twilight of the Gods*
CYRIEL BUYSSE *The Aunts*
JAMES CHAMPAGNE *Harlem Smoke*
FÉLICIEN CHAMPSAUR *The Latin Orgy*
BRENDAN CONNELL *Unofficial History of Pi Wei*
BRENDAN CONNELL *The Metapheromenoi*
RAFAELA CONTRERAS *The Turquoise Ring and Other Stories*
ADOLFO COUVE *When I Think of My Missing Head*
QUENTIN S. CRISP *Aiaigasa*
LUCIE DELARUE-MARDRUS *Amanit*
LUCIE DELARUE-MARDRUS *The Last Siren and Other Stories*
LADY DILKE *The Outcast Spirit and Other Stories*
CATHERINE DOUSTEYSSIER-KHOZE
　　The Beauty of the Death Cap
ÉDOUARD DUJARDIN *Hauntings*
BERIT ELLINGSEN *Now We Can See the Moon*
ERCKMANN-CHATRIAN *A Malediction*
ALPHONSE ESQUIROS *The Enchanted Castle*
ENRIQUE GÓMEZ CARRILLO *Sentimental Stories*
DELPHI FABRICE *Flowers of Ether*
DELPHI FABRICE *The Red Sorcerer*
DELPHI FABRICE *The Red Spider*
BENJAMIN GASTINEAU *The Reign of Satan*
EDMOND AND JULES DE GONCOURT *Manette Salomon*
REMY DE GOURMONT *From a Faraway Land*
REMY DE GOURMONT *Morose Vignettes*
GUIDO GOZZANO *Alcina and Other Stories*
GUSTAVE GUICHES *The Modesty of Sodom*
EDWARD HERON-ALLEN *The Complete Shorter Fiction*
EDWARD HERON-ALLEN *Three Ghost-Written Novels*
RHYS HUGHES *Cloud Farming in Wales*
J.-K. HUYSMANS *The Crowds of Lourdes*
J.-K. HUYSMANS *Knapsacks*
COLIN INSOLE *Valerie and Other Stories*
JUSTIN ISIS *Pleasant Tales II*

www.ingramcontent.com/pod-product-compliance
Lightning Source LLC
Chambersburg PA
CBHW020356110726
47899CB00006B/1738